To plan to see him and bowl him over was a very different matter from actually doing it. *Be witty and outrageous. He is a man who can't bear to be bored.* She was startled for a moment at her insight, but knew it to be true about him.

"It's a lovely day, Mr. Saxton," she said, allowing him to take her hand briefly. "I have come to rescue you from your labors."

Why, she is chasing me, he thought, both amused and intrigued. He waved toward the pile of papers on his desk. "Alas, I am but a miserable drudge. Behold my labors. I fear they will not go away without my personally dispatching them."

"I was told that you were a man of great resource. Perhaps, Mr. Saxton, you can forgo your labors, just for a short time. I, sir, will buy you lunch." At his look of surprise, Chauncey added in a mournful voice, "You see, sir, I have already received three proposals of marriage and I fear that eager gentlemen are even at this moment waiting for me to emerge. Have you no sense of gallantry, sir? I am, I assure you, a lady in distress."

"Somehow I cannot imagine you tolerating any distress, particularly from eager gentlemen. Are you always so forward?"

Her eyes sparkled. "Only when it is absolutely necessary."

Midnight Star

Catherine Coulter

A SIGNET BOOK

SIGNET
Published by the Penguin Group
Penguin Books USA Inc., 375 Hudson Street,
New York, New York 10014, U.S.A.
Penguin Books Ltd, 27 Wrights Lane,
London W8 5TZ, England
Penguin Books Australia Ltd, Ringwood,
Victoria, Australia
Penguin Books Canada Ltd, 10 Alcorn Avenue,
Toronto, Ontario, Canada M4V 3B2
Penguin Books (N.Z.) Ltd, 182–190 Wairau Road,
Auckland 10, New Zealand

Penguin Books Ltd, Registered Offices:
Harmondsworth, Middlesex, England

Published by Signet, an imprint of Dutton Signet,
a division of Penguin Books USA Inc.

First Printing, June, 1986
18   17

REGISTERED TRADEMARK—MARCA REGISTRADA

Printed in the United States of America

PUBLISHER'S NOTE
This is a work of fiction. Names, characters, places, and incidents either are the product
of the author's imagination or are used fictitiously, and any resemblance to actual
persons, living or dead, events, or locales is entirely coincidental.

To Jennifer McCord,
a friend indeed who has great ideas:

The Star Trilogy

Let's always go for it!

Prologue

Guildford, Surrey, 1852

"... *Ashes to ashes, dust to dust* ..."

Fresh clods of damp earth hit the coffin with dull, monotonous thuds. A single red rose glittered among the raw brown earth. *At least he is with Mama now.*

"... *The Lord Jesus Christ hath ordained that all of mankind must one day join him in everlasting peace* ..."

"We are so sorry, Elizabeth."

"If there is anything we can do, Elizabeth ..."

"... *We beseech our Savior to take unto him the soul of our departed friend Sir Alec Jameson Fitz-Hugh* ..."

"Your father was a gentle, loving man ..."

"Such a tragedy, Elizabeth, such a pity."

"Elizabeth!"

She shook her head, clearing her mind of the

vicar's soft droning words, clearing away the condolences of all her father's friends. She blinked as she looked up at Mr. Paul Montgomery, her father's longtime friend and solicitor. He cleared his throat, sending a reproachful look toward her Aunt Augusta, but Augusta Penworthy said more loudly, her voice imperious, "Elizabeth, you must attend! Mr. Montgomery has more important things to do than sit watching you daydream! And, may I add, so do your uncle and I!"

"Forgive me, Uncle Paul," Elizabeth said, ignoring her aunt. She knew her Aunt Augusta had to be here today for the reading of her dead brother's will, for she was his only living relative, other than his daughter. She glanced toward her Uncle Alfred, sweating profusely even in the chill afternoon of early April. Her father had despised Alfred Penworthy, calling him a miserable little weasel who couldn't drink a glass of port without Gussie's permission.

"Chauncey," Paul Montgomery said gently, using her nickname for the first time, "to be quite clear about all of this"—he waved at the stack of papers before him on her father's desk—"there is very little left. Jameson Hall will have to be sold, I fear, to pay the creditors."

"*What?*"

Aunt Augusta's screech brought Paul Montgomery to a startled halt. He frowned at the woman, bending his head so he could stare at her over his thick spectacles. "Madam," he said sternly, "it is to Miss FitzHugh that I am speaking."

"Alec died without a farthing? Is that what

you said, sir? It is impossible! He could not be so feckless!"

"Sir Alec left bequests, small ones, for the servants, madam." Mr. Montgomery shrugged his narrow shoulders. "Elizabeth," he continued, his expression so commiserating that Chauncey felt tears swim in her eyes, "I fear that your dear father made some rather ... questionable investments in the past couple of years. I tried to warn him, to hold him back, but it was no use. Also, I fear that he did not amend his will. That is another reason why your aunt and uncle are here today."

Chauncey stared at him, knowing what was to come, but asking nonetheless, "What do you mean, Uncle Paul?"

Mr. Montgomery carefully removed his glasses and began to polish the small circles on his shirt cuff. "I mean that he did not foresee that you would need a ... specified guardian until your twenty-first birthday. He assumed, of course, that you would be wed to Sir Guy Danforth long before he ... died. Since Alec did not so specify, your aunt and uncle, as your only living relatives, are your guardians."

"So," Augusta said in a disgusted voice, "I am to take the chit, feed her and clothe her, all without a sou from Alec's estate!"

"Now, my dear, poor Elizabeth has nothing to do with her father's lack of—" Uncle Alfred began, only to be cut off by poor Elizabeth.

"But I shall be twenty-one in a mere six months, Uncle Paul! I have no need of a guardian! What is there to guard, after all?"

And if there were something to guard, do you believe I would want my greedy aunt to have control?

"It is the law, my dear," Paul Montgomery said slowly. "But of course, there is another alternative for you, is there not?"

Chauncey lowered her head, seeing Guy Danforth in her mind's eye. He needed money badly, the dowry her father had promised him. Now there was nothing. "No, Uncle Paul," she said slowly, her voice growing stronger, "there isn't another alternative." She rose to her feet and shook out her heavy black wool skirt. "If there is nothing else, Uncle Paul, I will go and see to your comfort. Aunt Augusta, you and Uncle Alfred will be staying for the night?"

Aunt Augusta merely nodded, saying nothing more, and Chauncey walked quickly toward the library door, wondering if her aunt was at last thinking of her brother and regretted her unkind words. She closed it softly behind her, hearing as she did so Aunt Augusta's furious voice. "It is ridiculous that we should take the girl! Why, she's nearly a spinster! Certainly no gentleman will want to marry her now! What, I ask you, Mr. Montgomery, are we to do with her?"

Chauncey didn't wait to hear Uncle Paul's reply. So much for Aunt Augusta's brief bout of restraint.

"Miss Chauncey."

"Yes, Convers?" She turned to face the Fitz-Hugh butler, swallowing the hated tears and schooling her features to an impassive expression. "An excess of emotion in a woman is considered acceptable, I suppose," she could hear her father say. She saw him shrug, giving her his dear lopsided grin. "But it does allow others to know what is in her mind. And that is not always so very acceptable, is it?"

"Sir Guy is here, miss, asking to see you." At his mistress's hesitation, he asked softly, "Would you like me to tell Sir Guy that you are not receiving today?"

"No, Convers, I will see him. Is he in the Blue Salon?"

"Yes, miss. Are you all right, Miss Chauncey?"

"Of course. Please bring refreshments. No, wait, Convers. No refreshments will be necessary." Chauncey paused a moment before the silver-edged mirror beside the Blue Salon. The pale face that looked back at her little resembled the laughing, carefree Chauncey Jameson FitzHugh. Behind her was the great hall, its huge double oak doors open onto the marble entryway. She stared into the mirrored reflection at its magnificent high ceiling etched with geometric designs and baronial heraldry, at its stone floor covered with brightly patterned Turkey carpets. Heavy mahogany furniture, darkened from deep red to brown over the years, was set in austere groupings. Medieval arms, lances and longbows and helmets, graced the walls, never a patch of dust on them, for the FitzHugh servants were a conscientious lot. She closed her eyes a moment, remembering a little girl jousting with the highly polished suit of armor that stood proudly in the far corner of the hall. Jameson Hall, the home of three generations of FitzHughs, now to pass into the hands of strangers. No more jousts with the long-dead unknown knight, no more hoydenish swims in the placid River Wey that wound its way to the east of Jameson Hall. No more cozy talks with her father in front of the massive fireplace, her skirts tucked up as she sat on the floor beside his chair. She rarely sat in the smaller chair that stood beside his. It had been her mother's, beautiful, gentle Isobel, and she had always known that it remained Isobel's in her father's heart.

Chauncey felt a quivering shudder go through her body. "Thank God, Father," she whispered at her image in the mirror, "that you have been spared this." She tucked an errant strand of hair back into its prim coil at the back of her neck, squared her shoulders, and entered the salon.

"Elizabeth!"

She suppressed a frown. Guy could never bring himself to call her Chauncey. It smacked of a lack of breeding, she supposed, remembering when she had told him that her Irish nurse had dubbed her with the name when she was a little girl. It lacked a sense of self-worth. *But Father loved my nickname. He always said it softly, a kind of caress.* "Chauncey, my love," he'd tease her in a thick Irish brogue, "what the divil do ye think ye're doin, movin' the king's knight to that demned square? Be ye an angel, lettin' me win so easy-like?"

"Hello, Guy," she said, walking into the room. "It is kind of you to come." Chauncey allowed Sir Guy Danworth to take her hands in his and gently squeeze them.

"Of course I would come, my dear," he said gently. How pale she looks, he thought, staring a moment at the mauve shadows beneath her expressive eyes. The black gown didn't become her, making her face look thin and pinched. He didn't relish the months ahead, but of course he would do his duty with patience and tolerance.

Chauncey removed her hands from his grasp and walked to the far side of the salon to stand beside the white Italian marble fireplace, her dead grandmother's pride. She eyed him from beneath her lashes, wondering suddenly why she had consented to marry him. Certainly he was handsome, in an understated, ascetic sort of way. His thin, narrow face had once appealed to her, for she thought it mirrored his complexity, his sincerity. But no, she thought, her lips twisting briefly, seeing him with new eyes. He was a prig. Even at twenty-eight, he was unerringly pompous and rigid in his beliefs and behavior. And of course there was his incredibly narrow-minded mother. *Why did I not see him so clearly before? Was I so selfish and blind that I saw no one as he really was? Why didn't my father see him? Surely he couldn't have been so blind as I.*

"Elizabeth, please accept my condolences on this sad occasion. My mother also sends her regrets, of course."

"Of course," Chauncey murmured. "Thank you, Guy."

"My mother is concerned about you, my dear. She realizes, of course, that we cannot wed until your year of mourning is passed, and wonders what you will do. I mentioned to her that you would likely remain here at Jameson Hall, but she could not allow that to be proper. Not without a chaperon, at any rate. She has suggested that you stay with your aunt and uncle in London."

"Yes," Chauncey said, "I must stay with them, it seems."

"It will, of course, my dear Elizabeth, be my responsibility to work out an arrangement with your father's solicitor and look after Jameson Hall in the meanwhile."

"That won't be necessary, Guy." She looked at him straightly, seeing that he was, in fact, quite relieved that her father was dead, that he would now have everything. Must he even now eye the elegant furnishings of the Blue Salon with such a proprietary, almost greedy air? She wanted to laugh, but instead she said slowly and very clearly, "Jameson Hall will be sold shortly."

"I ... I do not understand, Elizabeth," Sir Guy said, his dark brows drawing together. Lord, he hoped she hadn't lost her wits after the past two days she'd spent in mute shock. But, he supposed, female hysterics would be worse. But no, she would never embarrass him with an emotional scene. "You are doubtless overwrought, my dear," he said with gentle condescension. "You may leave such discussions with the solicitor to me."

"Guy," she said, drawing off the engagement ring from her finger, "there is no money. My father left me nothing. Jameson Hall must be sold to cover his debts, as will everything else of any value. As I said, I have no choice but to ... live with my aunt and uncle until I am twenty-one."

"No money," he repeated blankly. "But that is impossible!"

She wanted to smile, for he sounded just like

her Aunt Augusta, shock, disgust, and condemnation clear in his voice. *He could not be so feckless!*

"That is correct, Guy. Here is your ring. I have no intention of holding you to our engagement." Oddly enough, the removal of the delicate emerald ring was like lifting a great weight from her shoulders. I must have been mad, she thought, somewhat dazed with the insight, to have agreed to marry him. *I would never have been Chauncey again.*

He took it, of course. She had never once expected that he would argue with her, plead with her, claim that he loved her, only her. She saw the shock fade from his face, watched his eyes narrow as he struggled to find some gentlemanly words to say.

"Elizabeth, this is unbelievable," he began. He felt a brief moment of absolute fury at the incredible shift in his fortunes. Damn Sir Alec! "You know that I care for you, but—"

"I know, Guy," she said, cutting him off. "Please give my thanks to your mother for her sympathy. I have many things to see to now. I must go. Good-bye, Guy. Convers will see you out."

She left him without a backward glance.

– 1 –

Bedford Square, London, 1852

Chauncey stared at her bedroom door, her eyes narrowing in anger. The knob slowly turned until the lock held it tight. She thought she heard a muffled curse, then footsteps walking away down the corridor.

She jumped to her feet, shaking her fist toward the door. That wretched Owen! How could that toad believe that she found him anything but utterly repellent?

She sighed, turned back to the bay window, and pressed her cheek to the cold glass. It was a dreary, foggy day, and she could barely make out the figures moving in the road below. God, how she hated London! How she hated living with her aunt and uncle! Her Aunt Augusta had even sold her mare, Ginger, along with everything else, and had refused to allow her to ride any of the horses in their stable.

"You are in mourning, Elizabeth," Chauncey could hear her saying in that sharp voice of hers. "You will behave like a lady."

Lady, ha! During the five months she had lived with her aunt and uncle she was more like a drudge, the obvious poor relation, running and fetching for her aunt, bearing with the noise and demands of the three young daughters of the house, and trying to avoid Owen.

"Really, Lizzie," she could hear fourteen-year-old Janine's whining voice chiding her in the second-floor schoolroom, "all this nonsense about history. What does a girl have to know about Gibraltar, for goodness' sake? You're just a silly old spinster!"

And Owen, mocking softly from the open doorway, "Now, little sister, dear Elizabeth must concern herself about something, hmm? After all, she doesn't have your advantages now, does she?"

"No," plump, strident eleven-year-old Alice shrilled, "she's just a silly old spinster!"

What will happen to me when I turn twenty-one?

It was a question that repeated itself unrelentingly once the shock and grief of her father's death had faded. Chauncey chewed on her lower lip. She was well-educated, at least when it came to England and her empire, but the thought of being a governess left her numb with dread. It was a role she detested. Were all girls like her young cousins? Completely uninterested in anything except the cloying verses to love songs? And what if she did become a governess? Would not her position in a household leave her open to slights? To unwanted advances from the men? Like Owen. Owen, twenty-three, slender as his father was plump, his chin sharp and his pale blue eyes devious and assessing like his mother's. She had been utterly stunned when he stopped her on the stairs the week before.

"How very sweet it is to have you here, dear Cousin Elizabeth," he had said, his hand reaching out to lightly touch her cheek.

Chauncey had known no fear. She jerked her face away and watched him drop his hand. "Really, Owen," she said sharply, "sweetness has little to do with it. I am here, and there is naught any of us can do about it, I least of all."

"Ah, but, Elizabeth," he said, giving her that assessing look that made her feel as if she were standing at the top of the stairs wearing nothing but her curiosity, "do not dismiss your . . . charms, my dear. I find them most invigorating. Soon you will be twenty-one, you know. And then what will you do? I can see that the thought worries you. Perhaps, my dear, if you would consider being . . . nice to me . . ." He saw her draw back, anger making her extraordinary eyes gleam. Their strange mahogany color fascinated him. "Yes, just be nice to me, Elizabeth. I can give you things, teach you things. I cannot believe that a husband of any worldly worth is in your future. But a husband is not a necessary commodity."

So different Owen was from Guy! Or perhaps he was just more honest. "Owen," she said calmly, "you are my cousin. Nothing else. Pray do not speak to me thus again."

Lord, but she was lovely, he thought, not at all deterred by her coldness. A bit on the thin side for his tastes, but even her confining corset couldn't hide the fullness of her breasts. He imag-

ined her slender long legs wrapped around him
and felt a surge of lust harden in his groin. But it
was her eyes that drew him. He could see the
slumbering passion in their depths. They flashed
an amber gold at this moment, lightened in her
anger.

"Proud little thing, ain't you, cousin?" He
laughed hoarsely. "You shouldn't be now. No
more living in a fancy house with servants bow-
ing to your every whim. And a doting father to
buy you pretty things. All you can hope for is a
. . . protector."

She laughed; she couldn't help it. "You, I take
it, are applying for the position?" She watched
his face pale in his anger, his eyes narrow. "Leave
me alone, Owen, do you hear me? And stay away
from the schoolroom." She added sarcastically,
"Perhaps even your sisters will learn something
of value if you're not there to scoff!"

"Perhaps," he said very softly, "you will quickly
change your mind." He reached for her, clasping
her against him, his movements so quick that she
did not have time to react. His hands were moving toward her breasts, his breath was on her
face. She did not think of laughing now. "Play
dead, my baby," she heard her old nurse tell her.
"Then give that Smith boy a pain he'll not soon
forget!"

She went limp. Owen, elated with her submis-
sion, eased his hold on her as he lowered his
head to find her mouth. Without a thought to the
consequences, Chauncey brought up her knee with
all her strength. Owen bellowed with pain and
fell back, clutching his groin. "You bitch!" he
snarled at her. "You'll pay for that!"

"I doubt it, you miserable toad," she said harshly. "We will see what your mother has to say about your molesting me!"

Chauncey had gone immediately to her aunt's room, filled with righteous anger. She shook her head now, still disbelieving her Aunt Augusta's attitude.

"Whatever are you talking about, miss?" Aunt Augusta demanded, breaking unceremoniously in on her recital. She rose from her dressing stool, flinging a jar of pomade onto the tabletop.

"I am talking about Owen, Aunt Augusta. He has behaved most improperly."

Aunt Augusta regarded her, her lips pursed. "Really, Elizabeth, such a tale ill suits you. I understand it, of course I do, but it won't work. You will cease flirting and teasing my son. He will not marry you."

Chauncey gaped at her. "You believe that I'm making this up? Marry Owen? I would sooner wed a waterfront pickpocket!"

Owen had stalked her after that, but Chauncey wasn't a fool. Would he never give up? she wondered. He appeared to enjoy stalking her, a cat-and-mouse game that left her always on edge. Thank God for the lock on her door!

What will happen to me when I turn twenty-one next month?

Chauncey stood quietly outside her aunt's bedchamber door, her hand raised to knock. There was so little time before her birthday, and she must speak to her aunt. Surely her father's sister must care at least a little about what happened to her!

Her uplifted hand froze as she heard her aunt say with spiteful clarity, "The girl has no notion of how to go along. Look what we have done for her, Alfred, and still she acts the proud heiress! And those lies she told about dear Owen! The poor boy was much shocked, I assure you."

"Was he now?" Uncle Alfred murmured.

"Indeed! And the girls aren't learning a thing from her. Poor Janine told me that Elizabeth had the nerve to scold her for not paying proper attention to her math lesson. Math, of all things! I put a stop to that! Such a pity that she didn't marry Sir Guy, but I suppose he jilted her when he learned the true state of things."

"No, 'twas Elizabeth who released him."

"So she said," Augusta scoffed. "Stupid of her, I say, if it is true, which I doubt. Just like her mother, she is. All proud and misty-eyed, and not a grain of sense! You can stop looking so misty-eyed, Alfred! Oh yes, I know that you looked sheep's eyes at dear, sweet Isobel."

Chauncey froze. Uncle Alfred and her mother? You're eavesdropping, my girl, and hearing things you shouldn't. She wanted to leave, but her feet seemed nailed to the floor. She heard her uncle sigh deeply. "Isobel is dead, Gussie. I admired her, yes, but so did most people."

"Ha! All she produced was one worthless girl. Treated her like a little princess until she died in childbed with another daughter. If Isobel had brought a decent dowry to Alec, perhaps today you and I would own Jameson Hall."

"Elizabeth would own Jameson Hall, not us, my dear."

"Had I been Alec's older brother, rather than

his sister, it would be I to own it! Lord knows you haven't made the wisest of investments, and you in trade! We've three daughters, Alfred, and husbands to find for each of them."

Alfred said mildly, "At least you've obtained a free governess for them, my love. That is a saving, I should say, to your houshold expenses. As for my investments, you know that Owen outspends his very generous allowance and brings in not a sou."

"Owen is a gentleman," Augusta said angrily. "He will marry well, I will see to it. And as for that haughty little niece of mine, I vow she wouldn't raise that proud little chin of hers at me if she but knew the truth about her dear father."

Truth? What truth? Leave, Chauncey, go now. But she still didn't move. She wondered wildly if her uncle were sweating under his wife's tirade.

"Leave it be, Gussie. The girl earns her keep."

"So, Alfred, you want to protect her, and I know why. Isobel's precious daughter, that's why! Well, if she dares to bring tales of Owen to me again, I will tell her that her dear father took his own life. Just see if I don't!"

Chauncey stared blindly at the bedroom door. *Her dear father took his own life. . . .*

"No!" It was a soft, agonized sound that tore from her throat. She doubled over, the pain so terrible that she thought she would die from it. "No!"

Mary, the one servant in Heath House who treated Chauncey courteously, found her huddled on the lower stairs to the third-floor servants' quarters. "Miss," she said softly, lightly

touching her hand to Chauncey's shoulder. "Are
you all right, miss?"

Chauncey raised dazed eyes to Mary's face.
"He could not have done such a thing," she
whispered.

"No, of course not," Mary assured her, having
no idea what Miss Elizabeth was talking about.
She saw the despair in the young lady's eyes and
wished there was something she could say to
ease her pain. It was likely the mistress and her
sharp tongue that had brought her to such a
state. Damn the old bitch anyway!

"Oh, Mary!" The tears gushed from her eyes,
and she sobbed brokenly, nestled against Mary's
ample bosom.

Chauncey raised her chin and quickened her
pace along the sidewalk. She had no money, and
the walk from Bedford Square to Uncle Paul's
office on Fleet Street was long and tiring. She
had worn a heavily veiled black bonnet, and it
protected her from the advances of the young
men, who took it for granted that a woman by
herself was asking for attention. She was perspiring and shallow of breath when she reached
the three-story brick building. For a moment she
couldn't make her legs walk up the shallow steps
to the entrance.

*Don't be a coward, Chauncey. Aunt Augusta is a
vicious old harridan. She was lying. Uncle Paul will
tell you the truth.*

Several black-garbed clerks were seated on high
stools, their heads lowered, their pens scratching
industriously on the papers before them. Chauncey
cleared her throat.

"Excuse me," she said, drawing the attention of one young man. "I wish to see Mr. Paul Montgomery. My name is Elizabeth FitzHugh."

"Have you an appointment?" the young man asked shortly.

Chauncey shook her head. "Please tell him that I am here," she said firmly, drawing back the black veil from her face.

The young man's eyes widened in admiration. "Be seated, miss. I will see if he is free."

Paul Montgomery emerged quickly from his office. "Chauncey! My dear, what a pleasant surprise! Come in, come in!"

Chauncey smiled back at him, her first smile of pleasure since her father's death. "I appreciate your taking time to see me, Uncle Paul."

"Nonsense, my dear!" He led her into his office and pulled back a chair for her in front of his massive oak desk. "Now, tell me what I can do for you."

For several moments she couldn't speak.

"You are looking lovely, Chauncey," he said as her silence stretched long. "I trust you have settled in nicely with your aunt and uncle?" Please let her say yes, he thought, forming the words in his own mouth that he wished her to speak.

"Uncle Paul, did my father kill himself?"

The stark words hung in the air between them. She saw him stiffen, saw the betraying gleam in his dark eyes through the thick lenses of his spectacles.

He slowly removed his glasses, cleaning them on the cuff of his shirt, a stalling habit Chauncey recognized. "Wherever did you get such a notion, my dear?"

"It is true, then," she said. "Please, Uncle Paul, do not lie to me. I . . . I overheard my aunt say it to my uncle."

"Stupid woman!" Paul Montgomery muttered. He studied her pale face intently, and seemed to come to a decision. "I am sorry, my dear. There was no reason for you ever to know. I had no idea that your aunt . . . But it doesn't matter now, does it?"

"It matters to me." Chauncey felt a trickle of sweat snake downward between her breasts. "He was given a Christian burial," she said numbly. "No one said anything. Not even Dr. Ramsay."

"I wasn't about to announce to the vicar that your father's death wasn't a tragic accident! Indeed, my dear, it was just that. Dr. Ramsay agreed with me. The overdose of laudanum . . ."

"Why, Uncle Paul? Why did he do it?"

His eyes fell to his slight paunch, held in by a stiff-clothed waistcoat. "I had prayed that I would never have to tell you this, Chauncey."

"I cannot believe that he would take his own life because of a few bad investments!"

"Not just that. It's a rather involved story, my dear." He paused a moment, as if collecting his thoughts. He saw the determination on her face, and said quietly, "Very well, Chauncey, if you must know. In the summer of 1851, your father met an American here in London, Delaney Saxton by name. Saxton was looking for investors. It seemed that he was quite wealthy, having made a fortune in gold in California, but he wanted to increase his wealth. He struck a deal with your father. Your father insisted that I and Saxton's English solicitor, Daniel Boynton, arrange for the transfer of twenty thousand pounds to Mr. Saxton. I should have realized that your father had mort- gaged everything to raise the money, but I didn't. Boynton and I drew up papers to protect your father's investment. If the quartz mine, a sure thing according to Saxton, did not produce the amounts of gold he had promised it would, Saxton agreed to sign over partial ownership of another operating gold mine to your father. He showed proof of the gold mine's profitability. Saxton left England several months later. We heard nothing, absolutely nothing. Your father was growing des- perate. Some two months before his death, Saxton's solicitor informed me that Mr. Saxton had writ- ten to tell him that the quartz mine your father had invested in had not produced the gold ex- pected. Saxton then refused to honor the agree- ment. Your father took it very badly."

"But that is incredible, Uncle Paul, unbeliev- able!"

"Not really, my dear. I must admit that I was somewhat skeptical about the entire business, but your father . . ." He shrugged. "He claimed that this Saxton had influential friends here in London. He trusted him."

"Just who are these influential friends?"

"I don't know. For some reason, your father refused to tell me who they were. I, of course, wanted to pursue the matter with them, but he insisted he would take care of it."

"Obviously they refused to help him. What about Saxton's solicitor, Boynton? Surely he must have known!"

"Again, my dear, I cannot tell you. You see,

poor Boynton died several weeks before your father, of apoplexy."

Chauncey stared at him blankly. If only, she thought vaguely, if only she had been her father's son, she would have been allowed to help him. She said slowly, "You sound as if you do not believe there ever was a quartz mine, Uncle Paul. That this was all a swindle."

"I think it quite likely. I fear we will never know."

"But what about the law? Why was nothing done about it?" Her voice rose shrilly.

"My dear Chauncey, Delaney Saxton lives in San Francisco, a city in California. It is many thousand miles distant. Believe me, once your father admitted to me that he would lose everything if Saxton weren't made to honor the agreement, I notified a banker friend of mine in New York City. He made inquiries, but could not discover anything. To continue would have cost a great deal of money. Neither your father nor I had it. There was nothing left, you see."

Chauncey closed her eyes a moment. Why hadn't her father confided in her? Didn't he realize that she would have done anything for him? To take his life because of money ... to leave her alone, at the mercy of her aunt. She felt a niggling anger at his cowardly behavior, but firmly quashed it. He obviously was not thinking clearly. He obviously assumed that she would wed Guy Danforth. She laughed, a harsh, rasping sound. "And there is still no money," she gasped. "Not any! And this crook, this abominable villain, Saxton, goes free!"

"Chauncey, my dear, you are overwrought. You

must calm yourself. I was an unthinking fool to have told you!"

She swallowed the rising hysteria. The world had never seemed more bleak than it did at this moment. She said aloud, "And I shall likely become a shop girl, sewing bonnets." She laughed again. "It is unfortunate, Uncle Paul, but I can't sew!"

"Chauncey, please. You will remain with your aunt and uncle. You will marry soon. In time, all this will fade, and you will forget. You will see."

Chauncey stood up, her shoulders squared, her back rigid. "No, Uncle Paul, I won't forget, ever."

Paul Montgomery looked at her distraught face. So proud and so helpless. She likely would not forget, but it wouldn't help her. No, he thought, nothing would help her, ever. He said not another word, merely escorted her from his office.

— 2 —

Chauncey could only stare openmouthed. "This is for me, Aunt Augusta?"

Augusta presented her with a wide, toothy smile. "Of course, my dear Elizabeth. It is your birthday, is it not? All this black you've been wearing, well, it's time for a change. We want to raise your spirits, my dear. I don't believe your dear father would have wanted you to go about for more than six months in such dismal clothes."

Chauncey was filled with a sense of unreality as she fingered the lavender silk gown. Aunt Augusta smiling at her? Giving her gifts? The world had taken a faulty turn! She stared blindly about her aunt's drawing room with its ponderous dark furniture, heavy fringed draperies, and the endless supply of bric-a-brac that filled every nook and cranny. "Such a scourge to dust all those things!" she could hear Mary saying.

"You will look very beautiful, cousin," Owen

said, moving toward her. "Though you are lovely just as you are."

Chauncey raised her eyes to Owen's face. He was gazing at her with the most sincere of expressions. But he is lying, she realized. He dislikes me heartily!

Uncle Alfred cleared his throat, but at a look from his wife, he kept silent.

"Dear Elizabeth," Aunt Augusta said slowly, "I realize that the past six months have not been particularly ... pleasant for you. Your poor father's death came as a dreadful shock. I will be honest with you, Elizabeth. Your uncle and I were taken aback that Alec had left you penniless. It was our own shock and disappointment, I suppose, that made us behave so unfairly. I can only say that we had been undergoing some financial problems and that quite turned our heads and our hearts. You are such a sweet girl. I pray you will find it in your heart to forgive us." Aunt Augusta smiled at her and gave her a gentle, affectionate hug.

Chauncey allowed herself to be hugged, and for an instant, warmth flowed through her. To be wanted, to belong again. It was all a mistake. They did care about her, they did want her to be happy.

Uncle Alfred cleared his throat again. "Elizabeth, my dear, we plan to celebrate your birthday this evening. A festive dinner and a play. Does that please you?"

"Yes, yes, of course, Uncle Alfred," she managed to say.

"Why do you not change, Elizabeth," Aunt Augusta said. "I have assigned Mary to you as your personal maid. I know you believed we had dismissed her after your little ... excursion last week, but we soon realized how very fond of her you are. She is waiting in your room to assist you."

Chauncey's feeling of unreality grew. The soft shimmering gown seemed as insubstantial as what had just occurred. "Thank you," she murmured, and left the salon in a daze.

Mary was waiting for her, just as Aunt Augusta had said.

"I don't understand it either, miss," Mary said, reading her thoughts exactly as she helped Chauncey remove the hated black wool gown. "When the agency told me I was to return here, I nearly swallowed my tongue! Turned off and without a reference, I was, and all because I tried to help you pay a visit to that solicitor of your father's without that old prune knowing about it!" Mary shook her head. "Of course, that miserable squealer Cranke found out and told her ladyship! Such a scene she made with me! A regular sharp-tongued fishwife, that one!"

Chauncey shivered, remembering her own scene with her aunt upon her return from Uncle Paul's office. She had been treated like a pariah until today, her birthday. Not that she had been particularly aware of it, for her mind had been in a tangle of confusion. No, she amended to herself, not confusion really, rather a cold numbness that had turned to blinding hatred for the man who had swindled her father and caused him to kill himself. She had understood everything Paul Montgomery told her, everything. And she felt so bloody helpless! Delaney Saxton was thou-

sands of miles away and here she was, stuck in
London, without a farthing to her name. She
became aware that Mary was looking at her ex-
pectantly, but for the life of her she couldn't
remember if Mary had asked her a question. "I'm
sorry, Mary, I wasn't attending. All of this"—she
waved her hand toward the lovely gown—"all of
this is such a shock! Aunt Augusta apologized to
me. Indeed, she even hugged me. I do not know
what to believe. It is all such a mystery."

"Indeed it is, miss. Mind you, I believe in
Christian charity, and how it should begin at
home, but in this house? Oh, I'm not blind by
any means, and I've seen well enough how they've
treated you these last six months. They must
want something. Aye, that's it. They want something. Sit down, miss, and I'll fix your hair before you put the gown on."

Chauncey sat on the brocade-covered stool in
front of her dressing table. "Mary," she said after a moment, meeting her maid's eyes in the
mirror, "what could I possibly have that they
would want? It makes no sense." *What I really
want is to believe them, to believe that they want
me.* "A cat remains a cat," Hannah, her old nurse,
used to say. "They're unaccountable creatures,
and pet them as much as you like, and listen to
them purr, they still never change. No, never."

Mary brushed a heavy tress of hair, curled it
deftly about her hand, then pinned it on top of
Chauncey's head. "Lovely hair you have, miss.
Every time I think I know the color, you stand in
a different light and I'll see some red or copper
or some brown. And so thick it is! Madam Prune
Face must hate to see you next to her pudding-

faced daughters! As I said, miss, I don't understand it, but I fancy you'll discover their motives soon enough."

"You don't believe then that they have perhaps ... changed?" *Please, Mary, say that it is possible!*

"Do oranges grow in London? I doubt it, miss. Now, stand up and let's see how you look in this gown. It's from Madam's own modiste too. I heard her dresser, Broome, say that it was fetched early this afternoon. Some other lady had ordered it and not paid for it. Lucky it fits you, miss."

The soft lavender silk caressed her shoulders, and a torrent of finely stitched lace spilled over her bosom. The gown fit her well enough. For a moment she felt like the Chauncey of a year ago, twirling about her father's library in a new gown, laughing when he assured her that she would break all the masculine hearts in Surrey.

" 'Tis lovely you are," Mary said, twitching an errant fold into place. "You watch out for that Master Owen, miss. So smooth and handsome he is, but he's a terror, that one! Cook told me last year that he'd tried to ravish one of the young housemaids, and in the water closet, of all places! Madam turned her off, of course." Mary shrugged philosophically. "It's the way of the world, I guess."

Mary sees things more clearly than I. I must stop being blind and seeing what it is I wish to see. I must grow up and stop being a gullible fool. "Do you know, Mary," Chauncey said, only a touch of bitterness in her voice as she slipped on the new pair of white gloves, "I think there must be something to that saying that you win more bees with honey. I think I shall be drippingly sweet tonight!"

Mary snorted. "Just see to it, miss, that you aren't the honeypot, and the bee stings you good and proper!"

Owen, Chauncey decided after but a fifteen-minute carriage ride, was definitely the bee. His new, very proper behavior stunned her, and it was all she could do to keep the niggling fear deep within her. He complimented her profusely, and listened to everything she uttered, which wasn't very much, with flattering attention. Evidently it was no longer his intention to trap her on the stairs. Her smile never faded. By the time the carriage arrived at the Russell on Albion Street, her jaw muscles ached.

"Ah, my dear," Uncle Alfred said, once they were seated around a charming white-lace-covered table, "you are the loveliest young lady present this evening. I see gentlemen already looking at Owen with envy. We will order champagne, of course, for your birthday, won't we, love? Ah yes, it is indeed a day to celebrate. Twenty-one. A marvelous age. One has all of one's life ahead of him . . . or her. You are most lucky, Elizabeth. You live with a loving family—"

"I believe I shall order the roast beef," Aunt Augusta announced, cutting off the effusions of her perspiring spouse. "You, Elizabeth, though you are as lovely as your uncle says, are a bit thin. You must order whatever you wish, my dear."

Why cannot I trust you? Why cannot I believe what you say?

"Thank you, Aunt Augusta," Chancey said aloud.

"I have been thinking, Elizabeth," her aunt continued, "that you should begin meeting with Cook. You were in charge of your poor father's household for several years, and I do not want your skills to grow rusty with disuse. You will, of course, tell Cook to prepare whatever meals appeal to you. I am certain your taste is excellent."

"I should enjoy eating whatever Elizabeth chooses," Owen said.

"Yes, well, it is decided then. Now, Alfred, where is our waiter?"

Chauncey started to tell her uncle to order for her, but stopped herself. No, she thought, stiffening her back, it is time that I am responsible for myself. She ordered what she thought to be the most expensive items on the Russell menu. At least she hoped, somewhat maliciously, that they were the dearest.

Owen's rather pale complexion grew florid as he downed his fourth glass of champagne. Chauncey swallowed a giggle, for Aunt Augusta was shooting him dagger glances.

Over a delicious dessert of blancmange and cream, Aunt Augusta leaned over and patted Chauncey's gloved hand. "My dear," she said sincerely, "I think it just as well that you did not wed Sir Guy Danforth. He likely would not have made you happy. You would likely prefer a more . . . gentle, yet sophisticated gentleman, one who is not so many years your senior. I believe, Owen, that you have consumed enough champagne."

Aunt Augusta gave a snorting laugh. "It is not, after all, your birthday, my dear boy."

Owen bestowed a lavish smile upon Chauncey. "Quite right, Mother. I fear I got carried away."

Why do I want to burst into laughter? Chauncey wondered. Even Owen, the toad, is amusing. Her thoughts turned again, unwittingly, to her father and to the villain who had murdered him as surely as if he had laced her father's wine with laudanum. She shuddered with reaction. If I hate him, she thought with sudden insight, I will destroy myself. But how, she wondered, her jaw tightening, could she simply forget? And now this ... mystery.

Uncle Alfred yawned delicately behind his hand. "Do you know, my dear," he said to his wife, "I believe I grow too old for all this jollity. Why don't you and I return to Heath House and let the young people go to the play by themselves?"

"My, what an excellent suggestion, Alfred."

In a pig's eye!

"What do you say, Elizabeth?" Owen said, dropping his voice to what he must have thought to be an intimate caress. "I will take good care of you. We will see *Romeo and Juliet.*" He gave her a grin fraught with meaning. "Of course, we aren't faced with their problems!"

We? My Lord, Chauncey thought, it is as I suspected. She saw the benign looks on her aunt's and uncle's faces. They want me to go with Owen! But why? It hadn't been too long ago that Aunt Augusta accused her of trying to trap her dear Owen into marriage. It was too much. Hannah had always accused her charge of tempting fate with her willful curiosity. But what was life without just a bit of risk? She had no doubts that she could handle Owen.

Chauncey very carefully placed her napkin beside her plate, folding it into a small square. She raised her head and flashed a wide smile to the three people looking at her. "Do you know," she said in a guilelessly innocent voice, "I should much like to see the play. It is so sweet of you to invite me, Owen. Are you certain that you don't mind, Aunt Augusta?" *I shall be as devious as the three of you!*

"Not at all, my dear. I ... your uncle and I want you to be happy and enjoy yourself. You may be certain that dear Owen will see to your every comfort."

"Oh yes, Elizabeth, I shall, I promise you."

The play was dreadful. The actors gesticulated wildly while they declaimed their lines to an increasingly restless crowd, and poor Romeo was at least forty years old. At least she wasn't bored, Chauncey thought, her lips thinning, for Owen had managed to brush his thigh against her several times. At the intermission, Chauncey allowed Owen to escort her to the large downstairs foyer for refreshments.

"May I have a glass of lemonade, please, Owen?" she asked.

"Your wish, my dear Elizabeth," he said, and gave her a flourishing bow.

When he returned with her glass, Elizabeth thanked him softly and began to sip the lemonade. She eyed him speculatively over the rim of her glass and said, "I fear the lemonade is too sour. Would you mind returning it, Owen, and getting me another glass?"

She wanted to laugh aloud at the brief look of anger that narrowed his eyes. It was gone quickly, to be replaced by what Owen must have believed to be a seductive, loving look, but Chauncey knew she hadn't imagined it. So, *my dear toad*, she thought as she watched him wend his way through the crowd back toward the refreshment tables, *your mother is making you dance attendance on me.*

When Owen handed her a new glass of lemonade, Chauncey took a small sip and handed the glass back to him. "Do you know, Owen, I fear I have developed a headache. Would you please see me home now?"

Such a pity, she thought, that the play wasn't a marvelous production, one that Owen would have liked to see to the end. As it was, her limpid request did not elicit more than a loving nod and a look of concern from him.

"Are you feeling better, Elizabeth?" he asked once they were ensconced in the hired carriage.

"Oh yes, Owen," she said sweetly, glad he couldn't see the gleam of purpose in her eyes in the dim light. "It has been such an exciting day, you know. I am in such a . . . whirl of pleasure!"

"Dear Elizabeth," Owen murmured, and gently squeezed her gloved hand. *I mustn't forget to scrub his touch off my hand.* "I am so pleased that you are happy," he continued after a moment, making Chauncey wonder if he were trying to recall a prepared speech. "It is my fondest desire to give you everything you wish, my dear." Again he paused. *Are you screwing up your courage for* something, Owen? she wanted to ask him. She waited patiently, a small smile playing about her mouth.

"Is it really, Owen?" she asked as the silence grew long.

"Indeed, Elizabeth. I realize it is perhaps too soon, your father being dead for but six months, but my heart compels me to speak. I have admired you for years, my dear, years."

My God, he really is going to ask me to marry him!

She couldn't allow it, for if she did, she would surely laugh in his face, and perhaps burst into tears at the betrayal. And Owen would never tell her why he was asking her. He would but prattle about his utter admiration of her. She realized with a start that she was afraid. *I would rather be a shop girl than marry him!*

"My ... headache, Owen, it has returned," she said abruptly. "If you don't mind, I would like to rest until we reach Heath House."

"Of course, my dear."

Did he sound the least bit relieved?

Chauncey thought furiously the remainder of the carriage ride to Heath House. There was no answer forthcoming. It appears, she decided, raising her chin in determination, that I am going to have to be an eavesdropper again.

She allowed Owen to kiss her hand, then quickly walked to her room. She sent Mary off to bed, then waited for a few more minutes. Slowly she eased her bedroom door open and peered up and down the corridor. No one was about. Stealthily she crept toward her aunt's suite of rooms. There was a light showing from beneath the door. She didn't even have to press her ear against the door, for her aunt's voice sounded through as clear as the proverbial bell.

"I am pleased you did not . . . rush things, my dear boy," Aunt Augusta said. "It is possible that Elizabeth would not think it likely that you could fall in love with her so quickly." She gave a deep relieved sigh. "I do believe that Elizabeth will forgive us for our lack of attention to her these past months. I had not believed her so malleable, but perhaps it is so."

Uncle Alfred said, "I really do not like this, my love. It is not that we are—"

Aunt Augusta interrupted him curtly. "Enough, Alfred. We haven't much time. Owen must be as attentive as possible to his cousin."

Why haven't they much time? Chauncey heard Owen say in a sulky voice, "I don't think Chauncey—"

"What an outrageous nickname! I pray you won't use it again, Owen!"

"Yes, Mother. As I was saying, I don't think Ch . . . Elizabeth particularly cares for me."

There was a stretch of utter silence. Aunt Augusta said grimly, "It was stupid of you to treat her like a housemaid, Owen! Quite stupid! You must gain her trust. Yes, that's it. The girl is lonely, but now we are her family. Her *loving* family."

Owen asked very softly, forcing Chauncey to strain to hear his words, "And if she doesn't come around, Mother? And in time?"

There were several minutes of utter silence. "It is something I would dislike above all things," Aunt Augusta said finally. "To compromise a young lady is most disturbing and quite ill-bred . . ."

Chauncey drew in her breath. Then she heard Owen laugh, covering the remainder of Aunt Augusta's words. She felt herself pale with rage. Oh yes, Owen would like to catch her unawares again! She would scratch his eyes out! She would tear . . .

"I don't like it," Uncle Alfred said. "Any of it."

"Forget Isobel," Aunt Augusta said harshly. "It must be done."

"Well, I am ready for bed," Owen announced.

Chauncey dashed down the corridor, managing to close her door just in time. She didn't fall asleep for a long time.

"Well, miss, here is your chocolate! It's a lovely day today and I want to know what you discovered."

Chauncey snapped awake. "Good morning, Mary," she said on a yawn. "I have quite a bit to tell you, and also a plan."

When she finished recounting the overheard conversation, Mary was gazing at her in consternation. "It is villainous! Suggesting that Master Owen compromise you! It is—"

"Yes, it is all that, Mary," Chauncey said, cutting her off. She stared thoughtfully for a moment into the dark glob of chocolate at the bottom of her cup. During the long, wakeful hours of the night, she had managed to repress her sorrow, her fury, and her unhappiness. All she had left was determination. "Will you help me, Mary? I have an idea. It is probably quite foolish, but I can't think of anything else for the moment."

"Oh yes, miss, anything!"

"I want you to find out if there have been any visitors in the past couple of days. Not any of Aunt Augusta's acquaintances, but a stranger. Can you do it?"

Mary screwed her eyes thoughtfully toward the ceiling. "That old sot Cranke might be difficult. But I've got ears, miss, and I can ask the staff, very subtle-like, of course."

"If there has been a visitor . . ." Chauncey shrugged. "Well, then we shall see. I can only believe that someone wants to remove me from here, and that for whatever reason, my aunt doesn't wish me to go. If there hasn't been anyone, then I would imagine that I am going to have to tread very carefully until I can leave this house and its loving occupants. Please bring me the paper, Mary—I think I should begin looking for a position."

What in heaven's name was going on? She saw them all objectively now, just as she had finally seen Guy. She had been nothing short of a fool to believe them, even for a moment. Chauncey sighed. She was likely a fool for thinking that someone, a stranger, had anything to do with Aunt Augusta's newfound devotion to her niece. She rose from her bed and began to bathe, wondering if Owen would be waiting for her in the corridor.

— 3 —

Two days passed in what Chauncey described to Mary as a state of siege, with herself being the fortress under attack. There had been a visitor, Mary had discovered, a "dried-up little man with the smell of the city on him," so Cranke told one of the footmen. But who the dried-up little man had been was still a mystery.

"Greed," Chauncey said. "There can be no other motive. Can you really believe, Mary, that Aunt Augusta would spend all this money for any other reason?" She waved her hand toward the two new gowns that lay on her bed in a froth of silk and satin. "She must view it as an investment of sorts."

"Then you think, miss, that this man is perhaps a business associate of your father's? That he is here to tell you that your father didn't lose everything after all?"

"I know it sounds farfetched," Chauncey said

on a tired sigh, "but for the life of me, I can think of nothing else."

"Don't chew your thumbnail, miss."

"Oh!" Chauncey regarded the ragged nail. "They are driving me distracted! And here I am hiding in my bedroom." She rose from the uncomfortable wing chair from beside the small fireplace and began to pace about the room. "I am being a coward, Mary, a miserable coward! I shall demand to know why they are treating me like a piece of prime horseflesh. I shall look Aunt Augusta straight in the eye—"

"I should suggest Master Owen instead," Mary said mildly.

"Well, yes, perhaps you are right. After all, they are certain to insist the minute dinner is over that Owen read me some poetry or that I play love songs to him, or some such nonsense. Then, of course, Aunt Augusta will yawn and nod and haul Uncle Alfred from the salon, leaving the 'two dear young people alone.' "

"Now, miss, you mustn't do anything rash. If this gentleman visits again, which you believe likely, I will know about it. Perhaps it is best that you simply wait them out."

Chauncey nodded glumly, and allowed Mary to dress her in another of Aunt Augusta's new gowns. It was a pale green silk cut fashionably low over her bosom. Too low, Chauncey thought as she stared in the mirror. No horse, she thought, ever looked like this. No, she looked more like a lovely piece of candy begging to be nibbled.

"Braids, Mary. Yes, I think a very severe style is in order for this evening."

Mary grinned at her young mistress, but the

resulting creation only made Chauncey appear all the more appetizing, in Mary's silent view. The thick band of braids fashioned high on her head made her slender neck look all the longer and more graceful. Mary sighed. It was too late to change it now.

"You take care, miss," she cautioned. "As long as you're playing the piano, you should be safe enough!"

"Thank you for the advice," Chauncey said dryly.

Unfortunately, it appeared that Aunt Augusta and Owen agreed with Mary. Did Owen believe that her new hairstyle was meant to entice him? Probably, she thought cynically, along with her bosom falling out of her gown.

"How utterly charming you look this evening, my dear Elizabeth," her aunt said. "So sophisticated with your hair like that. Don't you agree, Owen?"

"Oh, certainly, Mother, certainly."

"A beautiful new Penworthy," Uncle Alfred said.

Aunt Augusta tittered. Tittered! Chauncey felt her ears begin to tingle. She turned glittering eyes toward her uncle and said with forced calm, "I fear you forget that I am not a Penworthy, Uncle Alfred. I am a FitzHugh, a Jameson Fitz-Hugh."

"But not for much longer, I vow," Aunt Augusta said archly.

Chauncey did not miss the warning glance she sent toward Owen.

Aunt Augusta must have realized that the conversation had taken too forward a turn, and quickly retrenched. "You know, Elizabeth, your uncle and I have been thinking that your bed-chamber is a bit confining. With your marvelous taste, my dear, we have decided that you should have the Green Room and decorate it to your liking."

My marvelous taste? Chauncey wanted to laugh aloud. If Aunt Augusta was judging her taste by the dinner in front of her, her ability to spin falsehoods was indeed phenomenal. Stewed ham hocks in wine sauce, and boiled collards! Cook had gazed at Chauncey as if she had lost her mind. The Green Room. Chauncey blinked. It was a large, airy bedchamber that connected by an adjoining door to Owen's room. The siege had intensified. For a moment Chauncey felt raw fear well within her. She could expect no protec-tion from her aunt or uncle. She would have to go to Uncle Paul on the morrow. He would have to help her.

She smiled blandly. "I shall think about it, Aunt Augusta."

When Aunt Augusta and Uncle Alfred bid the young couple a hearty good night, just as Chaun-cey knew they would, she saw that Owen would make his declaration. He was sweating, beads of perspiration standing out on his broad forehead.

"Would you like me to play for you, Owen?" she asked, watching him rub his palms on his breeches.

She did not wait for him to reply, but moved purposefully to the piano and seated herself. She began to play a Mozart sonata, a very long one, she thought viciously.

Owen overcame his trepidation and interrupted

her during the second movement. "Elizabeth, my dear," he muttered close to her ear. She jumped at the feel of his hot breath against her cheek, and her hands came down on a discordant array of keys.

"I must speak to you. Please, Elizabeth, I find that I can hold back what I feel for you no longer!"

Chauncey turned slowly on the piano stool and stared up at him for a long moment. "How fluently you say your lines, Owen," she said.

He looked taken aback, but only for a moment. "I doubt I could ever be as fluent as you, my dear. Come, Elizabeth, and sit with me."

She rose and followed him to the high-backed sofa. But she didn't sit down. "What is it you wish to say to me?" she asked without preamble.

Owen laughed confidently. "You are so forthright, Elizabeth. As you wish." He shrugged, then sent her a blinding smile. "I want you to marry me."

Chauncey looked him squarely in the eye. "Why, Owen?"

"Why?" he repeated softly, his eyes caressing her face. "I love you, of course. I told you countless times in the past days that I have long admired you."

"Yes, that is what you have said. What I should like to know, Owen, is why you are asking me to marry you now, at this time."

"You have just turned twenty-one. It is time that you were wed."

"So, when my birthday dawned, you decided that you loved me."

"Not precisely, but close enough."

She thought for a brief moment that he would

have liked to add "damn you!" But of course he did not. "Owen," she said finally, still hopeful that he would slip and tell her something, "do you not recall that I am penniless? Hardly worthy wife material, I should say. Don't you agree?"

"There are more important things than money," he said.

"Not to your family, Owen," she said.

"You are wrong, Elizabeth, quite wrong! My mother and father think you are wonderful, and they do not mind that you do not have a dowry, I promise you."

He wasn't going to tell her a damned thing, Chauncey realized in disgust. He had been well-coached. "Owen," she said, "I have no intention of wedding anyone. I suggest you forget your newly acquired feelings for me."

"I cannot!" he said, his voice sharp now. He made a move to capture her hands, but Chauncey quickly whisked behind a chair. "It is not kind of you to . . . toy with my feelings."

"Owen," she said with great patience, "I do not wish to toy with anyone's feelings. I wish only to be left alone." She lowered her eyes a moment, and added, "Indeed, your parents' kindness to me has made me realize that I cannot continue to live on their bounty. I intend to find myself some sort of position."

"Position! That is ridiculous! My mother would never hear of such a thing. No, Elizabeth, for your protection, you must marry me."

"I remember, Owen, that you offered me your protection, without marriage."

"It was but a . . . jest, my dear. Aye, a jest."

"Good night, Owen," she said, lifting her chin.

"No, wait!"

Chauncey raised her skirts and ran from the salon. No, dear Owen, she thought as she ran up the stairs, I have no intention of being mauled by you!

"Elizabeth!"

He was chasing her! Chauncey made her room barely in time. She slammed the door and clicked the lock. She leaned against the door, painfully aware of her heaving breasts and pounding heart.

The doorknob rattled suddenly. "Elizabeth, let me in! I only want to speak to you. Come, unlock the door."

Where was Mary? Would her Aunt Augusta have the door broken down so Owen could compromise her? Try for a little deviousness, Chauncey, she told herself. You should have learned something about it from Aunt Augusta. "Owen, dear," she said softly. "I have a terrible headache. And you have surprised me mightily. I . . . I think my nerves are disordered. Can we speak of"—she couldn't bring herself to say "marriage"—"your feelings and mine on the morrow?"

There was utter silence for several moments. She thought she heard footsteps, and pressed her ear to the door. She heard her Aunt Augusta's voice, but could not make out her words. Then Owen said, "Of course, Elizabeth. You think my feelings for you are sudden, when in fact they are of long standing. We will speak tomorrow morning. Sleep well, my love."

Chauncey drew a deep breath. So Aunt Augusta had given her a night's respite. This is like something out of a melodrama, she thought suddenly, pained laughter bubbling up in her throat.

And Owen's acting is every bit as bad as poor Romeo's was! She no longer wanted to laugh, she was too frightened. She stood for several more moments, then walked purposefully to her armoire. She pulled out her large valise and began to pack her belongings. She stared a moment at the new gowns, then tossed them on the floor of the armoire.

When her valise was packed, she walked to the window and drew back the heavy curtains. The night was thick and uninviting, a heavy fog encasing even the tall trees in the park. This is all such nonsense, she thought, regaining her perspective. They cannot hold me prisoner, after all.

Chauncey awoke the next morning at a sharp knock on her door. She blinked away sleep and called out, "Who is it?"

"Mary, miss."

She heaved a sigh of relief and quickly rose to unlock the door. "I had thought it might be Owen," she said.

"Your valise, miss," Mary said, eyeing the bulging bag.

"Yes," Chauncey said. "I am leaving this morning, Mary. I am going to see my Uncle Paul. He will help me, he must."

At Mary's questioning look, Chauncey quickly told her what had happened the night before.

"Lawks!" Mary said. "Well, miss, after I've seen you dressed, I'll go pack my own things. And don't you worry, miss, we'll manage, you'll see."

I don't know how, Chauncey thought, but she

didn't have the energy to quibble. "Thank you, Mary," she said.

Chauncey didn't see Owen immediately, not until he said heartily from behind her, "Good morning, Elizabeth."

She jumped, feeling gooseflesh rise on her arms. "I am going to breakfast, Owen," she said, and made to walk past him.

"Not until we have reached an ... agreement, my love," Owen said, and closed his fingers around her wrist.

Chauncey stared down at his fingers.

"Tell me, promise me, that you'll marry me, Elizabeth."

His fingers tightened painfully. "Let me go, Owen."

"My parents have procured a special license, my love," he continued as if she had not spoken. "A minister, a Mr. Hampton, is already here to wed us. Say yes, Elizabeth."

"What?" she asked in a mocking voice. "We are to be wed before breakfast?"

"You will not toy with me further, Elizabeth," he snarled, and tightened his grip on her wrist.

Breathe deeply, Chauncey, she told herself. Be calm. "Owen," she said after a moment, "I will not wed you, not before breakfast, not ever. Indeed, I would not wed you if it meant I had to ... sell my body! Do you understand me?"

"Yes," he said, his voice dropping low, "oh yes you will, cousin." He slammed her against the wall, his hand clutching at the material at her throat. He jerked down, ripping her gown to her waist. She felt his mouth against her ear. "Oh yes, Elizabeth. I'll take you now. Then you'll have me."

She had imagined such a scene in her mind, but the reality of it left her momentarily stunned. Owen was kissing her, forcing his tongue into her mouth. She felt his hands grasping at her breasts. He was standing with his side turned to her, and she realized that he thought she would try to kick him.

Owen was dragging her toward his room.

Chauncey went utterly limp. She heard him draw in his breath in surprise, but he remembered what she had done to him the other time. "Oh, Owen," she sighed, and raised her mouth.

He clasped her hard against him, and his tongue was lunging against her closed lips. She opened her mouth. When his tongue thrust in, she bit him as hard as she could.

Owen yelled in pain. He fell back, clutching his hand over his mouth, and she could see blood between his fingers.

Chauncey grabbed her skirts and ran toward the stairs. She was hurtling down just as the knocker sounded at the front door. Owen was closing behind her, yelling crude curses at her. She realized vaguely that no one was about, none of the servants, not her aunt or uncle, not anyone.

She shouted at the top of her lungs, "Come in!"

The front door eased open, and a small man with bushy side whiskers thrust his head through the door. Chauncey shouted, "Yes, come in! Help me!"

Frank Gillette stared in astonishment at the young lady who was rushing down the stairs toward him. Her hair was disheveled, her gown torn to her waist. Behind her was a furious-looking young man who looked fit to kill.

Good God, he thought blankly, he had interrupted a rape. "What," he asked firmly, "is going on here?"

Suddenly the foyer seemed to erupt with people. Mrs. Penworthy and her rather unprepossessing spouse flew from the salon to his left. A man whom Gillette believed to be the butler came from the dining room to his right, his black coattails flapping.

"I repeat," Gillette said sternly, holding out his hand to the girl, "what the devil is the meaning of this?"

"What are you doing here?" Aunt Augusta yelled, her face pale with consternation. "You were not supposed to come again until tomorrow!"

Chauncey felt her terror begin to fade. This was the man with the smell of the city. "Who are you?" she whispered.

"Elizabeth, go to your room! I will come to you directly!"

Chauncey stared at her aunt and moved closer to the stranger.

"I am Frank Gillette," he said in a steadying voice. "Are you, by any chance, Miss Elizabeth Jameson FitzHugh?"

She nodded.

"I am delighted to find you in good health."

"I am always in good health, sir."

"Elizabeth, I will not tell you again," Aunt Augusta said, her jaw clenched. "Go to your room. Owen, see your cousin upstairs."

"Aunt," Chauncey said, stiffening beside her

rescuer, "I have no intention of going anywhere with any of you. I am leaving this house."

"Mr. Gillette," Aunt Augusta said, her voice supplicating, even pleading, "my niece is not herself. I pray you will ignore her disordered outburst and come with me into the salon. We will call the doctor for her immediately."

Money, Mr. Gillette thought, not overly surprised at what had obviously been transpiring—what it does to perfectly sane people! He was a fool, he realized belatedly, to have confided his purpose to this woman. "Madam," he said calmly to Aunt Augusta, "I am come to see Miss Fitz-Hugh. Now, if all of you will excuse us, we will take our leave."

"You are going nowhere, Elizabeth!" Aunt Augusta shouted, so frustrated she was trembling. "If you dare to leave this house, miss, you will starve in the street! We will provide you no more of our generous bounty!"

"But then again, Aunt Augusta," Chauncey said, drawing herself up straight, "I won't have to worry about being ravished by Owen, will I?"

"Liar! She is lying, Mr. Gillette! Pay her no heed!"

"Mr. Gillette, may I fetch my valise—'tis already packed—and my maid?"

"Certainly, my dear. If I am correct, I believe I saw a young woman who could be your maid waiting on the corner, with her bag. I will await you here." He touched her shoulder. "Miss FitzHugh," he said very softly, "you will not starve, I promise you that.

"Mrs. Penworthy," he continued to Aunt Augusta, "I will call the watch if the young lady isn't allowed to leave with me."

"No," Uncle Alfred said sternly, wiping his hand across his sweating forehead, "there will be no need for that. Augusta, you and Owen will go into the salon. It is over." He added almost as an afterthought, "I never really believed that Elizabeth could be coerced. She is too strong-willed." He turned away with those words, only to be brought up short by Cranke, who said in a faltering voice, "But, sir, what am I to do with the minister? He is drinking his third cup of coffee."

"Good God, man, set him to polishing the silver! I don't care!"

— 4 —

"A legacy! I have a legacy? I ... I don't believe it," Chauncey whispered, her eyes wide on Mr. Gillette's face. They were seated opposite each other in Chauncey's small sitting room in the Bradford Hotel. "Oh, I had figured out that all their machinations must have something to do with money, but I had no real expectations, you understand. You have said, Mr. Gillette, that you in no way represent my father. Then where does this legacy to me come from?"

"I believe you now recovered enough from your ordeal," he said, smiling at her. "Here is the whole story, Miss FitzHugh. Your godfather, Sir Jasper Dunkirk—do you remember him?"

"Why, of course I do, though it has been at least ten years since I've seen him."

"I am, rather was, Sir Jasper's solicitor. For the past nine years, he has resided in India. In fact, he made a great deal of money there. But, unfortunately, he lost both his wife and his son in one of the native uprisings. As a result, he made your father his heir, for there was no other family, either there or here in England. Sir Jasper died of a fever some months after your father. He had, evidently, read your father's obituary in a newspaper, for I received instructions from him shortly before his death. I suppose he knew of your family ties, for his instructions were quite clear. I was not to contact you about your inheritance until you turned twenty-one. You see, he wanted no relatives or guardians to have control of your wealth. I paid a visit to Heath House on your twenty-first birthday. I showed a lamentable lack of judgment, however. I told your aunt of my mission, then blithely accepted her word that you were ill and could see no one for a while. I was a fool, and I beg you to accept my profound apologies."

Chauncey gave him a twisted smile. "Had they not been so very ungracious to me before, I might not have seen through their ruse. You see, they became so utterly devoted to my welfare that I would have had to be a perfect ninny not to see through them." *But at first I didn't want to believe badly of them.* "And Owen. They wanted me to marry him, of course."

"Of course," Mr. Gillette agreed. "As your husband, he would have had complete control over your inheritance."

"Mr. Gillette, will my inheritance make me independent? It doesn't have to be too much, of course, just enough to keep me and my maid in simple lodgings."

To her surprise, Mr. Gillette leaned forward

in his chair and laughed heartily. For a moment Chauncey gazed at his nearly bald head, contrasting the pitiful few dark hairs that were combed carefully over the top of his plentiful side whiskers. "I have said something amusing, sir?"

"Miss FitzHugh," he managed at last, "not only are you independent, you are likely now one of the premier heiresses in all of England. My dear, you have inherited some two hundred thousand pounds."

Chauncey could only stare at him. "Two hundred thousand pounds," she repeated stupidly.

"Yes, my dear. At least I was wise enough not to tell your aunt and uncle the amount of your inheritance. I told them only that it was sizable. I imagine if I let slip the true amount, they would have whisked you willy-nilly to Gretna Green with their obnoxious son in tow."

"Two hundred thousand pounds," Chauncey said yet again. She rose jerkily to her feet. "It . . . it is too much! Oh dear, whatever am I to do?"

Frank Gillette was silent for a moment, watching the lovely young lady pace in front of him. "I believe you are an intelligent young woman," he said. "And you are twenty-one and in entire control of the money. I would suggest, my dear, that you have two alternatives: you can either find yourself a husband to control your holdings, or you can learn to manage for yourself."

"But I have never even seen *one* hundred pounds!"

Before Mr. Gillette could reply, Chauncey suddenly burst into loud laughter. "Oh dear," she gasped, hugging her sides, "surely I have stepped into the pages of some fairy tale, and you, sir, are my fairy godfather!"

"Well," Mr. Gillette said dryly, "this fairy godfather owns ten percent of your wealth." He downed the remainder of his tea and rose. "I suggest that you think about it, Miss FitzHugh. Rest assured that your inheritance is quite safe. Here is my card. When you have decided what you wish to do, please contact me."

After showing Mr. Gillette out, Mary returned to where Chauncey stood staring blankly into the small fireplace.

"Is there anything else you wish, madam?"

Chauncey, startled, looked at Mary, who stood stiffly in front of her. "You're acting awfully starchy, Mary," she said. "With all that money, I am suddenly become a madam instead of a miss?"

"Well, I only want to do what is proper—"

"Oh, Mary, cut line! Sit down and have some tea. You and I need to discuss what the devil I'm going to do with all my ill-gotten gains!"

The next afternoon, Chauncey, with Mary in tow, entered Mr. Gillette's office, not far from her Uncle Paul's, on Fleet Street.

The single black-frocked clerk was evidently expecting her, for he was on his feet in an instant. He bowed low to her, as if she were royalty. "Miss FitzHugh? Mr. Gillette is expecting you, ma'am. If you will follow me, please."

What servility, Chauncey thought, now that I am rich. She winked at Mary, and entered Mr. Gillette's office. It was large and dark, with heavy mahogany furnishings and two walls lined with bookshelves. Thick brocade draperies were drawn across narrow windows.

"Ah, my dear Miss FitzHugh. Welcome. Sit down."

"I have come to a decision, Mr. Gillette," Chauncey said without preamble, once she was seated across from his imposing desk.

"Yes, my dear?" he asked in a carefully neutral voice.

"I wish to control my own money. I have done a bit of studying in the past twenty-four hours, and have learned that a woman has absolutely no control over anything once she is married."

"That is quite true."

Chauncey lowered her eyes to her clasped hands in her lap. She toyed with the idea of telling Mr. Gillette of her plans, but decided not to. It really didn't concern him, after all. "I realize that in order to be able to handle my money with some astuteness, Mr. Gillette, someone must teach me about finance and business."

A thin dark brow arched upward.

Chauncey drew a deep breath. "I will apply myself, sir. I have allotted myself two months to learn what it is I need to learn." At his continued silence she added with some asperity, "I am not stupid, sir, nor am I a fluffle-headed female!"

"No. No, you are not," he said.

"I would imagine that most men would treat me in an odiously condescending manner were I to tell them what I wished to do. I ask you, sir, can you recommend someone who would help me, truly help me?"

"Yes, Miss FitzHugh, I know of someone who would help you." He grew silent again, and toyed with a pen on his desk. "You say you have chosen a time period of two months. May I ask what you intend to do when the two months have elapsed?"

Chauncey gave him a wide smile, but it didn't reach her eyes, which grew cold and hard. "Yes, Mr. Gillette. I am leaving England. I am going to ... America."

Mr. Gillette sucked in his breath in surprise. "This is quite a surprise, Miss FitzHugh—"

"Please, sir, call me Chauncey. My aunt thinks it is a dreadfully common nickname, but I am comfortable with it."

"Very well, Chauncey. Perhaps you will tell me why you have chosen America?"

"Perhaps," Chauncey said coolly, "I might just decide to live there awhile, and of course I understand it is a vast place. I shall doubtless travel." She shrugged. "We shall see." She leaned forward, her eyes intent on his face. "I trust you, Mr. Gillette. I wish you to remain my solicitor in England. But you will have to explain to me how I am to transfer a portion of my funds to America." A vast portion, she amended silently.

"I will be delighted to explain all that to you, Miss Fitz ... Chauncey. I would also be delighted to teach you myself, had I all the knowledge you need. But alas, I do not. Are you free this evening?" At her nod, he smiled. "Good. Expect me around seven o'clock tonight with a gentleman. His name is Gregory Thomas. He is one of the most astute and knowledgeable gentlemen of finance in all of England. I am certain that he will not disdain you because of your sex, my dear, I can promise you that!"

"I believe, sir," Chauncey said, grinning impishly, "that I should prefer you."

"Yes, I myself always prefer the known to the unknown. But you will like Mr. Thomas. He has much free time on his hands now, and will likely treat you like a beloved granddaughter."

After Frank Gillette had shown Chauncey from his office, he returned to his chair and sat down. He steepled his fingers and thumped them thoughtfully together. He was not blind. He had seen the implacable determination in her expressive eyes. What, he wondered, is the girl up to? Why does she wish to go to America? Perhaps, his thinking continued, if Gregory agreed to take the girl under his knowledgeable wing, he could discover what she was after. He disliked mysteries.

"Really, Chauncey, you must pay attention!"

Chauncey started guiltily and raised contrite eyes to Gregory Thomas. Indeed, she thought, taking in his thick wavy white hair and twinkling brown eyes, he did look like her grandfather. He had taken her under his wing with a good deal of enthusiasm, for, she guessed, he was very bored since he had left his business dealings in the hands of his son. "I'm sorry, Gregory," she said. "It's just . . ." Her voice broke off suddenly.

"Chauncey, what are you up to?"

No, she thought firmly, I won't tell him. No one is to be involved, no one but me. She smiled warmly, praying that she was convincing, for Gregory Thomas was exceedingly perceptive, making her feel on occasion as if her mind was a story eager to be read. "I was just thinking about my aunt and uncle, if you must know!"

He looked instantly diverted. "What have they to say this time?"

Chauncey gurgled with ready laughter. "You won't believe this, Gregory, but my Aunt Augusta has sent me a bill! For my room and board for six months. Also for the gowns and things she had made for me that fateful week."

"I trust you told them to go to the devil."

"Gregory, such language for a sweet young lady! No indeed, sir, I instructed Mr. Gillette to send them fifty pounds. I can just imagine the look on my aunt's face. She has been trying to blacken my name, you know. I find it most diverting."

"Wretched woman! I think we should put a stop to it, Chauncey. After all, a good name is quite important—"

"Particularly for a woman?" she asked blandly.

"Yes, I won't lie to you, and neither should you lie to yourself." He waved a slender hand. "Now that you have successfully gotten me off our fascinating subject, I must tell you that your aunt and uncle have been to see your father's solicitor."

"Uncle Paul? Good heavens, whatever for? When? I visited him last week, you know, and he mentioned nothing of it to me." Indeed, she thought, Paul Montgomery's kindness to her had turned to stilted formality during the past weeks. He had been hurt, she had thought in explanation, to learn that she had no intention of allowing him to administer her vast wealth. No, he hadn't mentioned anything about her aunt and uncle on her last visit. Indeed, he had seemed perturbed when she finally confided her plans to him.

"But you can't do that! 'Tis unheard-of, Chauncey! For God's sake, my dear, let it go!"

She had gazed at him intently, wondering at his unwonted display of emotion. "No, Uncle Paul, I shall never let it go. Delaney Saxton will pay. Once he is broken, once he knows that I, Elizabeth Jameson FitzHugh, am the person who has ruined him, I shall consider getting on with my life."

His jaw had worked spasmodically and he had paled under her intense gaze. "But, Chauncey—" he began.

"Uncle Paul, don't worry about me. I know what I am about, I assure you. And please don't tell me how much money it will cost. I can afford it, after all."

Chauncey, aware that Gregory was regarding her questioningly, shook off the memory of that meeting and asked more calmly, "What did they want with Uncle Paul, sir?"

"They wanted to discover if there were some way they could get part of your inheritance. Nearest relatives, former guardians, and all that sort of nonsense."

"I trust," Chauncey said tartly, "that he sent them to the rightabout!"

"Oddly enough, he didn't," Gregory said. "My sources of information tell me that he is quite busy at this moment trying to manufacture evidence, shall we say, that you were guilty of a breach of promise, that you had, in fact, been engaged to marry Owen Penworthy, and broke it off when you learned of your inheritance. These are some of the rumors they are busily spreading, my dear. I am surprised you did not know of them. But you needn't worry yourself about it, Chauncey. I have discussed the matter thoroughly with Frank Gillette. If such a charge were true, it would be likely that you could be sued for a good deal of money, but of course, it isn't true. Your *Uncle* Paul doesn't have a prayer of succeeding."

One thing Gregory Thomas had taught her during the past weeks was to sift calmly through facts when faced with a problem. She forced herself to do that now. After several moments she said, "I can understand my aunt and uncle's actions, for as my nurse Hannah used to tell me, a cat remains a cat. As to the rumors they are spreading, I had heard only that they were calling me coldhearted, an unnatural niece, and the like. What I do not understand is why Paul Montgomery would be willing to assist them."

Gregory Thomas shrugged elaborately. "Who knows? Money, as I'm certain you are discovering, my dear, makes people behave in execrable ways."

"You don't like Paul Montgomery," she said flatly.

"You are becoming much too perceptive, Chauncey. No, I will admit to it. I dislike the man heartily. I have for many years now. I do not trust him."

More facts to sift through. "Why?"

"My reasons have nothing particularly to do with you, my dear, thus I will keep them to myself."

"Very well, sir, I will not press you. None of it will really matter soon in any case. In exactly three weeks I will be sailing on the *Eastern Light* to America." She shrugged. "Who knows? Perhaps I shan't return to England."

He shook his head at her, perplexed.

"The *Eastern Light*," she explained kindly, "leaves from Plymouth on the thirteenth of November."

"Chauncey, stop playing games with me!"

"Games?" She raised an eyebrow. "I have told you often enough that I wish to travel. Now, enough about my plans, Gregory. You were quizzing me about contracts, remember?"

Gregory sighed. He wished Chauncey had confided her plans to Frank Gillette. He reluctantly drew himself back to Chauncey and her question. "Not exactly contracts, Elizabeth. A good lawyer can handle that. It's the people involved that are important. You must learn everything about anyone you intend to become involved with in a business venture."

"Yes," Chauncey said, nodding her head, "I understand that, Gregory." Indeed she did, she thought. Her eyes glittered. She could taste the revenge now. How she would savor it as she watched Delaney Saxton ruined!

"I do have several more questions about transferring funds, Gregory," she continued. "If I decide to travel around a bit in America, how can I be certain that my money will be available to me when I wish it?"

"It's a bit difficult, particularly in America. Not in large cities like New York or Boston, to be certain, but if one goes farther west of Chicago, honoring drafts becomes a bit hazardous. I, of course, will provide you with names of men whom

I trust, and banks that have endured during the currency fluctuations."

She was not that ignorant about San Francisco anymore. "If I decide to travel beyond Chicago, then it appears I should carry my money with me."

"It's true. What several people of my acquaintance have done when traveling to more uncivilized areas is to turn their money into gems. Diamonds most often. They're easy to hide, don't alert thieves, and are easy to turn back into currency. But, my dear, I cannot imagine that you would ever want to visit such places."

"Likely not," Chauncey said blandly. "But it never hurts to know about such things, does it?"

— 5 —

San Francisco, California, 1853

Delaney Xavier Saxton dismounted from the broad back of his stallion, Brutus, and stood on the corner of Second Street and Bryant, gazing with pride at his gray-stone-faced house, one of the most impressive additions to South Park. And it was nearly always sunny here on the southern slope of Rincon Hill, the San Francisco fog rarely wrapping it in a thick blanket of white. After nearly a year he still enjoyed contemplating the impressive structure with its wide portico and deep-set stone steps. He was pleased that the architect, Archibald Grover, had been able to reproduce his father's home in Boston from the rather amateur drawings Delaney had made for him. Although he hadn't thought so at the time, the devastating fire of June 1851 that had destroyed his first home had been something of a blessing. His new house had permanency; no fire would destroy it. It was a house that would become a home, with a wife and children filling the now-vacant rooms with laughter and joy.

The thought quickly turned his expression to a frown as Penelope Stevenson came to mind. Penelope, with her lovely face and dainty figure. She already treated his house with proprietary complacency, as did her mother and wealthy father, Henry Stevenson. Henry, known to his business cronies as Bunker, was beginning to press him, intimating in that brash, loud voice of his that his little girl could have her pick of eligible men.

It was true. There were still few marriageable ladies in San Francisco. The majority of women were whores, rich men's mistresses, or tight-lipped matrons who sought continually to improve the society of the city with their endless subscription balls, charity dinners, and Shakespearean productions. Penelope was quite pretty, Delaney thought objectively, pretty when her little mouth did not pout or turn down sullenly at the corners. And for some reason, she wanted him. Why was he still hesitating to ask that fatal question? He shook his head, knowing well the answer. He didn't love Penelope. She was eighteen years old, still childish in so many ways, capricious, vain, utterly spoiled by her doting father, and an outrageous flirt.

"Mr. Saxton, do you want me to take Brutus to the stable?"

Delaney turned at the sound of Lucas' deep, rumbling voice.

"Yes, please, Lucas. The old fellow needs a

good rubdown." He added ruefully, "And I've been a poor master, standing here like a fool, woolgathering."

"Miss Stevenson and Mrs. Stevenson will be here soon, sir, for tea."

Delaney snorted. "Tea, for God's sake," he muttered. "As far as I know, Mrs. Stevenson has not one whit of English blood in her fat veins."

Lucas' bland expression didn't change. "Lin Chou has made cakes, but I don't think they're particularly English. Made with rice."

Delaney laughed. "I suppose I had better see to improving my appearance. I'm certain Mrs. Stevenson won't approve of male sweat."

"Likely not," said Lucas. "You were at the post office, sir?"

"Yes. I've a letter from my brother in New York." He saw Lucas' face drop and said with more optimism than he actually felt, "Not a letter today from your sister, Lucas. You know the mails as well as I do."

"Aye, I know." But Lucas was disappointed. His sister, Julia, lived in Baltimore. Lucas had written her dozens of letters, begging her to join him in San Francisco. She would agree in one letter, only to put him off in the next.

Delaney patted Brutus' glossy neck and strode into his house. His booted steps sounded loud on the Chinese granite entryway, and the large chandelier overhead rattled with his movement. He climbed the beautiful carved oak staircase to the upper floor. His bedroom was enormous, the floor covered with several beautiful carpets from China. The huge bed was made of rosewood, as were the night table and armoire. Possessions, he thought, standing quietly for a moment in the middle of the room. At last I have all the possessions I could wish for, and still ... A large high-backed sofa faced the marble fireplace, with two wing chairs flanking it. Delaney sank down into one of the chairs and pulled his brother's letter from his waistcoat pocket.

"Dear Del," he read, "I hope this letter finds you in your usual good health. Actually I will be glad if this letter finds you! Giana is doing splendidly, as are Leah and Nicolas. My life is never dull, I can promise you." Delaney skimmed the next page of the letter that dealt with Alex's business and suggestions to Delaney on investments he might consider. "Speaking of investments, brother, I'm enclosing a clipping from the London *Times*. Wasn't Sir Alec FitzHugh one of the men who invested in your mine in Downieville? It appears he's quite dead, has been, as you can see from the clipping, for nearly ten months now. Unfortunately, Giana and I hadn't noticed it. In fact, she was wrapping a gift to send to her mother when she came across the paper, and wondered if you knew about his demise. I trust you were duly informed long ago by his lawyer." Delaney laid down the letter and gazed into the empty grate of the fireplace. No, he hadn't been informed by Paul Montgomery, Sir Alec's solicitor in London. Every month he sent a bank draft to Montgomery, quite large amounts, for the mine had proved a true find, as Delaney had known it would. Why hadn't Montgomery written to him? Perhaps he had, Delaney thought, remembering his comment to Lucas about the chancy mail system. Hadn't Sir Alec had a daughter? Was

Montgomery simply giving her the money now? Still, he should have notified me, Delaney thought, slowly rising from the chair. He had heard about his own solicitor's death, which had occurred before Sir Alec's. He didn't like coincidences.

As he bathed and changed into a frilled white shirt and a black frock coat, he mentally composed the letter he would write to Paul Montgomery. He was somewhat distracted when he greeted Penelope and her mother some thirty minutes later in what Mrs. Stevenson persisted in calling his drawing room.

"My dear Mr. Saxton, how delightful to see you again! Penelope has missed you sorely, sir! How nice of you to invite us for tea."

The woman was as loud and vulgar as her husband, but Delaney's smile never faltered. "My pleasure, ma'am. Penelope, you are looking lovely, as usual."

He took her small slender hand and raised it to his lips. He could see her preening at his courtly gesture. "Won't you ladies please be seated? Lucas, you may serve the tea and cakes."

Mrs. Agatha Stevenson was large-boned, her bosom overpowering. She persisted in wearing the most youthful of French fashions, gowns of daring colors decorated with quantities of ribbons and furbelows. Delaney silently hoped that the chair she chose would crack under her weight. How she and her equally large and clumsy husband had produced such a slender daughter was beyond him.

"English tea," Mrs. Stevenson said complacently, adjusting her bulk in the creaking chair.

"Did you not tell us once, Mr. Saxton, that you were in England several years ago?"

"Oh yes, Del, do tell us about it," said Penelope, her brown eyes wide with interest. "How I should love to go there."

"First the tea, ladies," Delaney said, signaling to the expressionless Lucas to wheel the cart to Mrs. Stevenson. "The cakes," he added blandly, "are Lin Chou's creation. I trust you will find them as delicious as I do."

"It could not be otherwise!"

"They look marvelous, Del!"

Delaney almost grinned when Mrs. Stevenson bit into the rice cake. Her jowls quivered, but of course she could say nothing now. Lin's rice cakes, flat and delicately browned, were more decorative than edible.

Why not impress the hell out of them? he thought, and with a nonchalant air said, "I returned to London in the company of my brother's mother- and father-in-law, the Duke and Duchess of Graffton."

"Oh," Penelope said, sitting forward in her chair. "Royalty!"

"Not quite, Penelope," he said blandly. "In any case, I spent an enjoyable several months in London, and managed at the same time to conduct a goodly amount of business." *With Sir Alec FitzHugh, among others, who is now dead.*

"Oh, Del, do tell me about the Tower of London," Penelope said in her breathless high voice. "Is there still blood about from all the people beheaded there?"

"No blood. The English are quite fastidious about things like that, you know." *It was Mont-*

*gomery who pressed for Sir Alec to invest. Why
didn't the man write to me of Sir Alec's death?*

Delaney felt a veil of boredom begin to descend. Surely teatime in England never lasted so bloody long! Did he really want to marry a chit who was only eighteen years old, and as empty-headed as a gourd? "Jesus," he muttered.

"What did you say, Del? ... Nothing? Well, let me tell you our news. Mama is giving a formal ball in three weeks and everyone will come! We're all going to wear masks—Papa insisted."

Delaney nearly spilled his tea. Masks! How could the girl and her mother be so ill-informed? Mr. Stevenson wanted everyone in San Francisco to attend his wife's ball, and that would necessarily mean that many of the ladies who would grace the function weren't ladies at all, but the men's mistresses. But Mrs. Stevenson did know, he silently amended to himself, watching the older woman shift uncomfortably in her chair as her daughter gibbered on. Anything, he thought, to fill the Stevensons' ballroom.

At last Delaney heard the Stevensons' carriage pull up in front of the house. He did not call for Lucas, but saw the ladies out himself. He returned Penelope's exuberant wave, walked back into the house, and made for the kitchen. The door was partially open, and he paused a moment at the sound of Lin Chou's giggle.

"I tell you, Lin," Lucas was saying to the slight Chinese girl, "the old behemoth couldn't say a word about the rice cakes. Mr. Saxton spiked her guns again, having her admit how marvelous they were before she took a bite."

Delaney could picture Lin nodding her head in

a quick birdlike movement. "Rice cakes are very delicacy, Lucas. Are you certain you not try another one?"

Delaney heard her laugh sweetly again, a sound he would not have heard from that of the silent, terrified girl he had rescued six months earlier from a filthy crib on Washington Street. He had bought her, as a matter of fact, at an auction. He had no idea if she had already been prostituted on her voyage from China. And of course he couldn't ask her. It would result in a loss of face that she could not endure. Thank God, Lucas had taken her under his mighty wing. Delaney grinned, remembering the gibe from Sam Brannan about Delaney taking in outcasts. "A chink whore and a one-legged pirate, Del! Jesus, man, don't you fear waking up with your throat cut? Or contracting some vile disease to rot off your privates?"

Delaney turned away from the kitchen and made his way to the library, his favorite room, built exactly to his specifications. It was a smaller model of the Duke of Graffton's library in London, replete with heavy dark leather furniture and three walls lined from floor to ceiling with bookcases. A thick red Aubusson carpet made the room less austere. It made it elegant. He tried for a moment to picture Penelope in this room and failed utterly.

For God's sake, man, he told himself silently, you're twenty-eight years old! You've got to marry someone, and Lord knows there are slim pickings in San Francisco. It occurred to him as he sat down behind his massive desk that if he did marry Penelope he would not give up Marie Duchamps, his French mistress. He spent several moments in vivid imagery of Marie, soft, beautifully white, lying naked on her bed, her arms open to receive him, her dark eyes dreamy with anticipation. She was faithful to him, at least he hoped she was, for the last thing he wanted was to contract the pox. He could already see her petulantly tossing her thick black mane of hair when he told her he could not take her to the Stevensons' ball. He shrugged, thinking he would have one of his employees escort her. Jarvis he could trust. Jarvis didn't like women.

He pulled out his stationery, dismissed both Marie and Penelope from his mind, and bent to the task of writing to Paul Montgomery in London.

— 6 —

Aboard the *Eastern Light*, 1853

It was an overcast day, chill and damp, but Chauncey was too excited to notice the weather. She stepped off the sidewalk onto the wide street, a bright smile on her face for an old woman who was selling apples on the corner. Suddenly she was alone on that street in Plymouth, watching a carriage race toward her, its high wheels bouncing on the sharp cobblestones. *What is the fool doing!* She saw the driver vividly, his face swathed in a black handkerchief, an old felt hat pulled over his forehead. She heard his hoarse voice yelling at the horses as his whip flailed their backs.

I am going to die! Crushed beneath the horses' hooves and the carriage wheels!

She smelled the thick steaming air blowing from the horses' nostrils, saw the flecks of foam

77

dotting their necks. She could feel their bodies hurtling against her, crushing her. . .

"No!"

Chauncey jerked upright in her bunk, trembling with the crushing fear of the nightmare.

"Miss Chauncey! Are you all right?"

She raised dazed eyes to Mary's concerned face, shadowed in the early-morning light. "I'm all right," she said, her voice quivering as violently as her body.

"You dreamed about it again, didn't you?"

Chauncey nodded as she ran her hands distractedly through her disheveled hair. "It was an accident," she said. The words were becoming a litany after each recurrence of the awful dream.

"Yes it was, in a sense anyway," Mary said, handing Chauncey a dampened cloth to wipe the perspiration from her forehead. "But it happened in England. Whatever madman it was who tried to run you down is many miles behind us. Lawks, miss, two oceans behind us, now that we're in the Pacific! There's no more need for you to fret about it."

"But why?" Chauncey asked in a thin voice, like a child who wants reassurance from her parent. "I've done nothing to anyone. Who would try to kill me? Not even Aunt Augusta or Uncle Alfred—"

"Now, you listen to me, Miss Chauncey," Mary interrupted in her no-nonsense voice, sitting herself beside her mistress on the narrow ship bunk. "That nice sailor saved you, and although he was just in the nick of time, you are alive and unharmed. It was a lunatic who drove that carriage.

We know those kinds of folk don't need reasons. Now, you will think no more about it."

But why would a madman be driving such a fine carriage? Why would a madman have his face hidden by a black handkerchief? Why would a madman, driven by insane, inexplicable forces, keep whipping the horses forward, leaving her in the gutter, held up by the sailor who had thrown his body against hers?

"I just wish it would stop." She sighed, lying back against the narrow pillow. She did not repeat her thoughts again, for Mary had no answers to the questions that haunted her.

"It will if you'll but let it," Mary said sharply. "Lord knows I've nearly forgotten it. Thank the Lord Captain Markham stopped in Los Angeles to bring aboard fresh supplies. If I never eat another fish again it will be too soon!"

Chauncey forced herself to clear her mind of the memory and swallowed the retort that Mary could well forget it. It wasn't she who had been nearly killed. She forced a smile to curve up the corners of her mouth. "I fancy the supplies he brought aboard from Valparaiso will bring him more of a profit."

Mary's full lips pursed into a thin line. "What an awful, depressing city that was! At least those trollops keep to themselves! It's a disgrace that women would willingly accept such conditions! The good Lord knows . . ."

Chauncey stopped listening, for Mary's outrage about the young women bound for prostitution in San Francisco was a theme with few variations. "Perhaps their lives will be better," she said mildly when Mary stopped her diatribe to take a breath.

"Harrumph," said Mary. "At least Captain Markham has the decency to keep them away from you."

"I am, after all, a paying passenger," Chauncey said.

"And a lady! I hope you've been paying attention to all Captain Markham's been telling you. Not all that many proper ladies in this so-called city we're traveling to. And another thing, Miss Chauncey. All your subtle questions about the wealthy men in San Francisco, Mr. Delaney Saxton in particular—well, I think you should go easy. He might begin to think that you have some sort of unhealthy interest in the man."

"I've learned all I need to about Mr. Saxton," Chauncey said. "At least, enough for the moment. I admit to being surprised that he is so young, and unmarried. Somehow one tends to think that a true villain must be older, paunchy perhaps, with a dissipated face."

"Many of the men in San Francisco are young and unmarried, and if they are married, their wives and children are safely back East. Why do you think these . . . trollops are in such demand?"

Off again, Chauncey thought. If only Mary knew the half of what Captain Markham had told her! At least she didn't have to be fearful of his motives, for indeed he seemed to regard her as a daughter to be protected. "So many young, boisterous men, my dear," he would say over the months they traveled together. "Wild, full of spirits, and dangerous upon occasion. Duels, fights, violence—they exercise little restraint. Practice

with the derringer I gave you, my dear. Even a
lady such as yourself must be prepared. San Francisco is not yet civilized like New York or your
home, London. Not, of course, that things haven't
changed over the last couple of years. More decent women now, but not that many more. The
Vigilantes helped quiet things down. Two years
ago, that was. Hanged some of those rotters, the
Sydney Ducks, scum, the lot of them! Villains
and criminals from Australia come here to rob
and murder. Aye, you'll stay far away from Sydney Town."

If Mary were to see the ivory-handled, very
deadly derringer, she would likely swoon, Chauncey
thought. She shot it well now. Over two months
of practice, when Mary was snug in her bunk for
her afternoon nap, had made Chauncey a competent marksman. Captain Markman's first mate,
Mr. Johansen, had been her instructor during
the past month. He was utterly in awe of his
captain, and so Chauncey felt as safe with him
as she would with the vicar from her home in
Surrey.

Mary became silent, seeing that her mistress
had fallen into a brown study. She does naught
but think about that man, she thought as she
smoothed out the sheets on her own small bunk.
It's unhealthy. Vengeance is mine, sayeth the
Lord. Mary frowned at her biblical turn of
thought. She could just imagine Miss Chauncey's
fine eyes darkening with implacable determination were she to say something like that to her.
"The Lord would likely take too long, if he ever
got around to it," she could hear Miss Chauncey
say in a cold, remote voice.

Actually, Chauncey was remembering her carefree life before her father's death. She wasn't certain now if she'd had two serious thoughts in her head then. "You're such a loving, sweet little soul," her father would tell her, ruffling her tousled curls. "But such a little scamp! What would your dear mother think, I wonder." That loving, sweet little soul had seemingly disappeared. The scamp was long gone too, as were both her parents. She shuddered, wondering whether she would now be wed to Sir Guy, living in his home and paying obeisance to his mother, if her father hadn't died in such circumstances. "There's always some good, no matter how bad things look," her old Irish nurse, Hannah, had told her as a child. But that was when a picnic was canceled because of rain. Poor Hannah, dying of cholera on a trip back to Ireland.

Three months aboard a ship is enough to drive one mad. I'm becoming maudlin and stupid. I must remember; I must plan.

"Is it time to get dressed for breakfast, Mary?"

Mary nodded briskly. "Just about. There's but a small basin of clean water, as usual."

"Ah, to be perfectly clean again," Chauncey sighed. "A real bath." She rolled out of her bunk and planted her bare feet firmly on the wooden floor.

"Well, it won't be long now. Captain Markham said we'll be arriving in San Francisco in but three days! It seems like ten years since we left New York, much less England."

"I doubt San Francisco will be anything like New York," Chauncey said as she drew her white bastiste nightgown over her head. "I was surprised at how ... civilized the city was." She fell silent a moment, remembering Rio de Janeiro, a city as exotic as any described in the Minerva Press novels. They had docked there for a week while repairs were made on the *Eastern Light*. Although there were many Europeans and Americans living in the city, it was the influence of the early Portuguese inhabitants that seemed to dominate. Chauncey would never forget shopping in the open-air stalls, watching the garishly dressed black women hawking all kinds of fruits as well as cloth, jewelry, tea, and coffee. She had brought enough gewgaws to fill a small valise. She smiled vaguely, now remembering how she would have gladly tossed away her exotic purchases when the ship floundered like a toy wooden boat in the cold, raging winds that gusted as the two oceans met at the tip of South America. Chauncey as well as the majority of the other passengers fell so ill with seasickness that she had wanted to die. Both she and Mary had even been hurled from their damp bunks several times by the ferocious hail-and snowstorms that pounded the ship. It had taken the *Eastern Light* an entire week to round Cape Horn. One of the great sails had been torn asunder, but Captain Markham hadn't seemed overly perturbed. "Slight damage, very slight. Fine sailing and a kettle full of luck" was what he said.

"Do you know how lucky we are, Mary? Mr. Johansen told me that many of the ships take a good eight months to navigate from New York around Cape Horn to San Francisco. And we're going to reach San Francisco in three months."

Three months of miserable food, cramped quarters, and near-death, Mary thought. "I suppose it's better than struggling overland through that awful-sounding Panama place with all its fevers and vicious natives! And just thinking about riding in those dreadful wagons across the interior of America, thirsting to death in the desert or losing your head to those red Indians—"

"Scalps, Mary, not heads."

"The result is the same, miss!"

"Indeed," Chauncey said absently, no longer paying attention, her thoughts inevitably going to the man in San Francisco. "Soon, Mr. Delaney Saxton," she said softly. "Soon."

The *Eastern Light* didn't pass through the Golden Gate until five days later. There was another storm to ride out, not so severe as the one that had sent the ship diving into the trough of incredibly deep waves off Cape Horn, its white sails beating against the savage burst of rain and wind. But still the rolling and bucking decks were enough to send Mary to her knees in devout and loud prayer and to make Chauncey's stomach roil in protest.

"Another trip safely done," Captain Markham said with simple pride as he stood by Chauncey on the quarterdeck as the ship neared its berth on what the captain called the Long Wharf. "More changes, I see," he continued. "Every time I return, the city has stretched itself outward. That area yonder—but two years ago it was still bay. A lot of bay has been filled in since the first argonauts arrived for gold in forty-nine, and more miles of wharf than you'd imagine. You'll find many streets paved with wooden planks now,

Miss Chauncey. Lucky they are, else after the rains you'd sink to your knees in the mud. And I heard that we'll have gas lights soon. Not a dismal little village any longer. No, as bustling a port as New Orleans."

"Just look at the hills," Chauncey said in some awe.

"That's Russian Hill," Captain Markham said, following her pointing finger. "And there is Telegraph Hill, called that because of the semaphore atop it. And there is Fern Hill. Houses are starting to creep up them now, but it's tough going. On the ocean side, there's naught but rolling sand dunes, no hills."

"The city looks quite modern. All the brick buildings."

"Aye, that's true. Used to be all wooden shanties, but fires have been a problem. Lucky in the long run, I guess. After each fire, San Francisco rebuilt better than before. Brick replaced wood. Makes men proud of their city."

It required another three hours before Chauncey and Mary, their luggage piled high in a dray, were on their way to the Oriental Hotel on Market Street at Battery. "The only proper place for a lady to reside," Captain Markham had told her at least ten times. She had bid the captain an affectionate good-bye, promising to dine with him two evenings hence.

Their dray made its way ponderously down a bustling street lined mostly with brick buildings and colorful signs proclaiming the type of business. "What a beautiful and ... unusual city," Chauncey said to their driver.

"Montgomery Street," their loquacious driver

told them. "All the bankers, assayers, gold buyers, and jewelers have businesses here."

Delaney Saxton's bank must be somewhere close. "Where is the Saxton, Brewer, and Company bank?" she asked.

"There, miss, on the corner of California Street. A good solid bank. You'll do well there."

You may be certain that I shall, she thought, her eyes darkening as she stared at the brick-faced building. She thought of the thousands of dollars' worth of diamonds carefully sewn into the hem of her gown. Oh yes, I will be giving Mr. Saxton a good deal of business.

"Forgive me, miss," the driver said, turning slightly to look at Chauncey. "You here to meet your parents?"

"I am here to visit your beautiful city," she said.

"Well, miss, San Francisco ain't as wild as it was in forty-nine, but if you don't mind me saying so . . ."

Another lecture from a well-meaning man, she thought, and cocked her head to one side, giving him her complete attention.

The Oriental Hotel was a pleasant surprise. Porticoes embellished its four-story facade and formed a shaded gallery on the entrance level. There was a wide wooden-planked sidewalk in front of the hotel and a gold-liveried employee met her at the front door.

On their short ride from the wharf, Chauncey had been aware of men who simply stopped in their tracks and stared at them. Some of them looked quite disreputable with their slouched hats and flannel trousers, and others, oddly enough to

Chauncey, looked like gentlemen straight off St. James Street in London, replete with frilled white shirts and black frock coats. It was no different in the lobby of the Oriental Hotel. There were a half-dozen gentlemen seated in comfortable chairs in the lobby, and upon her entrance she could feel their eyes studying her as if she were a rare and exotic specimen. The man behind the desk merely blinked at her once, then with a good deal of aplomb inquired politely what she wished.

I want to become quickly well-known as a young English lady of wealth, she thought, and informed the clerk that she wished the best accommodations available. She also informed him of her name in a rather carrying voice.

"Welcome to San Francisco, Miss Jameson."

There, she thought, following a young man and their luggage up the beautifully carved winding staircase, soon I should be the talk of San Francisco. I hope.

Chauncey wasn't aware that Mary, following in her wake, was waving her umbrella toward the hungry-eyed men who looked ready to follow her young mistress.

"Is the weather always so lovely and clear?" she asked the young man.

" 'Tis changeable, miss, if you know what I mean, it being March and all. You'll see fog soon enough. Thick white stuff that covers everything in sight, 'cept of course the tops of the hills. Now, when it rains, there's the problem. Always carry an umbrella, miss, and wear sturdy boots. The streets get real nasty. In fact, last month a gentleman was walking on the sidewalk, and before he knew it, the wooden planks sank and he was up to his knees in muck! Such language."

Chauncey's suite of rooms on the top floor of the Oriental was more beautiful than her rooms at the Bradford Hotel in London. Perhaps more gawdy, she amended, smiling at the vivid crimson draperies, held in place with thick loops of gold velvet.

"Lawks, Miss Chauncey," Mary breathed in awe after the young man had reluctantly taken his leave. "You'll not believe my room. It's a bloody palace! Prime, everything!"

Chauncey privately thought her own huge bedroom looked more like a harem suite than a hotel, but she held her peace. It was spacious and the view from the wide window was indeed beautiful. She could see all of the downtown area, the high-jutting barren hills, and the sparkling blue water of the bay, dotted with at least a hundred ships. So many buildings and so many people, she thought, trying to visualize a San Francisco of ten years before, a village of a mere one hundred souls. She walked to the vast bed and ran her hand over the soft dark blue velvet spread. Prime indeed, she thought.

"Look, Miss Chauncey," Mary said, "you've even a private bathing area behind this screen. Your own tub, too!"

"Prime," said Chauncey.

Chauncey paused a moment and looked up at the imposing bright-blue-painted sign: *"Saxton, Brewer, and Company."* For several moments her legs simply would not carry her forward. I am become a coward after all these months, she thought. What if he recognizes my name? Don't be a fool, she chided herself. Elizabeth Jameson is a stranger; he will never make a connection. She became aware suddenly that a group of men had stopped their progress along Montgomery Street and were staring openly at her.

She forced her shoulders back, raised her chin, and marched through the huge oak door into the vast interior of the bank, Mary close on her heels. It wasn't quiet, as were the banks in England, she thought, smiling to herself when she remembered she had visited but one. Men were arguing, talking in small groups clustered about black-frocked men, employees, she supposed, of the bank. Slowly the boisterous talk quieted as the men noticed her presence.

A tall, good-looking man, dressed in well-cut somber black, detached himself from a group and walked toward her, his face a study in curiosity and pleasure. He is young, Chauncey thought as he approached her, not much above thirty. Her heart began to pound and her mouth was suddenly dry.

"May I help you, miss?" the man asked, his voice pleasantly deep and vibrant.

Get a hold on yourself, you silly fool! "Yes, I am here to see Mr. Saxton. It is my intention to visit San Francisco and I wish to open an account in your bank."

He was silent a moment; then a wide smile split his mouth and she saw a small space between his two front teeth. "You are English," he said. At her nod, he continued, "I am Mr. Brewer, Miss . . ."

"Miss Jameson. Elizabeth Jameson."

"Yes, Miss Jameson. I am sorry, but Mr. Saxton is not here."

Chauncey felt like howling her disappointment. To come all this way and the wretched man was gone. "When do you expect Mr. Saxton, sir?"

Daniel Brewer pulled on his left earlobe, a habit of long standing. "He is currently in Downieville, visiting the mines, ma'am. I expect him to return in another week or so. May I help you?"

Mines? Her father's mines?

"Miss Jameson?"

"Ah yes, Mr. Brewer. Of course you may help me." She paused a moment, gathering her wits and suppressing her raging disappointment. "Let us go to your office, sir. And we will need the services of an honest jeweler."

Their business was transacted quickly and Chauncey was pleased with the result. The jeweler assessed several of the diamonds she wished to convert into cash at a slightly higher value than had the man in London. Mr. Brewer provided her with an account book, telling her that it was never wise to carry much money on her person.

"May I escort you ladies back to your hotel?" he asked solicitously.

Mary was not the least surprised when Chauncey gave Mr. Brewer a dazzling smile and agreed. She'll pry every bit of information out of the poor man, she thought, walking sedately behind Chauncey, her umbrella held tightly in her fisted hand.

"Would you like tea, Mr. Brewer?" Chauncey asked politely.

Mr. Brewer beamed.

Over tea, Chauncey, not one to rush her fences, inquired politely about Mr. Brewer and his antecedents. He was from Atlanta, he said, his father a clerk in a mill. He had been in San Francisco for two years now, and had no intention of ever returning to the South. After his second cup of tea, she asked casually, "You said that Mr. Saxton would not return for a week, sir?"

"That's right, Miss Jameson. I do know that he will be back for the Stevensons' masked ball. Promised to be here, and of course he wouldn't let down Miss Stevenson."

Miss Stevenson! She sipped her tea. "A young lady, I gather?"

"Yes, Miss Penelope is Henry Stevenson's only daughter. Pretty girl, and much sought after, as you can imagine, miss. It shouldn't be long before an announcement is made. Where did you meet Mr. Saxton?"

Chauncey's eyes flew to his face in momentary consternation. "Captain Markham of our ship, the *Eastern Light*, recommended him to me. He assured me that Mr. Saxton was a most . . . honest man."

"Del is that. He's one of the original argonauts and one of the few men to make a fortune in gold and not lose it. Now he's into banking and shipping, even politics. It's my pleasure to be his partner."

Chauncey sloshed the tea around the bottom of her cup. "And Mr. Stevenson? Is he equally as honest and well-to-do as Mr. Saxton?"

Mr. Brewer gave a loud belly laugh. "Honest? Well, Miss Jameson, that's indeed a relative term in San Francisco. Everything is freer out here, if you get my meaning. The biggest crooks are our politicians, but I guess that's true most anywhere. Mr. Stevenson now, he's rich, richer than Del as a matter of fact. He owns the bulk of the iron foundries, a lucrative business here, and one of the newspapers."

Richer than Delaney Saxton. How can I ruin him if he weds an heiress?

"I just arrived in your beautiful city, as you know, Mr. Brewer, and you are my first acquaintance. Perhaps it would be possible for me to meet Mrs. Stevenson and—"

"Of course, Miss Jameson, of course!" he interrupted her jovially. "A young lady like yourself needs to meet other ladies of your own standing. Perhaps you would like me to call with you at the Stevensons'?"

Chauncey gave him her most royal look, as if to say: *I call upon them?*

Mr. Brewer had not gained his modest fortune by being stupid. Not only was Miss Jameson an extraordinarily lovely young lady, she was also quite rich. An eccentric, he thought, excusing her. Undoubtedly Mrs. Stevenson would trade her jewels to be called friend by this rich young Englishwoman.

"On the other hand," he said, "perhaps I should instead tell Mrs. Stevenson of your arrival in our city. Then she could call on you . . . tomorrow? I am certain she would be pleased to present you with an invitation to her ball."

"Thank you, Mr. Brewer," Chauncey said in her most regal voice. She rose gracefully, extending her hand to him. "You have been most kind, sir. I trust I will see you again soon."

Mary showed Mr. Brewer to the door and turned to Chauncey, her broad forehead lined with a frown. "You didn't count on that, Miss Chauncey."

Chauncey didn't pretend to misunderstand her. "No," she said slowly, "I didn't. I am rich, Mary, but if Mr. Saxton marries this girl, the Stevensons' wealth combined with Mr. Saxton's will make things much more difficult." She fell silent and walked over to the wide bow window to stare down at the bustling activity below on Market Street.

"What are you thinking, Miss Chauncey?"

"I'm not certain yet, Mary," Chauncey said, not turning. "First I will make the acquaintance of Mrs. and Miss Stevenson. Perhaps it is just as well that Mr. Saxton is not here. I will have time to learn all about the lion before bearding him in his den."

— 7 —

Delaney stared meditatively into the mirror as he carefully arranged his cravat. He satisfied himself with his first effort and turned away to shrug into his black frock coat, held by a silent Lucas.

"This evening will be a bloody bore," Delaney said.

"Perhaps not," Lucas suggested. "Don't forget you've yet to lay eyes on that new English lady, an angel by all accounts."

"Only by Dan Brewer's account. According to Penelope, the girl's hardly passable and a true English snob."

Lucas grinned. "Well, you'll be able to judge for yourself." He handed Delaney a black velvet mask and a black cape.

"What utter nonsense," he heard Delaney mutter under his breath. "I suppose I'll be quite late. Bring the carriage back and don't wait up for me,

Luc. I'll get home with somebody, I'm certain. And drive slowly, I need to recoup my strength and my patience before I can be pleasant to Mrs. Stevenson."

Lucas did as he was instructed. Delaney leaned back against the stiff leather squabs and closed his eyes. There had been trouble at the Midnight Star, his mine in Downieville, and two men were dead as a result. Damned violence, he thought, still unable to accept it, as common as it had become in his life. And now he was on his way to play the gallant at a masked ball!

Miss Elizabeth Jameson, an Englishwoman. When he had arrived home two days before, Dan Brewer could speak of nothing else. The lady was wealthy, beautiful, and eccentric. Dan showed Delaney the finely cut diamonds in the vault. "She must be eccentric," Dan declared. "Why else would she come here, for God's sake?"

"Maybe she's hanging out for a rich husband," Delaney said.

"Ha! She wouldn't have to walk a block to find one!" He glanced at his friend and partner slyly. "Did I tell you, Del, that it was you she wanted to see when she first came to the bank?"

"No," Delaney said dryly, "you didn't. I don't know her from Adam . . . Eve, rather. I wonder why."

"She said something about the captain of the *Eastern Light* singing your praises."

An unmarried young lady was still something of an oddity in San Francisco, and Delaney was curious, he couldn't deny it. He grimaced, re-membering another bloody long *English tea* with Penelope and Mrs. Stevenson the afternoon before.

"Just imagine," Mrs. Stevenson had marveled loudly, "a real English lady here, and she will be at our ball. We enjoyed tea with her at the Oriental. Only the best suite for her."

"You make her sound like an exotic bird," Delaney said.

Penelope tittered. "Bird indeed, Delaney! Mama, does she not have a beak of a nose?"

"No breathtaking plumage?" Delaney asked.

"Well," Penelope grudgingly admitted, "she does have beautiful clothes. But she was rather cold and standoffish."

"Now, my dear," Mrs. Stevenson said, frowning slightly at her daughter, "Miss Jameson wasn't precisely cold. It is just that she is English. Very formal, but quite gracious in accepting our invitation. Did you not say, Delaney, that the English are far more restrained in their manners than Americans?"

"Something like that," Delaney agreed.

"I thought her quite old," Penelope said.

"Old?" her mother uttered. "My dear, she cannot be beyond her twenty-first year!"

Delaney laughed softly, picturing clearly Penelope's pouting little mouth. She could obviously not bear to have competition from another young lady. The carriage slowed as they neared the Stevenson mansion. Set on the gentle north slope of Rincon Hill, the impressive structure was aglow with lights from every window. Carriages lined the road, and Delaney called out to Lucas, "Stop here! I'll walk the rest of the way. Thank God it hasn't rained—I wouldn't want to soil my beautiful togs!"

Delaney fastened on his mask and swung the

cloak over his shoulders. He paused as he neared the massive front doors, and gazed up a moment at the sparkling stars in the clear sky above. He breathed the crisp cool night air deeply into his chest, wondering as he did so if Marie were already here with Jarvis, her escort. She would behave herself. She was French and utterly practical.

The Stevenson rendition of a butler, a man named Boggs, was a rough-looking character with a battered nose and a mouthful of broken teeth. His history was unknown, which was probably just as well for the peace of the Stevensons. Tonight he was decked out in formal evening dress and looked for the world like a mongrel dog among curled poodles.

"Good evening, Boggs," Delaney said. "It's elegant you are tonight."

"Thank you, Mr. Saxton," Boggs said grandly.

Delaney handed over his silk top hat and wandered upstairs to the huge ballroom. Glittering chandeliers cast dancing shadows on the guests, many of whom were whirling about in a rather fast-paced waltz. The small orchestra was settled at the far end of the ballroom upon a dais, playing their instruments with urgent gaiety.

Delaney recognized most of the guests immediately, though they were all wearing the required masks. As usual, there were more men than women present, even including some of the more questionable females. He saw Mrs. Stevenson, her iron-gray hair arranged in ridiculously tight ringlets about her broad face, two huge ostrich plumes rising at least a foot above her head. Penelope was surrounded by a group of

men. He could hear her tittering at their compliments from where he stood. He scanned the
crowd, realizing he was searching for Miss Elizabeth Jameson. He saw Marie dancing with the
stiff-kneed Jarvis. Penelope could learn something about style from Marie, as could most of
the ladies here tonight, he thought, unconsciously
nodding approval of her yellow velvet gown. Her
only jewelry was a diamond necklace he had
given her at Christmas.

There she was, the mysterious Englishwoman
in question—he was sure of it—standing next to
Dan Brewer, while Dan, bless his heart, appeared
to be shielding her from the onslaught of eager
gentlemen. She was wearing an elegant gown of
pale blue silk that fell away from her white shoulders. He scanned her form, objectively noting
her full breasts and slender waist. "I take it all
back," he murmured to himself. "There is style."
He could tell nothing of her face, but her hair
was lovely, an odd combination of colors, like the
leaves in autumn back in Boston, he thought. He
moved no closer, content to watch her for a while.
Only when Dan left her to go to the refreshment
table did Delaney approach. There were a half-
dozen other men closing in on her, but he deftly
made his way through their ranks until he stood
in front of her.

"It is my dance, I believe, Miss Jameson," he
said calmly, and proffered his arm.

Chauncey eyed the gentleman standing so much
at his ease in front of her. He was tall, slender,
and well-dressed. His hair was a light brown, the
color of rich honey, and rather longer than an
English gentleman would wear. He wore no side

whiskers or beard. His mouth was well-formed and his smile attractive.

At least he appeared utterly respectable, and he did know her name. A man of some importance, she supposed, for the other men had stood aside for him. Still, she frowned a moment before accepting him, her eyes going about the huge ballroom yet again. Where was Saxton? Dan Brewer had assured her that he would be coming.

"You know my name, sir," she said, bringing back her attention to the gentleman.

"Of course," he said. "I promise not to tread on your toes. Waltzing is one of my major accomplishments."

Chauncey grinned and accepted his arm. She found that he was a surprisingly good dancer, his movements easy to follow, and he did not attempt to draw her close.

"I do not know your name, sir," she said, gazing up at him. His eyes were a light brown, nearly the same color as his thick hair, with golden lights. Or were they more amber? It was hard to discern his other features because of his mask.

His eyes twinkled down at her. "I do not think you have a beak of a nose," he said.

"A beak! No, I trust not. What an outrageous thing to say, sir."

"True, but I was informed that it was indeed the case. By a young lady, of course. No gentleman, even if it were true, would so castigate an unmarried lady, at least not in San Francisco."

"I am beginning to believe that you would, sir!"

"I?" A mobile brown brow shot upward a good

inch. He smiled, revealing straight white teeth. "Never! I may be a blackguard, but I would never insult a lady who dances as well as you do."

"I do not dance with blackguards, sir."

"I beg to differ with you, ma'am. If you have danced at all this evening, blackguards have already numbered among your partners."

How slippery he is, Chauncey thought. At least he has wit and doesn't pretend that I am the most desirable creature in the world! She was silent a moment, remembering, and suddenly she missed a step.

"I suppose," her partner said pensively, "that I should have asked if you were a treader of toes."

"Not usually," she said a bit stiffly, miffled at his lack of tact. "It is just that I was wondering who that man is standing ... over there." She pointed distractedly toward a portly gentleman laughing immoderately with a woman wearing a rather pointedly garish red gown.

"No you weren't, not really," Delaney said. "In any case, the gentleman is John Parrot, one of San Francisco's esteemed financiers. Whom were you really looking at?"

"You are most forward," Chauncey observed, frowning up at him.

"No, actually, I'm the mildest of souls. Ah, the waltz is drawing to a close. But look, Miss Jameson, there is a flock of hungry birds—roosters, more aptly, gazing toward you. I will protect you for another dance."

Before Chauncey could say a word, he had swung her again into the next waltz. She started to protest, but her gaze was held by a short,

rather stocky young man who stood in the doorway of the ballroom. Was that Delaney Saxton?
He looked the part, at least from this distance.
He appeared utterly arrogant and conceited, as if
he were the royal prince surveying his kingdom.

She landed on her partner's foot.

"Oh dear, I am truly sorry," she gasped. "I
promise you I am not usually so clumsy."

"I suppose it is allowable, since you are an
eccentric."

Chauncey was startled into laughter. "Eccentric! Only very old, very wealthy people are allowed to be eccentric, sir. All others are simply
crazy."

"It is what I have been told, Miss Jameson.
Why else would you come to San Francisco?"

She fell awkwardly silent, and his eyes narrowed on her still face. "A world traveler, then,"
he said easily, disliking her sudden discomfort
even though he didn't understand it.

"Perhaps," she said finally.

"If you would but tell me whom you are looking for, you would likely spare my body further
pain. You just missed another step."

"Oh, very well," she said. "If you must know,
I am wishful of meeting my banker this evening."

"Your banker?" he asked carefully, his eyes
going briefly toward Dan Brewer.

"Yes, his name is ... Delaney Saxton. Mr.
Brewer told me he would be present this eve-
ning. After all, he is supposed to marry Miss
Stevenson. Surely he would not miss her ball."

Delaney was startled into silence. How could
a man Miss Jameson had never met before cause
her such distraction? There would be time enough

to tell her that it was he who was her banker. But not yet. He wanted to enjoy himself a bit longer. "Marry Penelope Stevenson?" he drawled. "Delaney Saxton? It is a strong possibility, I suppose. Tell me, did Dan Brewer give you all this information?"

Chauncey flushed just a bit. This man made her say things before her mind cleared them for utterance. "Well, not really. You see, Mrs. Stevenson and Miss Penelope came to visit me last week. It was they who told me of Mr. Saxton's . . . intentions."

"Hmm," said Delaney. "Why are you so anxious to meet this fellow? He's not at all prepossessing, you know. Terrible dancer, quite inarticulate, a buffoon in fact. Always laughs at stupid jests. Really, Miss Jameson, I beg you to forget the man. He's an utter bore, I promise you."

"Not an ounce of wit, then?"

"Less than an ounce."

"You are in fact not a friend of Mr. Saxton's, then?"

"Did I say that? Ah, such a pity the dance is over. I fear I must return you to your other admirers, ma'am. I wish you luck in fending off their attentions. But you really needn't worry. They all hold ladies in almost reverent awe."

"You don't appear to," she said sharply.

"But then, I'm something of a bore," said Delaney, smiling widely down at her.

She was striving to think of a retort when Dan Brewer bore down upon them. "You might at least tell me your name, sir," she said, goaded, "before," she added, "you take yourself off."

"Perhaps later, Miss Jameson. Good evening,

Dan. Did you come to provide protection for our newest lady?"

Dan Brewer smiled shyly at her. "Yes indeed. I'm glad you two have finally met. Miss Jameson, would you kindly honor me with this dance?"

"Met?" Chauncey exploded. "I have no idea who he is!"

Delaney gave her a devilish grin and wheeled about, striding confidently toward Miss Penelope Stevenson.

Dan Brewer laughed, shaking his head. "Ah, Del loves a good mystery! He's quite a jokester, Miss Jameson. You'll have to forgive him."

Chauncey became very still. "Del?" she asked, her voice thin and high.

"Of course," he said, cocking his head to one side. "My partner, Delaney Saxton."

— 8 —

"You're a fool, Chauncey, a hundred times a fool!"

"Ma'am? Forgive me, I didn't hear what you said."

Chauncey pulled herself together for her partner's benefit. He was a shy young man who was dancing with her as if she were a fragile porcelain doll. "I was just ... thinking aloud," she said, forcing a thin smile to her lips. She paused a moment and waved a negligent hand toward Delaney Saxton.

"I understand, Mr. Hewlitt, that Miss Stevenson and Mr. Saxton will soon be giving San Francisco a wedding celebration."

Mr. Hewlitt chewed on his lower lip, a nervous habit of long standing, Chauncey supposed. "I reckon so, ma'am. Miss Penelope is such a pretty little lady, and Del ... well, everyone wants him to have only the best. Yep, I guess they'll tie the knot soon."

Everyone sings his blasted praises! Has he never shown his true colors here? She shook her head slightly in answer to her own silent query, remembering the saying the folk of Surrey fondly repeated: "No thief ever steals from his own house."

The dance ended at that moment, and Chauncey again turned toward Delaney Saxton. He had just raised Penelope Stevensons' small hand to his lips. When he straightened, he looked directly at Chauncey and gave her a bow and a wicked smile. She froze, wondering if he were going to approach her again.

But he didn't. She danced until her feet ached. She met every lady worthy of that exalted title in San Francisco and endured every gentleman's fulsome compliments. It was past midnight when Dan Brewer claimed her again for a waltz.

"Doesn't everyone unmask at midnight, Mr. Brewer?" *I want to see his face, look at his eyes.*

Dan Brewer choked. "Well, no, Miss Jameson."

"Why ever not, sir?"

He mumbled uncomfortably, "It just isn't the tradition, ma'am, that's all."

It was Miss Penelope who told her why, some minutes later, when both young ladies had removed to the ladies' retiring room to refresh themselves.

"Oh, that," Penelope said, waving a small dismissing hand. "Mama couldn't allow that." She giggled at Chauncey's look of bewilderment. "Many of the ladies here tonight aren't ladies. Everyone knows it, but no one says anything if *they* are masked."

"*They?*"

"Loose women," Penelope said, quite unconcerned. "After all," she continued matter-of-factly, "there are so many men here. What are they to do? Even Delaney has a French mistress." She shrugged, not at all concerned. "Of course he'll give her up after we are married."

Chauncey was silent a moment, chewing over this startling information. "So," she said brightly after a moment, "when do you announce your engagement?"

"After Del convinces me, I suppose," Penelope said, eyeing the Englishwoman from the corner of her eye. She hadn't missed the two waltzes Del had danced with her when he had first arrived.

Penelope was rather silly and vain, Chauncey thought judiciously as she patted several strands of hair back into place, but still, she didn't want to hurt any innocent person. She forced herself to ask lightly, "You must be very fond of him. I thought him very . . . witty."

To Chauncey's surprise, Penelope shrugged her shoulders pettishly. "Oh, that! I can't understand some of the things he says sometimes, and he just smiles at me when I ask him to explain. I like him well enough. Daddy thinks he's quite a catch. And since he's been to England—indeed, even has English relations, royalty almost—Mama thinks the sun rises on him!"

Chauncey could think of nothing to say to this artless speech. *He has English relations.* So that was how he managed to trap her father! But why, she wondered, didn't Paul Montgomery know of these relations? She temporized. "I hope everything works out as you wish it to, Miss Stevenson."

Penelope gave her a superior, confident smile. "Oh, it will, Miss Jameson. I don't imagine that you will be in San Francisco much longer?"

Chauncey almost smiled at the hopeful note in Penelope's voice. "We will see," she said. "I find I am much enjoying your beautiful city."

Chauncey pounded her hapless pillow, but sleep eluded her. She doesn't love him, she thought over and over. I won't be hurting her heart, only her pride. She supposed she reached her decision just as the sun was beginning to rise over the city.

It was so simple, really. *So simple and final, you fool!* She climbed out of her warm bed and padded on bare feet to the windows. *I wonder if he is awake yet. I wonder if he liked me.* He certainly seemed to, she thought, even though he had avoided her the rest of the evening. *What if he loves Penelope Stevenson? What if I can't win him away from her?*

"Miss Chauncey! Up so early? Are you feeling well?"

Chauncey turned to see Mary, her dark hair disheveled, drawing the sash more tightly about the waist of her robe.

"No, I can see that isn't it at all," she continued, her eyes shrewd even as she yawned behind her hand. "You met Mr. Saxton."

"Yes, I met him—indeed, waltzed twice with him." She gave a self-mocking smile. "He is not quite what I expected, Mary. He does not look in the least . . . evil. At least I don't think so, since everyone stayed masked. And he acts in the most lighthearted way imaginable."

"Then why were you staring out of the window looking as if you had lost your last friend in the world?"

"I intend to marry him," Chauncey said baldly.

"So," Mary said thoughtfully, "the wind sets that way, does it? You are certain then that he intends to wed Miss Penelope?"

"It appears so. She is silly and vain, but her father is quite wealthy. It seems Mr. Saxton is an opportunist as well as a villain."

"You don't think he loves the chit?"

"I *know* she doesn't love him." She shrugged, but her voice hardened with resolve. "As for Mr. Saxton, whatever his feelings are, I fully intend that they will change."

Mary felt a wave of pity wash over her. It wasn't right that Miss Chauncey, now freed from the greed of her aunt and uncle, should be forced to go to such lengths. She sighed, knowing well that once Miss Chauncey had made up her mind, nothing would change it.

"Stop looking at me as if I were a wet kitten straggling in the rain! It will not be bad, Mary. I will marry him, ruin him, then we will return to England where we belong."

Miss Chauncey made it all sound so easy, Mary thought. But life wasn't like that. Life was a slippery road full of potholes and sharp turns. She looked toward her young mistress and heard her talking softly to herself. ". . . As his wife, I will know everything he plans, I will know exactly how to strike at him."

Mary muttered an utterly improper string of words and left Chauncey's bedroom.

*   *   *

"Del, you have a visitor."

Delaney looked up from the ledger he was studying, a mobile brow rising at the smug tone of Jarvis' voice.

"I gather it isn't fat old Mrs. Tucker wanting me to subscribe to her latest charity?"

"No, sir. 'Tis that Englishwoman, Miss Jameson. She asked for you specifically, Del."

"Is that so?" Delaney said softly, his expression becoming utterly bland. "Since the young lady is one of our prime customers, I suppose I should see what she wants. Do show her in, Jarvis. Oh ... and, Jarvis, you needn't listen at the keyhole!"

Jarvis cast his employer a wounded look, then took himself out of Delaney's office. Now, what does she want? he wondered lazily, leaning back in his comfortable leather chair. When Miss Jameson appeared in his doorway, he rose slowly, straightening his gray waistcoat as he did so, and for a moment felt intense pleasure simply looking at her. Even with her mask, he had had no doubt that she would be beautiful, and he was right. Her glorious hair was piled charmingly atop her head, with curling tendrils falling over her temples. Her bonnet was trimmed in yellow silk to match her entrancing gown. Her eyes were an odd mahogany color, but he suspected that like her hair, they shifted color depending on the light. And her mood, of course. He met her gaze and saw that she was assessing him as openly as he was her. "What an ... unexpected pleasure, Miss Jameson," he drawled, walking toward her. "To what do I owe this honor?"

Chauncey swallowed, taking in his thick wave

of honey-colored hair that fell over his forehead, and his twinkling eyes, fringed with thick dark lashes. Why couldn't he have a weak chin, at least? To plan to see him and bowl him over was a very different matter from actually doing it. *Be witty and outrageous. He is a man who can't bear to be bored.* She was startled for a moment at her insight, but she knew it to be true about him.

"It is a lovely day, Mr. Saxton," she said, allowing him to take her hand briefly. "I have come to rescue you from your labors."

Why, she is chasing me, he thought, both amused and intrigued. But his expression never changed. He waved toward the pile of papers on his desk. "Alas, Miss Jameson, I am but a miserable drudge. Behold my labors. I fear they will not go away without my personally dispatching them."

"Such a pity," she said in mock sorrow. "And I was told that you were a man of great resource. Perhaps, Mr. Saxton, you can forgo your labors, just for a short time. I, sir, will buy you lunch." At his look of surprise, Chauncey added on a mournful voice, "You see, sir, I have already received three proposals of marriage and I fear that eager gentlemen are even at this moment waiting for me to emerge. Have you no sense of gallantry, sir? I am, I assure you, a lady in distress."

"Somehow, Miss Jameson," Del said smoothly, "I cannot imagine you tolerating any distress, particularly from eager gentlemen. Are you always so forward?"

Her eyes sparkled. "Only when it is absolutely necessary. Now, sir, I find my ribs are rattling from hunger."

Delaney gave her a mock bow. "Your wish, dear lady ... Shall I ask Dan if he wants to join us?" He was further intrigued to see that his suggestion had taken her aback and that those extraordinary eyes of hers had darkened. "No," he said quickly, deciding to save her from further forwardness, "I imagine that Dan is in the righteous midst of making more money for us. I, on the other hand, will be pleased to eat some of our profits."

She laughed. "No, Mr. Saxton. It is I who will save your profits for you. The most expensive establishment, if you please. I am not at all niggardly."

"Particularly when you get what you want?"

Something suspiciously like pain glistened in her eyes, but she was laughing again, and he thought he must have imagined it.

"Particularly then," she agreed.

He gave her a flourishing bow and offered her his arm. He was aware of every male eye upon them as he escorted her out of the bank.

"The wood-plank sidewalks are a good idea," Chauncey said, eyeing the muddy street. The light rain had stopped early that morning, but the air was still damp and thick with fog.

"Yes," he said, moving to the street side to protect her.

"You men are lucky, sir, with your boots and trousers," Chauncey said, observing men walking in the wide street, oblivious of the mud puddles.

"And practical, Miss Jameson. Our vanities lie in other directions."

"I assure you, sir, that it is men and their

vanity who have forced women to adopt such ridiculous garments!"

"Acquit me, ma'am. I should much enjoy seeing you garbed in trousers and boots."

His drawing comment found its mark, but Chauncey quickly recovered. "Perhaps someday you may get your wish," she said blandly, shooting him an impish smile.

She turned away from him, absorbing the raucous noise that surrounded them. There is endless excitement here, she thought, gazing at the merchants, vendors, and myriad drays and wagons that filled California Street.

"Your city is alive, sir," she said. "Every sense is awakened."

"I have found other cities boring in comparison. I see you are wondering about all our modern brick buildings." At her inquiring look, he laughed. "Even if you weren't, you should. They are our defense against fire. All of the original argonauts, as we've been dubbed, have lost everything to fire in the past, myself included. Careful, Miss Jameson, that gentleman is a bit worse for drink."

"You do not appear to be suffering overly now, sir," Chauncey said, watching the stumbling man pass them.

"No," he agreed blandly, smiling down at her. "Have you attempted climbing any of our hills?"

"Yes, I visited the semaphore on Telegraph Hill. Most intriguing. As for the rest of them, I believe I will wait."

"Ah, here we are. Pierre's Culinary Establishment. A very upper-class restaurant, I assure you, ma'am. Quite draining on the purse."

The restaurant was a marvelously gawdy place, its huge front room hung with dark blue velvet draperies. Chauncey quickly saw that she was the only female present. Delaney greeted many of the other men, but did not pause.

"François," he said, smiling at the small pot-bellied man who was hurrying toward them. He added under his breath, "His real name is Jud Stubbs and he hails from Pennsylvania, I believe."

"Mr. Saxton, and the lovely new English lady. Such a pleasure, madame."

"Your fame has spread, even to the kitchens," Delaney murmured to Chauncey.

"I pray you will be polite, sir. After all, I am paying!"

François ushered them to a quiet table away from the windows, hovering over them as he gave them the menus.

"You will love the menu, Miss Jameson. François has himself endeavored to produce it in French."

Chauncey managed to contain her giggles until François had left them to themselves.

"François joined forces with a very real Frenchman, Pierre LeGrand, some six months ago. I assure you that Pierre does the cooking. Really, Miss Jameson, you must contain your mirth. I cannot imagine what all the gentlemen now staring at you must be thinking."

"Doubtless what they are thinking redounds to your benefit, Mr. Saxton."

"So sure of yourself, Miss Jameson?" he drawled. To his delight, she did not appear at all discomfited.

"Of course, sir. Have I not already received

three proposals of marriage in but a week and a half?"

Why, he wanted to ask her, do you appear to want me? He said nothing.

François handed Delaney a bottle of vintage Bordeaux wine. "This will doubtless be excellent, François. Thank you." To Chauncey he murmured, "All the comforts of London, ma'am."

When their glasses were filled, Delaney raised his and said, "Let us drink to you, Miss Jameson, and may you succeed in your endeavors."

She flushed; she couldn't help it. He is mocking me, she thought, and stiffened her spine. "Indeed, Mr. Saxton. To my success!"

"Why do I feel as though I'm a pig on the way to slaughter?" he remarked, giving her a crooked grin.

"You, sir," she said severely, "are already wallowing in your conceit!"

"But I shouldn't order the roast pork, hmm?"

"Perhaps a pig's jowl would be more suitable."

"Since we have covered everything except ham, Miss Jameson, I think I will direct you to the fish stew. I think you will find it quite unexceptionable. As to François's pronunciation of 'bouillabaisse,' it is better left unheard." He handed the menus back to François and gave him their order.

"I bow to your superior knowledge, sir."

"But not to my superior wit?"

"I believe you told me, Mr. Saxton, that the gentleman in question has less than an ounce of wit."

"You have hoisted me again, ma'am. It is not what I am used to." He smiled at her, a smile of

genuine warmth. Had he used the same unconscious charm on her father? She felt something
harden inside her.

"There are many things, Mr. Saxton, that one
must become used to," she said quietly.

"I feel you are plumbing depths while leaving
me to flounder in the shallows. You remind me
somewhat of my sister-in-law."

"Your sister-in-law? Now I am drowning, sir."

"Her name is Giana, and like you, she is English. She lives in New York with my brother,
Alex. She is quite a stubborn, strong-willed little
wench, but my brother has her under control
now, I believe."

He was drawing her, but she wasn't paying
attention. His sister-in-law was English, thus his
English relations. She sipped from her wineglass.
"What was her name, sir?"

"Sir? Since you insisted I accompany you to
lunch, ma'am, and in addition you have trusted
me with your money, perhaps you should consider calling me Delaney. I am not that old, only
twenty-eight to be exact. Not even the exalted
age of a loving uncle."

"What was her name . . . Delaney?"

"Van Cleave," he said, watching her closely.
He heard the tension in her voice and didn't
understand it.

"Van Cleave," Chauncey repeated thoughtfully.
"I am afraid that the name is unfamiliar to me."

"England is small, but not that small," he said.
For some reason, he didn't want to tell her that
Giana's mother was now Aurora Arlington, Duchess of Graffton. Did he expect her to gush over
him as did Mrs. Stevenson? No, she wouldn't do

that. Just exactly what she would do, he couldn't begin to guess.

There was silence between them for some minutes while François served the bouillabaisse. Delaney said thoughtfully, tapping his fingertip on his wineglass, "Everyone wonders why such a . . . lady as yourself is visiting San Francisco."

"You as well, sir . . . Delaney?"

"Of course. I was given to understand that you not only possessed a beak of a nose but also were a terrible snob. I am pleased that the former is not true. But the latter . . ?"

"Oh, a dreadful snob, I assure you," she said lightly. "This is quite delicious. I shall doubtless go to the poorhouse with a happy stomach."

"It is not that expensive, Miss Jameson. May I tell you that you are the first lady to invite me to lunch?"

"Perhaps you should cultivate your charm."

"But you did invite me, ma'am. I must not be that bereft of interesting qualities."

"Shouldn't everyone become acquainted with their banker?"

"You have a very agile tongue. I am not used to such quickness in a woman."

"As I said, Mr. Saxton, perhaps you should cultivate your charm."

"Back to 'Mister,' am I? I deserve it. Forgive me for insulting your sex. Then again, I am not quite used to having a woman seek me out."

He watched her closely, but she kept her eyes lowered to her plate until, he guessed, she gained control. Which she did very quickly.

To his utter astonishment, she grinned impishly and waved her fork at him. "Did you not wish to say 'blatant,' Delaney?"

"You, Miss Jameson," he said, sitting back in his chair and crossing his arms across his chest, "are an enigma."

"Do you dislike enigmas?"

"No. Such oddities add spice to life."

She flushed. "I am not an oddity!"

"How about a rich, well-bred oddity?"

"At least when I have afternoon tea, it is not an affectation!"

"Poor Mrs. Stevenson." He shook his head mournfully. "She does make such an effort, does she not?"

Before Chauncey could reply, a gentleman approached their table, his eyes never leaving her face.

"Ah, Tony," Delaney said blandly. "How many scathing articles have you written today?"

"Nary a one, Del," Tony said, his gaze still on Chauncey's face.

"Forgive me. Miss Jameson, allow me to present to you Anthony Dawson, one of the owners of our most sterling newspaper, the *Alta California*. He also has pretensions to writing."

Why won't the wretched man go away? Chauncey thought ten minutes later. She tried to be polite, but her voice grew more clipped by the minute.

Delaney merely smiled, appearing somewhat bored as he listened to the endless stream of compliments Tony was pouring into Miss Jameson's pretty ears. The compliments didn't surprise him. It was the utter lack of feminine response to the compliments that struck him. A handsome man, Tony, he thought, but Miss Jameson had no interest in him, none at all. Why me?

"I scent another proposal," Delaney said blandly as he escorted her out of the restaurant.

"I hope not," Chauncey said, a frown furrowing her brow.

"I suspect you will become quite used to them if you remain long in San Francisco. Tony Dawson is a good man, you know."

Good men don't interest me!

"Will you see me back to my hotel, Delaney?"

"Anything to keep the wolves at bay, dear lady."

He did not ask to see her again. She dallied, waiting, but he said nothing.

"Will you come up for tea, Delaney?" she asked at last in desperation. "Real English tea?"

He cocked a brow at her. "Forgive me, ma'am, but I must see to the safekeeping of your diamonds. I trust you will enjoy your visit to San Francisco." He tipped his hat to her and strolled away.

She felt her frustration mount. What was wrong with him? He had enjoyed her company, she was sure of it. Damnable wretched man!

— 9 —

Chauncey waited three days for Delaney Saxton to do something, *anything*. She saw him several times when she was shopping with Mary, but he merely greeted her politely and walked on.

"What is the matter with him?" she muttered, knocking a stone out of the way with the tip of her parasol. "Am I going to have to chase him down like a fox in the hunt?"

Mary didn't reply to this, too intent on the splendor of Portsmouth Square. "That, Miss Chauncey," she said, interrupting her mistress from her gloomy thoughts, "was the Jenny Lind Theater until just last year. Imagine that. All to praise the real Jenny Lind, but she never came here, you know. Bob, one of the porters, was telling me that it burned down three times! Finally Mr. Maguire sold it to the city. It's now the city hall of San Francisco."

"Doubtless good riddance," Chauncey said ungraciously eyeing the touted architectural ornament with its American flag.

"What I want to do is go inside the El Dorado. A real gambling house," Mary continued, pointing to the huge painted sign on the building next to city hall. She giggled. "It's hard to imagine a gambling saloon next to the government building."

"All right, Mary," Chauncey sighed. "I'll try to stop being an utter bore. Let's talk about the weather."

"So warm," Mary murmured. "I cannot believe it's February, and here we are wearing only light pelisses."

"Marvelous," Chauncey agreed. "Next you'll be waxing eloquent about the beauty of the bay."

"As sparkling as sapphires," Mary said readily. "Come now, Miss Chauncey, all isn't lost yet. You are going to a dinner party at the Newtons' tonight. Surely Mr. Saxton will be there."

"Yes," Chauncey said sharply. "As well as Miss Penelope Stevenson."

"Ah," Mary said.

That evening, as Mary arranged Chauncey's hair, Chauncey was cudgeling her brain for a likely strategy.

"Mayhap Mr. Saxton does love Miss Stevenson," Mary said, a refrain that now came with depressing regularity.

"Bosh," Chauncey said. "She has an insubstantial mind."

"But she is quite pretty, doubtless laughs at everything Mr. Saxton says, and can keep house. What man ever cared about a woman's mind, for heaven's sake?"

"The voice of experience?" Chauncey asked, raising an ironic eyebrow. "You are a year younger than I. Besides, your Miss Penelope doesn't even know when to laugh. It's accidental if she hits it right. What I need is a foolproof plan."

"You're going to abduct him?"

"If Mr. Saxton doesn't pay me proper attention this evening, I just might. Well, not quite, but—"

"Since Miss Stevenson will be present, you don't wish to be totally outrageous. You can't really expect the man to abandon his fiancée at the sight of you?"

"She is not his fiancée!"

"Yet."

"We will see" was all Chauncey said, her voice stubbornly set.

"Did I tell you I met Mr. Saxton's man this afternoon?"

"Mary!" Chauncey swiveled about on her dressing-table stool and gave her maid a wounded look. "How could you!"

"Lucas is his name and he's a likable fellow. Introduced himself, bold as you please, and offered to carry my one little package. He has the look of a pirate with that black eyepatch and his one wooden leg."

"Did you learn anything?" Chauncey asked with admirable patience.

Mary grinned. "Yes, miss, I did. He told me that there will be a big celebration for Mr. Washington's birthday this month in Portsmouth Square."

"Mary!"

"You've lost your sense of humor, miss. Very

well. Mr. Saxton rides every morning, early, usually on Rincon Hill."

"Ah," Chauncey said, her skeletal strategies at last beginning to gain meat.

Delaney Saxton was at his blandest at the Newtons' dinner that evening. There were only six guests, and he guessed that Mrs. Newton had invited Miss Jameson for Tony's benefit. Delaney gave his full attention to Penelope, half-hearing her amiable chatter, but his thoughts were on Miss Elizabeth Jameson. He laughed softly, remembering Lucas' words. "She's interested in you, Del. That maid of hers, a braw girl named Mary, pumped me until I felt like an empty well."

Lord, but she looked stunning, he thought, sipping at his wine. She was seated between Tony Dawson and Mrs. Newton, and he could hear her tinkling laughter down the table. His eyes fell to her breasts, full and milk white, rising above the double row of lace. He felt a surge of lust and determined, somewhat peeved by his reaction, to visit Marie after he left the Newtons'. Damn, he even liked her nose, small and straight, with nostrils, he thought fancifully, that were utterly aristocratic. And those full lips of hers.

"Del, didn't you hear a word I said?"

He turned to the lovely girl at his side, a lazy glint in his eyes. "Forgive me, my dear," he said smoothly. "Actually," he added, raising his voice a bit, "I was considering the impact of Spinoza's philosophy on the flora and fauna of San Francisco."

"That has nothing to do with my new gown!

Do you not like it, Del? Papa paid a fortune for it, I assure you!"

"But Spinoza, my dear . . ." Delaney protested.

"He's one of those Eastern politicians, I suppose," Penelope snapped.

"No," Delaney said slowly, "he's more in the nature of a vigilante, I should say."

Delaney grinned to himself at the sound of a strangled gasp from Miss Jameson and a hoot of laughter from Horace Newton.

"Del, you're impossible!" Horace said, wiping a spot of gravy from his chin.

"But life is so utterly boring without impossibilities."

Chauncey waved her fork at him. "Really, Mr. Saxton, you should not tell such plumbers! Why, everyone knows that Joe Spinoza is a remarkable example of the spurious logic propounded by the Tories to keep the dreadful Corn Laws in place."

"I fear, Miss Jameson," Delaney said, his eyes sparkling as he leaned forward to see her clearly, "that you have confused Joe Spinoza with his brother, Otis. Otis, as everyone knows, lived most of his life in trees, watching the leaves change color."

"Hold it a moment, Miss Jameson, Del," Tony Dawson cried. "I want to get some paper and write this down!"

"Please do not consider that, sir," Chauncey said kindly. "It would only embarrass Mr. Saxton when he discovers that Otis Spinoza, far from living in trees, spent the greater part of his life in Northern Africa studying the effects of the desert winds on the structure of sand dunes."

"I am certain, Miss Jameson," Penelope said

sharply, "that Del is not mistaken! He is very educated, you know, and reads scores of books."

"Surely not, sir!" Chauncey said in astonishment. "Not books! Miss Stevenson doubtless jests at your expense."

"My daughter never jests, Miss Jameson," Mrs. Stevenson said with stunning clarity.

"Forgive me, ma'am," Chauncey said with a charming smile. "Of course she does not."

"There are some things young ladies should never do," Delaney remarked to the table at large.

"Like show gentlemen up for idiots, Del?" Tony Dawson asked.

"Especially that."

"I suggest then that you don't stand up right away, Del," Mr. Newton said. "You may find that you're a good inch shorter!"

Delaney grinned directly at Chauncey, and raised his wineglass. "A toast to young ladies who seem to have forgotten that Americans have kicked the English back across the Atlantic two times in our short history."

"To Otis Spinoza, may he soon build a tree house!" Tony called out.

"To American gentlemen who cannot bear to be bested and must hark back to ancient history!"

"To the gentlemen," Mrs. Agatha Newton said, rising with a swish of silk skirts, "who will now be left to their port!"

Agatha Newton swept out of the dining room, trying to contain her mirth. Sally Stevenson had informed her that Miss Jameson was an utter snob. Sally always was a fool, she thought. She admitted that she had invited Miss Jameson because of Tony. He'd acted such a love-smitten sot that she couldn't bring herself to disappoint him. She met Miss Jameson's eye and gave a very ladylike snort. "My dear," she said, lightly touching Chauncey's arm, "I feared letting it continue. You would doubtless have left all the gentlemen's self-consequence in tatters!"

"I enjoy enlivening conversation, ma'am," Chauncey said, drawn to the older woman, who in some elusive way reminded Chauncey of her mother's sister, Lucy, who had died when Chauncey was fifteen years old.

"I did not find it so amusing," Penelope said.

"No," Agatha said soothingly, "of course you did not. You will play for us, will you not, Penelope? You present such a charming picture at the piano."

"She will wait for the gentlemen," Mrs. Stevenson said.

"You are right, ma'am," Chauncey said. "There is no reason to waste talent on us."

Agatha Newton was not at all surprised to see the gentlemen troop into the drawing room a very short time later. She was surprised, however, to see Delaney Saxton stroll immediately to Penelope Stevenson and stick to her like gum plaster. Odd, she thought. Very odd. Poor Tony. He hadn't a prayer with Miss Jameson.

Delaney could not explain his actions to himself. He found Miss Jameson utterly fascinating, her wit razor sharp. They had sparred like a couple of duelists, and he'd enjoyed the hell out of it. But he had drawn away from her. He grinned sardonically as he strode up the steps to knock on Marie's door, knowing full well that he intended to use his mistress's lovely body to assuage his lust for Elizabeth Jameson.

Even as he caressed Marie a short time later in her bedroom, he was picturing Elizabeth Jameson's white breasts in his mind. His fingers tingled.

"*Mon amour*," Marie whispered softly as she guided his hand downward, "how do you think?"

"I am thinking how much I want to be deep inside you," Delaney said, automatically translating her charmingly fractured English. He pulled Marie on top of him and plunged himself into her. "Ah," he said. "Now I'm not thinking anything."

His last thought before his body exploded in release was how Elizabeth Jameson would look astride him, her back arched and her hair flowing down her white back.

He didn't stay the night, somewhat to Marie's consternation. I didn't treat her very well, he thought as he rode through the quiet night back home, and it's all that little witch's fault.

What, he wondered, laughing softly, would she do next?

Two days later, Delaney joined Tony Dawson, Dan Brewer, and Horace Newton for lunch at Captain Cropper's.

"This damned fellow Limantour," Horace grumbled, forking down a bite of broiled terrapin. "You know, Tony, the scoundrel met with us at the Land Commission, filed a ton of documents and all that nonsense. He claims to own a goodly chunk of the city, Alcatraz, and Yerba Buena."

"Don't forget the Farallon Islands," Delaney said.

"It's all a swindle," Tony said. "No one is really excited about it yet, Horace."

"I wonder, though," Dan said. "I get the distinct impression that the man is going to cause us a lot of trouble in the long run."

Tony ordered another round of beer. When the frothy mugs arrived, he raised his. "Here's to your Midnight Star mine, Del. Dan tells me she's producing at a great rate."

"Well enough," Delaney said. "The ore is rich as hell, but I have a feeling that the quartz vein isn't going to last much longer." His thoughts skittered briefly to Paul Montgomery, and he frowned. It would be months before he heard anything. He'd made the decision that he wouldn't send any more money until he had heard from the man.

"Heard you had some trouble," Horace said, belching behind his hand.

"A bit," Delaney agreed. "A couple of Sydney Ducks more than likely, who had more greed than brains."

"At least the bastards are gone from San Francisco," Tony said. "Lord, Del, you missed all the excitement when the Vigilantes took over in the summer of fifty-one and you were over in England playing around."

"With the Midnight Star as the result," Delaney said dryly. He shrugged. "I just hope the claim jumpers will steer clear for a while. I don't particularly care for being both judge and executioner."

"Speaking of trouble, Del, when are you going

to take the plunge? I saw old Bunker Stevenson the other day and he's beginning to wonder if you're running shy." Horace gave him a wink over the rim of his glasses.

"Methinks," Dan said slyly, "that Del here is running, but who will catch him is another matter."

"I?" Delaney asked blandly, though he was aware of an increase in his heartbeat. "I never run, dear boy, at least from a two-legged filly."

"Well, Agatha can't say enough about the girl," Horace said. "I have heard her mutter, though, that she's too bright for her own good. Wonders what man would put up with that."

"Sam Brannan was telling me that Cory Miniver threw his hat in the ring, along with another dozen males in San Francisco," Dan said. "She turned him down flat."

"I'm taking her to Maguire's Opera House this evening," Tony said. "There's some Shakespearean drivel playing, and Miss Jameson being English and all, I thought she'd enjoy it."

"What is this, Tony?" Delaney asked. "I thought your finances were in good order. Surely you don't need to chase the heiress."

Tony sputtered his beer, and his handsome face darkened with sudden anger. "She's a lady, Del! I wouldn't care if she didn't have a bloody dime!"

"No, of course you wouldn't," Delaney said. "Maguire's Opera House, huh?"

"Yep."

"Marie has a yen to see some Shakespeare, I believe. I just might see you there tonight."

"Lord, Del," Dan said, sputtering over his beer.

"I wouldn't want to be in your shoes if Old Bunker Stevenson sees you there, and with your mistress!"

Ah, Delaney thought, smiling mischievously at his friends. But what will Miss Jameson think?

Chauncey was amused at the dagger glances the Stevensons sent Delaney throughout the rather impressive rendition of *The Tempest.* His mistress was lovely, she thought objectively. Chauncey met Delaney Saxton's limpid gaze but once, and gave him a broad wink. She was delighted when his eyes darkened. She chose to believe that his ire was due to the fact that he had expected her to show some jealousy, or at least some ladylike disapproval.

Tony Dawson scribbled down his thoughts during the performance for a short reveiw in the *Alta* for the next day.

"The theater is most impressive, sir," Chauncey said when the play was over and Tony was escorting her out of the building.

"I got the impression," Tony said, eyeing her closely, "that you were more interested in the people in the audience than the performers."

"Did you now?" she inquired, giving him an impish smile. "I must admit to being somewhat surprised that gentlemen flaunt their mistresses so openly. It is not done in London. At least I don't think it is."

"You really shouldn't know about such things," Tony muttered.

"Or speak of them?" Chauncey said lightly. "Innocent, utterly guileless young ladies, you mean? Well-bred and brought up to be blind and deaf as well as dumb?" She had the unwanted insight that Delaney Saxton would have been delighted to tease and jest about the ways of men and mistresses. "Forgive me, Tony," she said, wanting to exorcise any positive thoughts about Saxton. "I shall behave now, I promise you."

"Would you like to have a late supper at the Poodle Dog?"

"I have heard all about the fourth floor, sir," she said in a wistful voice. "I don't suppose I shall get to see it?"

"Miss Jameson!"

"There are special private rooms, are there not? And all sorts of gawdy furnishings? And a complicated system of buzzers to call for very discreet waiters? Oh dear, I've done it again. Behold, Tony, a studiously polite, quite deaf-and-dumb young lady."

"Miss Jameson, Elizabeth ..." he began, his voice so soft Chauncey had the unlikely thought that he could cut butter with it. He was very handsome, she couldn't deny it, with his dark thick hair and thick side whiskers. She quickly looked away from him. He was going to propose and she didn't want to hurt him. She heard him sigh deeply, and began to speak of one of his articles about the new amusement resort called Russ Gardens that would be opening soon near the Mission Dolores.

"Russ is a German immigrant, isn't he, Tony?"

"Yes," Tony said, sighing again. "Christian Russ is his name. It's going to be a family resort with band concerts and dining tables under the trees and the like."

"I haven't visited the racetrack there yet," Chauncey said.

"You enjoy horses, Miss Jameson?"

"I love to ride, Tony. I have bought the sweetest Arabian mare. Her name is Yvette." *And tomorrow morning Yvette and I are going to take a gallop very early on Rincon Hill.*

— 10 —

Chauncey breathed in the crisp early-morning air and reined in Yvette at Rincon Point. The view was breathtaking, with not a bit of fog blanketing the city. "Easy, girl," she said, stroking the mare's beautiful neck. "That, Yvette," she said, "is Russian Hill over there. And just look at all the houses! I should have Mary along. Doubtless she would know the names and addresses of everyone who lives there."

Her gaze clouded over. She knew it wasn't excessively intelligent of her to ride alone, but her derringer was snug in the pocket of her green velvet riding skirt. She turned in the saddle to look toward Delaney Saxton's house on the southern slope of the hill. She had seen him earlier talking to Lucas, at least she assumed it was Lucas, for he sported a black eyepatch that made him look utterly ferocious.

Where are you, Mr. Saxton? Damn you! She

had, despite her plan, given him two more days after visiting Maguire's Opera House with Tony Dawson, but he had done absolutely nothing. "Now, sir," she whispered to the cool breeze that teased her hair, "it is out of your hands." *I am right to do what I'm planning. I will not be a coward.*

She saw him. He was riding a thoroughbred palomino stallion whose golden mane shone in the brilliant early-morning sunlight. He rides very gracefully, she thought objectively, giving the devil his due. Soon he will see me, and we will show how gallant he is to a damsel in distress.

She click-clicked Yvette into a gallop. A little fall from your back won't hurt me, my girl, she silently assured her mare. She forced herself to let out a terrified scream, then dropped the reins. The mare lengthened her stride, and Chauncey slid around in the saddle. He had seen her! He was pushing his stallion into a gallop, leaning close to the horse's neck. Soon I shall heave myself out of the saddle and execute a very graceful roll on the grass.

There were few trees on the eastern slope of Rincon Hill, and Chauncey, swiveling back around, did not see the broad-branched pine tree until it was too late. Her shriek was very real. The branch struck her hard against her head and she was hurled violently from the saddle, striking the ground like a sack of potatoes.

Delaney's yell of warning died in his throat. He knew, of course, that she had ridden here to see him, but none of that mattered now. He felt fear course through him at the sight of her motionless body on the rocky ground.

He leapt off his stallion's back and rushed to her. He felt for the pulse in her throat. It was thready. He lightly slapped her cheeks. "Miss Jameson! Come, wake up!"

Chauncey's eyes fluttered open and she stared blankly up at him. "Damn," she said very softly, and tried to sit up. She moaned, raising her hand to her temple, and fell back. "It wasn't supposed to happen like this," she whispered.

"I know," he said calmly. "You struck your head, and must lie still. Do you hurt anyplace else?"

Chauncey felt a well of blackness drawing her down. She moistened her lips with her tongue, but could manage no more words.

"Elizabeth," Delaney said, fear curdling his guts. Suddenly he was aware that he was kneeling between her wide-spread legs. She had bent her knees when she had tried to rise, and their position was that of a man preparing to make love to his woman. He backed away, sweat breaking out on his forehead, and forced himself to straighten her legs and pull the frothy white petticoats over her beautifully laced drawers. "Jesus," he muttered. "I don't believe this! Elizabeth, hold still. Don't try to move. I'll be right back with help."

Delaney rose, knowing it would be dangerous to move her himself. He spotted Joe Thatcher slouched on the seat of his beer wagon, and frantically waved him down.

"Accident, huh?" Joe asked laconically, jumping down from his wagon. "Damn, Mr. Saxton, it's that rich lady from England."

"Yes," Delaney said, his voice clipped. "I'm

going to lift her into the wagon, Joe. I'll try to hold her steady. Drive us to my house. It's closest."

Joe spat a wad of tobacco, unfastened the hinges on the back of his wagon, and lowered it. "Here we are, Mr. Saxton. It ain't none too clean, but—"

"It's fine." He saw that she was conscious, but her eyes were tightly closed. "Hold on, Elizabeth. I've got to pick you up. Everything will be all right, I promise you."

He slipped his hands beneath her shoulders and thighs and slowly hefted her into his arms. She moaned softly, and he winced at the sound. He laid her atop some quite smelly old blankets in the wagon and jumped in beside her.

"Drive slowly, Joe. I don't know how badly she's hurt."

Joe spat again and whipped up his horse. Delaney held her shoulders steady, trying to keep her from bouncing about when the wagon hit the inevitable ruts.

It seemed an eternity to him before Joe pulled up in front of his house.

Delaney quickly stuffed a dollar into Joe's hand and shouted at the top of his lungs, "Lucas!"

The front door flew open, and Lucas rushed out. He took in the situation in a glance. "Shit," he said succinctly.

"Yes," Delaney said. "She got knocked off her horse by a tree branch. I'm going to carry her upstairs. Go get Doc Morris. And after that, Lucas," Delaney shouted after him, "Brutus and the lady's mare are wandering about on Rincon Hill!"

Lucas moved more quickly than Delaney had

ever seen, his peg leg in stiff gait. Lin met Delaney
in the entryway, her black almond eyes wide.
She muttered something in Chinese, but Delaney
didn't pause. He carried her quickly up the stairs,
kicked open the door to his bedroom, and strode
to his bed.

"Elizabeth," he said softly as he laid her gently
on her back. He lightly stroked his hand over her
pale cheek. Dirt covered the ugly swelling over
her right temple. He repeated her name again,
and Chauncey, hearing the sound vaguely, forced
her eyes to open. "I hurt," she whispered, biting
her lower lip.

"Where besides your head?"

"My ribs, I think."

He gently pulled off her dashing riding hat
and smoothed her hair away from her face. "The
doctor will be here very soon. No, don't try to
move."

"It isn't fair," she muttered, trying to stifle a
groan of pain.

"I know. I'll have that tree cut down immediately."

"Don't you dare try to make me laugh!"

"I'm sorry."

"It wasn't supposed to happen like that. I didn't
see that dumb tree."

He felt an unwilling smile curve up the corners of his mouth. "So, little one, you wanted an
accident, but not a real one."

*Shut up, Chauncey! Are you out of your stupid
mind?*

She turned her head away as she whimpered
softly and fell into blessed darkness.

Delaney eased down beside her and took her

limp hand in his. A lady's hand, he thought inconsequentially, studying the slender fingers with their immaculate buffed nails. He unfastened the brass buttons of her riding jacket, not that it would help ease her breathing much.

"Damn," he said softly, gazing at the fast-rising ugly bruise on her temple. Head injuries were serious business and he had never felt so damned helpless in his life. He was aware of every tick of the clock. Why wouldn't she wake up? "Elizabeth," he said softly, but she didn't stir. To his profound relief, he heard Doc Morris' stertorous breath as he climbed the stairs.

"Well, Del, what's all this?" Saint Morris asked as he walked into the bedroom. "It is the English lady. What the hell happened? Lucas muttered about a fall from a horse."

Delaney rose from the bed. "It's her head, and she whispered something about her ribs. She took quite a spill. A tree branch got her."

"Has she been unconscious the whole time?"

"No, in and out."

As Saint Morris spoke, he stripped off his frock coat and rolled up his shirt sleeves. "Let's take a look."

Delaney moved aside, watching with narrowed eyes as the very competent Saint, one of the few real doctors in San Francisco, gently prodded at the growing lump at her temple. Delaney had always thought of Saint as the most substantial man he'd ever known. He had more the look of a lumberjack—barrel-chested, huge shoulders. But his large hands were incredibly competent and gentle.

"She's alive," Saint said matter-of-factly. "Concussion, most likely. Damn all these ridiculous clothes women persist in wearing! Get me Lin Chou, Del. I can't examine her through all of these layers.''

Delaney felt a spurt of relief at doing something, anything, of help. Lin Chou was standing in the corridor with Lucas.

"Missy all right?" she asked.

"Right now Doc Morris needs to get her clothes off. I'll be out here when you're done. Oh, Lin, put her in that nightshirt of mine I never wear. It's in the bottom drawer.''

"Shit," Lucas said again, studying Delaney's face.

"Yeah," Delaney said, running his hand distractedly through his hair.

"What the hell was she doing out on Rincon Hill?"

"You should know," Delaney said. "Didn't you tell her maid all of my habits?"

"So that's the lay of it," Lucas said thoughtfully. "She wanted to meet you."

"So it appears. Damn, what's taking so long?" He swallowed convulsively, picturing her pale face and white lips. It was all his fault, he admitted. If he hadn't played the elusive fool, she wouldn't have been forced to go to such lengths.

"I'm a bloody fool," he said.

Lucas snorted at this, and said, "I'd best go get her maid, Mary. She's likely worried sick.''

"Good idea, Luc. And don't mind me. Saint said something about a concussion. I doubt Miss Jameson will be leaving here for a while. Have her maid pack Miss Jameson's things and her own. They'll be our guests.''

Delaney wanted a drink but he was loath to leave his post outside his bedroom door. He could hear Saint talking to Lin, but couldn't make out his words. It seemed a week passed before the door opened and Saint came out, rolling down his sleeves over his muscled forearms.

"Well? How is she?"

"The tree branch won," Saint said. "She'll live, Del, but you've got yourself a boarder for a while. Can't let you move her, not with that concussion. As for her ribs, as far as I can tell, she may have cracked a couple. She won't be feeling like waltzing much for the next couple of weeks."

"Is she conscious?"

"Nope, and it's probably just as well. Lin told me you've a store of laudanum. She'll need it."

"No internal injuries?"

"Doubtful. One thing about all those damned clothes, they did protect her somewhat. Now, Del, I'm ready for a glass of whiskey." He saw Delaney's worried gaze go back toward the bedroom, and shook his head. "There's naught you can do, Del. Lin will call if she comes around. When she does, I'll feel her belly and see if she has any pain there."

"I sent Lucas for her maid and clothes."

Saint shot his friend a sideways glance as they walked into Delaney's library downstairs. "Dan Brewer was telling me about the girl. Seems she has an interest in you, so Dan says."

"God knows," Delaney said. "She's quite a . . . handful."

"Lovely little thing. Never did like females who played the silent mouse. Not natural."

"Here's your whiskey, Saint." The two men

clicked their glasses together and downed the contents in one gulp.

"Will you stay until she comes out of it?"

"Can't, Del. Mrs. Cutter is birthing her third. Since she's an old hand at it, I came here first. I'll be back. Don't be so god-awful worried. Keep her calm and quiet when she comes around. A little laudanum in water. She's certain to need it."

Lin looked like a possessive little guard dog, Delaney thought when he entered his bedroom. She was standing still as a statue next to the bed, her eyes fixed on Miss Jameson's face.

The covers were pulled only to her waist, likely in deference to her ribs, and Delaney smiled at the sight of his nightshirt. I never would have looked like that in it.

"Missy not make a sound," Lin said.

"You can go downstairs now, Lin. Lucas should be bringing her maid along soon. I'll watch Miss Jameson."

"She's very beautiful," Lin said. "For a white woman."

"Speaking as a white man, I'd have to agree with you."

After Lin left, Delaney pulled over a chair and eased down into it. "Why, Elizabeth?" he said softly, studying her face. "Why are you so interested in me?" There was no response of course. He liked her name, aware for the first time that he had used it. Elizabeth Jameson, a very well-bred name.

Chauncey felt the sun shining on her face. It's time to get up, she thought hazily. I've been sleeping much too long. There's so much to be done. She opened her eyes and rational thought fled. What was he doing here in her bedroom?

"Hello," Delaney said, leaning forward. "I'm glad you're awake."

"But I always wake up in the morning," she said, then frowned. A bolt of pain shot through her chest, and she gasped aloud. "Something is wrong."

"Hold still, Elizabeth," he said, gently pressing down her shoulders. "You had an accident. Don't you remember?"

She nodded slowly, and the slight movement of her head made her very sorry. "I want to go home," she whispered, feeling tears sting her eyes.

"It's all right," he said quietly. "Do your ribs hurt?"

"Yes," she managed. "It hurts to breathe."

"Do you want some laudanum?"

"Oh no! My father died . . . laudanum."

He saw the frenzy of pain in her eyes. Pain from her body—and also pain from her father? "Hush," he said. "I won't let anything happen to you, Elizabeth. Just a little laudanum in water. It will make you feel better."

"My name is Chauncey," she whispered up at him, wondering why it was so important to make that clear.

"Chauncey," he repeated, his eyes lighting with a smile. "That is more like you than the formal 'Elizabeth,' I think."

"I . . . I can't help it," she gasped. He saw her fingers clutching frantically at the bedcovers.

Tears streaked down her cheeks, and he quickly flicked them away with his fingertips.

"I'm sorry. Here, I'm going to lift you just a bit. Drink a few swallows."

Delaney slipped his arm beneath her and felt the pain of her breathing. He placed the rim of the glass to her lips and tipped it. She tried to turn her head away, but he forced her to swallow.

Chauncey felt the rippling waves of pain engulfing her, drawing her inward. I hate tears, she thought angrily. "I don't want to be weak," she gasped her thoughts aloud.

"You should have heard me when I was shot last year. I yowled like a trapped bear." It was all a lie, but he would have said anything to ease her. "Hush now. I know it hurts dreadfully for you to talk. The laudanum will take effect in a few minutes."

"I don't want to die . . . not from laudanum."

"I imagine that you're going to live until you're ninety. Doc Morris will be back shortly. You'll believe him, won't you?"

She felt a veil of vagueness cloak her mind. She could feel the pain, could nearly taste it, but it was growing fainter, like an animal's fangs drawing out of her flesh. "I didn't want this to happen," she whispered.

"No one ever wants pain."

"I don't want to be . . . weak around you."

"You're not."

"I can't allow you to hurt me. Not until . . . not ever . . ."

He stared at her, not understanding her words, waiting, but her head lolled on the pillow and her eyelashes swept closed in sleep.

"Eliz . . . Chauncey," he began, suddenly frightened that he had given her too much laudanum. Surely she shouldn't sleep, not with a concussion.

He rose and strode toward the door, only to come to an abrupt halt in front of her maid, Mary, Lucas at her side. He said tensely to Lucas, "Go fetch Saint. She came out of it and I gave her some laudanum."

"How is she, sir?"

Delaney studied the girl in front of him. Her face wasn't precisely plain, for her gray eyes held a good deal of humor and common sense. Her mouth was too wide, her nose uptilted. She was plump and would likely be comfortably fat in later years. "What? Oh, Chauncey." Her expression altered, doubtless at the use of her mistress's nickname. "Listen, Mary. It is not an act. She was accidentally struck by a tree branch and thrown."

Mary shook her head, still expecting to see Miss Chauncey wink at her when she entered the bedroom. "Not an act," she repeated, trying to gather her scattered wits.

"I know that she set out to meet me, to have me execute a daring, quite needless rescue. I did, but she was hurt."

"Oh God," Mary whispered, swaying a bit. "How bad is it, sir?"

"A concussion and cracked ribs. The doctor will be returning shortly. He assures me that she'll be all right, with proper care."

Mary's tongue ran nervously over her lower lip. "How do you know it wasn't the . . . real thing?"

"She told me. Undoubtedly she didn't intend

to, but it slipped out. What is your full name, Mary?"

"Mary Leona MacTavish, sir."

"Thank you. It just occurred to me that I have put Miss Jameson in my bedroom. At least it's large and airy. You can sleep in the adjoining room. You will be my guests for a while."

"Thank you, sir."

Delaney turned about, only to ask abruptly over his shoulder, "But I get the impression that was what you planned on, Mary?"

"Of course not, sir!"

He frowned at her, and Mary, unable to control her limpid gaze, dropped her head and wrung her hands. "Oh, when Miss Chauncey gets the bit between her teeth! I'll go to her now, sir."

"Yes, certainly. We will share the nursing. You'll find her in one of my nightshirts. You can change her when she's well enough."

Delaney counted the soft chimes. Twelve strokes. Midnight. Mary was, he hoped, finally asleep in the adjoining room. He'd had to order her to get some sleep, and had gotten the distinct impression that she was afraid to leave her mistress alone with him. "I am not a rapist," he'd said sharply. "You won't be any good to her if you collapse from lack of rest."

It was Lucas, however, who had turned the trick. "Come on, girl," he'd said in the softest voice Delaney had ever heard from him. "I'll make sure you're called if she worsens."

"But her hair will tangle dreadfully if I don't braid it!"

"It already has," Delaney said. "You can worry about it tomorrow."

No, Delaney thought as the twelfth chime faded away, I'm not a rapist. But I should love having you in my arms, having you moan with pleasure when I kiss you and touch you. "Fool," he muttered to himself. "Ass." He was startled when she groaned softly. He immediately rose and bent over her. "There now, it's all right," he said, gently pulling tendrils of hair away from her forehead.

Her eyes opened. They were dilated, appearing nearly black in the dim lamplight. "Father," she whispered. She raised her hand, her fingers lightly touching his cheek. "Father."

"I'm here," he said. "I won't leave you, Chauncey."

"I was so stupid to believe I wanted to marry him. He's a prig, Father. But you never realized, never knew . . ."

She broke off, closing her eyes a moment.

"No, you won't marry him, Chauncey. A prig is not for you."

"Aunt Gussie was so angry," she murmured in an odd singsong voice. "You left me, Father. Left me in her care." She began to shudder, twisting her head about on the pillow.

"You're no longer in her care," he said firmly, speaking very clearly. "Do you hear me, Chauncey? Aunt Gussie has nothing to do with you now."

"They only wanted me when I became rich. And Owen. He's a toad. I didn't belong to anyone." Silent tears trickled from the corners of her eyes.

He wiped them away, listening to more rambling words. He had had experience once with a man who was delirious. He'd learned damning truths. But this gently bred girl. What damning things were in her past? Things that made her cry so hopelessly.

"Ginger, they sold her. Said I was in mourning and shouldn't ride. God, the months! Uncle Paul ... why are you doing that? They hate me ... hate me."

He couldn't hold her steady. He swung himself onto the bed beside her and turned her carefully against him, careful of her bandaged ribs. He stroked her hair, caressed her throat and shoulders, all the while whispering nonsense to her. She quieted finally, falling into an uneasy sleep, and he breathed a sigh of relief. She brought her hand up, fisting it against his shoulder as would a small child.

"I think your plan worked too well," he said ruefully, and lightly kissed her mouth.

— 11 —

"I can't breathe!" The words erupted from her throat, the pain they brought making them sound like a weak croaking sound. "The bandage, Mary, I can't breathe."

"You hold still, Miss Chauncey. I'll get help!"

Mary wheeled about and headed toward the door. It opened abruptly and Delaney entered.

"Sir, the bandage is too tight! She's hurting dreadfully!"

He felt the leap of fear and repressed it. "Let me see," he said calmly.

He sat down beside her, watching her face contort with each breath she drew. "Chauncey," he said firmly, drawing her eyes to his face. "Take shallow breaths. That's it. Slowly . . ."

It was his intention to loosen the bands of linen that Saint had wrapped around her ribs, but he realized belatedly that she was still wearing his nightshirt. He would have to practically

147

strip her to get the job done. "Mary," he said over his shoulder, "tell Lucas to fetch Doc Morris."

Delaney laid his hand lightly against her ribs, trying to determine if the cloths were too tight. He could feel each breath she drew. "No, more slowly, Chauncey. Light, shallow breaths. Good girl."

"I am not eight years old!" she said between gritted teeth.

"That's for damned sure. If you were, I wouldn't have to worry about offending your maidenly sensibilities. Now, do as I tell you."

She didn't care what he called her, not now. Every breath hurt, hurt so much she wanted to cry. He kept saying over and over, "Shallow breaths. That's right, shallow breaths."

And she obeyed his instructions.

"Well," Saint said, striding into the room, "Miss Mary here tells me our patient needs to have the bandages loosened."

Delaney turned at the sound of the doctor's booming voice. "Saint, glad you could come so quickly. Chauncey, in case you don't remember, this is your doctor, Saint Morris."

"Move aside, Del, and let me have a look." Without further words, he began to pull up Chauncey's nightshirt. Mary, with a gasp, planted herself firmly in front of Delaney.

Delaney walked quietly to the far side of the room and stared down at the garden Lin carefully tended. He had remonstrated briefly with her at the extra work, but she'd merely smiled at him and spouted about the inflated cost of vegetables. Everything was expensive, he'd pointed out reasonably, and he could well afford it, but she'd held firm. He turned his head slightly at the sound of Saint's stern voice.

"Now, young lady, stop fighting me. Take short, easy breaths, and don't fret. I'll have you more comfortable in just a minute."

Chauncey felt the vise about her chest ease slightly. "That's better," she managed.

"Good," Saint said matter-of-factly. "Miss Mary, give me a glass of water with three drops of laudanum."

"Please, no more laudanum. I . . . Please, no more."

"It'll ease your pain, girl. You'll do as I tell you, if you please."

Chauncey docilely drank the liquid. "I can't imagine why anyone would call you Saint," she said, staring at his bushy side whiskers.

He chuckled. "You'll be as good as new in no time. Delaney, you can come back now."

"It's a ridiculous name," Chauncey said clearly, trying to keep the laudanum at bay. "How ever did you get it?"

"It's ridiculous, is it, girl? Well, let me tell you a story."

He settled himself in the chair beside the bed. "Now, you listen to me. Back in the thirties, there was this young buck, Jim Savage was his name. Lived back in Illinois, he did. He married his sweetheart, and theirs was one of the first wagon trains to cross the plains headed for California. Unfortunately, the lass died after birthing a dead baby. Broke him, her death did. Broke him good. He made it here, ah, indeed he did. All sorts of rumors grew up about him, like him fighting in the Bear Flag Rebellion against Mexico, and teaming up with Frémont and Kit Carson. After gold was discovered, he disappeared again, and the story is that he took up with the Mariposa tribe and became their king! Well, it seems that some of the Indians turned on him, and things went from bad to worse. All the Indians went out of control. John McDougal made Jim Savage a major in the special Mariposa Battalion to put a stop to it. Savage marched his men up the banks of the Merced River into country no white man had ever seen before. One day, Savage reached the crest of this precipice. 'It's an inspiration,' Jim Savage said, shouting to a friend in awe. He was staring at cliffs a mile high, and two skinny waterfalls that plunged thousands of feet to the valley's floor. Named it Inspiration Point. Well, his legend grew, but it seems he was something of a noble fool and got himself shot, just last year."

There was utter silence.

Saint Morris studied her face. He saw the drug was taking effect, and smiled at her.

"What does that have to do with your being called Saint?"

"Your wits aren't begging yet, huh?" He patted her hand and rose. "You will sleep now, girl. As to why I'm called Saint, well, that's another story. Del, Miss Mary, take good care of my patient."

"You should be called a miserable storyteller, not saint," Chauncey called after him.

He chuckled and waved a huge hand at her.

"That was delicious," Chauncey said.

"It's one of Lin's special dishes for invalids. It's got an outlandish name—chicken-and-rice soup." he grinned widely. "And lots of unpronounceable things are in it. I will tell her you enjoyed it."

"Indeed," Chauncey said, giggling. "Perhaps she can sell the name to the rest of the civilized world."

He gave her an answering smile, but his eyes grew thoughtful on her face. She felt better, thank God. Her eyes were bright again and her color back to normal.

The lamps were dimmed and it was nearly ten o'clock at night. Saint hadn't been to see her today, having to attend a man who had been shot through the leg in a duel. Delaney sat in the wing chair next to the bed after he removed Chauncey's tray. "You had a number of visitors today," he said after a moment. "Gentlemen of all persuasions trooped through, hats in hand, mournful looks in their eyes, and the like."

"I trust you told them I wasn't receiving."

"Oh no, I brought them all up. You were taking a nap, of course, so I knew they wouldn't bother you."

Chauncey's hand flew to her hair, now brushed and braided. At his chuckle, she frowned. "You are a liar," she said.

"You are mending, thank God."

"And his Saint."

He leaned forward, his expression intent. "Any pain now?"

She stiffened, remembering her mewling weak groans. "No," she said in a clipped voice. Now she had only occasional twinges from the bruise at her temple, and her ribs were only a dull ache.

"I don't believe you, of course, but no more

laudanum until you're ready to go to sleep. Tell me, Chauncey," he continued without pause, "when did your father die?"

Her eyes flew to his face. "How ... how do you know about that?"

"You were delirious the night of your accident and spoke of many things. You thought I was your father."

"He died last April," she said. *Oh God, what did I say?*

"I'm sorry." He saw that she was regarding him with something suspiciously like fear, and wondered at it. Perhaps, he thought, she was in pain and didn't want to admit it to him. He rose and walked to the fireplace, picked up the poker, and stirred the glowing embers. He could feel her eyes boring into his back.

"You've been calling me Chauncey."

"You insisted," he said, turning back to her. "It suits you, you know. How did you get it?"

"My Irish nurse, Hannah, dubbed me that when I was only six years old. She said that for such a wee little mite I took too many chances. Her accent was a bit peculiar, you know, and the 'chances' sounded like 'chaunces.' "

"I trust you won't be taking more *chaunces* in the near future."

You were so damned elusive, what was I supposed to do?

He saw her flush, and smiled. "I find you most unusual," he said. "I was beginning to believe you a very sophisticated lady until your untimely accident."

"I am," she said.

"Oh no," Delaney said quietly. "You're strong-willed, and likely stubborn as hell, but not a blasé woman of the world."

Her eyes fell. She had planned this so carefully. Being in his house, being alone with him in intimate conversation. But still he seemed to elude her, even make sport of her. She must make him interested, dammit, she must!

"It came as something of a shock to me," she heard him say, "to find a soft, very vulnerable girl in my bed."

"I didn't mean to be," she said stiffly.

"Had your accident really been a fake, I can only imagine how you would have behaved. It boggles the mind, I assure you."

"It is unfair of you to mock me now."

He gave her a crooked grin. "I sense that if I don't take full advantage of the opportunity, you'll never allow me another *chaunce*."

She returned his smile. She didn't want to, but couldn't seem to help herself. "I am tired."

"Ah, that must mean that you can't find a sterling retort to put me in my lowly man's place. I don't suppose you're going to tell me exactly why you executed that charade?"

She looked him straight in the eye and drew a deep breath. "I like you and you persisted in ignoring me."

"I did rather ask you for an answer, didn't I?"

"Now you have one."

"Why me, Chauncey?"

"Why not?"

He stroked his chin thoughtfully. "Dan Brewer was wondering aloud what the devil a rich young lady was doing in San Francisco. We decided, all in facetious good humor, of course, that you were probably hanging out for a rich husband."

"I don't need a rich husband."

"That is what I find so fascinating, my dear."

My dear! She gave him what she believed to be a most seductive smile. To her utter chagrin, he laughed, a deep, booming laugh.

"I hate you!" she muttered, feeling a perfect fool.

"Love . . . hate, they are two sides to the coin, are they not?"

"Yes," she said, her eyes narrowed on his face, "they are."

"Tell me," he said abruptly, his tone utterly serious, "about your childhood in England."

She felt herself relaxing against the fat pillow. Here, at least, was safe ground. "I am an only child. My mother died in childbed when I was ten. I took care of my father until he . . . died."

"What about your Aunt Gussie?"

She tried to keep the rush of fear to herself. God, what had she said? "She is a terror."

"And Owen?"

"He is a toad, and her son."

"Ah, then who is the prig?"

"His name was Sir Guy Danforth. I had thought at one time that I would marry him. He and his mother lived near us in Surrey. I broke our engagement after my father died."

"Because he left you penniless?"

She stared at him, her hands fisting beneath the covers in an efort to keep herself calm. "It seems, sir, that you already know everything about me."

"No, just rambling bits and pieces. I have the

impression, though, that this past year has been a trial for you."

"Yes."

"Were you by any chance in London in fifty-one?"

"No, I was at home, in Surrey."

"It is unfortunate. I was visiting relatives at the time, but unfortunately I didn't see much of your country. I did meet many very interesting people, though, in London."

I'll just bet you did! "You mentioned that your sister-in-law is English?"

Delaney leaned his head back, but he regarded her intently beneath his lashes. "Yes. I was the guest of her mother and stepfather, Aurora and Damien Arlington. The Duke and Duchess of Graffton."

Chauncey felt a rush of fury. So they were the ones who sucked in her father! The ones who had refused to help him recover his money. And they were rich, damn them, very rich! "I do not know them," she said dully.

"Then why do their names upset you so?"

"Their names do not upset me," she said with perfect honesty.

"I repeat, Miss Jameson, you are an enigma." He rose and walked to the side table. She watched him pour water into a glass and add a bit of laudanum.

"I don't want that."

"I don't care at the moment what you want or don't want. You will drink it."

"I do not take orders from anyone," she said, cold fury lacing her voice.

He smiled at her, quite gently. "Do not force

me to hold you and pour it down your throat. You are in my house, in my bed, and in my care. Now, open your mouth."

She sipped until the glass was empty.

"Excellent. I was wondering if it was ever in your nature to be biddable. No, don't rip up at me. You've worn me to a bone and I've got some work to do before I can go to bed."

"I . . . I'm sorry."

He leaned down and lightly touched his fingertips to her cheek. "Don't make me feel like a cad, Chauncey. I am glad you are here. I would have preferred the circumstances to be different, but what's done is done. I want you to sleep now."

She raised her face and met his gaze. Unconsciously she moistened her lower lip with the tip of her tongue. She heard him draw in his breath. "You are not a prig," she said.

No, he thought, anything but. "Hold still, Chauncey," he said.

She watched the man bend over the woman, as though she were apart from them, observing from across the room. Apart from him until she felt his lips gently caress her mouth. She drew back, startled.

"So sophisticated," he murmured. "Has no man ever kissed you before?"

"Yes," she muttered. "Owen. It was awful."

"I dread to know what you did to him."

"I kicked him the first time. The second, I bit his tongue."

"Did the prig kiss you?"

"Of course not! He was a gentleman."

"Why did Owen kiss you the second time? Didn't the fellow ever learn?"

He watched the myriad expressions flit over her face as he awaited her response. He wasn't really surprised when she evaded him by asking impishly, "Why did you kiss me?"

"That was not really a kiss, my dear," he said, a devilish gleam lighting his eyes. "That was but a beginning . . . exploration."

"I cannot slap you. It would hurt my ribs."

"So I have you in my power. Doesn't that alarm you?"

She chuckled and almost instantly regretted it. "Please," she gasped, "don't make me laugh. And you, sir, should remember that I have a saint protecting me."

Delaney rose and stared thoughtfully down at her. He could see the laudanum drawing her into sleep, though there was still a pert challenge in her eyes. "Should I take my chances and kiss you again? After all, you didn't try to destroy my manhood."

She flushed, though he doubted she would have, had it not been for the laudanum dulling her control.

"Dare I believe I've had the last word?"

"I'm going to sleep," she said, and closed her eyes.

"Good night, Chauncey," he said.

She didn't open her eyes until she heard the door of the bedroom close very softly. Slowly she raised her fingers to her mouth. Her lips felt soft, somehow different. Tomorrow, she told herself, jerking her hand away, tomorrow I shall begin to question him about his holdings. He will show his true colors. He must! With no laudanum dulling my mind, I will also ask him more about all the very interesting people he met in London.

Chauncey, bathed, her hair arranged in lazy curls falling from a topknot, sat up in her bed, waiting for him to come. When she finally heard a man's footsteps in the corridor, she planted a dazzling smile on her face.

It was Saint Morris.

"My," he said, whistling, "I feel like the sun just broke through the fog and is shining on my miserable head. Well, girl, you'll not have need of me for much longer."

Chauncey wanted to ask him where Delaney was. After he examined her briefly, she asked in her most offhand voice, "Have you seen my host, sir?"

"Del? Hasn't he been up to see you, girl? He didn't deliver all these beautiful flowers from your admirers?" He waved toward the half-dozen bouquets placed about the room.

"No," she said. "Mary brought them all up yesterday."

"Well, there's a new batch downstairs. Doubtless Del will get around to bringing them up. He's a busy man. You rest, girl. Take the laudanum only if you really need it. Don't want you to become dependent on it."

"Why do they call you Saint?"

He grinned at her and wagged a meaty finger. "Another time, girl. It's an uplifting tale, and not one to be told lightly."

Alone, Chauncey glared at the bedroom door. So the cad was here in the house and hadn't deigned to come and see her! Oaf! Conceited, aloof swine! She suddenly pictured herself executing a series of daring accidents and Delaney Saxton shaking his head at her in exasperation. She started laughing.

When Delaney opened the door, it was to see his houseguest holding her sides and giggling. He raised a mobile brow at her. "I was only *thinking* the jest, Chauncey. Can you read my mind?"

She wiped her eyes. "I have tried, but there is naught there but a vast wasteland."

"You don't see any audacity lurking about in the wasteland? Ah, forgive me, ma'am, Penelope. Do come in. I'm sure Miss Jameson has been pining for feminine company."

Chauncey sucked in her breath, and said blandly, her eyes on Penelope, "Indeed, Mr. Saxton. After your . . . continuous attentions, it is a pleasant change."

"Miss Jameson," Penelope said in a high, shrill voice. "How very . . . pulled you look."

Delaney prepared himself to be amused, and moved well away to stand by the window, his hands thrust in the pockets of his trousers.

"Do I?" Chauncey said blandly. "It is doubtless all the late nights, Miss Stevenson."

Mrs. Stevenson sailed to the bed like the *Eastern Light* under full sail. She proffered a tight smile. "On the contrary, love," she said toward her daughter, "I believe Miss Jameson well enough to go back to her hotel. How do you feel, Miss Jameson?"

"Pulled, ma'am, but only on the inside."

"Won't you ladies be seated?" Delaney asked. But not too close, he thought as he arranged the chairs. He didn't want them to leave scorched around the edges.

"Everyone is talking about your accident," Penelope said, arranging her lovely yellow taffeta skirts around her. "Tony Dawson, the silly man, has been haunting the house, Del tells me."

Chauncey gave Delaney a drawing look, but he merely smiled, saying nothing.

"How nice," Chauncey said, "to have friends."

"Agatha Newton wanted to come with us," Mrs. Stevenson said, "but I told her it would probably overtire you to have too much company."

"Thank you, ma'am."

"I hear that dreadful man Saint Morris is tending you," Penelope said.

"My dear Penelope," Delaney said, his voice sounding to Chauncey's ears like a soft caress, "Dr. Morris is one of the few competent medical men we have in San Francisco. I do not understand your dislike of him."

"He is . . . not refined," Penelope said, tossing her head.

"Ah, that certainly puts him in his place." More than likely, Saint's only flaw was not paying sufficient masculine attention to Penelope.

Penelope blinked, uncertain how to take his words, but Delaney, knowing full well that Chauncey's eyes were glued on him, lightly caressed Penelope's hands. He straightened very slowly, wondering why he had done such a thing. He didn't love Penelope, now had no intention of marrying her, yet here he was behaving like an utter cad, leading her to believe herself important to him. He realized in that endless moment that she was even less important to him than just the day before. His eyes met Chauncey's. Such expressive eyes; if only he knew her well enough to read her thoughts in them. What would she say, he wondered, if he were to tell her that he probably wanted her more than she did him?

"Lin," he said, sheer gratitude in his voice, "the tea tray! I think, ladies, that Miss Jameson is a bit worn out. Why don't we have tea downstairs and let her rest?"

The triumphant look Penelope shot her made Chauncey want to grind her teeth. Polite departing words were exchanged and Chauncey was left alone with her tangled thoughts.

Lin returned shortly with tea and crisp almond cakes for Chauncey. "Do you like your tea plain, missy?"

"Yes, Lin. Thank you." Chauncey sipped at her tea. "The cakes are delicious. And all the other delicacies you've made for me. I appreciate it."

Lin paused a moment, then gave her a wide smile. Her teeth look like polished pearls, Chauncey thought. "The ladies left," Lin announced.

"Oh?"

"Mr. Saxton take Miss Stevenson to ride this afternoon."

Chauncey spilled her tea, wincing as the hot liquid scalded her palm. Lin bustled about, wiping her hand in a soft cloth, all the while thinking happily that the lady did want her master. She was sure of it now, and couldn't wait to tell Lucas.

Chauncey didn't curse until Lin left her alone.

— 12 —

Delaney forked the bite of braised chicken breast into his mouth. He could heard himself chewing, for it was the only sound in the room. Chauncey hadn't spoken above two words to him since he had come in with their dinner. He fancied he knew the reason for her snit, and was amused by it, and inordinately pleased.

"Don't you care for the peas?" he asked. "They're fresh from Lin's garden."

Chauncey didn't raise her eyes from her still-full plate. She had formed three little mounds with the peas. "They're very ... green," she said.

He cocked a mocking brow at her. "Green as in jealous green?"

She carefully laid her fork on the plate, wishing she could fling the peas in his miserable face. Jealousy be damned! She was frustrated, furious with him because she didn't know what to do, and he saw it as jealousy. She had no experience in the intricacies of men's minds, and had obviously chosen the wrong way to behave toward him. Did he really believe her jealous? His show of conceit put her back on firm ground, and she said amiably, "You are an arrogant swine, you know."

"That's better. You become quite tongue-tied when you're angry."

"At least it's a real emotion! I begin to wonder if you ever feel anything, beyond a joke, that is."

"Ah, Chauncey, ripping up at me? You behold a simple man who thought only to enjoy your company during dinner."

"You are so damned slippery!"

"But food is one of life's pleasures, my dear. I was but trying to explain it to you."

She regarded him closely and said abruptly, "You've a scar on your upper lip."

"The result of a slippery ax my father gave me for Christmas when I was eight years old. I have other scars, in more interesting places."

"You would doubtless be pleased to recount your bravery in the making of each one."

"Only if it would secure your admiration and soften you up a bit."

I can't and won't be soft around you! she wanted to yell at him. Instead she stifled an elaborate yawn and asked, "Did you enjoy your ride with Miss Stevenson?"

His mobile left brow shot up again. "Odd, isn't it, how I guessed you knew about that?"

"Oh, and you feel I am jealous because of it?" Take that, you cad, she thought, watching his eyes gleam with her unexpected retort.

"Penelope is a rather ... careful rider. Not hell-bent like you. Of course, she has kept her body intact as a result of her prudence."

He was toying with her, like a big lazy cat with a rib-bandaged mouse. The vivid picture that brought to her mind doused her ire at him and made her giggle.

"That's better. Will you share the jest with me?"

Why not? she thought. Nothing else seemed to work. "I imagined you a big furry cat pawing about a poor, helpless little mouse, one with bandaged ribs."

He grinned at her. "I wonder if there were no bandages which of us would be viewed as the cat?"

The mark hit home and she bit down on her lower lip. "I don't toy with you," she said stiffly.

"Perhaps not, but you have certainly chased me about in a grand manner. I am thinking that I should probably collapse in a heap and see what you would do with my exhausted body."

"That would certainly be a change," she said.

"Is it difficult being bound in your—my—bed, unable to chase your prey to ground?"

"Your potatoes are likely cold. Won't Lin be disappointed? You've hardly done justice to her delicious meal."

Delaney gazed briefly at the lump of mashed potatoes, then back over at her. "What would you say, my dear, if I were to collapse beside you in bed?"

Should she react coyly? Tease him? "Oh, damn," she said aloud, "I don't know!"

He burst into laughter, nearly upsetting the

tray in front of him. "You are a delight, you know that?"

She felt his words spiral through her body, giving her a brief feeling of utter triumph, and something else that nibbled undefined at the back of her mind. She shied away. "This delight wants to know what you did with your time today. Saint told me you were a busy man. Before Miss Stevenson came, were you involved in business?"

Thrust and parry, he thought. "Actually I was," he said, shoving aside the table and leaning back in his chair. "I'm expecting one of my ships to arrive from the Orient. It's due anytime now."

Shipping! How rich was he? "How many ships do you own, sir?"

"Three. My father was a shipbuilder back in Boston, as is my brother, Alex, in New York."

"I see," she said. "How . . . interesting."

He crossed his arms over his chest and stretched out his legs. "Is your question simply idle conversation, or do you want to know if I'm as rich as you are?"

"I'm very rich," she snapped. Could the wretched man read her mind? He disconcerted her, left her flapping in the breeze like a loose sail.

"And like me, you're a nabob. One of those deplorable specimens with pretensions to good breeding and good taste."

"I was definitely *old* wealth until my father died. Then everything was . . . different."

"Tell me how you came about your wealth."

No harm in that, she thought. Perhaps such a recital would gain his trust, his sympathy. "My godfather died in India. Some years before, his wife and son were killed in a native uprising. He made my father his heir. When my father died, he stipulated that all his money would come to me on my twenty-first birthday. He saved me, litterally. You see, I had no prospects save those of becoming a shop girl and garnishing bonnets, that or continue being a drudge in my aunt's house in London and fending off her son, Owen. I . . . I much enjoy my freedom."

"If that is the case, my dear, it would seem to me that the last thing you would want is a husband mucking about with your fortune."

He was doing it again, she thought, utterly vexed. She said stiffly, "America is not England, Delaney. Everyone is free here, including women."

"I suppose that is more true than not. You are a complex woman, Chauncey. Perhaps someday you will tell me why a very rich young English-woman decided to travel to this particular end of the earth."

"Have you not sailed on one of your ships to the Orient?"

"Yes, but that is not the point, is it?"

"No, you are right of course. It isn't the point."

He watched her intently a moment beneath the sweep of his lashes. Her thick hair was braided and pinned atop her head, with curling wisps framing her face. Her bed gown was frothy pale yellow lace, billowing up about her white throat. Even her hands were soft, white and graceful, the fingers slender and beautifully tapered. He glanced at his own hands and winced. They still looked like laborer's hands from the months spent in the mining camps.

He wanted her. It didn't overly surprise him, for she was a lovely woman. He had known women more beautiful, but none of them had drawn him like she did. It was that elusiveness about her that intrigued him. Thrust and parry, he thought again. She would lead him on shamelessly, then draw back abruptly.

"Have you any pain?" he asked.

"Just a bit," she said truthfully.

"But you refuse laudanum, right?"

"I do not like to be drugged."

"Chauncey, did your father die of an overdose of laudanum?"

She paled, her eyes dimming as if he had struck her. Yes, she wanted to howl in anguish at him. *Yours was the hand that thrust it into his mouth!* She closed her eyes, knowing that her fury and hatred of him were clear to see.

"I'm sorry," he said gently. "I did not mean to upset you. I will leave you now."

He rose and stacked the plates on the tray. "Sleep well, my dear. I will see you in the morning."

He left her in the quiet darkness, alone, to deal with her pain. Oddly enough, her last thought before sleep claimed her was that he was the complex one, an intricate puzzle whose pieces did not fit together to form the image of a man she must hate. She could not see shadows of corruption beneath his teasing smile.

Delaney spoke briefly with Lin and Lucas before retiring to his library to work. But concentration eluded him. He smiled, remembering Lin's guileless words. "Missy likes you," she had said slyly. "She's a real lady, that one."

He tried writing a letter to his brother, Alex, but realized after a good fifteen minutes that he had succeeded in producing but one inane sentence. He cursed softly, knowing well what it was—who it was—that was distracting him. He doused the lamps and walked quietly up the stairs. He paused a moment in front of her bedroom door, knowing he should curse himself for his lustful thoughts, when a piercing scream froze his rampant desire.

"Chauncey!" He flung open her bedroom door and rushed into the dark room, expecting perhaps to see a villainous creature ravishing her. Instead, all he could make out was her writhing body on the bed. Her low, guttural sobs filled the stillness of the room.

"Chauncey," he said again, more softly this time, realizing that she was caught in a nightmare. He sat on the side of the bed and clasped her shoulders. "Come on," he whispered softly. "Wake up, Chauncey. Wake up!"

"No!" she moaned, trying to thrust him away. He could feel the power of her fear, and it shook him.

"Wake up, dammit!"

He drew her into his arms, tightening his arms about her back. "Come on, sweetheart. It's all right now."

The door to the adjoining room flew open, and Mary, still drawing her bed robe about her, rushed in, her fat braids flapping up and down on her shoulders.

"It's all right, Mary," Delaney said quietly. "She had a nightmare."

Mary drew a deep breath, coming no closer. "It's been a while," she said. "I'd hoped it would leave her alone."

"It's the same nightmare?" He felt Chauncey stir in his arms, her sobs now dissolved into erratic hiccups. Instead of pulling away, she burrowed closer to him, as if trying to hide herself.

"Yes. Before we left England, she was nearly run down by a madman driving a carriage. A sailor saved her at the last minute."

"I see," he said. "Go back to bed, Mary. I'll stay with her until she calms."

Mary nodded and walked back into her room, closing the door behind her. It didn't occur to Delaney at the moment that it was most unexpected for a maid to leave her mistress alone in the arms of a man who was not her husband. "Chauncey," he whispered against her temple. Unintentionally his lips formed soft kisses. She nestled closer and he felt a shock of desire at the feel of her breasts pressing against his chest. His hands were stroking her hair, kneading the taut muscles of her neck. "Sweetheart," he said, his lips forming the endearment against her cheek.

Chauncey felt the terror slowly drain away. She realized with something of a start that she felt quite safe tucked against him, his firm hands kneading away her fear. She struggled back, angered not by his holding her, but by her own thoughts. "I am not a weak fool," she muttered. He loosed, but continued to keep her in the circle of his arms.

"No, of course you are not. Everyone has bad dreams."

"It wasn't just a bad dream," she said sharply. "He tried to kill me. I'm not crazy."

"The man who drove the carriage?"

She pressed her face against his shoulder, nodding. Her movement made him suck in his breath. His hand longed to caress her breast.

Damned horny goat! He quickly untangled her arms and pressed her back into her pillow. She was in his house, in his bed, and he would not take advantage of her.

She seemed oblivious of his distress and his ragged breathing. "I'm all right now," she said, barely a tremor in her voice. "I'm sorry to have disturbed you. The dream does not come often now."

"I was passing your room when I heard you scream." He gently pushed a tendril of hair away from her forehead, his hand shaking slightly. "You scared the hell out of me."

At that moment, Chauncey shook off her fear. She was utterly aware that he was alone with her, and she was wearing nothing but her nightgown. Should she pull him down to her? Ask him to stay? Stay and do what? She suddenly saw Owen, his intent to compromise her, and she sucked in her breath, her entire body stiffening, hating herself.

"Don't be afraid of me, Chauncey," he said quietly, misreading her reaction. "I would never harm you. Would you like a glass of water or milk?"

"No," she said, her voice sounding suspiciously like a child on the verge of tears.

He rose and methodically straightened the covers. Say something, you fool! "If Saint says it is all right, would you like to take a carriage ride with me tomorrow?"

"Yes," she said after a moment. "I would like that."

She lay in the darkness, staring toward the closed door. She heard him down the corridor, pause, and retrace his steps. Then he was striding down the front stairs and out the front door. Where, she wondered, frowning, was he going?

Delaney spent the next three hours with Marie, giving his body exquisite relief. But not his mind. He was broodingly silent as he rode Brutus through the dark streets of San Francisco.

"Yes indeed," Saint said, smiling at his patient's obvious enthusiasm, "but mind you don't gallop those horses of yours, Del! It's a beautiful day, not a whiff of fog. Take her to see the ocean, but careful you don't overtire her."

How free and unfettered it felt to wear a gown without a corset, Chauncey thought as she tilted her face back to bask in the warm sunlight. This must be what men feel like. She turned her head slightly to look at Delaney seated beside her. Lucas was driving a bay gelding whose name was, ironically enough, Stud.

"Thank you," she said. "The landau is perfect. I feel utterly spoiled and cosseted."

"The landau is on loan from the Stevensons," he said, giving her a wicked grin.

She drew in her breath, then smiled back at him. "I will not allow you to draw me, not today!"

"You are warm enough, Chauncey?"

"If you pile another blanket on me, I shall roast."

Delaney gave her a long look, thinking he would like to make her roast all right, but with his body, not a damned blanket.

Lucas guided the horse through the maze of

wagons, pedestrians, and vendors down Market Street. "All the new building," Chauncey said, gasping slightly as a Chinese nearly stumbled into the path of the carriage, weighted down with several heavy boards.

"It never ends. Lucas, let's drive past the Mission Dolores. When you're well again, Chauncey, we'll visit the Russ Gardens. You know about them, don't you?"

"Oh yes," she said pertly. "Tony, dear Tony, told me all about them."

"Touché, witch. This, my dear Chauncey, is the plank road that was built in 1851 to connect the center of San Francisco with the Mission Dolores. We now have a racetrack there. All the comforts of civilization."

"I've never been to a racetrack before," Chauncey said somewhat wistfully.

"What? Not even Ascot?"

She shook her head, her lips pursing primly. "Father didn't think it proper."

"Now that you're an independent woman, will you deem it proper?"

"Perhaps," she said, giving him a coy smile, "with the proper escort."

"I'll ask Tony if he's free," Delancy said blandly.

"You—"

"Did you know that San Francisco got its name only six years ago? Washington Barlett was the *alcalde,* or mayor, then. He ordered the name changed from Yerba Buena to San Francisco in our first newspaper, the *California Star.*"

"Yerba what?"

"Yerba Buena. It means 'good herb.' Supposedly because of an aromatic shrub that grew about the shore. Everyone, you know, wanted to claim California—the Russians, the French, even you British. We Americans, of course, won out in the end. The Spanish ceded California to us in 1848, when we won the war, only five years ago."

"When was gold discovered?"

"It's ironic. The treaty was signed early in 1848. Only nine days earlier, Marshall had picked up the first flakes of gold at Sutter's sawmill. All hell broke loose a few months later."

"With you as one of the ... what are you called? The argonauts?"

His expression clouded for just an instant. "That's right," he said matter-of-factly. "I traveled overland from Boston. Quite a hazardous journey in those days. In fact, it still is."

"You came to California because of the gold?"

"As my brother, Alex, is fond of telling anyone who will listen, I was a rebellious sort, not content to follow in my father's and grandfather's footsteps. It took the lure of gold and the challenge of making my own way to get me off my butt."

"It must have been ... difficult for you," she said.

"Nary a bit of romance in it, that's for sure. Rather hard work, really. I was very lucky, unlike most of the men who came here."

"I imagine it was more hard work, rather," Chauncey observed dryly. "Is it a rule among men that they make light of grueling experiences? Prove that they're invincible and all that?"

He laughed. "Would I impress you if I told you about all those bloody mosquitoes that attacked my poor body? And the discomfort of standing in waist-deep water panning for gold?"

"Oh look," Chauncey said suddenly. "There's no one here! Sand dunes everywhere!"

"I can't get too close, Mr. Saxton," Lucas said over his shoulder. "The wheels will get stuck in the sand."

"Stop at the next rise, Luc. I'll assist Miss Jameson down to the shore."

The rough path was covered with swirling sand despite the scraggly bushes someone had planted alongside it to keep it clear. The air was cooler, and suddenly Chauncey could smell the ocean.

"It's beautiful," she breathed, waving at the sea gulls hovering overhead. "And no one is here. It is all ours."

"Yes," Delaney said, "yes, it is. Right here is fine, Luc."

Lucas pulled Stud to a halt atop the last rise. Spread in front of them was the Pacific Ocean, sparkling blue, like winking sapphires under the bright midday sun. The sound of the waves breaking toward shore was the only sound, that and the occasional squawk of a sea gull.

"Oh my," Chauncey said, gazing about her in stunned awe. "I feel like I'm the first person to see it. I wonder if this is what an explorer feels like."

"I'm glad you can see it now. Who knows? In ten years, even five, perhaps men will be out here building wildly all along this stretch. We're indeed lucky today. Most often this area is blanketed with fog."

Chauncey swiveled about to stare at a rugged

tree-covered cliff. "That is where I would build my house," she said.

"Mighty damp, ma'am. And the fog is no respecter of beautiful views. Shall we go down to the beach?"

Chauncey's ribs were still sore, but not that sore, she decided. As for walking, she refused to think about it. "Lead on, sir."

Delaney tossed one of the blankets over his shoulders and walked to her side of the carriage. "Miss Jameson," he said formally, then winked at her, and gently drew her into his arms.

"Really," she began, "I am quite all right, Delaney!"

"Hush, my dear. It is my pleasure, I assure you."

She didn't mean to, but her hands curled around his shoulders. She felt his taut muscles rippling beneath her fingers. A strange, completely unexpected warmth curled in the pit of her stomach. At least she thought it was her stomach. "I must be hungry," she muttered, confused.

She felt the rumbling laughter in his chest. "If we have a picnic out here, the sea gulls will bombard us. They have no pride."

Just for a moment, she told herself, as she relaxed against him, just for a moment. She breathed in the salty air and felt the ocean breeze tear at her hair.

Delaney set her down reluctantly, just a few feet beyond the tide line. He unfolded the blanket and spread it on the sand. "Your sofa, ma'am."

She glanced at him beneath her lashes, wondering why the odd feelings that were centered well below her waist had calmed somewhat. "I

don't understand," she muttered, and carefully
eased herself down on the blanket. She arranged
her skirts primly about her legs.

Delaney lay on his side next to her, propping
himself up on his elbow. "What don't you understand?" he asked.

"I'm not hungry anymore," she said, still
puzzled.

"Why did you think you were? I recall you
stuffed yourself at lunch."

She gazed out over the water, unaware that he
was watching her face closely. She shrugged, then
winced at the slight pulling feeling in her ribs.
"It's silly. But when you were carrying me, my
stomach felt empty, and rumbly, sort of."

His eyes glittered. "So sophisticated," he said.

"What does that mean?" she asked, turning to
frown at him.

"Not a thing, Chauncey." He sat up and began
to sift sand between his fingers. "I come here
when I want to think things out," he said, seemingly intent on the piles of sand he was building.

"And are you thinking important things now?"

"I believe so," he said vaguely, the damned
sand holding all his attention. "Things seem to
become clearer out here, and more simple."

He shifted his position slightly, and Chauncey
found herself looking at his long legs, outlined
snugly in dark brown flannel trousers. His thighs
were well-muscled, and her eyes followed their
line upward. She shocked herself when she looked
blatantly at the taut outline of his groin. She
blinked, aware that the silly feeling was back in
her stomach again.

"Chauncey," he said, his voice heavy with feeling. Her eyes flew to his face and she felt herself grow quite red.

"I'm sorry," she blurted out. "I ... I don't know what's wrong with me! You must think I'm awful."

Suddenly he lay back on the blanket and spread his arms wide. His gaze held hers and she noticed in the bright sunlight the dancing golden flecks lighting the liquid brown of his eyes. "I have decided," he announced grandly, "that I have been run aground. Behold a collapsed man. Do with me what you will, Chauncey."

She ran her tongue nervously over her lower lip, and Delaney wondered frantically if he would embarrass the both of them, for he could feel the nearly painful swelling of his manhood.

"What do you mean?" she asked at last, her eyes, thankfully, still on his face.

"So it is my total surrender you demand?"

He looks as if he wants to consume me, she thought with blurred insight. She was suddenly frightened, and quickly turned her face away from him. Where was her burning hatred of him? Where was that unyielding part of her that had been her anchor for so very long?

"More thrust and parry?" he asked gently, the irony of his tone reaching her.

"I am ... afraid," she said, and he couldn't mistake the honesty in her voice.

"Don't you remember my telling you last night that I would never harm you? I might be a brash American, my dear, but I am not lost to all honor."

She felt her breath catch harshly in her throat. She wanted to yell at him that she wasn't afraid of him. It was herself she feared. Her mind fastened on his words. *Not lost to honor.* But he was, damn him, he was! Dear God, she wanted to hate him, plunge a dagger into his chest! She realized that she was getting exactly what she wanted. How many weeks had she been set on her single-minded course to bring about this moment? You must take advantage of the situation, she told herself angrily.

She turned back to him and gave him a dazzling smile, trying desperately to exude a wanton promise in her eyes. To her utter chagrin, he laughed softly.

"Oh, Chauncey, you haven't the ... experience to play the seductress."

She stiffened alarmingly, frightened that he seemed to see so easily through her.

"Nor is there any need," he continued. He sat up, turning gracefully toward her. Gently he cupped her chin in his hand.

"I never before realized how it would feel to let another person become so important, so vital to me."

"Then why have you been so ... elusive, as if you were mocking me?"

"I've wondered the same thing myself, believe me! It all started the night of the masked ball. You were such fun to tease, never at a loss for a stinging retort. I suppose I wanted to see how outrageous you would become."

"So outrageous that I nearly killed myself!"

"And what man could ignore such a dramatic gesture? You please me, Chauncey, as no woman has ever done before. You delight the imagination." He wanted desperately to kiss her, to pull

her down with him on the blanket. He dropped
his hand from her chin.

"You become the poet," she said with forced
lightness, but her voice was shaking in spite of
herself.

He waved away her words. "I'm twenty-eight
years old, Chauncey, not too much older than
you. I'm a rich man, and have no need for your
money."

"Penelope?" she whispered.

"That young lady will suffer nothing more than
a bout of wounded vanity."

Chauncey moistened her lips again, not wanting to ask, but compelled to. "Your . . . mistress?"

He frowned. "How do you know about that?"

"Penelope told me. She said you would give
her up, once you were married to her."

Delaney thought about Marie's giving soft body,
her French practicality, her basic kindness. He
remembered the brooding anger he had felt at
himself that night before, when he had thrust
into her body, all his thoughts on Chauncey lying
in his bed.

"Penelope shouldn't have told you anything
about her," he said.

"It is something I really don't understand. Do
all men have need of . . . well, mistresses?"

"Indeed so," he said gravely, his eyes twinkling as his sense of humor came to the fore.
"But it's not quite the same thing as having a
wife."

"Then I suppose it must be all right. Penelope
was being selfish then?"

He howled with laughter, unable to help himself. He held his stomach, gasping for breath.

"I do not see what is so funny!"

"You, Chauncey," he said, wiping his eyes with his sleeve. He saw that she was genuinely confused, and said very seriously, "I want you for my wife. I don't want a mistress. I want you to be furious at the thought of my touching another woman. I want you to be quite selfish. Now, my sophisticated girl, will you please say yes and get me out of my misery?"

"Say yes to what, sir?" she asked pertly, enjoying having the upper hand at last.

"Complete and utter surrender," he sighed. "Will you marry me?"

"Do you know," she said thoughtfully, studying his face, "I think it just might be a good idea."

"A quite good idea," he said. It occurred to him on their ride home that neither of them had mentioned love. He frowned at Lucas' back. Surely Chauncey must love him, to have gone to such lengths. Why hadn't she said anything? My sophisticated lady is shy, he thought. All in good time. As to his own feelings, he dismissed the notion of love. He wanted her; she pleased him. Love would come in due course.

— 13 —

"All right, Del," Dan Brewer said, thumping down his frothy mug of beer, "you've dragged me out of the bank, twisted my arm to come into the El Dorado, and forced me to drink this damned beer. Will you now tell me what's going on?"

"*Forced?* You have foam on your upper lip, Dan."

Dan swiped the back of his hand across his mouth. His eyes suddenly narrowed. "It's nothing to do with Miss Jameson, is it? She is doing just fine now?"

"Oh yes, she is all pert and sassy-mouthed again, and I'm going to marry her."

"*You're what?*"

"I trust that you aren't going to be heartbroken, along with a dozen other men?"

"Good God! Congratulations, Del!" He shook his head, bemused. "I'll be damned. But not surprised, no, not really." He leaned forward in his chair and cocked an eyebrow at his friend. "Having her in your house did it, huh?"

"I'm certain," Delaney said softly, only a hint of menace in his voice, "that you aren't picturing any . . . improper scenes?"

"No," Dan said, "I'm not. At least, if I was, I'm not now!"

"I knew I could count on you, Dan."

Delaney sat back in his chair, briefly scanning the group of men in the most flamboyant gambling saloon in San Francisco. It was late afternoon, and the regulars were already hunched over circular tables, their cards fanned out in front of them. A tinny piano was blaring in the background, blending in with jovial male voices at the huge mahogany bar and sounds of poker chips flicked onto the tables. There were only a couple of garishly dressed women present at this time of day. Their efforts were saved for the night.

"Do you know something?" Del said finally, almost as if speaking to himself. Not waiting for a response, he continued, "I have come to believe in the past two hours—that is the length now of our engagement—that it was somehow inevitable. Sounds rather idiotic, doesn't it?"

"Does this mean when I decide to marry I'm going to begin waxing philosophical?" Dan asked, grinning. He watched Delaney swallow a generous portion of his beer. "Inevitable? Well, Miss Jameson did come in asking for you the same day she arrived in San Francisco."

"Do you think my fame as the brilliant lover lured her over from England?"

"I'd like to be a mouse in your pocket if you asked her that!"

"Oh, I probably will. No blushes from her, I'm sure. She'd probably tell me she heard I needed instructions." But that wasn't true; he knew it now. She was incredibly naive, her working knowledge of her own sexual responses to him, a man, nonexistent.

"What about Penelope Stevenson and Tony Dawson?"

"The two flies in the ointment? Well, set your mind at ease about Penelope. I told her yesterday when I took her riding that I was going to marry Chauncey."

"Chauncey?"

"Elizabeth's nickname. I find it rather ... endearing."

"Quite confident about the lady's feelings, weren't you?"

"Perhaps. But it didn't really matter. I would no more marry Penelope Stevenson than sign over my ownership of the bank to you!"

"How did Penelope react to your announcement?"

"Let me put it this way. I never knew that an eighteen-year-old girl, supposedly raised in the most proper way imaginable, could spout such colorful language. After she finished raking Chauncey up and down, she lit into me. Her parting shot was to tell me to go to hell. I spoke then to Bunker. He surprised me. No bluster at all. Merely sighed and wished me well. Told me in a wistful voice that I was a lucky man."

"It's not as if you were engaged to the chit, for heaven's sake, Del."

"True, but Penelope has a high opinion of herself and her charms. I had heard that she was spreading the word that it was she who was holding me off. Amazing, absolutely amazing."

"You know, Del," Dan said thoughtfully, "you really don't know Miss Jameson very well. She's been here under a month."

"Yes," Delaney said slowly, gazing into his beer mug, "that's quite true." He gave Dan a rakish grin. "I will now have years to get to know her. She is a puzzle that I will delight in solving, but slowly, very slowly."

James Cora, owner of the El Dorado, strolled over to their table, his habitual cigar dangling in the corner of his mouth. A tall man, he was floridly handsome, his wide, white-toothed smile always slightly suspect, at least in Delaney's jaundiced view. "Del, Dan, how are you boys doing?"

"Making money, but I doubt at your rate, Jim," Delaney said, shaking the older man's hand. "I don't need to ask you how your business is faring."

"Nope," James Cora said, turning his head to proudly survey his opulent kingdom. "How 'bout I buy you boys another beer? On the house?"

"Sure," Dan said. "But I don't intend to stay around and lose all my money playing poker with you."

"I'll live, son, I'll live, which is more than I can say about that fool Jack Darcy. Stupid ass."

"I heard he accused Baron Jones of cheating," Dan said.

"Not a smart move," Del said, shaking his head, remembering his own duel with Baron more than two years before. "The man's an excellent shot and something of a sadist to boot. Is it true he moved in on Darcy's mistress before the man was even buried?"

"Yep," James Cora said. "Nice piece," he added, dismissing quite coldly the entire incident. "You boys keep out of trouble." He nodded to them and strode over to greet Sam Brannan.

"That man is going to come to a bad end," Dan said, shaking his head.

"You're doubtless right, particularly with Bella and her rages. I heard she threw a vaseful of wilted flowers with slimy stems right at his head just last week."

"Let us trust that a wife is less violent than a mistress! Incidentally, Del, what about Marie?"

Delaney gave him a twisted smile, remembering Chauncey's innocent questions regarding men and their need for mistresses. It occurred to him that she had said not one word about his giving up his mistress. She hadn't even seemed overly impressed that he'd willingly offered to give her up.

"I'll speak to her soon, Dan. I doubt she'll have any difficulty at all finding a generous new protector."

They spoke of business for a while; then Delaney pulled out his vest watch. "I'm having dinner with my future wife. Keep my news under your hat for the time being, though I doubt Bunker Stevenson will show such restraint, particularly if he has informed his wife."

"Have you set a date yet?"

Delaney shook his head. "No. Chauncey was exhausted from our carriage ride to the ocean. I left her sleeping soundly. I'll talk to her about it this evening."

* * *

Delaney carried his future wife downstairs to the dining room for supper. When he eased her into a chair, he whispered in a wicked voice, "Tell me you've got that funny feeling in your stomach again."

She smiled up at him, clearly puzzled. "I *am* hungry," she said.

He couldn't wait to show her the source of her hunger, and the thought of caressing and fondling her made his body tense with desire. He wanted to whisper to her that she would learn all about funny sensations on their wedding night. But he said nothing. She was so bloody innocent about sex, and he drew the line at embarrassing her in that way, at least until they were married.

When he was seated and Lin had served their dinner, Delaney raised his wineglass to her. "To us, Chauncey."

She hesitated almost imperceptibly, then raised her own glass. "Yes, to us."

"While you were having pleasant dreams this afternoon, I was with Dan. He sends his congratulations."

"That is kind of him. Umm. Lin makes the most delicious pork. And all these crunchy fresh vegetables."

"She uses a Chinese ingredient called soy sauce. And ginger. Did I mention that you look utterly delicious yourself this evening?"

"Yes"—she grinned at him—"you did. And you, sir, do not exactly look like a chimney sweep yourself. Very dazzling, I should say, in that black frock coat. It makes your eyes look like dark honey. You do have very expressive eyes, you know, Delaney, but I imagine that many women have told you that before."

"Certainly," he said blandly. He felt inordinately pleased to hear it from her, the woman who would be his wife.

"Conceited man," she teased him.

"At least now I have justification for it. The most beautiful woman in San Francisco is going to marry me."

For an instant she felt choked with misery. And something else. Guilt. Stop it, Chauncey! You must do it, you have to! He deserves it!

"I do not wish to be simply a ... decoration, Del," she said, her falsely light voice not fooling him for an instant. "A wife who exists only through her husband."

"Have I asked that of you?"

"No. But I know what Englishmen are like. I realized after I broke my engagement to Sir Guy that he thought me a brainless, silly female, good only to run his household in the ever-present shadow of his dear mother."

"I am not English, my dear, and there are no shadows in this house."

She fiddled with her fork a moment, making designs in the small pile of vegetables left on her plate. "I ... I do not want to lose control of my money." She raised her eyes to his face and saw that he was regarding her intently, his eyes puzzled. "What I mean to say is that after I came into my inheritance, I spent two months with a man of business in London learning how to ... well, how to handle money. He told me that in America, just as in England, when a woman marries, she loses control of her money. She becomes an appendage, completely dependent upon her husband. I don't want that."

"Your money is yours, Chauncey," he said with quiet deliberation. "I want nothing to do with it. Did you think I would demand that you turn your funds over to me? A dowry of sorts?"

"I don't know," she said, looking at him straightly. "I am not much used to men and their ways."

"I think you are somewhat used to men, but the variety you've known were not particularly sterling specimens. Your uncle, Sir Guy the prig, and Owen the toad. Perhaps, if you wish, I can point you to some wise investments." He shrugged, and her eyes were drawn, despite herself, to his shoulders, firm and muscular. She swallowed convulsively and reached blindly for her wineglass.

"I told you, Chauncey," he continued after a moment, not understanding her sudden abstraction, "that I would never harm you. Nor will I ever try to make you into something you are not. All I will ever ask of you"—his lips twisted into a crooked smile—"is that you will be happy as my wife."

"Yes," she said firmly, "that is what I want too." *But I will harm you! I must!*

"Tell me, my dear, does reality taste as sweet as the dream?"

"I . . . I don't know what you mean."

"Reality, dear one, is me as your husband. The chase was the dream."

"Perhaps," she said a bit unsteadily, "you should ask me that after you are my husband."

"I will, you can count on it. There was something else I wished to say to you, Chauncey. You are English. Until five months ago, England was all you knew. I want to assure you that if you wish to spend some time in England, we will go together. Wives adhering to their husbands is all fine and good, but I would never demand that you forget all that you were before you came to me."

Her hand tightened about the stem of her wineglass. She spoke aloud her confusion without considering. "Why are you so ... nice? So considerate and reasonable?"

He cocked a mobile brow at her. "Did you expect me to be otherwise?"

Yes, damn you!

She smiled brightly, a false smile. "No, of course not, you simply took me off-guard. There is really nothing left for me in England. But you, Del, you have those illustrious relations, do you not?"

"Yes."

"Were you not thick as ... thieves with them when you were last in England? When? Fifty-one?"

"Yes, in 1851. The duke and duchess certainly introduced me to a lot of people, as I told you. I believe the duchess's not-so-hidden motive was to find me a nice English wife. She will doubtless be utterly delight to hear that she has succeeded, all without lifting a finger."

Oh God, will she recognize the name Jameson? If she doesn't, will she want to know who the devil I am? Will Delaney ask questions I cannot answer?

"It takes dreadfully long to send and receive letters from England, doesn't it? Good heavens, your precious duke and duchess won't know of your marriage for at least three months."

"True. I wrote to both to them and to my

brother this afternoon after I returned home from my visit with Dan. My brother has long urged me to take the fatal step."

"I don't think I like the sound of this fatal-step business!"

"Man talk, Chauncey, nothing more. Men tend to boast aloud of their freedom all the while wishing desperately for permanency: a wife and home and family."

Permanency. Will I be gone in six months?

"A family," she repeated suddenly, her eyes going blank.

Delaney's wineglass paused at his lips. "It is normally something that follows quite naturally from marriage, you know, my love. Do you not want children?"

She swallowed, unable to meet his eyes. "I don't know. That is, I am young!"

"Many women have their first child when they are only sixteen or seventeen."

She moistened her dry lips with her tongue. "Must children follow marriage, Delaney? Right away, I mean?"

What the devil was wrong? he wondered, keeping his expression impassive with difficulty. "No, I suppose not. Most husbands and wives desire children." He wanted to tease her, tell her that the probability of her conceiving would be high, since he likely wouldn't let her out of his bed for six months. He wondered if she even knew how babies were made, and decided not to pursue the subject until after they were married. "If you wish to wait, I suppose it can be arranged." He pictured himself asking Marie what she used to prevent conception, and nearly choked on his wine at the thought.

"Yes," she managed, "I think I do wish it." She knew that husbands and wives were intimate, knew that they took their clothes off around each other and slept together. And kissed and other things. She shook her head, refusing to think closely about it. Whatever she had to do as his wife, she would do.

Delaney was devoutly relieved he was sitting down, for whatever she knew or didn't know, he doubted she could be unaware of the bulge in his trousers were he to rise. "When will you marry me, Chauncey?" he asked, trying to distract himself.

"Whenever you would like," she said, toying with her vegetables.

"Next week? At St. Mary's?"

"For a man who has cherished his freedom for twenty-eight years, you are very anxious, Mr. Saxton, to get yourself chained!"

He grinned at her. "True, too true," he said. "Also, my dear, I won't want you moving back to the Oriental." He lowered his eyes and murmured softly, "Saint told me you'd be in fine fettle in another week."

"Wretched man! Do you know why he is called Saint?"

"Indeed I do, but it is his story, not mine." He wanted to tease her that Saint would likely tell her when she was in labor with their first child. He remembered suddenly the terrible fear he had felt when his sister-in-law, Giana, had gone into labor while out walking with him in New

York two years before. Perhaps, he thought, they could wait.

"Do you know something?" he asked after a moment, laughing.

"Many things, sir, but likely this is going to be at my expense!"

"No, not really. It's just that I haven't asked you properly to marry me. I discount asking you while we wallowed in the sand at the beach. Will you marry me, Chauncey?"

"May I assume that you are metaphorically lying prostrate at my feet?"

"A dead fox, ma'am. Or at least a collapsed one. You have run me to ground."

She frowned at him. "You make me sound like some sort of Amazon. I am not, you know."

"What are you, Chauncey?"

"I, sir?" She raptly studied the fine linen napkin in her lap. "I am merely a woman who ... wants you, above all other men."

"*Want*, Chauncey? Such an staid word, quite functional as a matter of fact. And I, my dear, am a romantic. You might remember that."

And I am a realist! She felt a strange emptiness as she gazed at him beneath lowered lids. There was humor in his eyes, and tenderness. Directed at her. Surely, she thought, he did not expect her to tell him that she loved him! She said very softly, "Yes, Del, I promise to remember."

"Excellent. Now, my dear future wife, would you like me to teach you how to play poker?"

Delaney finally settled on his back in his temporary bed, pillowing his head on his arms. Life was damned odd, he thought, frowning into the darkness. A month ago he was contemplating marriage to Penelope Stevenson. Without love. Lord, but he had been an utter fool even to have considered it. Elizabeth Jameson. Chauncey. She was everything he wanted in a wife. What he'd said to Dan was true. She satified the imagination. And she wanted him. Words he said in passion to Marie. Functional words. He told himself again, his mind sliding into sleep, that all would come in time.

— 14 —

"She looks skinny and pale, like a frumpy old lady!"

Tony Dawson raised a pained brow at Penelope's ludicrous comment. Surely soon she would run out of nasty things to say about Miss Jameson. His mind froze on that thought. No, now she was Mrs. Delaney Saxton. Tony sighed, wishing Penelope would somehow disappear and leave him to his misery. But of course she didn't.

"I can't believe Del would be taken in by the likes of her!"

"Likes, Penelope? What do you mean by that?" Keep your damned mouth shut, he chided himself. Here he was asking for more virulent remarks.

"Some English lady," Penelope hissed, aware that that old bitch Agatha Newton was staring down her nose at her. "No one really knows who

194

she is or where she comes from. All she has is money."

Tony looked pensively into his champagne glass. "She does have money," he said finally in a non-committal voice, then added, "If one listens carefully to her speech, I venture to say that England is the only place she could come from."

"That isn't what I meant," Penelope said, "and you know it!"

Tony ignored this accusation, looking around frantically for help, but saw none forthcoming. The bride and groom were being toasted by Sam Brannan and Reverend Barkeley by the wide bay windows. Chauncey did look pale, he thought, his heart wrenching slightly at the sight of her. He sighed, hearing Penelope's shrill whisper.

"You do know, don't you, Tony, that she *slept* here, in Delaney's bed, for the past two and a half weeks? He was forced to marry her!"

"I think it was more a case of Del being a Good Samaritan, Penelope, don't you? After all, she was quite ill."

"Ha!" Penelope said, sniffing. "She will learn soon that Del is like all the other men in San Francisco. A tomcat with a mistress!"

Agatha Newton shook her head, feeling sorry for Tony Dawson, his disappointment as well as his obvious trial in Penelope Stevenson's company. Ridiculous little snit! Didn't she realize that she was but making herself look foolish? As for all the other guests, they were warmhearted and full of good wishes for Del and Chauncey. The small wedding at St. Mary's, she and Horace and Dan Brewer the witnesses, had been quite elegant, Reverend David Barkeley having managed to stow all his hellfire and brimstone for the ceremony. Here in the Saxton home at least one hundred people had strolled through during the afternoon to wish the couple the best. A magnificent buffet had been set out in the dining room, compliments of Lin Chou and Armond Arnault's catering service. Agatha met her husband's eye and nodded slightly. It was getting late and Chauncey looked ready to drop from weariness. Agatha's gray eyes softened with memory as she gazed at the lovely white satin gown, designed and sewn by Monsieur Daneau himself, all in one short week. The bodice fit snugly and was heavily trimmed with exquisite white Brussels lace. A half-dozen petticoats supported the endless rich yards of the heavy satin skirt. The long white veil was sewn with delicate seed pearls and fell gracefully down Chauncey's back. It was fixed to the crown of her head with a circle of orange blossom. Around her slender neck was a beautiful single strand of pearls, similar to those Agatha had worn twenty years before at her own wedding.

"Ready, my dear?" Horace asked quietly, coming to stand beside her.

Agatha sighed. "Doesn't she look glorious, Horace? Ah, how all this makes me remember our own wedding day."

Horace Newton scratched his gray head. "Lord, Aggie, you remember that far back? And here I've tried to forget all of it."

Well used to her spouse's teasing, Agatha ignored his drawing words and asked, "Do you think, Horace, that I should perhaps speak to Chauncey?"

"Whatever for?" her husband asked in some surprise. "Thought you'd already proffered all the right sentiments."

"Her mother died when she was a little girl," Agatha explained as if to a dull-witted child. "I shouldn't wonder if she were quite ignorant about the more intimate parts of marriage. Maybe as an older married woman—"

"Lord, Aggie, leave off! Del can handle all of that. He's not a randy boy, after all. I doubt the girl's all that naive in any case."

"She's English," Agatha said with some asperity. "You know how well-bred girls are raised there."

"No, I don't, but no matter. The last thing she needs is an old battleax like you advising her!"

"Uncouth bore!"

"Well, I suppose you could tell her that she'll have the time of her life."

Agatha poked him fondly in the ribs. "Well, I refuse to leave until that silly little fool Penelope Stevenson is safely out the door. And Sally Stevenson! You'd think the world has come to an end."

"All right. I'll go collar Bunker. He's beginning to look the worse for wear. Excellent champagne, and all Bunker has swilled is brandy."

"And I'll rescue poor Tony from Penelope." Agatha smiled politely to the remaining guests, keeping on course to where Tony stood, a look of long suffering on his handsome face. "How are you, Tony, Penelope?" she asked brightly. "What a lovely wedding it was, don't you think? And this magnificent reception. I vow I've eaten enough for three days!"

"The wedding cake was too dry," Penelope said. "I'll bet that Chink cook of Del's made it."

"You know, Penelope," Agatha said thoughtfully, staring down at the girl, "there is nothing more repugnant than a show of bad manners, particularly when the show derives from jealousy. Don't you agree?"

"You'll see," Penelope said stiffly, looking from Agatha Newton, silly old cow, to a flushed Tony Dawson, "Del will tire of her quickly enough. Then he'll be sorry." With that obscure parting shot, she turned and flounced toward her mother.

"Thank you for the rescue, Agatha," Tony said fervently, swallowing the remainder of his champagne.

"My pleasure, dear boy." She patted his hand. "We're leaving now. Would you like to accompany us?"

Tony gave her a crooked grin. "Why? Do you think I'll say something repugnant if I remain?"

"Oh no," Agatha said cheerfully. "It's just that it's sometimes better to spend time with friends than alone."

"Just so, but not this evening, thank you."

"Damned fine filly you got, Del," Sam Brannan was saying to Delaney as he walked him to the front door.

"Thank you, Sam. I agree, you may be sure."

"The poor girl looks quite tired," Sam continued, unable to contain the leer that made his full lips pout. "Lord, I hope she won't be exhausted tomorrow!"

Delaney stiffened, his smile forced. "I'm glad you could come, Sam," he said.

After a sharp, jovial poke in Delaney's stomach, Sam Brannan took his leave, followed by the Stevensons and the Newtons.

Chauncey, finally released from the proselytizing endeavors of Reverend Barkeley—"the Church of England, indeed, ma'am!"—and still reeling from all the people she had met for the first time, eased herself into a comfortable velvet chair and leaned back, closing her eyes.

She heard Delaney's smooth voice from the entryway, deftly turning the more suggestive comments from the single men and complimenting the ladies on their apparel as they filed out the front door.

"I am Mrs. Delaney Saxton," she murmured, her voice revealing the shock of it. "I don't believe it."

"I imagine that you will soon enough."

Her eyes flew open. Tony Dawson was smiling down at her, but his left hand was fisted at his side.

"Ah, Tony," she said, regaining her control quickly. "I thought you'd left."

"I am going now. I wanted to wish you well again, Elizabeth."

"Please, Tony, call me Chauncey."

He lifted a well-formed eyebrow. "Del won't mind?"

"Whatever does he have to say with my name?"

"He is now your husband. I imagine he will have a lot to say about many things."

"Well," she said pertly, rising from her chair and smoothing the full skirts of her white satin gown, "so will I! And I think I can outtalk him most of the time."

"Is she tossing down the gauntlet, Tony?" Delaney said, smiling at his wife.

Tony saw the softness in his friend's gaze and winced. "I'll be going now," he said somewhat stiffly, disregarding Del's jesting question. "Will you be traveling out of the city for a wedding trip?"

"We haven't decided anything specific yet," Delaney said. "Doubtless my fast-talking wife will inform me soon what she wants to do."

"All I want to do," Chauncey said on an artless yawn, "is go to bed."

Both men whipped about to stare at her. "Ah, my dear," Delaney said finally, a wide grin revealing straight white teeth, "you must learn to keep your more interesting wishes to yourself. Or at least whisper them to me very softly."

"Oh!" Her face flushed a bright red. "I didn't mean ... that is ... you're terrible, Delaney Saxton! Tony, come, I'll show you out! We will leave this wretched tease to himself."

Tony paused at the front door after accepting his top hat from Lucas. "I do wish you the very best, Chauncey," he said, smiling down at her. "Del is a fine man. You will be happy with him, I am certain." He looked as if he would say more, and Chauncey held her breath for a moment, praying he would not.

"Thank you, Tony. You must come over to dinner soon. Lin makes the most delicious concoctions." She laughed lightly, hoping to break the tension she felt emanating from him. "I have learned never to ask her the ingredients."

"Yes, I should be delighted," he said, and turned quickly on his heel.

"He'll survive, madam. Don't trouble yourself."

Chauncey turned at Lucas' shortly spoken words. "Yes, I know." She smiled ruefully. "If Tony were in a more equally populated city, I fancy his feelings would never have been engaged."

"As to that, I couldn't say. Ah, here is Mr. Saxton."

She felt his hands on her shoulders, gently kneading the taut muscles. "Better?" he murmured, leaning to lightly kiss her temple. He slowly turned her to face him. "How do your ribs feel?"

"Just a bit sore," Chauncey said, her voice sounding dry and crackly. *Get a hold on yourself, you fool!* She laughed, a completely artificial sound that didn't fool Delaney for an instant. "Monsieur Daneau was quite voluble about my not wearing a corset."

"Yes," Delaney said gently, "you told me about it already. You really don't have anything for a corset to contain. The man's an idiot."

"Fashion," she said, tilting her chin upward. "If it weren't for you blasted men, I daresay we wouldn't be so confined, cramped, and otherwise encumbered."

He smiled at her, understanding her nervousness and wishing he could lessen it somehow. Chauncey, in the short time he had known her, always resorted to argument when she was uncertain of herself. "I agree completely," he said. "Shall I go fire Monsieur Daneau's very fancy store?"

She moistened her lips with her tongue until she became aware that Delaney had grown very still, watching her. "My lips are dry," she said sharply. Was that what coquettes did to attract men?

He cocked a mobile eyebrow. "It's the champagne," he said blandly. "It's dark," he added, as if to himself.

"Where is Mary?" Chauncey, for the first time in her short life, turned a cold shoulder to the beautiful star-studded sky.

"She, Lucas, and Lin are in the kitchen enjoying themselves. I'll be your lady's maid. Come, wife."

Wife!

She stood as still as a statue. In a single lithe motion, Delaney scooped her into his arms. I feel like I'm carrying a soft board, he thought vaguely, smiling toward the top of the stairs. When he reached his bedroom—their bedroom now—he gently lowered her to the floor, turned, and firmly closed the door.

He watched her a moment, standing stiffly in the middle of the room, her arms wrapped around herself as if in protection.

Delaney made no move toward her. He leaned against the door, crossing his arms across his chest. "Do you know, my dear," he said after a moment, "I told you that I would never harm you. Do you remember?"

She nodded, her eyes fastened on the swirls of color in the carpet at her feet.

"Did I also tell you that you are the most beautiful bride I've ever had?"

Her head whipped up. "I am your only bride!"

"Excellent. I hate to see you acting like a frightened puppy. Now, wife, let me help you with that gown."

She felt his fingers deftly unfastening the long row of satin-covered buttons down her back, and forced herself to stand still. I am his wife, she repeated over and over to herself. I must behave like a happy bride. He must never suspect . . .

The gown slipped from her shoulders.

"Turn around, love, and hold onto me. I can think of no other way to get you out of this thing without destroying it."

Soon, her many petticoats tossed carelessly over a chair back, she was standing in her lawn shift, so femininely embroidered with yellow rosebuds, and her lace-trimmed drawers and silk stockings.

"You look utterly adorable," Delaney said, gently cupping her chin between his thumb and forefinger. "Underthings and a veil. Yes, utterly adorable. Come sit down at the dressing table, Chauncey, and I'll free your hair."

While Delaney unfastened the long veil and gently pulled the many pins from her hair, he set himself to relaxing her and distracting her. "I heard some of the snide little remarks from Penelope. Were you so lucky?"

"Indeed, I would have had to be deaf not to! I think she would have liked to stick the cake knife into my ribs."

"All's well that ends well, I say," he said, picking up her brush and slowly stroking through her thick hair. "I must thank you for rescuing me from that grubby little chit. Although I doubt now that I ever would have wed her. Even before you arrived, love, she was wearing on the nerves."

Chauncey's eyes flew to his face in the mirror. Not married her! Had she done all of this for naught? She shook her head, bemused. No, it was better this way. Despite all the husbandly demands she would have to endure, she would be living in his house, reading his business papers, and listening to his plans. And *ruining* him.

"You have beautiful hair, Chauncey. Perhaps I should initiate a Lady Godiva Day and place you in the starring role."

He was so damned likable! "It is not long enough," she said.

"Perhaps in a year or so, then. Now, my dear," he continued, turning to the armoire, "I have a surprise for you. And not from Monsieur Daneau's shop."

She watched him warily as he pulled down a gaily red-ribboned box and handed it to her. "I hope you will enjoy it as much as I will." He kissed her lightly on her pursed lips and immediately straightened.

Chauncey pulled away the ribbon and lifted the lid. Nestled in layers of tissue paper was a silk nightgown and peignior that resembled nothing she had ever seen, much less worn. It was nothing but sheer nonsense, light yellow trimmed with swansdown. "It's beautiful," she managed. "But there's not much to it."

"No," he agreed, "not much. But likely more than too much for me." He kissed her cheek and turned to walk to the bedroom door. "Do put it on, Chauncey. I'll be back in a moment."

Chauncey rose when the door closed behind her husband, the flimsy nightgown clutched in her fists. Mechanically she smoothed out the material, her eyes falling to her wedding ring. It was a magnificent piece of jewelry, a single large diamond surrounded by three rubies held in a

delicate gold setting. She stood silently, staring
toward the warm embers in the fireplace. Suddenly she whirled about. He would return soon.
The last thing she wanted was to be standing in
the middle of the room still in her underwear!
Quickly she stripped off the remainder of her
things and slipped the nightgown over her head.
It floated loosely about her body, the silk almost
caressingly tender. She stared at herself in the
cheval mirror, feeling like some sort of fluffy
dessert.

She heard the door open and turned quickly,
unaware that the light from the fireplace illumi-
nated every curve of her slender body.

Delaney sucked in his breath. "My God," he
said softly. "You are exquisite."

"You are too, Del," she said lightly, forcing
herself to remain still as he strode toward her.
He was wearing a heavy dark blue velvet dressing gown. She hadn't realized before how broad
his shoulders were. "Except for your feet," she
added, trying to jest.

"Now that we are both shoeless, I'll see exactly how you fit against me."

He stood a moment in front of her, then slowly
drew her against him. She felt his hand on the
back of her head, pressing her face against his
shoulder. "A perfect fit," he said softly against
her temple. She felt him trembling and wondered at it. "I'm going to make you very hungry
tonight, Chauncey, very hungry. Now, I want
you to wrap your arms around my shoulders and
stand on your tiptoes."

She did as he said, suddenly aware of the
strength of him. She felt his hands stroke down

her back to her hips, and stiffened, a soft uncertain cry breaking from her mouth. "Hush, sweetheart. Relax. That's better. Can you feel me, Chauncey?"

How utterly odd, she thought vaguely, her lower regions beginning to tingle at the pressure from the hardness of his body. "Feel what?" she asked.

"My desire for you, love." He cupped his hands beneath her buttocks and lifted her.

"Oh!" She flung her arms about his neck to steady herself, burying her face against his neck.

Slow down, he chided himself as he drew a deep, steadying breath. All night, you've the entire bloody night.

Delaney gently lifted her into his arms and carried her to the bed. He laid her on her back and straightened over her. "Do you know," he said thoughtfully, stroking his chin, "I'm already quite tired of that bit of fluff you're wearing."

"But I've nothing else!" she exclaimed, drawing her legs up.

"Oh yes you do, sweetheart, more than you can possibly imagine." He stepped back and untied the sash from about his waist. He heard her draw in a sharp breath and paused. Would she find his man's body distasteful, repugnant? His manhood was swollen and hard, thrusting outward. Would she be shocked and frightened of him?

He was going too quickly, he decided, and dropped his hands. He gave her a rakish grin and gathered her into his arms again.

What was he going to do to her? Chauncey wondered frantically. When he eased himself down into a wing chair near to the fireplace, arranging her comfortably on his lap, she breathed a brief sigh of relief.

"You would like to talk?" she asked hopefully.

"Of course. I discovered I'm really not too tired. Tell me, wife, what you were thinking during our wedding this morning."

Her mind willingly focused on his question, distracting her momentarily from the light touch of his hand on her shoulder.

"I was thinking that Agatha might burst into a mother's tears at any moment."

His right hand paused a moment, then continued trailing down her arm. "Ah, Chauncey," he said in a complaining tone, "did I not tell you that I'm a romantic? Here I was expecting you to confide that it was the happiest moment in your life."

His mouth was smiling, but his eyes were gazing at the outline of her breasts, at the smooth nipples. He realized that he wanted to caress her through the flimsy silk until her nipples were taut. Without his mind's permission, his fingers lightly touched her breast, sliding over the smooth roundness to cup it in his hand.

She was very still, holding her breath. She wanted to yell at him to stop, but of course she could not. He was her husband; her body was his, legally. And she was his, willingly, to his mind. She felt him squeeze her breast very gently and jumped. "Contraception!" she burst out.

Delaney's hand quieted and he cocked his head sideways to better see her face. "I do not believe you are endangered by my hand," he said in a teasing voice.

"But men and women never do this . . . sort of thing unless they're married."

Ah, such innocence, he thought. In truth, he had forgotten to speak to Marie about preventing conception. Indeed, he had spent an entire evening with her, trying to explain about Chauncey. He had been a trifle amused at her smug assumption that he would be returning to her soon enough.

"My dear, trust me for this evening. It takes time to make a baby, so I'm told. No need tonight to resort to artificial methods."

Trust him? That was impossible. She shook her head, a frown marring her forehead with the realization that when she was not thinking directly about her reasons for marrying him, she automatically did trust him. She felt his hand caressing her breast again, circling closer to her nipple. She drew in her breath, utterly chagrined when she looked down to see that part of her body rising pertly even before he touched her.

"You're seducing me," she said in an accusing voice, willing her body to show no enthusiasm for him.

"I decided," Delaney said, "that if I did not, I might well spend the next twenty years as a virgin." His fingers touched her now taut nipple and he smiled. "Perhaps I was wrong. You are quite responsive, my dear."

"I don't mean to be! Truly I . . . You are wretched, Delaney Saxton, to tease me so. And you aren't a virgin!"

His hand glided smoothly from her arcing breast downward over her ribs. "Actually," he said softly, tightening his hold on her, "the last thing I want to do right now is tease you. Kiss me, Chauncey."

She lifted her face and felt his warm mouth touch hers. He tasted of champagne and lobster and a very sweet man taste. "Just relax, love," he murmured against her lips.

She felt his tongue glide smoothly over her closed lips, and she felt a rush of warmth deep in her stomach. "Oh," she said in soft surprise. His tongue slipped into her mouth. It was the oddest feeling, and for a moment she let herself react to his exploration. His fingers were splayed over her belly, gently kneading. She arched upward against him, sending his fingers lower.

Delaney felt her reaction and gloried in it. His mouth left hers and he kissed her nose, her chin, her high cheekbones. His hand pressed down against her, and he could feel the warmth rising from her body. "Let's go to bed, Chauncey," he said hoarsely against her ear.

"I am not certain that I want to," she said in a shrill voice, wishing he would move his damned hand. She had the embarrassing feeling that she was growing damp beneath his probing fingers, and was unnerved by it. Surely it wasn't natural!

"We will go very slowly, I promise." He hoisted her up high in his arms and carried her to the bed.

"You are very strong," Chauncey said, her voice a high nervous squeak, knowing that the moment of reckoning was quite near. It can't be too bad, she thought wildly. So many people are married!

"And you, my love, are adorably soft," he said as he laid her on her back in the middle of the bed and eased down beside her.

"This bed is so small," Chauncey gasped, feeling the heat from his body even though he wasn't touching her.

Delaney smiled ruefully. He wasn't a randy young boy, but his control was sorely tried. And his bride was very nervous. Well, he decided, ignorance definitely wasn't bliss, particularly in the marriage bed. He said slowly, "Chauncey, the size of the bed isn't at all important at this moment. I'm going to make love to you now. Just relax and trust me. All right?"

She nodded, swallowing convulsively. *Make love!* What an odd thing to say. His lowering head blocked out the light from the single lamp. She felt his mouth caressing hers, felt his hand stroking down her body, learning every inch of her. "Damned thing," he muttered, and rose to a sitting position. "Enough of this nonsense."

She wanted to protest, but instead tightly closed her mouth. In but a moment she felt the cool air touching her flesh, saw him toss the nightgown to the floor. Her hands went instinctively to cover her breasts.

Delaney said nothing, merely turned and shrugged out of his dressing gown. When he looked back at Chauncey, he saw that her eyes were tightly closed. He pressed his body against her side, balancing himself on an elbow above her.

He drew in his breath at her beauty. "Lord," he muttered softly.

"Lord?" Her eyes flew open. "You are praying?"

"No, I am admiring you. You are lovely. No, don't try to hide yourself from me. I'm your husband, remember?"

He laid his hand on neutral territory at her waist. "Shall I tell you what I'm seeing?"

He didn't await a reply. "Your incredible eyes are the color of my waxed mahogany desk, and in this dim light your hair is like rippling waves of thick reddish, brownish, blondish—"

She giggled. "It is a stupid color, and you are running out of 'ishes'!"

Her mirth died in her throat when his gaze shifted suddenly downward, and she gasped slightly, her hands fisting.

"Your breasts, my dear, are your high point, so to speak. I wonder if your nipples taste pink?" He lowered his head and gently circled a nipple, then took it into his mouth.

Chauncey lurched upward. "Oh no! Please, Delaney, you mustn't. You can't—"

"Hush," he whispered, his warm breath making her shudder. "You mustn't interrupt my study." His tongue lapped and her nipple throbbed. He raised his head and looked into her dazed, very bewildered eyes. "I think you like that. There is much more, love. No, don't pull away. Forget any foolishness you've heard about lovemaking from prune-faced old biddies, and let your body react naturally."

His eyes returned to their study. "Now, as for your ribs, they're colorful still. The dull purple is most enchanting." Lightly his fingertips outlined her ribs. "A bit skinny, but I'm not complaining, mind you. You don't strain my back when I'm carrying you." He realized that his voice was shaking a bit and closed his eyes a moment, drawing on a fast-disappearing control.

"I can feel the length of you against me,"

Chauncey said, and Delaney trembled. "You feel very hard and hairy." Just the sound of her voice, not to mention the words, shook him terribly.

"You can explore me later," he managed. He laid his hand on her belly. "So white, like the snow in the Sierras before men's boots tromp over it." Lord, you fool, that was about as seductive as an emetic! "Do you know, Chauncey, what lies beneath this soft thatch of hair?"

"Please," she gasped, so embarrassed that she tried to jerk away from him. She drew suddenly still, for his fingers were gently probing through the soft tangle of curls, touching her wetness. She sucked in a shuddering breath. "This is awful," she said, more to herself than to him.

He stroked her swollen flesh, reveling in the softness. "Ah, love," he whispered, lowering his head, "it is a wonderful awfulness, for both of us." He kissed her deeply, forcing her lips to part as his fingers rhythmically stroked her. He felt her hips move briefly against his fingers, then still. Damned repressive way girls were raised, he thought, frustrated. He knew he couldn't wait much longer. Surely she could feel him pressing painfully against her thigh, throbbing and hungry for her.

His fingers left her a moment, and he was delighted to hear her moan of disappointment—at least he chose to think it disappointment. He circled her small entrance, and could feel her flesh pulsating, warm and inviting. Slowly he inserted his forefinger, testing her, stretching her to ease his way.

"Delaney!" she burst out, lurching up and

trying to expel his probing finger. "I cannot believe that you would . . . No, 'tis impossible!"

He knew he should begin again, ease her, make her relax and want him once more, but he feared he would release his seed before he entered her. "Hush," he ground out. He pressed her back and rolled over on top of her. He balanced himself on his elbows and looked down into her wild eyes. "Feel me, Chauncey. I want you. Just close down that active mind of yours and let yourself respond."

"Oh no," she whispered, feeling his hardness pressing against her closed thighs.

He began to move slowly over her. The feel of her soft breasts against his chest drove him distracted. "Chauncey," he said, his voice breaking on a moan, "I cannot wait, love."

She felt his knee forcing her legs apart, and she gazed up at him helplessly, now frightened. Every warm, delightful intriguing sensation fled. She lay stiffly as he reared between her legs. He was looking at her, seeing her body in intimate detail. She raised her hands and pressed them against his shoulders, trying to push him away.

Delaney gazed at her delicate pink beauty. Better just to get it over with before he lost all control. He slowly guided his manhood into her, feeling her tense, stiffen. I will not hurt her, he thought silently. I will not hurt her. But in the next moment, he butted against her maidenhead. He cursed silently. With all her damned horseback riding, he'd hoped she would have lost that commodity. Now that he was buried firmly inside her, he stretched on top of her, careful to go no deeper until she relaxed somewhat.

"You are driving me wild," he said, unable to relax himself. "Chauncey, open your eyes, love. Now, kiss me." His mouth closed over hers, his tongue lightly probing to meet hers. At the moment of contact, he thrust forward, tearing through the thin barrier and hurtling into the depths of her. He caught her cry of pain in his mouth. Even though her fingernails dug into his shoulders, he could not prevent himself from driving into her, claiming her, becoming part of her.

Tears blurred her eyes, and pain from deep inside her made her whimper. She felt utterly helpless, betrayed somehow, for he had promised her that he wouldn't hurt her. Slowly, to her utter surprise, the sharp pain disappeared and the elusive warmth began to build within her once again. Her arms, of their own volition, hugged him to her, and her back arched upward.

Her movement broke his last vestige of control. He moaned deep in his throat. "I'm sorry, love," he gasped, and drove his full length into her. Chauncey felt him stiffen, watched his eyes close over a violent emotion that she didn't comprehend. Her own growing interest was long gone. She felt a burst of wetness inside her. It was from him, not her.

She waited, her body tense, her mind frozen until he quieted. He eased himself on top of her, seemingly exhausted. She frowned over his shoulder. She thought vaguely that the soft lamplight made the ends of his hair lighten from brownish blond to gold.

He is my husband, she told herself. I had no choice. I have done my duty.

Delaney, his wits returned, slowly raised himself on his elbows and looked down at his wife's face. "Will you forgive me?"

"For hurting me? It doesn't hurt anymore, just stings a bit."

He looked rueful. "That and leaving you."

"Leaving me where?" she asked, puzzled.

He shook his head, bemused. "Once you reach the destination, you will know, I promise you."

"You are no longer as you were," Chauncey said, frowning slightly at the changing feel of him inside her.

"No, I suppose not." He gently drew back, easing out of her. He saw her wince slightly.

"Better?"

She nodded, flushing suddenly at their intimacy. How often would he enter her body? she wondered wordlessly. Was it a thing that men wanted to do once a month? Once a year? Her eyes stared at him when he said blandly, "Good. We'll sleep a bit before we try again."

"*Again!* But surely you can't mean to—"

"It is a tradition for couples on their wedding night to make love at least six times."

"You can't mean it!" Her appalled look made him release his held-in laughter.

"Oh, Chauncey, you are such an innocent delight!" He kissed her again, tenderly, without passion. "You're a bit sore, right? It was that wretched maidenhead of yours. Now the bloody thing is gone, thank God."

"No, I think you should rather give yourself that congratulation." She looked at him closely, then frowned. "I feel sticky and . . . wet."

"Chauncey," he said fervently, lightly caress-

ing her cheek, "I am so glad you married me."
He wondered if he should offer to help her clean
herself, but he pictured her mortification at such
a suggestion and held his peace.

"I really had little choice in the matter," she
whispered, her bitterness and confusion from
what had just happened to her buried snug in
her mind, and let him draw her against his side.
She laid her cheek against his chest and fell into
a deep sleep, his hair tickling her nose.

— 15 —

"Chauncey. Come on, love, wake up, it's time for breakfast."

She moaned, yanking the soft pillow over her head to block out the insistent voice. The dream drew her back, and she was once again dangling upside down from an apple-tree branch behind Jameson Hall, laughing delightedly at the faces Jem, the stableboy, was making at her. Hannah was scolding her, coming into the orchard at an ungraceful gallop. "Yer drawers, miss!" she was screeching.

"Sweetheart," the voice came again. She felt a hand on her shoulder, lightly squeezing.

"No, please," she muttered, but the dream was gone now. She felt the pillow pulled from her grip and sun shone onto her face. Chauncey opened her eyes and gasped. "Delaney, what are you doing in here? And you're not really dressed properly. Surely . . ." Her voice broke off suddenly, and she felt a scarlet flush rise from her throat to the roots of her hair. Good God! He was her husband!

"Oh," she said, molding the covers around her like a shroud over a mummy. She was completely naked under the sheet and two blankets.

"Good morning, wife," Delaney said softly, wishing now that he hadn't left the bed and had awakened her and loved her while she was still partially asleep. Now her barriers were back up. She had looked at first bewildered, then shocked, and now utterly embarrassed.

"G-good morning, Del," she said. She couldn't, wouldn't meet his eyes, imagining the knowing gleam, the complacent smugness.

He took pity on her and handed her one of her own depressingly modest dressing gowns. "There's a nip in the air, sweetheart. Here, put this on."

Chauncey grasped the bed gown but didn't move. Delaney sighed and turned his back to her. He was arranging their breakfast on the small table when he heard the bed creak as she rose.

He made his face expressionless and slowly turned to look at his bride. If it weren't for her wildly tousled hair, framing her face and tumbling down her back in abandon, she would look like a modest little schoolgirl in that wretched dressing gown. My sophisticated woman of the world, he thought wryly, encased in a fortress of high-necked muslin.

I will not let her freeze up on me, he thought, and moved to take her into his arms. She made a small sound of protest and held herself stiff against him. He kissed her lightly on the forehead while his fingers sifted through her hair, easing out some of the tangles.

"It's a mess. I usually braid it, or Mary does."

"Never again, if you please." He smiled against her ear, ignoring the embarrassed thinness of her voice. "You have the look of a woman who has . . . slept well."

"I'm hungry!"

He stood back to look down into her face, not releasing her from the circle of his arm. "True," he said sadly. "I didn't see to your hunger properly last night."

"You are speaking nonsense, Del," she said, and pushed her hands against his chest. He was wearing a white shirt, open over his chest, and a pair of black trousers. His feet were bare.

"Always," he said, his light brown eyes taking on the familiar teasing gleam. "Anything to ease you, love."

She felt the dried stickiness on her thighs and flushed, annoyed with herself. "I have to . . . that is, I must go to . . ."

"Ah, certainly." He released her and watched her hurry behind the screen on the far side of the room. "Lin brought you fresh water while you were still sleeping," he called after her. He would have enjoyed bathing his seed and her virgin blood from her himself, but he wisely refrained from calling out that suggestion. He sat down beside the table and set himself to drinking the hot coffee.

Chauncey gasped, stared down at herself, her eyes wide with fear. Dried blood covered her

220 *Catherine Coulter*

inner thighs. *Her* blood! He had hurt her, killed her! She cried out, unable to help herself.

"Chauncey! Lord, what's the matter?" He strode across the room, only to halt abruptly as he came around the dressing screen, and stared at her. She was clutching the bed gown to the front of her, and her eyes were wild with fear. "What's wrong, sweetheart? Did you hurt yourself?"

"No," she gasped. "You did it! I don't understand. I don't hurt, but all the blood!" She clutched the gown closer, not knowing what to do.

He wanted to laugh at her ignorance, but her obvious fear smote him. "It's all right," he said gently, walking slowly toward her. "It's but your virgin blood, love, nothing more. It's very natural the first time, when your maidenhead is ruptured. I promise it won't happen again."

She shuddered with relief, then felt ready to sink with mortification. "I . . . I didn't know," she stammered, feeling like an utter fool. "No one ever told me that this would happen."

"No, of course you wouldn't," he said, his voice pitched low to soothe her. Damn, he thought, he should have told her what to expect, but it simply hadn't occurred to him that she would be so appallingly ignorant. "Would you like me to help you, Chauncey?"

She shook her head, mute. Did he really expect her to say yes? To strip naked in front of him and let him bathe her? She shuddered at the image that came to her mind. "Please, just leave," she muttered, her voice tight.

Delaney returned to the table and sat down again. He rubbed his hand over his brow. Damn him for a fool. He shouldn't have left her to discover the blood for herself. He glanced over at the bed and saw more evidence of her virginity, dark splotches of blood stark against the white sheet.

"Chauncey," he called out, "are you all right?"

"Yes, certainly."

Ah, no more fear, he thought, amusement lacing his relief. Her voice was firm and aggressive, as if she expected him to make sport of her, and was ready to give as good as she got. He reluctantly gave up on the very pleasant notion of making love to her this morning . . . and this afternoon . . . Well, perhaps this evening . . .

"Ah," he mused aloud, "the endless responsibilities of a new husband."

"What does that mean?"

Delaney grinned up at her militant expression. "Sit down, Chauncey, and try one of these delicious croissants. Lin fetched them from the French bakery on Kearny especially for you."

He watched her ease into the chair opposite him and reach for a croissant and butter. "You weren't in the wrong, Chauncey," he said, unable to keep the teasing gleam from his eyes. "There's no need to become all sorts of defensive and mount an attack on my poor self."

She took a vicious bite from the flaky croissant, swallowed it before she should have, and choked.

"Here, love," he said, laughter lurking in his voice as he handed her a glass of orange juice.

Chauncey glared at him over the rim of the glass. When she got her breath, she said more calmly, "You have the knack of making me feel like a fool."

"I?" He raised a mobile brow at her.

"You," she said firmly. "Now, tell me what you meant by that obnoxious thing you said."

"Which obnoxious thing?"

"Your responsibilities as a new husband. It sounded quite condescending to me."

"No, not really," he said, shaking his head. "Actually, I was feeling very sorry for myself. You see, my dear"—he waited until she'd taken another bite of croissant—"it was my intention to make love to you all day, but you're likely not up to it. Most disheartening, but I assure you I do understand."

Chauncey felt the soreness between her legs and shifted uncomfortably in her chair. He had seen her, touched her, and thrust inside her body. She flushed, wishing she could disappear, wishing he would disappear and that she could despise him. Why wouldn't he act like the knave he was? Why didn't she feel degraded after he'd taken her? "I don't like you," she said in a militant voice.

"Ah, Chauncey," he said, clearly amused by her, "you will never bore me."

"But you bore me, sir!"

"In that case, I should forget about your soreness and make love to you." He half-rose from his chair, but stopped as Chauncey gasped and shot up, tipping the table.

He grabbed it, laughing as he did so. Once it

was steadied, he sat down again and steepled his long fingers together, eyeing her over the tips of them. The silence stretched between them, and Chauncey squirmed in her chair. What an idiot she was to let him draw her!

Unexpectedly he asked, "Will you tell me now why you came to San Francisco?"

She stared at him stupidly, her wits having gone begging. *I came to ruin you, you miserable bastard!* She licked her suddenly dry lips. *But you don't act like you're supposed to and I don't understand!* "Wanderlust," she said succinctly. "London bored me. I wanted adventure, to see new things and places and people."

"I see," he said. "That is certainly an interesting reason." He saw from her expressive eyes that she was formulating more outlandish reasons, and said quickly, "I thought, my dear, that you might enjoy taking a riverboat to the city of Sacramento. It's grown tremendously the past couple of years, become quite an interesting and cultured city as a matter of fact. In all likelihood it will become the capital of California in the near future. What do you say? With all your wanderlust, you must want to see more of California than just San Francisco."

"Indians," she said, grasping at the first straw that came to mind. Dammit, she had to stay here and make plans!

"We're not going overland. If you see any, they'll be on the shore, a goodly distance away."

"There's water all the way to Sacramento?"

"Yes, all the way. Truly, love, I think you'll enjoy yourself. A riverboat is nothing like the ship you traveled from New York on. It's the height of opulence, and if we weren't married, we'd likely gain a good deal of weight from all the delicious food."

Chauncey could well picture the exercise involved in remaining skinny. She shrugged inwardly. It would be the same in any case, and there was nothing she could do about it. Why didn't she feel more put upon? "Yes," she said, realizing that a happy bride should want a wedding trip, "I should like to visit Sacramento."

"Excellent. They endured a huge fire just last year, but like San Franciscans, they rebuilt the city bigger and better. We will leave this afternoon, if that suits you, love."

"Everythng is already arranged?" she asked, raising a brow at him.

"Indeed. I want you never to be disappointed about anything."

"Ah," she said, wiping her hands on the linen napkin, "the responsibilities of a husband."

The *Scarlet Queen* was like no boat or ship Chauncey had seen before. "American steamers are the finest imaginable," Delaney told her as he escorted her down the wide wooden Clay Street wharf. "Many visitors call them water palaces. As opposed to water closets, of course." Chauncey ignored his jest and stared at the steamer. It did look more like a house than a ship, several stories high, with large doors, windows, and what looked like many galleries. "At night on the water, the *Scarlet Queen* will look like an enchanted castle, for there are lights blazing from every window and the chimneys look like volcanoes belching fire."

"You become a poet, sir," she said, secretly very impressed. She turned at the sound of a man shouting. The wide wooden dock was filled with workers loading and unloading crates from several other ships docked there, and horses neighed as drivers whipped them up, navigating their wagons and drays through the throng of people. She shivered, for the afternoon was chill and overcast, wispy fog curling about the long wharf.

"Chilly? Let's get on board." Delaney quickly eased her out of the way of a Chinese who was balancing two buckets of shrimp slung on a long pole over his shoulders. "Lucas already delivered our trunks," he continued. "You will like the captain, I promise you. His name is Rufus O'Mally, and he has a poet's smooth Irish tongue with the ladies, but a greater martinet I've yet to meet."

"You sound like you know him well," Chauncey observed, not really paying attention, for the activity on the wide deck of the *Scarlet Queen* held her eye. She supposed that she should, by now, be accustomed to seeing ladies in silks and gentlemen in top hats and fancy suits alongside rough-looking men garbed in baggy trousers and slouched flannel hats. She thought of such a scene in London and nearly laughed aloud at the incongruity of it.

"He works for me," Delaney said smoothly.

His words sank in and she whirled about, gazing at him in some consternation. "You *own* this boat?" she asked slowly.

"Actually, Sam Brannan and I are partners. Sam has his fingers in more pies than I care to count, including many in Sacramento, and he talked me into this venture. It's paid off very well." He saw that she was frowning, and added in some surprise, "Aren't you pleased that your husband can afford to provide well for you?"

"I am not some kind of pet monkey to be kept in a gilded cage!"

"No, and your mixed metaphors are charming."

"I don't need you to provide for me."

He still did not understand her obvious upset, and chose for the moment to ignore it. "The *Scarlet Queen* carries primarily passengers bound for Sacramento, but there are many stops along the way. Perhaps on another trip we'll go to Grass Valley and Marysville and visit General Sutter. I think you'd enjoy Hock Farm. If you like, we can visit the Yuba River. I have a gold mine there."

I'll just bet you do, she thought, kicking at a coiled hemp rope.

"It's still quite rough and uncivilized," Delaney continued, nodding to Colonel Dakworth and his wife as he steered Chauncey aft toward the glassed wheelhouse. "A great variety of men live there—Germans, Swedes, Chinese, even some English." He suddenly grew silent, his lips thinning into a white line.

"Well, if it ain't Mr. Saxton and his little bride! Howdy, ma'am!"

Chauncey eyed the dark-haired, powerfully built man standing in front of her. She blinked when Delaney said abruptly, "Baron. I'm certain you'll excuse us."

He gripped her elbow in an iron hold. "Baron?" she asked, puzzled. "Who is he? Why do you so dislike him?"

"He is not a nice man, Chauncey. In fact, I don't think I'd trust him if he were surrounded by harp-playing angels in heaven. Ah, Captain O'Mally."

Chauncey blinked at the very short little man who was dressed in an ornate scarlet uniform. His bald head was round as his stomach and he had a wide mouth filled with unevenly spaced, very white teeth. His eyes were a twinkling light blue. He looked like a good-natured, thoroughly harmless leprechaun.

"Rufus, this is my wife, Elizabeth. My dear, Captain O'Mally."

He clicked his heels together and his smile widened even further. "Charming, ma'am, and charmed, I assure you!" His blue eyes studied her face. "So you're the lovely English lady who caught our Del."

"She did indeed," Delaney agreed blandly.

"I am pleased to meet you, Captain," Chauncey said, extending her gloved hand. His hands were as small and delicate as her own, but she felt the iron strength as he clasped her fingers.

"And this is Mr. Hoolihan, ma'am," Captain O'Mally said, straightening to his full diminutive height. Chauncey nodded to the tall, very dark-visaged man who had come out of the glassed-in wheelhouse. He too was dressed in a scarlet uniform of sorts, but without so many gold braids and brass buttons. On him the uniform looked very dashing.

"Mr. Hoolihan just joined me just last week," Captain O'Mally said. "This is only his second trip. Came to us very highly recommended, of course."

The men exchanged what Chauncey decided was boat talk. She realized after a few moments that Mr. Hoolihan was gazing at her from the corner of his dark eyes. His look held no admiration, no warmth. Indeed, he appeared to be studying her like a specimen butterfly to be pinned in a collection. She shook off the fanciful image. Suddenly there was the sound of a loud whistle, and she jumped.

"Ah, we're ready to go," Captain O'Mally said. "Will you join me for dinner, Del?"

"Perhaps," Delaney said, shooting a teasing smile toward Chauncey.

The captain nodded his bald head and said smartly to Mr. Hoolihan, "All right, boy, let's earn our keep! Ma'am," he said, and stepped aside as Delaney escorted Chauncey from the wheelhouse.

"Our stateroom is on the top deck," Delaney said, pointing to the wide wooden stairs upward. "The dining room, gambling hall, and first-class cabins are on this deck."

Chauncey avoided the stairs and turned to walk to the railing. "Everything is so lavish, so polished," she said, running her fingers over the sparkling brass.

"Yes," he agreed. "Belowdeck, things aren't quite so laudable. It's not nearly as bad as the steerage in ships, but there aren't any velvet appointments."

The racket grew as more passengers crowded to the railing to wave good-bye to friends and family on the dock. Sailors flung the heavy shoring lines to men on the decks. The loud whistle sounded again. Slowly the steamboat eased away from the dock.

Delaney waited patiently until Chauncey had had her fill. Their fellow passengers began to disperse to their cabins or to the gambling hall or to one of the two salons. He lightly touched her shoulder. "Come, love," he said.

"But there is so much to see! Look at the hills, Delaney. They're so much greener than those in the city. And the islands, are they inhabited? Indians?"

"A few and maybe. You're shivering, my dear. I don't want you to take a chill."

Chauncey turned reluctantly from the railing, refusing to meet her husband's eyes. It seemed to her that he now held all the power, and she was frightened. She vaguely remembered the rippling, quite pleasurable sensations of the night before, and took a deep breath. She raised her chin and walked briskly toward the stairs.

Their stateroom was beyond anything she could have imagined. The walls were solid mahogany, the furniture dark and rich. A crimson carpet covered the floor, and the windows were draped with crimson velvet. Her eyes were drawn to the wide bed on the port side of the room, its spread as scarlet as blood.

"Like a floating bordello, isn't it?"

She ran her tongue over her lower lip.

"Sam picked out the decor. I think it fulfilled

all his fantasies." She felt his hands lightly caressing her shoulder blades, moving up under the thick chignon to knead her neck.

"Del, I—"

"It's all right, love," he said quietly.

"It's just that I feel more embarrassed than I did last night." She gave a shaky laugh. "That probably sounds quite silly to you."

"No, not really." He turned her gently to face him and cupped her chin between his thumb and forefinger. "Now you know what my body is like and what lovemaking is about." He grinned, unable to keep from teasing her. "At least, I think you know something about my body. Did you keep your eyes shut all the time?"

She shook her head against his shoulder.

"And now you know what it's like to have me inside of you. To be honest, Chauncey, I've thought of little else all day. You are adorable, do you know that?"

Damn you! I don't want to become close to you! I don't want to spend time on this wretched boat!

"Now, sweetheart, I'm going to undress you and make very slow, very thorough love to you. If you're still hungry later, well, I'll send to the kitchen for something."

She was afraid, but he couldn't guess the true reason. She was afraid that he would make her body respond to him. It had begun the previous night, until he had hurt her. But it wouldn't hurt anymore. His hands were lightly caressing her sides, moving slowly upward until his fingers were stroking the sides of her breasts. Slowly he lowered his head and gently pressed his mouth against hers. His lips were warm and soft and she thought vaguely that he tasted sweet, so sweet.

Fight him, you fool! You can't stop him, but you don't have to enjoy it!

She felt his tongue glide over her lips, tracing lightly, then gently probing to gain entrance. His hands held her head steady, and he continued kissing her until he felt her begin to ease. His tongue lightly stroked hers, and he felt her shudder. Progress, he thought, at last. Now for all her damned clothes.

"Do you like the way that feels?" he asked softly in her mouth.

Chauncey's eyes were tightly closed, and it was a battle not to clasp him more closely against her. Her head nodded, without her permission.

Delaney stepped back, his fingers on the fastening hooks of her blue velvet mantle. Her eyes flew open and she stared up at him helplessly. Back to the beginning, he thought, kissing her again as his fingers finished their work.

By the time Chauncey was standing in the middle of the luxurious stateroom clad only in her lacy drawers and shift, she was pale with anxiety. She turned away when Delaney began to remove his own clothes with great rapidity. She was fingering the soft velvet draperies, staring blindly out over the water, when his hands closed over her bare shoulders.

She closed her eyes again. *I'm supposed to be in love with him. I can't let him suspect!*

She felt his arm slip around her thighs and she clutched at his bare shoulders as he swung her up into his arms. His flesh felt so very warm and smooth. He held her with one arm while he swept back the velvet bedcover.

He laid her on her back and she found herself staring into his eyes, momentarily shaken by the deep tenderness she read in the golden depths. And something else. Desire. Her eyes drifted downward to the pale golden tufts of hair on his chest, to the ridges of muscle over his belly. She drew in a sharp breath at the proof of his desire. His thick swollen manhood thrust from the dense hair at his groin. "Del," she said, her voice jerky and pathetically wavering to her own ears.

He slipped onto the bed beside her. "No, love, don't be afraid. Just lie still and enjoy. All right?"

She didn't reply, nor did he really expect her to. A husband's responsibility, he thought ruefully. Seducing his wife. He wanted her naked against him. Now. She didn't fight him as he slipped off her shift and eased her drawers down her hips.

When he pulled her naked against the length of him, he felt her stiffen, then become pliant, like a rag doll.

"No, I won't let you be a martyr," he said hoarsely.

She felt the determination in his every kiss, every movement of his hands. His fingers were gliding over her buttocks, splaying inward to touch her. She caught her breath at the explosion of warmth in her belly.

"Del, please, don't! Please . . ."

Now his fingers were stroking upward toward her belly, burrowing into the soft mat of curls, probing her gently until she felt her body begin to take on a will of its own. He dipped his head to gently nuzzle her nipples before drawing on them, suckling her.

"Please don't what?" he teased her gently as his finger slipped inside her. He sucked in his breath. She was hot, her soft woman's flesh moist and inviting.

"I don't know!" she gasped, staring in bewilderment into his eyes. "I don't like that!"

"Liar." His forefinger eased in more deeply. He could feel her muscles contracting about his finger, and his manhood pulsed in response against her thigh.

"No more pain, sweetheart," he whispered, pushing his finger a bit deeper. He began to caress her with his thumb, and to his delight, she shuddered, and her thighs grew utterly lax. Her face was burrowed against his shoulder, and she breathed in his scent. *This is terrible! I don't want to feel anything! Please, no!*

She moaned his name, pounding her fists against his shoulders, wanting to push him away but drawing him nearer.

"That's it, love," he said, satisfaction in his deep voice, his eyes glittering into hers. "Come for me now. I want to see your eyes, taste you when you let go." He could feel her resistance, see the struggle in her dazed eyes. "Let go, love," he said, and felt her body tense, then begin to convulse in climax. He kissed her deeply, taking her cries of pleasure in his mouth, then eased back to watch her face. She arched her back, her head lolling on the pillow, tangling her hair around her face. Her eyes, filled with dazed surprise, met his. He wanted to weep with the pleasure of it. He continued to caress her and stroke her as intense pleasure convulsed her body.

"Ah, that was sweet, so sweet," he said. Quickly, before her climax ebbed, he knelt between her thighs. He parted them wide, his breath quickening at her willingness. He guided himself inside her, feeling the heat of her enclose him. To his surprise and undoing, her hips thrust up, drawing him deep within her. "Raise your legs around my hips," he managed to grind out between clenched teeth.

She did as he bid her, and he was lost. He thrust deep, and felt his body explode in incredible pleasure. He cried out her name, murmuring sex words, love words.

He felt a surge of tenderness, and yes, satisfaction as he collapsed on top of her. Another moan escaped his lips as her thighs tightened around his hips, holding him deep within her.

He managed to pull himself up on his elbows. "You are some woman, wife," he said softly, pushing deeper.

Chauncey blinked up at him, her mind working furiously. "I don't understand," she whispered, unable to accept what her body had forced upon her. "I didn't want to feel so—"

He dipped down his head and kissed her lightly on her lips. "Do you have any idea how soft your breasts are?" he asked, smiling at her bewildered, confused expression. "How can you blush, love?" He grasped her and rolled onto his side, bringing her with him. His thoughts stretched toward the future, a future filled with passion. It was a pleasing thought, and he squeezed her more tightly against him.

Chauncey felt numb with shock. She tried to remember the Chauncey who hated this man, the Chauncey who smiled cruelly at the thought of destroying him, bringing him to his knees, the Chauncey who was in control of everything.

She burst into tears.

— 16 —

Captain O'Mally's dining table provided an interesting assortment of people and an array of equally fascinating foods. Heavy chandeliers glittered above the long, rather narrow room. Gilt-framed paintings covered the three oak walls, the other being all glass. The tables were covered with pristine white cloths and graced with sparkling silver cutlery and fine English china.

"Most impressive, Captain," Chauncey said as he held her chair.

"Del insisted on the best," Rufus said, giving her his most charming leprechaun grin. "As he usually does," he added, sweeping his gaze admiringly over her peach silk gown.

The dinner menu was printed in a flowery script, and many of the myriad dishes were unfamiliar to Chauncey. Broiled plover, hare chops in salmi, venison steak ... The list seemed endless.

Delaney saw her blink and said softly, "The brains, love? Please, forgo those if you wish. I already dread that you have a surfeit. I would recommend the braised chicken with oyster sauce."

"Thank you," she said, not meeting his eyes. She could still see him staring at her aghast when she had burst into tears but two hours before. He had held her, not demanding an explanation, not demanding anything from her. He had already taken everything, she thought now, her thoughts confused and desolate.

Delaney gave his order to the white-coated waiter who stood at his elbow, then leaned back in his chair, a crystal goblet of dry white wine in his left hand. He responded equably to a question from Colonel Dakworth, and commented suitably on the rather stormy situation now brewing over which city should become the capital of California. But he didn't give a damn about any of it at the moment. Such a puzzle she was, he thought, listening to his wife's soft voice as she asked the waiter for the braised chicken. A beautiful, responsive puzzle. He saw Brent Hammond, a friend, a gambler, womanizer, and something of a pirate, eyeing her speculatively. You haven't a prayer, old man, he wanted to tell him, his lips curling sardonically. Not a prayer. Brent hadn't been able to come to their wedding. And Captain O'Mally's first mate, Mr. Hoolihan. His look wasn't at all speculative in the manner of Hammond's; it was rather assessing, and utterly emotionless. Odd man, Hoolihan, he thought. If he could force his mind away from Chauncey, he wanted to find out more about him.

Dakworth, the blustering old fool, was expounding in fine style to Reverend Divine about the thieves and villains the viligantes had routed out of San Francisco two years before. Delaney didn't care what exaggerations the bewhiskered old man propounded, he just wanted the damned meal over with and Chauncey back in their stateroom.

The talk remained animated throughout the long meal, with tales from Reverend Divine about his trials with the filthy, savage Indians. "Ugly brutes" seemed to be his sniffing refrain. Chauncey, Delaney observed silently, ate next to nothing. What was she thinking? he wondered. Was she mortified that she had experienced sexual pleasure with him? Was that the reason for her tears? Surely she hadn't been raised to believe that ladies were simply to endure their husbands' brutish demands and, that to feel anything was ill-bred. Her obvious ignorance indicated that no one had told her anything about sex.

Chauncey was pulled from her roiling thoughts by Captain O'Mally's cheerful lilting voice. "A moment, everyone! I propose a toast. To Delaney and Elizabeth Saxton, our newlyweds."

Brent Hammond's black brows arched upward and there was a decidedly wolfish gleam in his dark eyes. "To the lovely bride," he said, his deep voice bland as the white rice.

"May your union be blessed," Reverend Divine added in a pompous voice.

Chauncey's eyes flew to his face. Blessed! He must mean children! She felt her temples throb. Delaney had promised her, had assured her . . .

She could feel his seed explode deep within her body, filling her. "Oh no," she whispered.

"What, Mrs. Saxton? Another toast?"

It was Mr. Hammond's smooth, mocking voice. Damn him! She lifted her chin, looked at him full in his darkly handsome face, and announced in a thankfully calm voice, "Yes, indeed, Mr. Hammond. A toast to the *Scarlet Queen*. And to my husband's excellent taste in wineglasses."

Chauncey couldn't face the array of sweet desserts, and nibbled on a small bunch of grapes. She could feel Delaney's concern, his puzzlement. God, she wanted to be alone! When the meal was finally over, she heard Captain O'Mally ask to speak privately with Delaney about some urgent business matters. She turned swiftly, schooled her features into what she hoped was the understanding-wife look, and said, "I shall be fine, Del. Indeed, I think I should like to walk on the deck for a while. It is a beautiful night."

Delaney wasn't fooled for an instant. Very well, his expressive eyes told her, I shall leave you be for the moment. "Soon, my dear," he said, patting her hand. "Your stateroom, Rufus?" he asked.

Chauncey drew a relieved breath as she made her way to their stateroom to fetch her velvet mantle. A few minutes later, she was walking past the gaming salon. She heard the laughter, and snatches of gay conversation. She walked forward, relieved that the one remaining couple on deck was leaving. She was alone with her thoughts at last. What thoughts? she asked herself facetiously. The night was beautiful, she thought vaguely, leaning her head back to gaze up at the quarter-moon and the array of bright stars overhead. She could see little of the shore, just the black outline of trees and hills. Not a soul out there, she thought, just savage, uncivilized land.

She leaned her elbows on the brass railing and stared down at the rippling dark water of the Sacramento River. She wondered what kinds of fish were below the murky surface.

I am changing, she thought, finally admitting it to herself. I am losing my purpose, succumbing to a man who is responsible for my father's death. Her hands gripped the railing until her knuckles showed white. But it was the beautiful wedding ring that caught her attention. She closed her eyes a moment, trying to recapture the awful pain and bitterness she had nourished for the past long months. "I cannot falter," she said softly, the words merely forming silently on her lips. "I must be strong, I must . . ."

The vow died in her mind. A strong arm closed about her waist, a hand clamped hard on her mouth. For an instant she was too startled to struggle.

"Sorry, ma'am," she heard a guttural voice growl in her ear. She felt herself being lifted. Dear God, no! her mind screamed. He's going to throw me overboard!

She twisted frantically, jerking her elbow back into the man's stomach. He grunted in pain but did not release her. She bit down on the hand, and screamed, a high, thin sound escaping. His hand fisted and slammed hard into her jaw. She saw dancing lights before her eyes, and felt a searing pain. But still she fought frantically, tangling both of them in her swirling heavy mantle.

He was cursing her, drawing her upward to the railing. I am not strong enough. I am going to die, drown!

She felt the man's hand close over her breast and pause a moment. He squeezed, but her mind was too clogged with terror to feel any pain. His breathing was harsh now and she wondered wildly if it was from his lust or her struggles.

She heard a shout and the clomp of running boots. Oh God, help me! she screamed silently. The man gave a mighty heave, but Chauncey's mantle caught between his legs. She heard him cursing, felt the instant he realized that someone was coming. He pushed her violently into the railing, clouting her back with his fists.

"What's going on here? Hey, stop!"

Suddenly he let her go, and Chauncey sank to her knees on the smooth deck, gasping for breath.

"Mrs. Saxton! Good God, ma'am. Wh-who is that fellow?"

It was Brent Hammond, now crouched down next to her, his hands clasped strongly about her shoulders.

"I'm all right," she managed, her body shuddering. She raised her white face to his. "He tried to kill me."

Brent cursed softly and fluently. "Come, ma'am. He's gone now." He hoisted her up into his arms.

"Del," she whispered. "Please, my husband . . ."

"What the hell!"

Delaney halted in his tracks, stunned at the sight of Chauncey in Brent Hammond's arms.

"Your wife, Saxton," Brent Hammond said calmly. "She's all right, thank God."

Chauncey turned wild eyes to her husband's

set face and felt a flood of sheer relief surge through her body. She struggled free of Brent Hammond's arms and he set her on her feet. "Del," she cried, and stumbled toward him.

Delaney enfolded her against his chest, his hands automatically stroking down her back, soothing her. He looked up and met Brent's dark eyes. "What happened?" he asked quietly.

"It appears that someone—a man—tried to throw your wife overboard." He lowered his voice, adding, "Perhaps it was an attempted rape."

Chauncey felt her husband's arms tighten almost painfully about her back. "It's all right, sweetheart," he said. "I'm here now. It's all right."

His calmly spoken words brought reality to the nightmare, and memory. She raised her pale face. "Was it the same man who tried to kill me in England?"

His pause was almost imperceptible, but she felt it and didn't understand it. "I don't know, Chauncey. Brent, did you see his face?"

Brent lit a cheroot, blowing out the smoke before replying. His smooth brow furrowed in thought. "He was dressed roughly, a wool cap pulled down over his forehead. When he heard me coming, he ran toward the steerage stairs."

Chauncey's fingers clutched and fretted with the lapels on Delaney's frock coat. "I didn't see him, Del. He was behind me, and I didn't recognize his voice."

"What did he say, love? Do you remember?"

"Something like 'I'm sorry.' "

"A criminal with regrets," Brent murmured.

"I believe we'd best speak to Rufus about this. Can you manage it, Chauncey?"

She nodded, more in reflex than in truth. She was terrified, fear curdling in her stomach, making her want to retch. "Who, Del? Who wants me—?"

"We'll find out," he interrupted her quickly. "Brent, would you please ask Captain O'Mally to come to our stateroom?"

Brent Hammond nodded, and watched Delaney lift his wife into his arms and stride away with her. He stared thoughtfully after the couple, then tossed his cheroot over the side, into the still dark water.

Delaney felt Chauncey clinging to his neck as if he were her lifeline. Jesus, he thought, what if Brent hadn't come along in time? He felt his muscles tensing and realized his forehead was covered with a fine sheen of perspiration. He tried to remember every detail now about her nightmare. He hadn't really believed it, not then. He realized that he really didn't know all that much about Chauncey and her past in England. Whoever wanted her dead came from her past. An attempted rape? He didn't think so.

He set her down in their stateroom. A steward had lit the lamps, and for the first time he could see her face clearly. She was utterly without color, her eyes dazed, the pupils dilated. An ugly bruise was darkening on her jaw. He could see her swallowing convulsively, and quickly led her to the basin atop the commode. He peeled off her mantle and held her shoulders while she retched up the little dinner she had eaten. He left her a moment to pour her a shot of whiskey, and she sank to the carpet, her beautiful silk gown now wrinkled and soiled, spread around her.

He dropped to his knees in front of her. "Here, Chauncey, drink this."

She took a cautious sip of the whiskey and fell into a paroxysm of coughing as the fiery liquid burned to her stomach.

"A bit more. That's good, sweetheart."

He laid her on the bed and fetched a damp cloth and placed it on her forehead. "Lie still a moment, love." He gently ran his fingers over her jaw. Nothing broken, thank God. He saw her eyes lose their wild, frantic look, and felt himself ease a bit. "Better?" he asked softly.

"Yes," she whispered. "I'm sorry I made such a fool—"

"Hush, love." He lifted her limp hand and kissed her fingers. "You scared the hell out of me. Listen to me, we'll find him, I promise you."

There was a sharp rap on the stateroom door, and Delaney raised his head. "Come in," he called.

Captain O'Mally, looking utterly bewildered, came into the stateroom. "What's going on, Del? Hammond said something about rape and murder and—"

Delaney squeezed Chauncey's hand and rose, interrupting the captain sharply. "Sit down, Rufus. We've got a problem."

Get a hold on yourself, you weak fool, Chauncey chided herself as she listened to her husband speak calmly and precisely. She sat up, swaying just a bit, and planted her feet on the carpet.

"Can you tell the captain exactly what happened now, Chauncey?" Delaney asked, moving to stand beside her, his hand resting on her shoulder.

She did, drawing strength as she spoke. She

realized vaguely that her husband was gently kneading her shoulder as she spoke, comforting her. "I never saw his face," she concluded after a woeful few moments, knowing her story would be of no help in locating the man. "You know, though," she added, "his accent was odd, blurred."

Delaney looked at her sharply. "What do you mean?"

She tried to find the right words but couldn't. She shrugged, quivering slightly with remembered shock.

Rufus O'Mally fretted with his captain's hat. He wanted to curse, but couldn't, of course, not in front of a lady. "I don't understand this," he said finally. "Who on earth would want to harm you, ma'am? Well, no matter now, we're wasting time! I'll get my men together and make a search, but ..." He shrugged, knowing the odds. His eyes met Delaney's. It would be useless, both of them knew that. "Do you want to come, Del?"

Delaney felt Chauncey's fingers clutch about his wrist. "No, I didn't see the fellow. Brent Hammond is our best bet, I think."

"Very well. I'll come back as soon as I can." Rufus turned to Chauncey. "I'm really sorry, ma'am. Most distressing. I can't believe that ... well, enough of my nattering! I'll be off now."

Delaney said nothing until the door closed on the captain. He slowly drew Chauncey into his arms. He felt her heaving breasts against his chest, felt her fingers gripping his shoulders. "Let's get you out of those clothes and into bed," he said, his voice somewhat shaky. Damn you for a rutting pig, he cursed himself silently. He rose, turning away from her for a moment to regain his control.

Chauncey was blessedly numb. She felt him unfastening the long row of buttons on her gown and obeyed him silently when he told her to turn around. She still wore no corset, and was soon standing before him clothed in only her lace-edged linen shift.

"Into bed now, love," he said, giving her a gentle shove.

She raised bewildered eyes to his expressionless face. "But my nightgown," she protested.

"Yes," he said, nearly choking. He walked like a mechanical man to the built-in armoire and fetched her the most modest gown he could find. When he turned around, she was standing still as a statue where he had left her, watching him.

The last thing she needs is a horny idiot gaping at her, he thought, trying not to look at her soft breasts thrusting against the material of her shift. To his utter surprise, Chauncey grasped her shift and lifted it over her head. He froze.

She raised her head and looked into his blazing eyes. "Please, Del, help me," she whispered. She felt his eyes roving hungrily over her naked body. "Please, don't leave me."

"Jesus!" He tossed the nightgown away and jerked her into his arms. "Chauncey, love," he said, his fingers frantically pulling the pins from her hair. Thick mahogany waves flowed over his fingers down her back. She doesn't want sex, he told himself, willing himself to believe it. She's frightened and needs reassurance. She needs to reaffirm that she's alive.

He managed to hold to his reasoning until

Chauncey suddenly thrust her belly against him and grasped his face between her hands to bring his mouth to hers. "Please," she whispered wildly against his lips, her body moving frantically against his.

He knew she wasn't thinking clearly, knew she was trying to wipe out what had happened. It was all shock, reaction. It was ... Her tongue thrust into his mouth and he moaned.

"You're my wife," he gasped, the simple truth making him wild with need. "My wife."

He felt her hands on the buttons of his shirt, tugging frantically. Without another word, he lifted her into his arms and laid her on top of the velvet spread. He stepped back, his eyes searching hers, and practically ripped off his clothes. He stood naked beside the bed for a moment, and watched her eyes rove down his body. They widened at the sight of his thrusting manhood.

"Please," she whispered, and held out her arms to him.

He covered her body with his, kissing her wildly, and she responded mindlessly, her hands digging into his shoulders, stroking down his back to his buttocks. Over and over she whispered, "Please, please ..."

His hand slipped downward to probe the softness between her thighs, and he quivered at the hot wetness of her woman's flesh. She was nearly beyond herself when he thrust into her. The instant he filled her, her body burst with her release. Her climax was so powerful she nearly bucked him off her, harsh cries erupting from her throat. She screamed his name and held him to her when his body exploded with his own climax.

Delaney felt as though his soul had been ripped from his body. He couldn't stop kissing her, caressing her, telling her how much he needed her. Slowly she relaxed beneath him, her thighs easing from their grip on his flanks. He stared down into her face and saw that her eyes no longer held the blind, dazed look.

He watched her pink tongue nervously wet her lower lip. "I don't understand," she whispered.

He did, but for the moment, words were beyond him, words and rational thought. He kissed her again, deeply. To his besotted surprise, he felt her respond, felt her thighs tense.

He rolled onto his back and set her astride him. He watched her face as his member, hard and ready, thrust up, deep into her. Shock, bewilderment, and rampant desire. He grasped her narrow waist and moved her up and down on him, teaching her the rhythm. Her full breasts, their taut pink nipples thrust out as she arched her back, quivered when he caressed them. When his fingers glided downward to probe and find her, her dazed mind, emptied of all fear, released her yet again and she cried out harshly, her hands splayed on his chest, clutching at him as her body released her.

Her wild response triggered his own body, and he held her fiercely, plunging deep within her.

Slowly he eased her forward until she lay stretched flat on top of him, her luxurious hair flowing over them both like a silken blanket. She seemed senseless, beyond passion now, beyond her fear. He stroked her back gently, saying nothing, and soon her breathing evened into sleep. Good Lord, he thought as his dazed wits returned to normal. Never before had he made love with such involvement, such . . . commitment. It had not really occurred to him that Chauncey would be unresponsive to lovemaking, but this . . . this utterly wild abandon . . . He shook his head slightly, stilling when she moaned softly in her sleep. Don't be a fool, Del, he told himself, smiling crookedly. It was her fear, her need to escape for however briefly from what had happened, that had erased all her inhabitions. Still, he felt an overwhelming sense of pleasure and male accomplishment. A woman's pleasure, a precious, elusive thing, a challenge to any man. Not much of a challenge this time, he thought ruefully. It had been she who had taken him.

He wrapped an arm around her back and eased upward, grabbing a blanket to pull over them. She burrowed against him, and he laughed softly at his own predictable response. He did not sleep, for his mind quickly began to sift through all that had happened. He didn't know how much time had passed when he heard a soft rap on the stateroom door. He gently eased a sleeping Chauncey away from him and rose quickly, grabbing his dressing gown.

He opened the door and looked into Captain O'Mally's worried face. "Well?" he asked quietly.

"Nothing, Del, nothing. Jesus, he might even be one of the crew for all we could discover. Could Mrs. Saxton tell you any more?"

"No, she's sleeping now. I'll speak to her again in the morning."

Rufus shook his head. "I have to agree with Brent Hammond. It's a damnable mystery. Look, Del, all of us have enemies. Do you think someone could have tried to hurt your wife out of revenge, to get back at you?"

"It's possible," Delaney said, but he didn't believe it.

"What about Baron Jones? I know you had a run-in with him ... what, last year? I heard about the duel. I saw him on the dock today. Perhaps he's on board ..."

Delaney flexed his shoulder unconsciously, his body remembering the pain of the bullet that had torn through his flesh. As for Baron Jones, he would limp for the rest of his miserable life. "No," he said shortly, "he didn't stay." He smiled crookedly. "Anyway, I can't imagine the baron running. He's a fool and a bully, but not a coward. I'll speak to you tomorrow, Rufus. Thanks for checking."

Captain O'Mally nodded and took his leave.

Delaney turned thoughtfully to see Chauncey, her hair tumbling about her pale face, struggling to a sitting position. "What is going on?" she asked, her voice vague with sleep.

"Nothing, sweetheart," he said, forcing his eyes away from her bare breasts. "Let's get some sleep."

"All right," she said, and sank back against the pillow.

— 17 —

"Here, sweetheart, drink this."

Chauncey eyed the cup and saucer held out to her and shimmied up to a sitting position.

Delaney gulped. Still half-asleep, she was oblivious of her nakedness. "What time is it?" she asked on a yawn. Suddenly her eyes widened and she flushed. She yanked at the covers, drawing them to her shoulders. "Oh dear," she gulped, eyeing him from beneath her lashes.

"English tea," he said abruptly, and she took the saucer. She sipped at the blessedly hot tea, flavored with lemon, just as she liked it.

"What time is it?" she asked again, forcing her eyes to her husband's face. He was seated in a chair next to the bed, wearing a deep burgundy velvet dressing gown, his long legs stretched out in front him, crossed at his bare ankles.

"About nine o'clock. Do I take it that you slept well?"

"You must know that I did!" Memory in exquisite detail filled her now clear mind, and she took another gulp of her tea. How could she have acted so . . . Her mind sought a sufficiently insulting word to apply to her appalling behavior, but failed. Her response to him the second time he had taken her was bad enough, but this!

"Do you know that I can tell what you're thinking now?" he asked, his twinkling eyes in the dim morning light of the cabin more golden than light brown. "Now, that is, that I know you so much better," he added. He saw that she would argue with him, and quickly raised a quieting hand. "Nah, darlin'," he said in his best Southern drawl, "yah'll just shut yah pretty mouth an' forget all those wicked thoughts."

"I can barely understand you!" she snapped, knowing he was teasing her and hating it. But only for a moment. Very carefully she set her empty cup into its saucer and laid it on the side of the bed. "I am afraid," she said, looking at him straight.

"Yes," he said, equally as serious as he sat forward, clasping his hands between his thighs. "So am I. I think it's time we had a very detailed discussion. Are you up to it?"

For a brief moment she was drawn to his hands, strong and brown, his fingers long and tapered. She could for that brief instant feel the calluses of his fingertips stroking over her. *Stop it, Chauncey! This is ridiculous!* She forced herself to nod.

"Good. Now, first, tell me again about that fellow who tried to run you down in England."

She did, quite calmly, for it was months in the past and the terror had faded. As she talked, she was aware of his mobile brown brows arching or drawing together as if they mirrored his thoughts.

"You have no idea who he was?"

"No, as I said, he wore a black handkerchief over his face."

"All right. Now, last night."

Chauncey ran her tongue over her lips. "Can I have some more tea, please?"

He obliged, and Chauncey thought vaguely that it looked odd to see his strong tanned hand pouring tea from the delicate china teapot. Her thoughts veered sharply again to his hands on her body, and she squirmed.

This time he read her thoughts easily, and frowned slightly. He gently cupped her chin in his hand, stroking his forefinger along her jaw. "Sweetheart," he said very calmly, "what happened between us last night was perfectly normal ..." *Not really, you fool!* "You are my wife and I want you to realize that it is your duty to feel pleasure with me, your husband."

"I ... I acted so wild," she burst out.

His eyes crinkled with amusement. "I loved every minute of your wildness." He drew a deep breath and moved back to his chair. "I think it best that we set that aside for the moment. Tell me again what happened."

This was more difficult for her, but finally, after many questions from Delaney, she finished. She sighed and leaned back against the pillow, watching him.

"What we have is someone who wants you removed," he said quite emotionlessly, "someone from England, not here. Your aunt and uncle would inherit your fortune were you to die?"

"Yes, but it can't be them, Del! Aunt Augusta is greedy and really awful, but I can't believe she would try to *murder* me!"

"All right. Tell me about your father."

She shook her head numbly, knowing full well that she could say nothing about her father or about Paul Montgomery or about Delaney's now deceased solicitor, Mr. Boynton.

"Chauncey!"

His voice was sharp, and she blinked at him. "My father was involved in some rather shaky business dealings," she said finally, giving him as much of the truth as she dared. "But he was a good man, a very good man." Her voice broke. Here she was defending her father to the man responsible for his death! It was too much. She turned her face away on the pillow and sobbed softly.

Before Delaney could move to take her into his arms, she stiffened and whirled about to face him. "What about you?" she demanded harshly. "You are my husband now. It is you, not anyone else, who would have all my money were I to die! Not my aunt or uncle!"

He felt a muscle jerk in his jaw. He immediately clamped down on his anger at her ridiculous accusation, and realized that once again she was presenting him with a puzzle. He sat back in his chair and crossed his arms over his chest. "But I didn't know you in England, wife," he said with precise calm. "You believe there are two people out to remove you? Me and some other luckless fool?"

But what about my father?

She shook her head numbly. "I . . . I'm sorry," she muttered.

"I want you to listen to me, Chauncey, very carefully. I care for you quite a bit, you know, otherwise I would not have married you. You are . . . keeping things from me, things from your past. You can be certain that I will do my damnedest to protect you, but for God's sake, you must be completely honest with me! I don't want us having to spend our lives looking over our shoulders wondering who the hell is trying to kill you."

He had never before spoken to her so coldly. There was no lurking laughter in his voice, no soft warmth in his narrowed eyes.

"I'm waiting," he said, his voice even more ferociously calm and cold.

"Please, Del, there is nothing more I can tell you." Her voice broke, not purposely, but it gained her time from his relentless demands.

"All right," he said, sighing. *Dammit! What was she keeping from him?* "Now, we're going to pack our things. We'll be stopping at Marysville early this afternoon. You and I are returning to San Francisco."

She blinked at him.

"The man who tried to kill you is in all likelihood still on board. We'll take no more chances. We're going home." *And I am going to make inquiries, my love.* But Lord, he thought, it would take months to get any answers, if there were any to be had!

* * *

Marysville, Delaney told her, was a much newer place than Sacramento, but already there were a good six thousand inhabitants. Chauncey thought it looked like a dismal place, but the setting was lovely, the town lying at the fork of the Feather and Yuba rivers.

Their return trip was on the steamer *Wildfire*, a rather antiquated vessel that had been refitted to carry the continual stream of passengers into the gold country and back to San Francisco. Their cabin was small and sparsely furnished.

Delaney did not leave her side for a minute, and she was aware that he was watching her, questions in his eyes. She wanted to yell at him that even if she did tell him all the truth about herself, it wouldn't solve the puzzle of who wanted to kill her.

They dined in their cabin. Chauncey, who had expected the food to be as dreadful as their accommodations, was pleasantly surprised at the delicious broiled trout. Would the questions never leave his eyes? she wondered as she chattered on about inconsequential things. Eventually she became as silent as her husband, her mind forcing her back to England. She thought of her "Uncle" Paul, of Frank Gillette, of Thomas Gregory, the only three people outside of her relatives who knew of her fortune. But they had nothing to gain, nothing whatsoever! It made no sense, and she wanted to scream with frustration.

"Chauncey."

Delaney's voice broke her tumbled thoughts and she stared at him blankly.

"Time for bed, my dear."

There was no screen in the cabin and Chauncey

was forced to undress in front of him. She eyed the bed. It was lumpy and quite narrow. She could practically feel his amusement when she slipped her nightgown over her head over her shift. She knew he was laughing at her during her contortions to remove the shift and keep herself covered at the same time. She didn't once look at him, for if she did, she knew she would likely blush.

She crawled to the far side of the bunk and pulled the covers to her chin. She closed her eyes tightly, not opening them even when she felt the mattress give under Delaney's weight.

"Come here."

She started at the curt sound of his voice.

"I . . . I'm awfully tired," she managed to say in a thread-thin voice.

"I'm not, and I promise you that you won't be in a few moments. Come here."

She didn't move. She jumped when she felt his fingers lightly stroke over her still-sore jaw. Slowly his fingers explored her in the darkness, her lips, the line of her nose, her throat. When his mouth sought hers, she forced herself to lie quietly. I will not become a wild thing again, she swore to herself. I will not let him make me feel . . .

She gasped when his hand lightly settled on her breast. She held herself rigid, fighting the growing response. She locked her legs together, wishing that the interesting ache between her thighs would disappear. Fool that she was, she'd believed she was hungry! "No," she whispered against his lips.

His tongue lightly stroked hers, and he said

very softly, "I will not let you fight me, Chauncey, not when I know the passion you have for me." She felt his hand ease beneath her nightgown and move gently upward. "So soft," he said, stroking her inner thighs. When he cupped his hand over her, she tried desperately to ignore the sheer feeling that was taking over her mind. She arched up, trying to pull away from his hand, but he eased his finger inside her, testing her, probing her.

His eyes darkened in a satisfied gleam, for she was growing wet from his caressing fingers. "You see," he said as he nibbled her ear, "your body knows the pleasure I can give you. Stop fighting me. More important, stop fighting yourself."

"I don't want . . ."

She moaned, shamelessly raising her hips to press closer to his fingers.

"Ah, yes you do. Touch me, love. Touch me as I'm touching you."

Her fingers obeyed his command. They glided tentatively down his chest to his flat belly, then lower to tangle in the bush of hair at his groin. She sucked in her breath when lightly her fingers touched his manhood. His flesh was hot, swollen, and throbbed in her hand. He moaned softly into her mouth as she explored him.

"You feel like hard velvet," she whispered.

She felt him lurch against her at her words. He was trembling, and for a moment she was awed that she could bring him to such a point. Then his fingers became hot and deep, and she forgot everything.

"Let go, love. That's it. Yes, open to me." Delaney could feel her resistance. Her mind was fighting her pleasure. When she tensed, unable to control the rampant sensations coursing through her body, he saw a moment of wild fear in her eyes. He forgot his questions as her hands clutched his shoulders, and he plunged deep inside her, his own need overtaking him.

He held her until her breathing quieted, then rose, his body unutterably weary, to douse the lamps. When he eased beside her again, he felt her withdrawing from him. He clasped her to him and said, half in anger, half in frustration, "If you cry again, I'll not let you sleep until you tell me why."

"I won't cry," she said against his shoulder.

He raised his hand to push her hair back from her forehead. "Will you tell me why you fight yourself, then?"

She grew very still. His fingers were lightly exploring her face, even now exquisitely careful of her sore jaw. Her own hand, for want of anyplace else to go, lay open-palmed on his chest.

She felt him sigh deeply. "Do you realize how very odd your behavior is, Chauncey?"

She swallowed at his question, but no words of explanation or denial were forthcoming. She was relieved that it was dark and he couldn't see her eyes. Damn him, he always saw too much!

"I suppose you do," he continued after a moment of her silence. "It is likely, you know, that I would have gotten around to chasing you. But the fact of the matter is that I didn't have to. You wanted me and made that quite clear from the moment I met you. You got what you wanted, my dear, and now you fight me and yourself. I would like to understand you. I am your husband. If you can't bring yourself to trust me, then I wonder what is to become of us."

"You . . . you are not what I expected!" she blurted out.

Delaney blinked. Slowly he eased onto his side, facing her. He held her close, aware of his body reacting again to her. Stop it, he told himself sternly. Jesus, now is not the time! "Just what did you expect?"

His voice was soothing, gentle, but her mind shied away from what she had unwittingly revealed to him. "You are an American," she said.

"Well, that is certainly true, but you knew that, love."

Think, you silly fool! "Del, I won't become pregnant, will I?

She felt him tense and his hand stilled on her back. He said in blank surprise, "Is this . . . resistance of yours what this is about? This is why you fight me and yourself?"

"Yes," she said baldly. "I do not wish to be pregnant . . . just yet. It frightens me."

He could hear the ring of truth in her voice. He thought of the sponges and the vinegar solution in his trunk, and the instructions Marie had given him. Jesus, he thought, he hadn't kept his word to Chauncey. In truth, he'd forgotten all about it. "I understand, love," he said, gently kissing her temple. "Before we make love again, I will show you what to do."

He heard her sigh of relief, felt her thick lashes brush against his throat, and wondered yet again if that were all of it.

He lay quietly after she slept, staring into the

darkness, this time his thoughts more humorous, drawn to the scene with Marie.

"You what, *mon cher?*" She stared at him, her hurt for the moment quashed in utter surprise.

"I need your advice on contraception, Marie. My wife doesn't wish to become pregnant too quickly."

She burst into laughter, hugging her sides. "It is too funny," she gasped. "You ask your mistress for help with your wife! *Dieu!* You men!"

He'd laughed too, appreciating the humor of the situation. He remembered Marie telling him about a woman's cycle, and wondered if Chauncey were about to start her monthly flow. He counted in his mind the number of times they'd made love. "Damn," he muttered into the darkness. He'd just as soon forget the whole business, but he had promised. He grinned suddenly, picturing how he would instruct Chauncey in the use of the sponge.

They spent the remainder of the return trip on deck, Delaney pointing out the sights. "This is the Carquinez Strait," he said. "Soon we'll be in the San Pablo Bay, then dead south to the San Francisco Bay."

"At least there are trees lining the shores," Chauncey said, eyeing the oaks, ashes, and willows. "Captain O'Mally told me how luxuriant and beautiful nature was here, but really, Delaney, look beyond! There's nothing but sandy, dusty plains. Surely he speaks in comparison to San Francisco."

Delaney grinned at her. "I suppose to some used to the civilized, tamed, and otherwise cosseted nature of England, you would think that San Francisco is rather desolate."

"Harrumph," said Chauncey. She tightened the bow of her bonnet against the stiff wind. "There are so many islands," she observed after a moment. "Are they all uninhabited?"

"For the most part. Occasionally, Indians and trappers visit, but there aren't enough vegetation and animals to support life."

"It is certainly unlike England."

"True. The first time I traveled by boat inland, I realized I'd never felt so free in my life. It was wide open, wild—uncivilized, if you will. The thousands of gold seekers have brought great change. I sometimes wonder how long this vast land would have remained untouched if gold hadn't been discovered. Fifty thousand souls now live in San Francisco. When I arrived in 1849, there were but a thousand. You know that Mexico ceded California to the United States some five years ago. Our touted progress and men's greed will shortly bring the Californios to extinction. Already their land grants are being tossed out of our corrupt courts, their cattle stolen and butchered, their acres taken over by squatters."

"Who are these Californios?"

"For the most part, they are either Spanish or Mexican and have wielded great power in the near past. They are the old aristocracy of California, feudal landlords, more or less. Their land-grant *ranchos* many times exceed two hundred thousand acres. Then we Yanquis poured in." Delaney paused a moment, his jaw hardening and his eyes narrowing in anger. "It amazes me that *we* have such contempt for peoples with different languages, different cultures. Most the men I know call them 'greasers.' The Chinese are called 'diggers.' Pleasant, isn't it?"

Chauncey frowned up at his set profile. "No, not particularly, but to be honest, Del, I've never thought about it. I know you saved Lin from a dreadful fate, but these Californios. You seem to take their problems personally."

"I suppose I do. They're a proud, easygoing people, and a man's word is considered his bond. They live and die by their honor, and thus they will not survive. One family I know quite well. Don Luis Varga saved my life once back in fifty. Unfortunately, when I was out of California in fifty-one, his family lost some of their lands to gold seekers, their cattle to rustlers, and the rest to banks. They were forced to take residence in Monterey. Don Luis was brutally murdered when he tried to protect his cattle from the bandits. As I told you, they are a proud breed of people, and they believe in honor above all else. I suppose you think I've painted a perfect people with no flaws at all." He smiled ruefully. "Actually, they love to gamble and are wretched at it. Those Californios who have found gold have lost it just as quickly. In many ways, they're simple as children, with no clear concept of high interest rates or rampant inflation or . . . Still, what's happening to them makes me mad as hell, and there's little I can do about it."

"I should like to meet the Varga family. I've never gambled, but I'm probably wretched at it too."

"Perhaps you shall, one day."

How very honorable he himself sounded, she

thought, her softened mouth tightening into a thin line as she remembered, She said flippantly, baiting him, "It seems to me that you could do something for them. After all, aren't you very rich?"

Delaney turned his head to stare at her thoughtfully. "Yes," he said slowly, "I am rich, but not rich enough. And there's a matter of power. One man can't wield enough power to turn the tide of what is happening, and corruption is rife, both in the cities and in the state government." He smiled wryly. "Did I tell you that a group of our most civic-minded men in the Pacific Club want me to run for the Senate?"

"You are considered so honest, then?"

"Isn't that rather an odd question from a loving wife?"

"Come, Del, haven't you ever . . . cheated anyone to gain an advantage?"

She was watching his face closely, and drew back at the sudden fury in his eyes. Then his thick lashes covered his expression and he said curtly, "No."

"Not even during your travels? To England for instance? After all, it's a great distance away. It seems to me that you could have promised anything and there wouldn't be any retribution if you didn't make good."

He studied her silently. She spoke lightly, as if in idle speculation, but he felt tenseness radiating from her. "Would you care to explain, Chauncey?" he asked quietly.

She shrugged elaborately and turned her attention to the willow trees whose dipping branches nearly touched the water at the edge of the river some fifty yards away. "I was just making conversation. Theoretical questions, that's all."

She was lying, of that he was certain. But why the questions about his honesty? A woman wouldn't marry a man she didn't believe in and trust, would she? "Perhaps those are the theoretical questions you have about your aunt and uncle. What did you say their name was?"

"Penworthy," she said without thinking.

She sucked in her breath, realizing the information she had just given him. Fool, she screamed at herself silently.

But he seemed to have lost interest. She breathed a sigh of relief. Still, she sought to distract him. "I noticed a scar on your shoulder. How did you get it?"

She is so transparent, he thought, turning again to face her. "I fought a duel with a rather gruesome individual named Baron Jones. Yes, I can see from the expression on your face that you remember him."

"A duel," she repeated blankly. "That is . . . barbaric!"

"Indeed," he said dryly. "Unfortunately, out here it is sometimes unavoidable."

"Did you try to kill him?"

"No, but I probably should have. He still occasionally presents me with . . . problems."

"Why the duel?"

To her surprise, he flushed.

"You didn't like the cut of his coat?" she asked.

"Actually," he said, goaded, "he tried to force himself upon Marie, my mistress. That's why I got you out of his sight as quickly as possible."

"How distressing for both of you," she managed, both surprised and furious at herself for the bolt of jealousy that shot through her. He grinned widely at her and she realized that she'd given him the upper hand.

"A man doesn't like other men to poach on his preserves."

"Preserves! What an uncivilized, arrogant—"

He dipped his head down and kissed her pursed lips.

"I am not your *property,* your—"

He kissed her again.

There was a muffled guffaw from a fellow passenger. Chauncey jerked away, her face flaming.

"Have I the last word, do you think, sweetheart?"

"I don't suppose there are any sharks in these waters?"

He threw back his head and laughed heartily. "Weak," he said, shaking his finger at her. "Very weak, but I should make allowances, shouldn't I? You are but a woman, after all."

— 18 —

Chauncey cocked one eye open and frowned at Mary, who was humming an Irish ballad off key, as chirpy as any bird.

"It's awfully early for such high spirits," Chauncey said on a wide yawn when Mary reached the end of her verse. She swung her legs over the side of the bed, realized she didn't have a stitch on, and felt her face burn. Damn him, she cursed silently. Mary began singing again. "Have you been visiting the bottle, Mary? Your mood is just too nice."

"My, my, aren't you in a twitty mood," Mary said, turning from the armoire to face her mistress. "Would you like a robe?"

"Of course I would!"

"It is rather chilly this morning. Just look at that rain! Coming down in sheets! You know,

Miss Chauncey, you should ask that husband of yours to give you a nightgown before he leaves you in the morning."

"Mary," Chauncey said, gritting her teeth, "why are you trying to make me scream?"

"Lucas has told me quite a bit about Mr. Del," Mary continued calmly as she assisted her mistress into a yellow velvet dressing gown. "He's not a bad man, Miss Chauncey."

Chauncey snapped fully awake, and stared incredulously at her maid. "I just don't believe you! You're ready to dismiss what he did to my father after living three weeks in his house? Oh yes, I know, he's so *bloody* charming, isn't he? Or is it Lucas' charm?"

Mary felt her cheeks grow warm, but she was ready to give as good as she got, and said blandly, "It seems to me that you're quite charmed with him too, particularly in bed."

Chauncey chewed vigorously on her lower lip. "That," she said bitterly, "is a weakness. It has nothing to do with anything."

"It occurs to me, miss, that this weakness can quite rapidly result in a child."

"Oh no! That is, I will take measures to ensure it doesn't." Perhaps tonight, she thought, wondering just what these measures would be. She closed her eyes a moment, remembering the previous night when they'd arrived back in San Francisco. More of her husband's damned charm. She'd never seen such a wide smile on Lucas' pirate face. And Lin, hovering about, chattering like a berserk parrot everything that had happened in their three-day absence. And Mary, smiling fondly, with that gleam in her eyes. To her surprise, her husband hadn't initiated lovemaking with her after he'd stripped off her nightgown. He'd merely kissed her and held her until she'd fallen asleep. She could sense his preoccupation, but asked him no questions.

"By the way, Miss Chauncey, Mr. Del told us this morning what had happened and why you returned so quickly. He told Lucas not to let you out of his sight when he wasn't with you. You will cooperate, won't you?"

"Of course," Chauncey said. "I'm not a complete fool." She fell into brooding silence.

"Mr. Del asked me all about your aunt and uncle. He's worried, Miss Chauncey. Lord, here I'd almost convinced myself that that accident in Plymouth was really just that."

Chauncey's head snapped up. "You didn't tell him about Paul Montgomery, did you?"

"No, but I wanted to. I'm worried too, Miss Chauncey. This entire situation is cockeyed! Here you are trying to hurt Mr. Del, and someone else wants to hurt you, and Mr. Del could get himself killed trying to protect you."

"Mary, listen to me, please. I've thought and thought, but I can't think of anyone who would go to such lengths to do away with me. I know Paul Montgomery was somewhat disturbed that I didn't allow him to handle my money, but that wouldn't make him want to kill me, surely. Good grief, he was one of my father's best friends."

"Unless your aunt and uncle promised him some of your inheritance," Mary said, cocking her head thoughtfully to one side.

"I've thought of that," Chauncey said on a sigh. "In fact," she added on a crooked grin, "I think I'll write to them and tell them I've lost everything. Plead with them to let me come back to England and live with them."

"Actually, Mr. Del mentioned something of the sort this morning. He's ready to try anything, Miss Chauncey." Mary began fidgeting with Chauncey's hairbrush. "He's guessed that there's something you're keeping from him. He just kind of sighed when I finished telling about the Penworthys. He didn't push me, but he knows there's something you're not telling him."

"I know. Whatever else he is, he isn't a fool."

"You know, Miss Chauncey, whoever the fellow is, he'll probably try again."

"Yes, I know. I'll not step a foot out of the house without my derringer. Perhaps," she added with false brightness, "I can catch him myself."

Mary fell silent and began to unpack Chauncey's trunk. "Mrs. Newton came by yesterday afternoon," she said. "Such a nice lady, but you know, she asked me all sorts of questions about you. When I looked a bit put off, she told me that that little twit Penelope Stevenson was still holding a grudge toward you. She told me she wanted to spike their guns. You know, tell everyone where you're from in England and who your parents were."

That aroused Chauncey from her gloom. "Let them all go to the devil," she said.

"Perhaps so," Mary said stiffly, "but you don't want Mr. Del hurt by any talk."

"Here you go again! Of course I want him hurt, dammit!"

"Don't use bad words, young lady!"

"For God's sake, *Miss* Mary, you're younger than I!"

"And just maybe I see things more clearly than you do!"

"Ha! Do you know that your Mr. Del fought a duel over his damned mistress?"

"Well, he wasn't a married man when he did. Lord knows," she added on a chuckle, "Mr. Del isn't a celibate!"

Chauncey closed her eyes for a long, pained moment. Mary had defected to the enemy camp. She'd never felt so alone. She jumped off the bed. "I want a bath."

A half-hour later, Chauncey was seated in front of her dressing table staring vacantly into the mirror as Mary brushed out her hair. She jumped at the sound of Mary's voice.

"What are you going to do now?"

"Always carry my derringer about, as I told you."

"That isn't what I meant, Miss Chauncey, and you know it!"

"Perhaps I shouldn't tell you. After all, you're so in love with Mr. Del, or is it Lucas the pirate?" She sounded nasty and mean and sarcastic, but couldn't help it.

"I'll tell what I would do," Mary said, unmoved. "I'd talk straight to my husband. I'd tell him the truth, all of it."

"Lovely idea! I can just picture it now. I'd be on the next ship back to England and he'd be free as a bird!"

"What is this about a ship back to England?"

Both women froze at the sound of Delaney's voice.

"Good morning, Mary, Chauncey. Or should I say afternoon?" He strode over to Chauncey and gave her a fond kiss on her cheek. "You're not planning to leave me, are you?"

"I thought you'd gone," Chauncey said, "for the day."

He raised a brow. "I leave you? This is our honeymoon. Besides, it's raining buckets. Mary, leave her hair down. Lin's kept your breakfast warm for you. Are you about ready?"

Over a breakfast of eggs, bacon, and crunchy toast, Delaney told her about a meeting that evening at the Pacific Club. "Horace isn't going to let me get off, I fear," Delaney said. "They want someone as honest as a virgin for senator. Perhaps," he added, his expressive eyes twinkling, "they'll find a dank skeleton somewhere lurking in my checkered past. Then I'd be off the hook. Maybe I should invent one."

"But you want this, don't you?" Chauncey asked slowly. "You want to be in politics."

She watched his strong fingers curl about his coffee cup. "Yes, I suppose I do. You're getting to know me too well, love. But I don't want to end up in Washington. I want to do something here in California. I've been a part of several committees and found it most exhilarating. I would like to be one of the men to set up these committees, select the members, and see that a decent job is done. Paul Donner died a couple of months ago. What I would like to propose to Horace and the other gentlemen is that I run for the state legislature."

"How would it work?"

He grinned at her. "I forget that you're English and used to a very different system. Well, perhaps not too different. I'd have to have the party's nomination and then tromp around to various towns in California to convince men to vote for me."

"It would take a great deal of money, wouldn't it?"

"Indeed it would. A good deal of my money, and sizable contributions. Would you like to be a politician's wife, Chauncey?"

Although his voice was light, she sensed the seriousness in him and knew without a shadow of a doubt that this was something he wanted above anything. Was this the way to ruin him? She gave him a dazzling smile. "I should love it."

The excitement faded from his expressive eyes. "First things first. There's the matter of the idiot who wants you dead."

"Yes," Chauncey said, her voice very calm, "Mary told me how you'd pumped her this morning. I don't think I care for your methods."

Delaney very carefully set his coffee cup in its saucer, rose from his chair, and strode to the wide bow windows in the dining room. He seemed mesmerized for many moments by the rain lashing against the windowpanes. He said over his shoulder, "No, I don't imagine that you would, but then, a husband must feel somewhat odd when his wife doesn't trust him."

"You're weaving fantasy into a cloth that doesn't exist, Del. Why on earth wouldn't I trust you?"

"If I knew the answer to that, I could take more direct action, couldn't I?" He turned from the window to ace her. "I'm tired, Chauncey, tired to the bone of your evasiveness. Even now you're tensing up on me. Your face is far too expressive for your own good, sweetheart."

Prove to him that he's wrong! Chauncey planted a smile on her face and walked to her husband. She stood on her tiptoes and kissed him firmly on the mouth. She felt his surprise, felt his drawing away from her, and clutched the lapels of his frock coat. His lips parted, as if against his wishes, and she whispered softly into his mouth, "You are my husband. I must have traveled halfway around the world to find you."

He grew very still.

"My . . . evasiveness, if there is such a thing— why, it's probably due to the newness of my situation. Everything is very different from England."

He wanted to believe her, she could see it in his eyes. She felt a surge of guilt and closed her own eyes. He saw too much. Always too much.

Chauncey paced through the dining room, across the wide entrance hall to the drawing room. How can I ruin him? She'd discarded several wild ideas during the past few hours. She glanced toward the clock on the mantel. Ten o'clock. He'd be home soon from his meeting at the Pacific Club, and she was no closer to coming up with a plan that could possibly work. I am not a schemer, she decided reluctantly. She slammed a fisted hand against her open palm and forced herself to review again one of her less fantastic ideas. Even if she did manage to circulate scandal stories about him, it wouldn't make him one whit poorer, just deprive him of his political hopes.

And his bloody assets were simply too diverse. How could she ruin him?

Chauncey sat down on the sofa and leaned her head back. Everything was becoming so difficult, almost impossible, really. She simply didn't have the freedom of movement even if she did come up with something that could succeed. She shivered, remembering all too clearly the man who had tried to haul her over the rail and into the murky night waters of the Sacramento River. Who?

And Delaney. He was becoming too real to her, too important. Damn him, why didn't he behave the way she'd thought an evil man should behave? Why couldn't he be mean, nasty, and awful? She wanted desperately to hate him, to loathe him.

"I am becoming a hysterical female," she said aloud to the empty room. "All I have are myriad questions and a dithering mind." And she was afraid. Afraid to be alone, yet afraid when he was with her. Afraid of herself and what she was beginning to feel for him.

She rose and resumed her fruitless pacing. "If only there were someone I could trust," she muttered. She shook her head even as Agatha Newton's face came to her mind. No, all the people in San Francisco would be loyal to Delaney, not her, a foreigner.

"I think I see the beginnings of a hole in the carpet," Delaney said, coming into the room some fifteen minutes later. "Come here and let me kiss you. It will keep you in one place and save our belongings."

She saw the sheen of raindrops on his thick

hair, darkening it a rich honey color. His eyes, as rich a honey color as his hair, were filled with anticipation and that odd tenderness that he seemed to reserve just for her. She gulped.

"Hello," she said, not moving. "Are you to be the new power in the state of California?"

"I really don't give a damn at the moment. Come here."

She went to him and nestled her cheek against his shoulder. His arms went about her, squeezing her tight.

"I missed you. I'm a rotter for leaving you alone during our honeymoon. Forgive me."

She felt his fingers lightly caressing her jaw, then cupping her chin. She wished she needed to force herself into acting the loving wife, but at the moment she didn't. She raised her head wanting him to kiss her. "Do you know how beautiful you are, Chauncey?" His voice was soft, beguiling, but still he didn't kiss her, merely ran the tip of his finger over her lips.

"You're just saying that because you have to," she said, her voice gruff.

"How true. Your body now—"

She poked him in the stomach. Obligingly he grunted and pulled her tightly into his arms again. "I want to make love to you, sweetheart. Actually, I've thought of little else all evening. I was a complete bore. Now, let me tell you what I'm going to do to you." He whispered his quite explicit plans into her ear.

She felt her heart rate increase, felt the strange, utterly swamping sensations build in her body, felt her mind grow languid.

"I don't want to feel like this," she muttered,

her voice sounding so worried that he wanted to laugh.

"I know, but you will. Come, love, I want you naked."

By the time they reached their bedroom, Chauncey had regained something of a hold on herself. She shivered as she knelt in front of the hearth and built up the fire. Despite her half-dozen petticoats and her heavy burgundy velvet gown, she could feel his hands stroking her, feel his tongue curling . . . Stop it, you witless idiot!

Her breasts were heaving slightly when she finally rose. He was standing in the middle of the room watching her, stripped down to his black trousers. The firelight cast enticing shadows on his chest downward to his flat belly, and her eyes were drawn to him like a moth to a flame.

"I don't know about all this, Delaney," she began, feeling like a complete and abject fool. She jerked her eyes away and looked up at the ceiling. "I am mentally negligible," she said.

He laughed, and she watched unwillingly the play of muscles over his stomach. His eyes never left her face as he pulled off his trousers. He knew she was studying his body, and the intense look on her face pleased him. He felt himself becoming aroused. "Come, love, it's my turn to drink my fill of you."

Her gown and piles of petticoats lay on the carpet in but a few minutes. He kissed her lips lightly as he pulled down the straps of her satin chemise. "Ah," he said, pulling her against him, "there can be nothing this side of heaven like a soft woman."

"Just any woman?"

She could feel him smiling at her sharp tone as he nibbled on her throat. She felt herself easing, her body responding quickly to his caressing hands, his mouth, the pressure of his member against her belly. She sighed, standing on her tiptoes to fit herself better against him. Suddenly he stilled. "Damn." He pulled away from her and gave her a rueful look. "I did promise, Chauncey."

She looked at him, a bit dazed. "What?"

"Children. You don't wish to become pregnant too quickly."

"Oh," she said. "Do you mean that you won't—"

"Never that," he said with sincere conviction. "Stay put a moment, love, and I'll fetch the necessary items."

When he showed her the sponge and the liquid a few moments later, she said blankly, "I'm supposed to bathe with this? Drink it?"

"Well, not really. Actually, the liquid goes on the sponge and the sponge goes deep inside you."

She felt embarrassed now standing in the middle of their bedroom without a stitch of clothing on, staring at the stupid sponge. "I am to do what?" she gasped, backing away several steps.

He smiled at her incredulous tone. "First of all, don't put on a dressing gown, it's the last thing we need. We need to have ... easy access, so to speak. Come lie down and I'll show you what to do."

She scampered to the bed and immediately pulled the cover over herself. She stared up at him wide-eyed, watching as he poured the clear liquid over the sponge. "It's primarily vinegar," he said when she sniffed. "Love, please don't look at me as if I'm going to do reprehensible things to you." He set the sponge on the night table and sat down beside her. "It won't be bad, you'll see. You'll not be able to feel it"—he smiled wickedly—"and neither will I." Slowly he pulled the cover away. "Onto your back, Chauncey."

"I don't want to," she said in a thin voice, her eyes glued to the sponge.

"All right, we'll wait awhile." He eased down beside her and drew her now stiff body against him. "Now, what's all this? There's no reason for you to be so embarrassed. I am your husband, you know."

His thoughts, for the most part, remained with the sponge as he kissed her and stroked her. When his hand drifted to her belly, he felt her stiffen, not with fear, but with anticipation, and he smiled. He teased her until she clutched her hand about his neck and forced his face down to hers. Her hips arched upward and he felt her shudder when his fingers found her and began to move sensuously over her.

Her soft flesh swelled under his fingers, growing warm and moist. "Ah," he whispered into her mouth. "That is so very nice, Chauncey."

She whimpered, pressing against his hand, her body squirming to meet his. He nearly consigned the sponge to limbo.

He moved away from her and slowly eased her thighs apart. "You are so lovely," he said, "so very lovely, and ready for me." He quickly grabbed the damned sponge. "Don't move now, love."

Chauncey shuddered with need when she felt him touching her. But the cold sponge slipping inside her made her jerk upright. "Shush," he said, concentrating on the task. "There now"—he smiled at her—"that wasn't too bad, was it? Now, back to the business at hand."

His mouth replaced his fingers and within moments Chauncey felt as if she were going to scream with the pleasure of it. He took her to the very edge, then quickly reared over her and buried himself deep in her body.

Her cries he caught in his mouth. As her trembling eased, she stared up at his face and watched as his climax overtook him. She felt an odd surge of joy at the intense pleasure she had brought him. When he collapsed on top of her, she held him close, small quivers of pleasure still washing through her.

"Del," she cried out suddenly, "I cannot . . . that is, I don't . . ."

"What, sweetheart?"

"Nothing," she said, biting down on her tongue. Dear God, she'd almost blurted out everything! She felt utter misery, and burst into tears.

Almost, he thought, almost she told me. Very gently he pressed her, "Come, love, what is it you cannot or don't want to do?"

Chauncey buried her face into his chest. "Nothing," she sobbed. "Nothing. I told you nothing, dammit!"

"Very well," he said, holding his frustration in check. "It's time to sleep now, Chauncey." He pulled away from her, balanced himself on his elbow, and gently wiped the tears away with his fingers.

"You know," he said, staring intently down

into her face, "most things are easier to bear if they're shared." She merely stared at him, her anguish clear in her eyes, and he wanted to shake her until she spoke the truth to him. But he didn't. Time, he thought. Whatever it is will just take more time.

He rose from the bed and doused the lamps.

He stood over her a moment, listening to her sniffing down her tears. "The sponge must stay inside you until tomorrow morning," he said matter-of-factly.

— 19 —

Agatha Newton smiled toward her hostess. "Please tell Lin that her dinner was excellent. "I doubt I can move!"

"Yes, indeed," Horace Newton said, wiping his mouth on his napkin and folding it neatly beside his very empty plate. "If the old girl doubts she can move, I dare swear I'll be sitting here three days from now!"

"It wasn't exactly what you were expecting, I'll wager," Chauncey said, grinning. "Yorkshire pudding, roast beef, and boiled potatoes."

"With just a touch of ginger and soy sauce," Delaney said. "Lin assured us that it was necessary to make the foreign fare edible."

Chauncey glanced toward the tall clock in the corner. "Oh dear, we must be on our way. I'm certain the gentlemen don't want to miss a moment of Lola Montez' performance!"

"Not even an instant," Delaney agreed. "Ah, the Spider Dance! It boggles the imagination."

"I wonder if she'd let me into her web," Horace said, wriggling his thick gray brows provocatively at his wife.

"You're a lecherous old satyr!" Agatha said as she rose from her chair.

They traveled in the Newtons' closed carriage to the American Theater. It was Chauncey's first venture from the house since their return to San Francisco two days before. She knew Delaney carried a derringer, for she'd seen it. As for her own, it was safe inside her reticule.

"I heard that folk had to spend up to sixty dollars a ticket," Horace said as they wended their way through the hectic crowd inside the two-story brick theater. There were few women in the audience, Chauncey saw as Delaney assisted her into their box, and many of them were as garishly gowned as the interior furnishings of the theater. The men were that unusual mixture found, Chauncey guessed, only in San Francisco: elegantly dressed gentlemen just as she'd seen in St. James in London, side by side with flannel-trousered men in rough work shirts who looked as if they'd just come in from the goldfields. There was much good-natured jesting and a certain amount of rowdiness. Their box, procured, Delaney had told her, from Sam Brannan, who'd already been seen escorting Lola Montez, held but four crimson-velvet-colvered chairs. Chauncey's gown covered Delaney's legs.

Chauncey found herself again marveling at the audience. "A true democracy," she said to Delaney.

"You're right," he agreed, grasping her gloved

hand in his and drawing it on his lap. "You never know if the rough-looking fellow on your right might be carrying a fortune in gold. Indeed, tomorrow he could buy me out."

"Del, who is that woman in that box over there? The one in the yellow velvet gown who is smiling toward us? She looks familiar. Oh, she just waved at you."

Delaney met Marie's eyes and nodded in greeting. He felt a tinge of color on his cheeks but forced himself to shrug at his wife's question. "Just a . . . lady, my dear."

Just a lady my foot! It was his French mistress, Marie, she realized in that moment. Chauncey could see the intimate gleam in Marie's lovely dark eyes from twenty feet away. She felt a strange churning anger and a feeling of absolute inferiority. Marie was so bloody gorgeous!

"I know who she is," she said in a tight voice. "After all, I did see you with her before." She wanted to box his ears, yell like a fishwife, but the moment was lost: the crimson curtains parted on the stage and Lola Montez appeared. Anything Chauncey could have said would have been lost in the thundering applause, loud whistles, and calls from the men in the audience.

Lola Montez wasn't classically beautiful, Chauncey decided, but she exuded a raw kind of sensuality that even Delaney wasn't immune to, for he sat slightly forward in his seat. She was tall, voluptuously built, and her costume was nothing more than judiciously placed gauzy veils. Her eyes were snapping, vividly alive, appearing nearly black, and her thick black hair was wound in elaborate coils about her head in a decidedly Spanish fashion.

Oh well, Chauncey told herself, best to simply sit back and enjoy it. When Lola spoke, it was in charmingly lisped English. The men roared after every utterance she made.

Delaney whispered to Chauncey, "Lord, all she has to do it simply stand there! But I do believe, my dear, that her charms are a bit overripe for my taste."

Chauncey gave him an incredulous look. "I think Horace is beginning to perspire," she said.

The Spanish dancer more than made up for her lack of acting ability when at last she reappeared onstage to perform her famous Spider Dance. Chauncey heard her own small gasp of shock. She was wearing pratically nothing. During her pantomime, she shook whalebone spiders from her skimpy costume and stamped on them. The crowd went wild.

"You are enjoying yourself a great deal too much," Chauncey hissed in Delaney's ear. "That smile of yours is so vacuous, you'd be confined in Bedlam if you were in England."

He gave her a wolfish grin. "My body isn't feeling at all vacuous."

"Cad!" she said, poking him in the ribs. "Such a thing would never be allowed in England!"

"Don't bet on it, sweetheart."

When her performance was finished, Lola Montez was deluged with flowers, and to Chauncey's wide-eyed surprise, gold nuggets were tossed onto the stage at her feet.

"I wonder," Horace said, "how much gold she'll be depositing in your bank tomorrow, Del."

"The vault will be bulging," Agatha said.

"Actually, love," Delaney whispered in Chauncey's ear as Lola Montez took her tenth curtain call, "I was just imagining you wearing that bit of nothing and seducing me with well-placed whalebone."

"Ah, look," Horace said, saving Chauncey from making a suitable retort, "there's Pat Hull. I hear he's head-over-toes in love with Lola, and she isn't particularly uninterested in him."

"Pat who?" Chauncey asked. But she didn't hear his reply, for her eyes suddenly lit on a man who was looking directly at her from his slouched position in a dim corner of the theater. It was Hoolihan, the sailor aboard the *Scarlet Queen*. The moment she recognized him he quickly turned away, melting into a crowd of still-stomping and applauding men. She felt a *frisson* go through her body, raising gooseflesh on her arms. I'm becoming a dithering hysteric again, she tried to tell herself, but the feeling remained.

She was markedly quietly during the carriage ride home. For the life of her, she couldn't remember what she'd said to the Newtons.

"All right, Chauncey, what is it?" Delaney asked the moment they walked into the drawing room.

She stripped off her long gloves and tossed them onto a chair back. "I'm probably seeing ghosts and imagining things—"

He interrupted her with a sharp slash of his hand. "Cut the bull, Chauncey. What made you withdraw into yourself?"

"All right," she said on a sigh. "Do you remember Captain O'Mally's new man—Mr. Hoolihan, I believe his name was?"

"Yes."

"I saw him at the theater. He was staring at me. When he realized that I saw him too, he made off. Shouldn't he be on board the *Scarlet Queen?*"

"Why the hell didn't you tell me immediately?" He strode to her and grasped her shoulders, shaking her slightly.

"I thought I was just being ... crazy." Her voice broke. "I *felt* something, Del. Something frightful. I ... I can't explain it." She raised wide uncertain eyes to his face. "If he didn't mean anything, why did he act so furtive?"

"All right," he said, his voice cool, his control back. "You're completely safe here." He began rubbing her arms, soothing her, bringing her warmth. "Do you recall Captain O'Mally telling us that Hoolihan was quite a new man?"

"I'm not sure."

She shivered and he pulled her against him. "No more of that. Tomorrow I'll find out soon enough just who this Hoolihan is and if he's still in my employ. If he is the one responsible for all this, I'll have him taken care of."

She nodded, mute, against his shoulder. *I am trusting him to protect me. I want him to protect me.*

"You know," Delaney said over her head, "I think I remember that Hoolihan had an odd accent. English perhaps?"

"English," she repeated, leaning back against his arms and raising her eyes to his. "Oh no! It makes no sense, Del. There is no one in England who would despise me enough to—"

"It does make all sorts of sense, unfortunately, and you know it. Don't forget what happened in Plymouth. Incidentally, I saw the letter you had Lucas post yesterday to your aunt and uncle in England."

"Yes, I wrote to tell them that I was once again dreadfully poor and begged them to take me in." She smiled crookedly at his admiring grin. "It was either that or tell them that I was married. I thought they'd be more pleased to hear the former."

"Well done, my girl. Well done indeed. If money is at the root of all this, you can believe that your fall from fortune will quickly get around."

Her eyes fell. But it wasn't money, she was certain of it. It was another *feeling*. Just who wanted her removed and why was still a damnably elusive mystery.

"No," Delaney said, easily reading her thoughts from her shifting expressions, "I don't believe it has anything to do with money either." He added in some surprise, "You really don't have any idea, do you?"

"No, I don't. I told you I didn't."

He saw fear and something else he couldn't fathom in her eyes. Guilt? He shook his head. It made no sense. But then again, he thought, her lack of trust in him made no sense either. "It's all right, love," he said gently. "Why don't we go upstairs now and you can seduce me with whalebone."

Her fear made her as wildly abandoned as she'd been aboard the *Scarlet Queen*. I've been used, he thought when at last he held her in his arms and she slept. Used to still her fear and make her forget for at least a little while. She awoke in the middle of the night, fighting free of Delaney's arms and the heavy covers. She cried out once, feeling the cold fathomless waters closing over her head, drawing her down.

"Oh, God," she whispered as he held her, rocking her against his warm body. "Please, Del, make it stop!"

He did. She responded feverishly and he took her quickly, almost roughly. He felt a stab of guilt until he felt her body tense beneath him and felt consuming cries of pleasure against his shoulder.

This has got to stop, he told himself, angry at her even as he took his own release.

"Hoolihan jumped ship the day after we left the *Scarlet Queen*," Delaney said matter-of-factly the following evening over dinner. "I hired six men today to find him."

The tasty shredded pork turned to ashes in Chauncey's mouth. She slowly, very precisely laid down her fork.

"Luckily," he continued, "I found one of his boat mates and got an excellent description. I even had a sketch made of him. If he is still hanging about San Francisco, I'll have him, and quite soon."

Still, she simply looked at him.

"Also, if you happen to see a giant of a man with blond hair outside the house, he's a Swede by the name of Olaf. I've hired him to share duties with Lucas."

"You are going to a lot of trouble for me," she said finally. "Thank you, Del."

His fork fell with a clatter onto his plate. "You're my wife, damn you, Chauncey! Just what the hell did you think I'd do? Ignore the situation? Issue an invitation to this scum asking him to come and take you off my hands?"

She stared at him helplessly, her face devoid of color. His anger startled her, for it was so unlike him. But she understood it. She could think of nothing to say.

He willed her to speak to him, to trust him, but she lowered her eyes and stared at her plate.

He tossed his napkin on the table and scraped back his chair. "You're driving me crazy. I'll see you later."

He strode from the dining room without a backward glance.

A picture of Marie's intimate smile at Delaney flashed suddenly through her mind, and she called out, her voice shrill, "Where are you going?"

He said curtly over his shoulder, "Out."

"Don't you dare go to that woman!" she yelled at him, jumping up from her chair.

He stopped cold at the jealous fury in her voice. "Why the hell not?" he asked softly, turning to face her. "After all, my dear, I let you use me last night—twice, as a matter of fact. Why shouldn't I go use her?"

She cringed at the memory of her wild response to him. Had she really used him? Chauncey was stunned by her own reaction. "You . . . you wouldn't, you can't—"

"My dear wife," he said very slowly and very calmly, "I wouldn't have married you, despite your relentless and elaborate pursuit, if I'd only wanted sex from you. God knows, it requires quite a bit of ingenuity and persistence just to make you willing. Except, of course, when you want a man's body to keep your nightmares at bay. You're entirely selfish, Chauncey, in bed and out of it. If you decide you want to give me more, let me know. Good night, madam."

And he was gone.

"I hate you!" she shouted after him, but the words came out as a broken whisper. "At least I'm not a swindler and a thief!"

Chauncey had no idea that she even possessed such wild, uncontrollable emotions, the gamut of which she had totally exhausted throughout the long night. She was drained, utterly limp and listless the following day. She wandered about the house like a ghost, not really caring, not really thinking about anything at all. She ignored Mary's questioning looks and sent Lin's breakfast back to the kitchen untouched.

When Lin appeared in the doorway of the drawing room that afternoon, her almond eyes narrowed in concern, Chauncey merely looked at her, saying nothing.

"Miss Chauncey, Lucas like to speak to you."

"Send him in, Lin."

Lucas limped into the room. "Excuse me, ma'am. Mr. Del's ship the *Jade* just docked. I wanted to tell you that Olaf is outside, if you need him. I'm going to help unload the ship."

Chauncey stared at him. "Which warehouse, Lucas?" she asked very calmly.

"He had a new one built, off the end of Sansome Street."

"I see." Indeed, she did see, everything. "I should like to accompany you, Lucas."

He looked taken aback, but for only a moment. Miss Chauncey needed to get out, and he would be there to protect her. She couldn't stay indoors all the time, after all, until they'd caught that man Hoolihan. Still, he felt a bit of uncertainty, concerned about what Mr. Del would think when he saw his wife. "Certainly, ma'am. Could we go shortly?"

"I'll just be a moment, Lucas."

Ten minutes later, Lucas helped Chauncey to mount her mare, Yvette. The afternoon was overcast, with thick fog drifting over the hills toward them.

"You warm enough, ma'am?"

"Yes, indeed," Chauncey said, and urged Yvette to a trot. At last, she thought. At long last. She saw Lucas tip his hat to Olaf as they rode from the house. She'd spoken only briefly to the big Swede. He looked as fierce as Lucas in his own way, and like Lucas, he seemed as gentle as a puppy.

As usual, the downtown area of San Francisco was filled with men, wagons, and horses. She could hear the tinny piano music from a saloon on Kearny Street. She found herself scanning the men's faces as they rode past, almost smiling in anticipation. Come on, Hoolihan, she thought, her fingers curling about her small derringer.

When they reached Delaney's large warehouse, she wanted to shout with glee. It was set apart, newly built, a massive wooden building that, she thought, her lips tightening, would burn quickly and completely. She knew well enough every

San Franciscan's fear of fire, but just this warehouse would burn, nothing else. Only Delaney would be hurt. She had learned something of shipping from Thomas Gregory during her two months with him in London. Given that the *Jade* was returning from the Orient, it must have many, many thousands of dollars' worth of goods.

They dismounted near the large entrance to the warehouse. Dozens of men, many of them sailors from the *Jade*, were hauling wooden boxes into the building.

"Chauncey! What the hell!"

She turned at the sound of Delaney's sharp, surprised voice. He had shed his frock coat and rolled the sleeves of his white shirt to his elbows. Sweat glistened on his face. He strode over to her, his eyes narrowing on Lucas' face.

"Don't blame Lucas, Del," she said quickly. "I . . . I wanted to get out of the house. Please, let me stay."

As she spoke, her eyes veered to his ship, a large clipper, modern and sleek.

He looked at her closely, seeing the excitement in her eyes, and sighed. It was true, he thought, she couldn't remain virtually a prisoner. "All right," he said, smiling at her, "but just for a few minutes." She appeared to have forgotten their virulent argument of the previous night.

All I need is a few minutes! She could feel the blood pounding and surging through her body. She ignored the brief pleasure the sight of her husband had brought her. He'd left her the previous night and gone to his precious mistress. He'd finally shown her his true colors. He wasn't honorable, not at all. *I will feel no guilt. None at all.*

"Tell me about the goods you've brought over," she said, her voice bright.

He conducted her through the warehouse, opening some of the crates to show her bolts of incredibly beautiful silk, old and ornate furnishings, and vases from Chinese dynasties she'd never heard of. So many beautiful things that would cease to exist. Soon. Very soon.

She was charming, radiant, and hung solicitously on his every word. He allowed her to stay longer than he'd planned. When finally she rode away with Lucas, he stood staring after her, his eyes narrowed, his expression thoughtful.

— 20 —

I'm finally revenging you, Father! Finally I'll do what I must.

Chauncey stilled all guilt, all doubts, and concentrated on her dinner.

"You're looking very thoughtful this evening," Delaney said as he lifted his goblet of wine to his lips.

"Am I?" she asked brightly. She smiled at him, a dazzling smile that made his body leap in response. "I was just thinking about the *Jade* and what a beautiful ship she is. And all that cargo! When will you move it, Del?"

"Beginning tomorrow. Don't look so surprised, love. The ship was late, and merchants have been awaiting the goods for nearly a month now."

Tonight. It must be tonight!

"I suppose the cargo must be worth a great

deal of money." *Careful, Chauncey, don't act too interested.*

"Yes, a great deal," Del said.

Worth enough to ruin you?

"The warehouse is most impressive. Thank you for showing me through it."

"The warehouse too is worth a great deal. It was just finished six months ago. Others will begin building on the wharf soon. Sam Brannan . . ."

Chauncey heard Sam Brannan's plans with half an ear. I am hurting no one, she told herself yet again. No one save Delaney Saxton. Would he come to her for money, she wondered, when it was all over?

"I must go out for a while, love," Del said, interrupting her thoughts. "I won't be long. though." He paused a moment, looking at her thoughtfully from beneath his lowered lashes.

Was this to be a repeat of last night? "Where are you going?" Her voice sounded shrill and she fought for control. "This time, that is."

He cocked an interested brow at her. "Do you really wish to know?"

She ground her teeth. "Can't you simply answer a question? No, it's more amusing for you to taunt me! You won't go to her again tonight, Delaney! You mustn't! Surely you are too tired?"

"I suppose I am somewhat tired," he said in the blandest of voices. He watched her with a mild show of interest.

Chauncey rose quickly from her chair and stamped her foot. "Did you sleep with her last night?"

Delaney sat back in his chair and studied her

flushed face thoughtfully. The silence stretched long between them. "Would it bother you if I had?"

"You are my husband!"

"It pleases me that you remember."

She wanted to scream at him, hurl her chair at his head. "You didn't answer me, Del. Did you sleep with her last night?"

"Not much—sleep, that is. She was warm, giving . . . a woman, Chauncey. Unselfish and honest in her needs."

Suddenly her reason for not wishing him to leave was lost in her fury. She hadn't really expected him to admit seeing his mistress. She jerked backward, feeling disoriented. She heard her own voice, low, filled with pain. "You wouldn't. You are not that kind of man—"

"No, I am not. It infuriates me, my dear, that you would even ask me such a question. Now that we've enacted this charming little scene, I'm leaving. I will be home within two hours. If you wish it, I'll make love to you when I return." He walked slowly to her, lifted her chin with his fingers, and studied her upturned face. "Wait up for me, love. You'll see that I'm not too tired to see to your pleasure."

He kissed her lightly on her mouth, turned, and left the dining room.

So he hadn't visited his mistress. So what? It didn't change a thing, damn him. Wretched elusive beast!

She was ready for him two hours later, dressed in the delicious confection of nightgown and peignoir he'd bought her for their wedding night. He will suspect nothing, she thought.

"Hello," she said softly when he quietly entered their bedroom.

"Hello yourself," he said. He rubbed the back of his neck. "Lord, I'm tired."

"Not too tired, I hope," she said, trying for a seductive tone of voice.

He grinned at her. "Never too tired for you, love."

She watched him strip off his clothes, then handed him a glass of wine. "Did you put an aphrodisiac in this?" he asked her in a teasing voice.

"No," she said.

"To us, Chauncey."

"To the . . . future," she said, and sipped her wine.

He drank the entire glass and set it down on a table. "Come here, wife. I want to kiss you."

He must have no doubts, she thought, no doubts at all. She felt guilty and afraid, but walked quickly into his arms. She tried to detach herself from the outwardly warm and loving woman in Delaney's arms.

Del was nuzzling her neck, his hands kneading her full hips. He felt a sudden wave of overwhelming fatigue wash through him, and yawned deeply. "I'm more tired than I thought," he said, shaking his head.

"Come to bed then," she said, drawing her hand through his arm.

"I'm sure to lose my fatigue once I'm on my back . . . or you're on yours."

But he didn't. Tiredness drew down his lashes, numbed his mind and his body. The physical labor he'd done today on the dock shouldn't have had such an effect on him, he thought, his mind hazy. He felt Chauncey's warm body pressed against him, but his desire for her was fading as the deadening sleep overtook him.

Chauncey didn't move for a good five minutes. She stared down at his sleeping face, listening closely to his even breathing. She waited another hour, until the clock downstairs chimed twelve strokes. Resolutely she slipped out of the bed.

She was trembling as she quickly dressed in an old muslin gown. She left off all her petticoats and pulled on stout shoes. Delaney mumbled something, and she froze. He turned onto his side, his sleep unbroken. She was being silly. The laudanum she'd put in his wine would keep him sleeping soundly all night.

She drew a deep steadying breath and stealthily slipped into the darkened corridor. Lucas' room was downstairs. Surely by now he was sleeping nearly as soundly as his master. As for the Swede, Olaf had left earlier in the evening. She slipped out the kitchen door, careful to keep it unlocked for her return.

The stables were dark, but she'd studied her route this afternoon, and her steps were sure. Yvette nickered softly and Chauncey quickly rubbed her velvet nose, speaking to the mare quietly. "Come, girl, it's a midnight ride for us. You must be surefooted and brave." I'm talking to myself, she thought, trying to give myself courage and resolution.

She slipped a bridle over Yvette's head and led her from her stall. No saddle this night. She hoisted herself onto her mare's back and quietly urged her forward.

The night was overcast, with only a few stars glittering through when the clouds shifted. A thick fog blanketed the wharf area, making the air cold and damp. She pulled her cloak more closely about her, careful to keep the hood well over her head. She rode toward the Sansome Street wharf from the south, avoiding most of the still brightly lit gambling saloons. There were still men on the streets, and each one made her quiver with fear. Was that Hoolihan slouching in the ally between those two buildings? No, he was Chinese. But what about the man reeling into the road in front of her?

"Stop being a damned coward," she said aloud, the sound of her own voice making her more confident. "Hoolihan would have no idea that you left the house. He might even be long gone from San Francisco. Concentrate on what you must do. Concentrate."

Twenty minutes later, Yvette's hooves were clomping loudly on the wooden wharf. It was ghostly quiet. The *Jade* rode high at anchor at the end of the wharf, her high bare masts looking eerie in the thick fog. The warehouse loomed up huge and dark. Chauncey slid off Yvette's back, afraid to ride closer, and tethered her to one of the wharf posts. Her teeth were chattering with cold and fear as she drew into the shadow of the warehouse. Suddenly she stopped cold, rooted to the spot. There were two men wrapped in blankets slumped against the wall of the warehouse, obviously asleep. Of course there would be guards. How could she have been so stupid as not to realize that? She stood perfectly still, watching them and thinking. She didn't want to hurt them.

She drew a deep breath, loud and raspy in her own ears, and stealthily walked toward the large double doors, her back pressed against the building. Just a little farther.

There was a thick crossbeam holding the doors closed. She stared at it for a long moment, the snoring of the two men loud in the quiet. Slowly she tugged the bar upward, at the same time moving it to the side, in its slot. The bar creaked. One of the men snorted, then began a staccato series of loud snores.

Carefully, move very carefully, she told herself. At last one of the doors was free of the heavy bar. She slipped her fingers into the opening between the doors and gently pulled. It groaned on its hinges and she felt gooseflesh rise on her arms. "Please," she whispered. "Just a few more inches."

She slipped through the narrow opening. Huge crates loomed before her, covered with pale tarpaulins, like shadowy ghosts. She stopped and looked about her. The warehouse was nearly filled. Thousands upon thousands of dollars' worth of goods were here. She pictured the shimmering bolts of Chinese silk, the exquisite vases and paintings. All of it belonged to Delaney Saxton, the man who had sent her father to his death. Her husband, the man who would give his life to protect her.

"Stop it!" she hissed aloud into the utter stillness.

I have to do it! I have to!

Angrily she pulled the matches from her cloak pocket and struck one. It made a harsh sizzling sound before illuminating the small area where where she stood.

Like an automaton, she walked down the narrow aisle to the middle of the warehouse. The match burned out, and she struck another. She held it outward over a tarpaulin that covered some goods on the floor. Her hand shook. "Oh God," she whispered, "I can't do it!"

The match light flickered and went out, burning her fingers.

"Delaney." His name was a soft, agonized cry. She struck another match, willing herself to act.

I love him. The thought seared through her mind and body. *I cannot betray him.* But what of your father? He died because of this man! No, her mind screamed silently, he died because he couldn't face what had happened.

She felt salty tears streaming down her face, felt a numbing pain, a pain so great that she moaned softly. But she couldn't do it. The match flickered and she threw it from her. Home, she thought. She wanted only to go home. Home to Delaney; home to lie in his arms and accept his love. Suddenly she was surrounded by gunfire. Quick, loud reports cracked at her. She screamed, dashing toward the door. She whirled about, staring behind her. The tarpaulin was aflame and bright-colored sparks flew upward, popping, sizzling, making odd shapes before flickering away.

The damned match! She had to put out the fire! But the noise—what was it? Suddenly she heard men's loud voices and the doors flew open. She lurched behind a large crate and sank to her knees. She couldn't be found here!

"Jesus!" one of the men yelled. "Quick, Damon,

we can beat it out. It's those damned Chink fireworks!"

She watched the men rush to the flaming tarpaulin, ripping off their blankets as they ran. She quickly made her way behind the crates and slipped unseen from the warehouse. Her heart was pounding so loudly she was certain they would hear her.

She reached Yvette, sobbing for breath, when she heard a loud explosion. Oh God, no! She scrambled onto her mare's back and whipped her down the wharf. A dozen men were running toward her and she shouted, "Quickly! There's a fire in the warehouse! Hurry!"

What have I done?

The refrain spun in her mind, giving her no peace. She had no thought of Hoolihan as Yvette galloped back toward South Park. The horrible sound of the explosion sounded again and again in her ears. She deserved to be in that warehouse. She was the one who deserved to die, if die someone must. If any of the men were hurt, she didn't know what she would do.

The stables appeared so normal, as if nothing at all out of the ordinary had occurred. She slipped off Yvette's back and forced herself to do what she must. All her movements were utterly mechanical. When she finally slipped through the bedroom door, she felt faint with fear. She jerked off her clothes and stuffed them under the bed.

"Mr. Del! Wake up! It's a fire!"

Chauncey stared wide-eyed toward the door, seeing Lucas surge into the room. Delaney moaned softly beside her.

"Mr. Del!" Lucas limped to the bed, ignored Chauncey, and began shaking his master. "Wake up!"

Delaney jerked awake. His head felt stuffed with cotton. He blankly at Lucas for a moment. "Fire?" he repeated, trying to shake the heavy veil of weariness from his mind.

"The warehouse! Damon is downstairs. Quickly!"

Delaney jumped from the bed, oblivious of his nakedness. He pulled on his trousers, shirt, and boots in rapid succession.

"What is it, Del?"

"A fire, love," he said, turning to regard his pale, disheveled wife. "I'll be back soon. Don't leave the house, Chauncey. Lucas is staying here with you."

Even with this emergency he doesn't forget his protection of me. She felt numb with guilt. Swiftly Delaney leaned down and kissed her. "Stay put," he said again, then strode out of the room, leaving her to gaze after him with pain-filled eyes.

She heard the front door slam. Such a final sound. *What if he is killed? What if . . .?*

Chauncey dressed quickly. The house was well lit by the time she made her way downstairs. Mary was talking to Lucas, with Lin hovering beside them, wringing her hands. It was four o'clock in the morning.

"Make tea and coffee, please, Lin," she said, shocked at how calm her voice sounded. "Mr. Del should be back soon. He'll need it."

What if the laudanum makes him slow? What if there's another explosion? What if . . .?

She wasn't aware that she'd moaned until she

felt Lin's thin arms wrapped around her shoulders. "Mr. Del be just fine, Miss Chauncey. Just fine. You see."

She sobbed, deep racking sounds. She felt Lucas' strong arms go around her, and she leaned against him, all her guilt and anger at herself flowing out, like a dam bursting. She banged her fists against Lucas' solid chest, sobbing over and over, "No! Please, no!"

Lucas said nothing, merely held her. Over her head he mouthed the words "Some hot tea" to Lin. Gently he led Chauncey into the drawing room. He efficiently laid a fire and lit it.

"Do you know anything, Lucas?"

He frowned at her flat, emotionless voice. The tears and loss of control he understood, but this?

"No, ma'am. Damon just said they'd nearly got the fire out and he came to get Mr. Del."

"I see."

Lin brought in the tea, and Chauncey sipped at the scalding liquid. She wasn't aware that her hands were trembling until she spilled the blistering tea on her forearm.

"Oh!" It was a burn. Fires burned. Flesh. People died in fires, horrible deaths.

Lucas took the cup from her hands and set it on the table beside the sofa. He saw the dazed fear in her eyes and prayed that Mr. Del would return home soon. He had no idea how to handle this situation.

The minutes went by with agonizing slowness. Chauncey was huddled on the sofa, her knees drawn up to her chest, staring unseeing into the fire.

Lucas heard approaching horses and quickly

let himself out of the house. If Mr. Del was hurt, he wanted to know it first. Thank God, he thought when he saw him dismount. He was covered with soot, black smudges on his face, but he was fine, just fine.

"We didn't lose too much," Delaney said, managing a smile for Lucas.

"Lord, I'm glad you're back in one piece! Miss Chauncey is in a bad way, Mr. Del, a very bad way."

He felt a surge of fear. "What the hell do you mean?"

"Upset about the fire and you. You're all right?"

"Yes, of course. Please see to Brutus, Luc."

Delaney strode into the house. He felt both exhilarated and exhausted.

Chauncey stared at him. He was filthy and his white shirt was burned at the shoulder. She let out a cry and launched herself at him.

"What is all this?" he teased her gently, stroking her tangled hair. She was trembling and he drew her closer, forgetting how dirty he was. "Hush, love. Everything is all right, I promise you."

"I'm sorry," she sobbed, clutching at his neck, choking him. "Oh God, Del, I'm so sorry!"

"Sorry for what?" he asked, kissing her temple.

"I . . . I shouldn't have let you go! Not alone!"

"I know. It was selfish of me. Come, sweetheart, I survived. All of us survived. Even most of the goods survived. It was just a minor disaster."

He gently pushed her back so he could see her face. She was utterly without color, her eyes huge and dilated. There were now two black smudges of soot on her cheek. There was something different about her; he sensed it. Not just her obvious fear for his safety, but something else.

"I couldn't have ... continued if you'd been ..." The words choked in her throat and she pressed herself hard against him, burying her face in his shoulder. "I can't hate you, I can't!"

Delaney grew very still. Why in the world would she even think of hating him, for God's sake? She had chased him down, not the other way around. It had taken the damned fire to make her realize that she didn't hate him? He shook his head, bewildered. "I know you don't, love," he said. "Perhaps someone should have set that fire sooner," he added, more to himself than to her.

"Someone set it?" she whispered.

"So it would appear. The warehouse doors were open. One of my men found some burned matches on the floor. Fortunately for me, the fellow must have accidentally tossed a match onto the Chinese fireworks and panicked. They make a god-awful noise. There's some smoke damage, but for the most part, the bulk of the goods are in good shape."

Her hand touched the rent in his shirt. "You're hurt! Damn you, you told me you were all right!"

"It's my shirt that's hurt, sweetheart, not my body." He cupped her face between his palms. "Now, stop carrying on like a mother hen who's afraid her chick is in the soup pot. I am perfectly all right. I suggest we both go upstairs and clean up." He rubbed the black smudge on her cheek with the tip of his finger. "You're adorable, but a bit dirty."

To his utter astonishment, her eyes fell and she began to twist her hands together. The words trembled on her lips. Dear God, what was she to do? She'd failed at every scheme she'd attempted, except marrying him, her enemy. Only now she loved him. Deep inside her, she could no longer accept that he could be guilty of swindling her father. He simply couldn't do anything like that. "Delaney, I must tell you . . ."

"Chauncey, love, what is it? What's wrong?"

"I . . . I love you!"

"Ah," he said with great satisfaction, "finally."

His odd words jerked her from her roiling thoughts. "What do you mean, 'finally'?"

"Perhaps," he said very softly, "perhaps someday you'll tell me. Now, let's get bathed and back to bed. I don't know what's the matter with me, but I feel ready to drop."

He didn't see her face twist with guilt.

— 21 —

Delaney was gone when she awoke late the next morning.

"Mr. Del have plenty mess to clean up," Lin told her as she served breakfast.

"Yes," Chauncey said dully, "I suppose he did."

She wanted to ride to the warehouse and assess the damage she'd done, but Agatha Newton arrived and she was compelled to listen to the good woman carry on about the Sydney Ducks, the brutes most likely responsible for the fire. "At least," Agatha said, "Del's men kept the looters at bay, thank God!" By the time Agatha gave her a hug and left, Chauncey was ready to yell her frustration and guilt.

Lucas caught her just as she was preparing to have Olaf drive her to the wharf.

"Ma'am, Mr. Del sent me," he said, swinging toward her. "He needs some papers from his desk. Insurance papers."

Chauncey nodded and walked back into the house. She'd been in Delaney's library only once, and she'd thought then how very English it looked with its paneled walls, bookcases, and huge maghogany desk. She walked to his desk and pulled the top drawer open. Her hand stilled. By God, she thought, what a fool I've been! She found the insurance papers quickly and sent Lucas on his way.

She returned to sit behind the impressive desk. She opened each drawer, thumbing carefully through the papers and letters within. Nothing about her father. In the bottom drawer was a locked wooden box. She picked it up and shook it. There were papers inside. Slowly she pulled a pin from her hair and fit it into the lock. It finally clicked and she raised the lid. For a moment she was afraid to examine the papers and letters. She realized that she didn't want to confirm that Delaney was guilty. There was a folded piece of paper on top, and resolutely she pulled it free. It was obviously a copy of a letter he had written some four months earlier. It was to Paul Montgomery. She read it slowly, the neat black script blurring as the truth became obvious. She studied each copy of the bank drafts to her father over the past months. Huge amounts of money going to him. Delaney was innocent. Paul Montgomery had lied about everything.

The money never reached her father.

Chauncey sat back in Delaney's high-backed leather chair and closed her eyes. It was all too incredible; incredible but true. Paul Montgomery had cheated her father of all the money. No wonder he'd acted so strangely when she told him she was coming to San Francisco! He knew she would discover the truth. He knew she would realize Delaney wasn't the scoundrel he'd wanted to convince her he was.

Paul Montgomery is the one who wants me dead.

But to kill her simply because she would discover that he was a crook and a liar? She rubbed her hand wearily over her forehead.

You've got to tell Delaney. Everything.

She moaned softly. Dear God, she loved him. If she told him the truth, he would despise her, send her back to England without a second thought. He would hate her for her deception. And she wouldn't blame him a bit.

She sat staring blindly toward the thick tomes in the bookshelves against the opposite wall. She heard the front door open, footsteps on the marble entryway, masculine steps. Delaney. She quickly stuffed the papers and letters back into the box and shoved it into the bottom drawer.

"Whatever are you doing in here, love?"

She gazed at him clearly for the first time. She would willingly die for him. His face was shadowed in the dim light, except his beautiful eyes, like clear honey, filled with tenderness for her.

The enormity of her situation hit her hard. She couldn't seem to speak, only stare at him, memorizing his features. She couldn't bear to see the tenderness change to outrage, to utter fury, to hatred.

"Chauncey? Are you all right?"

I'll make him love me, make myself indispensable to him, then confess the truth. I'll conceive his child. He wouldn't send me away then. Oh God, another deception.

"I'm fine, Del," she said. She rose from the chair and walked as in a dream toward him. She stopped inches away from him and looked up into his face. Slowly she glided her fingertips over his jaw. "You are so beautiful," she whispered.

Delaney blinked, and one mobile brow shot up. His thoughts throughout the morning had veered to her and her strange behavior of the night before. He didn't understand her. She had changed.

"Am I now?" he said, his eyes locked to hers. "What brought this on?"

What if he discovers the truth before I tell him? What about Paul Montgomery? I don't want to die!

"Oh no," she said, unaware that she'd spoken aloud. She knew now there was no choice. She had to tell him the truth. She stopped abruptly. No. She wanted one more day and night with him, with the husband who cared for her, laughed with her, loved her so completely with his body and soul.

"Are you feeling all right?" She felt his hands stroking gently over her arms.

"Yes," she said. She leaned forward, resting her forehead against his shoulder. "Aren't we still on our honeymoon?"

"For the next twenty years, I'd say."

"Must you go to the bank today? Or back to the warehouse?"

"What did you have in mind, sweetheart?"

She stood on her tiptoes, fitting herself tightly against him. "I want you to stay . . . with me."

"I think that can be arranged," he said, and gently kissed her.

*   *   *

"Mr. Saxton! We've got him!"

Delaney turned from his conversation with Dan Drewer at Jed Randall's excited voice.

"What's all this about, Del?" Dan asked. "Got whom?"

"Nothing to concern you, Dan," he said to his partner. "I'll be back later. A Mr. McIntyre is coming to see me about a loan. Would you deal with it? The file's on my desk."

"Certainly," Dan said, staring after Delaney as he quickly accompanied the other man from the bank.

Delaney said nothing until they'd stepped outside the bank into the street. "Hoolihan?" he asked.

"Yes, sir. Actually, it was Monk who found him. He was in bed with a whore on Washington Street—Hoolihan, that is."

"Where have you taken him?" Delaney asked, not bothering to inquire what Monk was doing at the brothel.

"To your warehouse, sir. Monk had to rough him up just a bit, but not too badly."

Delaney nodded and increased his pace. Just as long as Monk Dove hadn't broken Hoolihan's damned neck, he didn't mind what he'd done to him. Monk was a mountain, his strength incredible.

Ten minutes later, Delaney and Jed were at the warehouse. Men were working outside, replacing burned wooden planks, loading ruined merchandise into drays. The interior still smelled of smoke and the peculiar acrid odor of the Chinese fireworks.

Three men were standing in front of the tattered Hoolihan. Monk saw Delaney, and his mouth split into a wide grin, showing broken yellow teeth. "Got him, sir!"

"Excellent, Monk," Delaney said, his eyes on Hoolihan's face. The man was obviously frightened, his light-colored eyes dilated, his beard-stubbled jaw working spasmodically. When he saw Delaney, he paled even more and drew back.

"Now, now, mate, don't be so shy," Monk said, twisting his arm just a bit.

"Good work, Monk," Delaney said. "Now, gentlemen, if you would leave us alone for a moment. Mr. Hoolihan and I have quite a bit to discuss."

Delaney waited until the men had moved a respectable distance away. "Now, Hoolihan, I have just one question for you, and you will answer it, my friend. If you don't, I will have Monk and his other friends shred you into small pieces. Do you understand me?"

"You've made a mistake! I don't know what you want!"

"Do you understand me?" Delaney repeated very calmly. He read the violent, desperate attempt in Hoolihan's eyes and added, "If you try to take me, I'll shoot you. In your legs, both of them. I don't want you dead, Hoolihan, but if you try something stupid, I'll make you feel a great deal of pain, more than your poor mother when she birthed you. Now, I'm growing bored with this. Who hired you to kill my wife?"

Hoolihan licked his lips but remained silent.

Slowly Delaney drew out his derringer. "Your left leg first, Hoolihan. Your knee, to be specific. I wonder if your whore will like you as a cripple—

if you don't die of blood poisoning first, that is."
He carefully aimed the small pistol.

"No!" Hoolihan shrieked. "I don't know! I swear
it!"

"After the left knee, I'll put a bullet through
the right. Perhaps James Cora will let you sit on
the sidewalk outside the El Dorado and beg for
money, for you'll not be walking." He pulled
back the hammer.

"Listen to me," Hoolihan said, desperation and
defeat in his voice. "It was a man I don't know.
He paid me a thousand dollars to sign on the
Scarlet Queen. He knew you'd be traveling to
Sacramento. I swear it. I don't know his name."

Delaney gently caressed the barrel of the small
derringer. "Was the man English?"

"He talked funny, if that's what you mean.
Not like the blokes from Australia, more proper-
like. Dressed like a real dandy."

He's telling the truth, Delaney thought. "Tell
me, Hoolihan, what reason did he give you for
killing my wife?"

"All he told me was that the lady had to be
shut up. She knew too much. About what, I swear
I don't know!"

"What does he look like?"

"If I tell you, will you let me go?"

"Trying to bargain, Hoolihan?" Delaney asked,
his voice sounding coldly amused. "Let me be
blunt, my friend. I won't turn you over to our
local authorities. You'd be free in twenty-four
hours if I did. No, if you don't tell me everything
you know, I'll kill you. If you do cooperate, on
the other hand, you'll not be killed. But you will

take a nice long trip on one of my ships. Hong Kong is really quite nice this time of year."

Shanghaied, Hoolihan thought, forced labor of the lowest sort, but better than being six feet under with worms eating your flesh. He drew a deep breath, wincing slightly at the pain in his stomach. "He was old, and wore spectacles. Kind of heavyset, but soft-looking, like he'd really lived a grand life."

"How old?" Age in San Francisco was a very relative term. Most of the male population were under thirty-five. Any man over forty was considered old.

Hoolihan thought frantically. "In his fifties, I'd say. Graying hair, thin on top."

Delaney felt a surge of elation. Chauncey had to know who he was from Hoolihan's description. "Just how, Hoolihan, did he plan to ensure you'd carry through with your part of the bargain? I can't believe he simply handed you a thousand dollars without some sort of collateral."

"He gave me five hundred," Hoolihan said simply. "Told me I'd get the rest when he confirmed that your wife had fallen overboard and drowned."

"All to be a tragic accident, then," Delaney said more to himself than to the fidgeting man. "So our heavyset gentleman is still in San Francisco."

"I don't know. I came back here . . ." Hoolihan swallowed, his eyes dropping before the fury in Delaney's.

"Yes, you returned to arrange another accident. Well, Hoolihan, I've decided that your trip to the Orient can wait awhile. You, my friend, are going to keep very close company with Monk. You're going to find this man for me. Do you understand?"

Hoolihan nodded readily, so relieved that he couldn't speak for a moment.

"Monk, Jed!" Delaney turned to look at the men ambling toward him. What a collection of utter villains, he thought with grim amusement.

Delaney didn't return home right away. Instead he called his loyal assistant, Jarvis, into his office and gave him instructions. He was to visit every hotel in San Francisco and inquire after the Englishman. He gave Jarvis enough money for bribes and sent him on his way. Bless Jarvis, he thought. He'd asked no questions, merely nodded.

Delaney walked back to South Park, deep in thought. He tried to concentrate on all Hoolihan had told him, only to have Chauncey's passion-lit eyes appear in his mind. Until yesterday she'd never before initiated their lovemaking, much less touched his body with such excited and dedicated interest and possessiveness. Even when she'd turned utterly wanton after her fright, she'd been passive, letting him bring her release, staying somehow separate from him. But not yesterday, not twice during the night. He smiled briefly, picturing her as she'd caressed him, not really understanding his body well enough to know how to pleasure him. He'd taught her a bit, and she had reveled in it. He was sure of it. There had been no hesitancy in her, only excitement and love and tenderness. She'd given herself to him completely.

And she'd stopped him when he mentioned the sponge. The thought of her wanting him to plant his seed deep in her body had made him wild with passion.

No, he thought, clearing his mind. Not completely. There was still something hidden, something that held her back. Soon, he thought, he'd know. He would see it in her eyes the moment she recognized the Englishman from the description Hoolihan had provided. He stopped suddenly, uncertain if he wanted to know what she was keeping from him. Don't be a fool, he told himself firmly. Whatever it was couldn't be that bad.

She held me tightly, keeping me deep within her, keeping my seed deep within her. "God, I'm thinking like a randy goat," he said aloud, and watched a pigtailed Chinese eye him oddly as he passed.

He found her drinking tea with Agatha Newton in the drawing room. She sucked in her breath when she saw him. Joy filled her face, and she jumped to her feet, rushing to him.

"Good afternoon, love," he said, giving her a quick kiss. "Hello, Aggie. Any interesting gossip?"

"Oh Lord, isn't there always?" Agatha grinned at him. "I'll be sure to pass along that Mr. and Mrs. Delaney Saxton are still on their honeymoon."

"That," he said, squeezing Chauncey, "is nothing less than the truth." *But how much longer will it last? What will she say, how will she react when I confront her?*

"Well, I can see that my presence is the last thing you two want at this moment." Agatha rose and shook out her burgundy skirts. "I'll see you tomorrow, Chauncey—that is, if your husband will allow you out of his sight."

Chauncey flushed, smiled, and murmured something unintelligible.

"Give my best to Horace, Aggie," Delaney said. He released his wife and walked with Agatha to the front door. She paused a moment, planting her bonnet firmly over her gray hair. "You're a lucky man, Del," she said. "Very lucky."

"Yes," he said, grinning down at her, "yes, I know that."

"Just don't forget it, young man," she said, poking him in the stomach. "Lucas," she called out, "fetch my man for me! He's likely ogling the new maid at the Butler's house!"

Delaney returned to the drawing room. Chauncey was standing in the middle of the room, her eyes narrowed on the carpet, her shoulders slumped.

He took her into his arms. "Do you know, I like that yellow silk gown. You're the only woman I know who looks almost as delightful with clothes as without."

"I . . . Thank you, Del. I wasn't expecting you home so early."

"I enjoyed your greeting."

"Well, I was surprised."

He gently pushed her back and studied her face a moment before saying baldly, "My men found Hoolihan."

She sucked in her breath. "Hoolihan," she repeated blankly.

"Yes. I had quite a long chat with the fellow.

Indeed, sweetheart, although he didn't know the name of the man who'd hired him, he gave me an excellent description. He is English, of course. I imagine that he followed you here after his failure to eliminate you in Plymouth."

Paul Montgomery. He's going to describe Paul Montgomery! She jerked away from him and planted herself behind a chair, her fingers gripping the back until her knuckles showed white. *Oh God, what am I going to do?* "Tell me," she said tersely.

He did, carefully and precisely, his eyes never wavering from her face. *She knows who he is, he thought. She knows.*

"Tell me his name, Chauncey," he said.

She looked at him wildly. She couldn't tell him, not like this! Not without . . . *Without what, you fool? Without making him love you first, without giving yourself a chance to make him understand.* She felt trapped, helpless and afraid.

"Hoolihan is going to help us find him," Delaney said after a long moment. "It would help, sweetheart, if you'd tell me who he is." The silence was thick between them. He had to push her. He said very calmly, "If you don't tell me, Chauncey, I'm putting you on the next ship back to England."

"No! Please, Del, you can't!" She gulped. He would do just as he said, she knew it. "Very well," she said. "His name is Paul Mont . . . Montsorrel. He is . . . *was* my father's solicitor. I've known him since I was a child."

"Why would he want you dead, Chauncey?"

She was rubbing her arms, her movements jerky. "Greed," she burst out. "He was furious when I didn't allow him to handle my money. Indeed, my aunt and uncle went to him, blackening my name, trying to have me sued for breach of promise."

"Chauncey," he said very quietly, "Hoolihan said this Paul Montsorrel indicated to him that you knew too much. That doesn't seem to have anything to do with greed."

"No, no, it doesn't," she said numbly. "But I can't believe he would try to kill me!"

"Tell me the rest of it. Now."

If I tell you all of it, I'll be on my way back to England before the end of the week! "Very well," she said. "I . . . I discovered that he was cheating my father. Indeed, I shouldn't have been a pauper upon my father's death, but he'd stolen all the money." It was the truth. And it didn't make sense. "Why, Del? Why would he want me dead?"

"Why didn't you tell me this before?"

She flung her hands before her as if to ward off his words. "I don't know."

She knew what his next question would be. "Just how did you discover what he'd done, Chauncey? And upon discovering it, why didn't you have the man arrested?"

"I couldn't prove anything, nothing! I wanted only to leave England and him and all the awful memories."

He knew her well enough to realize she was mixing truth with lies, but he didn't know which was which. Jesus, would he ever unravel all of this mess? One thing he did know: Chauncey wasn't a coward or a frightened, timid female. If she'd believed this Paul Montsorrel guilty, she'd never have left him unpunished. Montsorrel. In-

deed, was that the man's real name? He sighed
deeply and ran his fingers through his hair. He
simply had to gain her trust.

When Lucas returned from the post office the
next morning, bringing him a letter from his
brother, Alex, he realized trust had nothing to do
with anything.

— 22 —

Alex's bold handwriting blurred a moment before Delaney's eyes. One meager paragraph, he thought in ironic amusement, perhaps only a hundred words. Those words written by his brother could have been about anything: Nicholas, his nephew, as black-eyed as his father; or Leah, his lovely niece; or ... *Stop it, you bloody fool! You wanted to know the truth!* But he'd wanted Chauncey to tell him. He forced his eyes downward and read yet again that meager paragraph that had suddenly changed his life.

"Incidentally, Del, Giana received a letter from her mother shortly after I wrote to you. It seems that that Englishman, Sir Alec FitzHugh, indeed left a daughter. What's more, he left her penniless! I believe the plot thickens. Then, like Cinderella, the girl received a huge inheritance from a Sir Jasper Dunkirk. Funny thing is that the young lady left England very soon thereafter. The duchess says the girl's aunt and uncle Penworthy were screaming breach of promise for their son. It would be interesting to know, the duchess suggested, just why Sir Alec's solicitor, Paul Montgomery, had turned colors so quickly and maligned the young lady himself, since he'd known her all her life and was supposedly loyal to the Jameson FitzHugh family. Further, she wondered where all the money you'd faithfully sent had gone."

Paul Montsorrel. Paul Montgomery.

"Jesus," he said softly. "Elizabeth Jameson FitzHugh." His first thought, oddly enough, was whether his marriage was valid. Chauncey hadn't provided her complete name.

He reread Alex's final words. "I have already written to the duchess and assured her that you've been sending money like a regular trooper, supposedly to Sir Alec. I doubt not that she'll see to that damned bounder Montgomery."

Delaney slowly lowered the letter to his desktop and calmly folded it back into its envelope. So many damned twists and turns! But Chauncey knew that Paul Montgomery was swindling her father. Then why had she come to San Francisco? Why had she so assiduously sought him out?

"You stupid ass," he said to himself, "she believed that you were the guilty party! Montgomery must have convinced her of it." She'd come to San Francisco to get her revenge upon him. He made an effort to close off all the myriad impli-

cations of her act, at least for the moment. Montgomery was the immediate problem. Certainly
he had to realize that she would discover the
truth eventually. Why murder? *My father died
from laudanum.* He froze. Dear God, had the man
murdered Sir Alec? Certainly Sir Alec must have
wondered where all the money was going. Had
he confronted Montgomery?

I discovered he was cheating my father.

So Chauncey had read the papers in his desk
and knew he was innocent. He thought about her
nearly uncontrolled outburst over the fire at the
warehouse. Had she been responsible? Her revenge against him? But she discovered the truth.
Very slowly he opened the bottom drawer in his
desk and pulled out the box containing all the
records and correspondence. He examined the
lock closely; she'd done a good job of it, but it
had been picked. The papers inside were neatly
in place, but he knew. He knew she'd read them.

*She hated you so much she was willing to marry
you to gain her revenge.*

That hidden part of her, always puzzling to
him, always elusive, was now explained. He closed
his eyes a moment against the pain, anger, and
utter outrage he felt. He rose very slowly from
his chair, placed the box under his arm, and
walked upstairs to their bedroom.

Chauncey was seated before her dressing table, Mary braiding her thick hair into a fat plait
to be wound atop her head.

"Leave us, Mary."

"Oh, Mr. Del! Certainly, sir." It was the time
of reckoning; Mary knew it. She sent her mis-

tress a quick encouraging smile. Very quietly she left the room, closing the door firmly behind her.

In the mirror Chauncey saw the box under his arm, and grew very still. She'd been so careful. He couldn't know!

"Good morning," she said in a bright voice, turning on the brocade stool to face him. "It's a beautiful day, isn't it? Not a bit of fog. Lucas was telling me that during the summer—"

"Shut up," he said very calmly.

She searched his face. It was closed to her, expressionless, but she felt the fury radiating from him.

"You know," she said dully.

"Yes, I know. Perhaps I know more than you do, wife."

She flinched at the emphasis he'd placed on "wife." Sarcastic and cold. She rose and clasped her arms over her breasts. His eyes, always filled with humor and tenderness for her, were narrowed and glittered like molten gold. "Del, please, you must listen to me. You can't really understand, you can't—"

"I'd suggest that you keep your tongue between your teeth, Chauncey, and listen to me instead. You know," he continued in an even, detached tone, "I never could really understand why you chased me so assiduously. Indeed, from the moment you arrived in San Francisco, you were searching for me. Tell me, why did you decide to go to such lengths as to talk me into marriage?"

She found herself wringing her hands, and quickly flattened her palms against her dressing gown. "I understood that you were going to marry Penelope Stevenson. I couldn't allow that. The money from both families was too much. I couldn't have . . . ruined you. But, Del—"

"Ah, perfectly understandable," he interrupted her, his tone one of polite interest. "You staged that charming accident with your mare, only it backfired on you. You let that much slip, remember? I was very flattered, I suppose, that you would go so far to get into my house, to be close to me. I just had no idea how deeply the waters ran." He raised a stilling hand. "No, I am not finished yet, wife. Let me tell you that I am not quite a fool, though through your eyes I may appear to be the most gullible creature alive. But had you faked an injury, I would have seen through it, so even your concussion and cracked ribs worked in your favor. After all, what is a little honest pain compared to the prize you wanted? Remember your nightmare? I held you in my arms, wanting nothing more than to ease your fear and make you happy. Ah, and think of our wedding night. Did your skin crawl when I, your sworn enemy, touched your body? Took your innocence? Because I was your sworn enemy, was I not?"

"Yes." *I have to make you understand!* "I wanted to tell you everything, I swear it! Please, just listen to me for a minute. It all began in London when I was living with the Penworthys. I overheard my aunt tell my uncle that my father hadn't died of natural causes, but rather committed suicide. I went to see Paul Montgomery to demand the truth. It was then he told me about you and what you had done to my father. Of course I believed him! I'd known him all my life!"

"Did you come here to kill me or just ruin me?"

"I never wanted to kill you, I couldn't! I am not that . . . kind of person."

"Ah, my dear, perhaps not. But you are the most cold-blooded bitch it has ever been my privilege to encounter. No, please do not try my patience further with your protestations. You did set fire to the warehouse, didn't you? I can see the answer in your eyes. How very . . . driven you were, to risk your own life to hurt me."

"It was an accident, Del! When I was standing in the warehouse, I knew you couldn't be guilty, but guilty or not, I couldn't do it because I loved you! I couldn't hurt you. I thought the match was burned out, but it fell on those awful fireworks!"

"And then"—he placed the box carefully on a tabletop—"then you read the correspondence. Yesterday, I would gather. I wondered at your . . . sweetness and enthusiasm, my dear. You became a positive wild thing in my bed. No, don't interrupt me, Chauncey. I don't believe I could stand hearing how you really wanted to make love to me, to prove to yourself and to me that you'd forgiven me what I'd never done!"

"But it's true!" She crossed the few feet between them and clutched at his lapels. "Del, please, I know that what I've done makes it difficult for you to trust me now, but I believed Paul Montgomery! I—"

He took her hands from his coat and shoved her away. "All you had to do was ask me, Chauncey, confront me."

"Confront you! And if you had been guilty,

what would you have done? Admitted everything to me and begged my forgiveness? Marched to jail? I doubt that, Del! More likely you would have had me removed permanently!"

"Yes," he said slowly, "I suppose I would have had you killed, killed just like Montgomery probably murdered your father."

Her eyes widened with shock, and she whirled away from him, holding her arms tightly around her body. "Oh God, no!" Her voice was a thread of sound, anguished and disbelieving.

"I deduced it only a while ago. I couldn't believe that Montgomery would want you dead simply because you would discover that he'd swindled your father. No, it had to be something more. I don't understand why you didn't figure it out, my dear. Your mind, I have discovered, is quite creative."

"It didn't occur to me," she said, raising her head. "It still seems impossible." Her eyes were dazed, haunted. "He killed my father all because of money? A man he'd known for years and called friend? An 'uncle' who never forgot to send me gifts at Christmas?'

"And now this man wants you dead. It seems believable enough to me. He has to be pretty desperate to have followed you from England. With you gone, my dear, he could return to London and live quite well his ill-gotten gains. I imagine he isn't too happy that you married me, for if you had been killed in Plymouth, your aunt and uncle, not I, would have inherited all your money. Doubtless he would have managed to get his hands on a goodly portion of your funds before turning over the rest to the Penworthys. But regardless, he would have been safe. At least he would think himself safe. My brother, Alex, has already written to the Duke and Duchess of Graffton telling them of Montgomery's perfidy. Odd, isn't it, that he would lose after going to all the trouble of removing you?"

It is just as I thought it would be, Chauncey realized, staring fixedly at her husband but not really hearing his words. He hates me now. He wants to hate me.

"I did what I believed right!" she burst out, her hands fisted at her sides. "What would you have done, damn you?"

Delaney stroked his jaw, studying her flushed face. "I already told you what I would have done," he said matter-of-factly. "I would have confronted you—something, my dear, that you didn't have the guts to do. Had I believed you guilty, I would have killed you."

"I am a woman! What did you expect me to do? Challenge you to a duel? Damn you, Delaney! I sought to ruin you, as I thought you had my father. Only I couldn't figure out how to do it. Your holdings are too dispersed."

"But you hated me enough to take the risk of riding out in the night to the warehouse, knowing that someone wanted you dead. Your notion of revenge, my dear, is chilling. Even if you had burned all the goods and the warehouse to the ground, I wouldn't have been a begger—surely you realized that. After all, you are my wife, privy to the knowledge of where my money is. As your loving husband, I kept nothing from you."

"Yes, I know that. But I felt so guilty." Her

voice broke. "I was falling in love with you, yet I knew that I had to revenge my father. Even then, you won. The damned fire was an accident. Can't you believe that?"

Suddenly he started to laugh, a rumbling sound deep in his chest. "How deflated you must have felt," he gasped, "when I told you I'd never had any intention of marrying Penelope! By then you were stuck with me as your husband. Poor Chauncey! Tell me, wife, what were your thoughts then?"

"No, I wasn't deflated," she said. "You told me before we were married. I am trying to tell you the truth, Del, all of it. I decided to marry you because I would, of course, be close to you, live in your house, and be able to learn of all your business plans."

"Didn't you realize that I would want you as my wife in every way?"

"Yes, but I wasn't certain what it was all about." She raised her chin in defiance. "I decided I could bear anything, that I had to bear it."

"As I recall," he said, his voice thick with mockery, "after the threat on your life aboard the *Scarlet Queen*, you very nearly ravished my poor body. Did you despise yourself afterward for being such a wild bitch?"

"Yes."

"Well, that is honesty of a sort. And after you'd ruined me, what was your plan?"

"To leave you. Tell you that it was I who had ruined you, and why."

"Ah, your profound desire to avoid conceiving my child. Do you know, dear wife, that I asked my mistress about contraception? Marie thought it a great joke."

"I could be pregnant with your child at this moment, Del."

He was drawn up at the soft pleading in her voice. "Yes, I suppose you could," he said slowly. "Let us hope that I am not so virile, my dear. It would not be particularly pleasant for you to return to England carrying a babe in your womb, would it?"

No, she would't accept it. It couldn't be over. She lowered her head in silent supplication. "I . . . I don't want to leave. I want to be your wife. I want to have your children."

"Chauncey, I have been a great fool."

She raised her head, hope in her eyes.

"If I were to allow you to remain, I would be that much greater a fool. All this time, I wanted you to trust me. Oh yes, I knew you were keeping something from me. But now I really don't give a damn if you trust me or not, because you see, my dear, I don't trust you."

He turned abruptly and strode from the room.

"Del, wait!" But he was gone.

He did not return the rest of the day, nor that night. The following morning, he came into the bedroom.

"What are you doing?"

Chauncey whirled about at the sound of his voice. She gestured helplessly at the open valise on the bed. "I'm packing my things."

"You will need different things where we're going."

She stared at him, hope once again building in her. "What do you mean?"

"When it rains, it pours, it would appear. I received a message late yesterday that there were more troubles at the Midnight Star mine in Downieville. This is the mine, you doubtless know, that earned such great amounts of money for Paul Montgomery. I can't leave you here—I'm not that great a villain. You'd probably be found drowned in the bay within the week. I think it somewhat ironic that you should see the property that started this entire charade. You'll need sturdy clothes. I'll send Mary to you."

He turned at the doorway. "I am hoping that by the time we return, Lucas and my men will have tracked down Montgomery and . . . taken care of him."

She had gained more time. She felt dizzy with relief.

"Then, my dear," he added quietly, "you can return to your packing. Incidentally, wife, it is entirely possible that Mary won't be leaving with you. It appears that she and Lucas have found that they care for each other. Life can sometimes be very simple and uncomplicated, can it not?"

Delaney kept his face carefully expressionless even when she looked as if he'd struck her. Thank God he'd never told her that he loved her. He felt himself weaken. Words, cruel words, erupted from his throat as he watched her. "Of course I shall initiate divorce proceedings here. England is quite a bit more difficult, I understand. Because I am a gentleman, I shall take the blame. Adultery, perhaps."

"That probably won't be untrue," she said bitterly.

"Ah yes, I keep forgetting that you know me so

very well. I shall be certain that my next wife will allow *me* to court *her*. We leave early in the morning, Chauncey. No," he added thoughtfully, "not Chauncey. Elizabeth Jameson FitzHugh shouldn't have such an intimate, carefree nickname. Yes, Elizabeth. By the way, we are legally married. I checked with my lawyer. Even though you omitted your complete name, we are tied to each other—for a short time, at least. There is something else, my dear. It is quite possible that the agreement I signed before we were married, allowing you to keep control of your money, isn't valid. Misrepresentation, I believe my lawyer called it. Wouldn't that be ironic? But trust me, my dear, not to send you back to England a pauper. Not a complete pauper, in any case."

The following morning they boarded the beautiful steamer *Senator* for the hundred-mile journey to Sacramento. Chauncey was wearing the only lovely gown she'd brought. She was thankful for the warmth of the burgundy velvet mantle, for the morning was chilly, with fog blanketing the city. How different this will be from our last trip, she thought, staring vaguely around her. Her eyes searched the crowds of people. Was Paul Montgomery there somewhere, watching her? Probably not. Delaney had been too careful.

Delaney was carrying their valises, only two of them, for he told her that they would be traveling light once they'd left the steamer to journey inland. She'd spent several strained and silent hours the day before with Mary, Lucas, and Olaf following discreetly, buying the sturdy clothes Del had ordered. She had bought two split skirts in heavy wool and two loose-fitting linen blouses. Even her underthings were utterly practical. And stout boots. She paid with her own money.

Late that evening the steamer turned into the Sacramento River, but Chauncey wasn't aware of it. She dined alone in their stateroom, her thoughts in turmoil. Delaney had simply withdrawn from her. He was polite—oh yes, chillingly so.

"You will stay here, my dear. I trust you have sense enough to obey me in this."

"Yes," she said, "I will stay here." She raised her chin slightly, her eyes searching his face. "And you?"

"I think I will do what most men do—gamble a bit, smoke a cheroot, and drink a good glass of port."

"You will not dine with me?"

"I believe it would be best if I did not. My civilized veneer just might peel away by the second course. I will see you later, my dear."

Oh yes, so polite.

She ate little, though the terrapin was doubtless delicious, the green beans fresh and crisp. It was several hours before she fell into a restless sleep, her thoughts moving ahead to the trip they were taking. They would be alone, away from civilization. Please, she prayed to herself, let him forgive me. She wondered if his reaction would have been different had she told him herself who she really was and why she'd come to San Francisco, told him before he discovered it for himself. Would it have made any difference?

She was jerked awake by an insistent hand shaking her shoulder.

"We are getting off, Chauncey. Wake up and dress warmly."

"But it's not even daylight," she said vaguely, pushing her hair out of her face.

"The steamer docks at five o'clock. We will board another, smaller steamer for Marysville. 'Tis but fifty miles, but I don't want to lose any time."

"We're in Sacramento?"

"Yes, but you won't see much of the town. We'll board the *Miner* at seven o'clock."

She couldn't prevent herself, and asked, "Where did you spend the night, Del?"

She made out his sardonic expression in the dim cabin light. "I don't believe you really want to know, my dear."

"No," she agreed, "you are probably right."

Thirty minutes later, she stood beside her husband on deck as the *Senator* docked in Sacramento. She could make out little of the town, save that it had a very unfinished look due to the terrible fire of the year before. There were no vast sandy hills, just flat stretches with row upon row of wooden buildings. Even this early in the morning, the wharf area was chaotic with vendors, merchants, builders, drays, and every sort of wagon.

Delaney took her arm firmly and guided her down the gangplank onto the wide wooden wharf. "The *Miner* is close by," he said, pointing over to the next long plank of wood stretching into the river.

Again Chauncey found herself marveling at the mix of people: Chinese men with their raven-black hair braided down their backs, Spanish men in colorful sombreros and vests, and black men, tall and muscular in their loose-fitting white shirts. But the majority of the men wore jackets, many of them torn and disreputable-looking, and dirty boots pulled up over their trousers.

They remained in the main salon of the steamer. At least Delaney didn't leave her side. She watched the men playing cards and chewing tobacco. Even young boys!

"At least they don't spit!" she said, remembering the times she'd winced at the sight of men, even well-dressed gentlemen, spitting in any corner available.

"No, but watch," Delaney said. He was smiling slightly, but not at her. She followed his gaze to a boy no more than twelve years old. The lad was chewing tobacco. He pulled out a pocket handkerchief and spit the revolting brown wad into it.

The passage to Marysville took longer than expected, for the river had had little rainfall and there was the constant danger of becoming stuck on barely submerged sandbanks. Chauncey stood at the railing, watching everything silently. Occasionally some hills came into view, and here and there were glimpses of a mountain chain. For the most part, though, the scenery was monotonous. Pale green hills dotted with occasional scraggily bushes and scrub oaks.

"We won't be stopping at Hock Farm," Delaney said. "General Sutter and his sons are interesting men. Due north is Mount Shasta, the highest point of the Sierra Nevada Mountains."

Chauncey listened to the sound of his voice, not really caring what he said. He sounded tired, and she felt waves of concern. How ironic, she thought. How very ironic.

She jumped at the sound of a shout from one of the sailors.

"Marysville!"

— **23** —

Chauncey stared toward the small town coming into view. It was a motley collection of tents and wooden structures haphazardly set down, it seemed to her, with no rhyme or reason. There was not one tree within fifty yards of the town, cut down, she supposed, during the winter for fires. Still some hundred yards away, she could already feel the excitement and that particular sort of chaos that she'd sensed when she first arrived in San Francisco. There were men standing on the long dock wildly waving their felt hats toward the steamer. Chauncey moved closer to Delaney, for the passengers were spilling out onto the deck. Mrs. Dobbs, a most fascinating woman with the reddest hair Chauncey had ever seen, brushed by her.

"Excuse me, dearie. Quite a crush, ain't it?"

"Yes, ma'am. I find it most interesting." She turned to Delaney. "Actually, I feel like I'm in a different world."

Delaney well understood what she meant, but to him Marysville had changed immensely over the past three years. Gold seekers had scored the virgin land, making it look raw and ugly as sin. That was doubtless what she'd meant. She scorned it. He refused to let himself be drawn to her, to understand her, to smile at her. The past day and a half had been a trial and he'd asked himself over and over why he had brought her here. He hadn't believed she would be in any real danger in San Francisco.

It is likely she's in more danger here in the wilds.

He refused to think about it and he refused to smile. He asked in a cold, indifferent voice, "It is not like your decadent, overripe England, is it?"

"No," she said slowly, her brief excitement crushed, "it is not."

He's fighting me. He's fueling his anger. She understood, but his flippant words hurt, hurt badly.

She looked toward Mrs. Dobbs, now waving wildly toward the men on shore, laughing and shouting. "I hope her family is here to meet her," she said.

Delaney laughed coldly. "So you don't recognize a kindred spirit?"

"What do you mean?"

"Your Mrs. Dobbs is a whore, of course. She's like your England, a bit overripe and blown, but the men in Marysville will welcome her with open arms, so to speak."

At last he had drawn her. Her fingers itched to strike him, but she didn't. She drew a deep breath and asked calmly, "Is a wife who responds to her husband considered a whore?"

"Doubtless, if she does it for a reason other than . . . affection. I would at least consider you an honest whore had you demanded money from me."

"Very well. How much should I charge you?"

"You've already taken all I would ever consider paying you."

It was no use, she thought. He's keeping me at two arms' lengths. She forced herself to shrug and look back at the town. "I cannot help but wonder what it will look like in, say, ten years. Surely the gold will be gone by then. Do you believe the people will stay and build up the town?"

"It isn't quite so bad as you think, my dear. Last time I was here, there were a good six thousand folk living in Marysville and they boasted a theater and two newspapers. More culture than most of your English towns have, I daresay. Why, there are nearly as many goods available in the stores as there are in Sacramento."

"What are the names of the rivers?"

"We're at the head of the Feather and the Yuba. We'll spend the night here, then leave tomorrow morning on horseback for Downieville."

"There are many gold mines here?"

"Indeed, and quartz mines as well. On the average, the quartz yields about thirteen percent of gold. Fascinating, isn't it?"

His voice was mocking, but she didn't respond, only said quietly, "I should like to see how it is done."

"Perhaps, if you ever decide to visit again, you

will see all the fascinating shafts and galleries, even the gold washings on the Yuba River. Shall I continue about the wooden channels?"

"No, I cannot picture your words in my mind."

"But I've begun to believe you very inventive, my dear, particularly in bed. I vow that with more intense practice, you could rival even Marie."

She flinched, and did not reply.

Marysville did boast a number of shops, stores, and countless gaming saloons. Chauncey walked beside Delaney down the main street of the town, careful to keep the hem of her gown out of the wide mud puddles. It was warm and she soon felt a trickle of sweat between her breasts. She was constantly aware of men stopping to stare at her, open admiration in their eyes. She found herself wondering if it was all worth it, the frantic search for gold, living in such primitive conditions, without the comfort of a family.

"We will stay here tonight," she heard Delaney say.

The Golden Goose was a two-story hotel that appeared to have just been built. It looked raw and unfinished. A very old man stood behind the narrow counter. Too old to search for gold, Chauncey thought. He kept rubbing his lower back.

Their small room was on the second floor and overlooked the main street. There were a narrow bed, a basin on an old commode, and a doorless armoire against one wall. Delaney would have to sleep with her tonight, she thought, and wondered what she would do.

He was wondering the same thing. He needed

a good night's sleep, but knew at the same time that it would be misery to lie beside her and not take her in his arms. He cursed softly under his breath. He saw her stare at him, her expressive eyes showing uncertainty and bewilderment at his unexpected spate of foul language. There were many things he had to do, but he wasn't quite so cruel as to force her to remain in their room the rest of the day.

"Change into something more appropriate, my dear," he said finally, "and we will see the town and buy supplies."

There was no screen, nothing. Chauncey said quietly to Delaney's back, "I need your help with my buttons."

He ground out his cheroot and turned from the window. "Not much of a frontier wife, are you? Helpless without a servant to take care of you."

"With the new clothes I bought, I'll not need a servant, shall I?"

He felt like a fool, drawing her and baiting her. He frowned at her back as he fiddled with the tiny buttons. He wanted her to fight back, not respond to him with such damned reasonableness, as if she didn't even care.

"I see you still aren't wearing a corset."

"No," she said, trembling slightly at the touch of his fingers against her bare back.

"Perhaps you should consider it. It improves a woman's figure immensely." *Damned liar! You can span her waist with your hands!*

"Surely you would not wish me to wear one now?" she asked, wondering how her voice could sound so very calm and self-assured. "We will be traveling by horseback and camping in the open, won't we?"

"Yes," he said, forcing his eyes away from the nape of her neck. "It will be an experience for you, the perfect little lady from England trekking about in the wilderness. Tell me, do you think you can even light a fire outdoors?"

She shoved the gown from her shoulders and let it fall to the floor at her feet. Did she hear him suck in his breath? "You must know the answer to that," she said, bending down to pick up her gown. She straightened and turned to face him, clutching her discarded gown over her breasts. "You must also know that I can learn, and I will. I won't delay you, Delaney, or be a burden."

Why was she hiding her body from him? he wondered perversely. He said aloud, wanting to get a rise from her, "Really, my dear wife, such modesty. Isn't it a bit late for this maidenly display?"

She looked at him for a long moment, and came to a decision. Slowly she lowered the gown and tossed it to the back of the lone chair. She pulled the straps of her chemise from her shoulders and felt the soft satin glide down to her waist.

Delaney stared at her breasts; he couldn't help himself. His body responded, and he whispered softly, "Damn you, Chauncey."

"Is ten ounces of gold too little to ask?" She stared at him straightly, drawing back her shoulders so that her breasts thrust toward him. "Should I perhaps ask more?"

He turned on his heel and strode to the door of

their room. He said over his shoulder, not looking at her, "I'll be back soon. Go to bed." He slammed out.

He returned late that afternoon, telling her shortly that he'd seen to buying the necessary supplies. He took her to the *Colleen* Restaurant, owned, he told her, by two Irishmen. After a silent meal of delicious beef stew, he took her back to the hotel and left her at the door of their room.

She slipped between the cold sheets and felt her body slide toward the middle of the lumpy mattress. She couldn't seem to find a prayer that covered all the problems she faced, and settled for a "Please, God, please make everything all right."

She heard Delaney come into the room a good hour later. He moved about quietly, but she heard the sound of his boots dropping to the wooden floor. She said nothing, pretending sleep.

When the bed gave under his weight, she held her breath. He rolled against her, cursed long and fluently under his breath, and struggled back to his side of the bed.

The next morning, it was Chauncey who awoke first. She struggled to a sitting position and gazed over at her husband. He was lying on his stomach, his face turned toward her on the pillow. His soft honey-colored hair was tousled, and the angry lines she'd become accustomed to seeing the past couple of days were smoothed out, making him look younger and as vulnerable as a boy. Without her conscious volition, her hand reached to touch his jaw lightly. Light brown stubble scratched against her fingers. Dear Lord, she loved him so much! But it was too late, much too late. It had been too late before she had ever met him.

She wondered vaguely when she had begun to love him. She could still picture his twinkling eyes when he had danced with her that first night at the Stevensons' ball, when she hadn't yet known who he was. He had baited her, mocked her, and teased her. He had made her laugh. She thought of his hands on her body, stroking her, giving her such pleasure, and she shuddered. She had long forgotten the pain and mortification of her wedding night, but even then, she thought now, he had been tender and careful with her, careful not to offend her, careful not to hurt her. She felt a wave of utter hopelessness wash through her, and lowered her head.

"Don't cry, damn you!"

She sniffed, not looking at him. "I'm not crying."

"Good, for I've given you nothing concrete to weep about!" He thrust back the covers and slid out of bed. He was naked. "You like what you see, wife?"

She recoiled from his sneering voice. "Yes," she said, raising her face, "I do. I always have. You are very beautiful."

Delaney turned his back to her, unable to think of a retort. He did not bother dressing until he'd shaved and washed. "Well," he said, turning to her, "it's time to get up. We're leaving within the hour. And wear your sturdy clothes."

She did as he bid her. Once they were both dressed, they regarded each other with surprise. He was garbed as she'd never seen him: buckskin pants, black boots, and a full-sleeved white shirt with vest and jacket. He strapped a gunbelt about his waist.

"You look so different," she said.

"And don't you look the perfect little prairie maiden," he said coldly, but secretly he thought she looked beautiful dressed in her wool split skirt, white blouse, her hair braided into a thick plait down her back.

"I trust it will be appropriate," she said.

"Keep your jacket out. It will get chilly in the mountains."

"Very well," she said.

They packed their valises in silence, then made their way downstairs to eat in the small dining room in the hotel. "Eat up," he said. "From now on we'll be cooking for ourselves. Since you know nothing about it, I'll be the chef."

The old man who had been at the counter served them a platter of scrambled eggs, bacon, and a pile of dry toast.

"Yer goin' inland?"

Delaney nodded. "To Downieville."

"Chancy weather, I heard. Long ride."

"A good seventy miles overland. Any Indians about?"

"Always are. Bloody beggars are always gettin' their dander up and causin' trouble. Yer missus travelin' with ye?"

"Yes."

"Awful purty, beggin' yer pardon, ma'am. Don't see too many ladies like ye about. Ye dress warm, ma'am."

Chauncey smiled at him, for his were the first kind words she'd heard in many days.

"Buy yerself some gloves, else you'll regret it."

Delaney frowned. He'd forgotten about gloves. He looked at her soft white hands.

"It's all right, Del," she said quickly. "I know you want to get an early start. I don't need gloves."

"Of course you do. I'll wake up old Joe Cribbs at the general store. Now, finish your breakfast. It will be the last good meal you'll have in about three days."

She lowered her head and ate.

Why, he asked himself yet again, had he brought her? And why did he want to travel overland to Downieville? More time alone with her, you ass.

They rode northeast, Delaney setting a brisk pace. They stayed within sight of the Yuba River, passing miners standing knee-deep in the water, and small camps. Delaney didn't stop, nor did he speak to her. The sun was high in the sky when he finally called a halt. Chauncey slipped down from her mare's back and felt her legs wobble a bit. She hadn't ridden for such a length of time since she was sixteen. She stamped her feet a bit and wandered to the edge of a bluff that overlooked the Yuba River. God, but it was beautiful! She flung her arms wide, embracing the grandeur of the giant fir trees that studded the hills all about them. The gentle barren rolling hills had ceased about an hour before. "I feel as if I'm the first person ever to be here," she said aloud. "Like I'm an artist who sees a painting no one else has ever seen."

Delaney well understood her awe. He felt it himself each time he journeyed to Downieville overland. He said, "Wear your hat. The sun is hot and you're burning."

She shot him a look from the corner of her eye. "Excuse me," she said, and walked toward a clump of bushes.

When she emerged, Delaney handed her a thick slice of bread spread with a dubious mixture. All she recognized were beans. She ate, not wanting to know the ingredients.

"I smell like a horse," she said.

"You'll not notice how either of us smell by tomorrow."

"It is so peaceful here."

"Yes."

"Will all the scenery be so beautiful, the land so wild?"

"No, not unless we go inland from the river. Even now, we're but two or three miles from a mining camp."

"Will we see Indians?"

"Most likely."

"What are they like?"

"For the most part, they're harmless, and helpless. It seems that for every one of us to come to California, one more of them dies. There are renegades, but to survive, they live deep in the forests. Are you finished eating?"

She handed him her plate, and he simply looked at it. "Rub it out with sand. I doubt there are any servants within hearing distance."

"You have but to tell me what to do, Del," she said, looking at him steadily.

"Rub it out with sand," he repeated.

Together they repacked the supply bags. Chauncey felt her muscles beginning to tighten and looked askance at her mare, Dolores. But Delaney had mounted gracefully and was giving her a silent, mocking glance.

She climbed into the saddle. At least she was riding astride. She couldn't begin to imagine enduring in a sidesaddle.

They moved a good mile inland, and there were no trails. For the most part, their horses walked, avoiding the thick brambles. Chauncey no longer heard the birds singing. She was growing less enthralled with the grandeur of the hills and forest. Her bottom felt raw, her legs numb.

She said nothing. She had promised she wouldn't slow him down, and she had no intention of complaining. She'd fall off her mare first.

Delaney saw her exhaustion and pushed another mile. He halted in a small clearing beside a glitteringly clear creek. "We'll stop here for the night. Rub down the horses, Chauncey, and see that they're well-tethered."

He paid her no more attention.

She sent a scathing look toward his back, gritted her teeth, and dismounted. Her legs collapsed and she clung to the pommel. Muscles in her thighs that she'd never dreamed existed were screaming.

"See to it, Chauncey! And collect some firewood. I'm going hunting."

She whirled around, her tortured muscles momentarily forgotten. "No," she called after him in a panic. "Don't leave me alone!"

Delaney turned and shifted his hat back on his forehead. "Even proper little English ladies have to pay for their supper. I'll be back soon. Just stick close to the horses after you've done your chores."

She stared after him as he disappeared into the trees, his rifle tucked under his arm.

"Sneering, unfeeling bastard," she said under her breath. "All right, Dolores, off with your saddle! Hank," she continued to Delaney's bay stallion, "you're next. Stop snorting at me and don't be so impatient."

An hour later, Chauncey was grinning to herself and warming her hands over the small fire she'd built. The bedrolls were laid out, the horses tethered close by, and at least her face and hands were clean. She sat cross-legged by the fire and leaned forward, cupping her chin against her fisted hands. The sun was near to setting. She tried to concentrate on the beauty of her surroundings, but failed miserably. The air grew chill, the silence deafening. She cried out at the sudden sharp report of a rifle.

"Talk to yourself, idiot. Yes, that's it. Hello, Dolores, Hank. Is the grass good? I don't think you need any more water."

Dolores whinnied.

Chauncey rose quickly to her feet, and weaved where she stood. Her muscles had tightened and cramps ripped through her. She was rubbing her bottom when Delaney emerged into the small clearing, a dead rabbit held in his hand. It was all Chauncey could manage not to flinch away.

She gulped and took a step backward, her expression appalled.

"Don't worry," Delaney said, "I won't ask you to soil your pretty hands. Nor do I want you to vomit on our dinner."

She couldn't help herself. She simply couldn't bear to see him skin the rabbit. She walked around the perimeter of their camp, trying to avoid looking at him and his revolting task, and easing her muscles.

"We'll eat in about twenty minutes," she heard him say. "Come here, and keep turning the rabbit on the spit. I'm going to bathe."

When he returned, he was shrugging back into his shirt. The water was frigid. Had he stripped and jumped in?

"I built the fire," she said, her voice a bit sharp. Damn him! She wasn't about to admire the play of muscles across his chest.

"Yes, I see. Matches are a great invention, are they not? Next time, build it more loosely, so air can circulate beneath. Like this."

She watched silently at he took several sticks and balanced them upright so they came together in a cone.

"The rabbit is done," she said.

"Burned to a crisp, rather."

"I set out the dishes and bedrolls."

"And talked at great length to the horses."

He'd heard her! "They are about the only amiable company I've found!"

He squatted in front of the fire and began to pull the burned meat from the bones. "Didn't you open any beans?"

"No." She stared at the rabbit meat, burned on the outside and quite rare on the inside.

"Watch me do it," he said.

They ate in silence. Chauncey didn't want to talk; she wanted to curl up, wrap herself in the bedroll, and groan her muscles to sleep. She eyed her bedroll laid out on the other side of the fire and moaned at the thought of getting to it. Perhaps she could crawl, or maybe roll.

"Next time, keep turning the meat."

"I thought it delicious," Chauncey snapped, her fingers tightening around a bone.

"Are you finished?"

"Yes."

"I'll sand out the plates while you collect more firewood. There are all sorts of interesting beasts in the forest. I don't want to share my bedroll with any of them."

Collect more firewood! She pulled herself to her knees. There wasn't a bush or anything to use as a support. Didn't he feel any discomfort at all? He was striding about as if he'd just gotten out of bed after a wonderful night's sleep. Get up, Chauncey!

She did, but found after leaning over to pick up some dead branches, that she couldn't move. She tossed her small collection beside the fire and collapsed on her bedroll.

Delaney's eyebrow shot up. He knew she was in agony. His muscles were a bit sore, and he was used to riding goodly distances. He strode to his valise and withdrew a small jar. He tossed it onto her lap. "It's liniment. It smells like manure, but it works. Rub it on your thighs and your bottom."

"Thank you," she said.

He went to collect more firewood, leaving her alone. She managed to pull off her skirt, boots, and underthings. She opened the jar and was rocked back at the dreadful smell. Manure! More like three-day-old dead fish! Still, she dipped a glob on her fingers and resolutely began to rub the chilly cream into her screaming thigh muscles.

She finished her legs and sat feeling like an utter fool. How the devil was she to do her bottom?

"Turn over on your stomach."

He was standing over her, legs spread, his hands on his hips. He looked like some kind of desperado, a word she'd heard Lucas use.

"More modesty? I've made a thorough study of your charms. Did you not promise that you wouldn't delay me? You won't be able to sit your mare tomorrow without my . . . assistance. Now, turn over."

She tugged her shirt over her thighs and slowly eased onto her stomach. She reared up when she felt her hips bared.

"Just hold still." He straddled her, his knees on either side of her thighs. She felt his fingers coated with the cream touch her buttocks.

Delaney stared down at his wife's beautiful white hips and saw the beginnings of bruises. He didn't gentle his touch, but kneaded her soft flesh deeply and firmly. She groaned, but he pressed his hand into the small of her back to keep her from moving. God, but he wanted her! He sucked in his breath and continued rubbing her, stroking her. His fingers slid between her thighs, and he felt the heat of her.

All he had to do was flip her onto her back and take her. He quickly wiped the liniment from his hand. His finger found her and slowly began to ease inside her.

She wanted to cry and yell at him at the same time. She heard his jerky breathing, felt his finger probing. "How much do you intend to pay me?"

His finger thrust deep within her.

"Stop it! Damn you, don't!" She tried to jerk away from him, but his knees were on either side of her thighs, and she couldn't move.

"You're my wife, and I'll take you when and where I want to."

"You don't want me, you just want to punish me and hurt me!"

His finger eased out of her and he pressed his hand under her to cup her. "Yes, I want you, wife, and if you would but touch yourself as I am doing, you'd see that you are as ready as a bitch in heat."

He moved his palm to her belly and she felt her own wetness on her fingers. Why not? she thought blankly to herself. At least for a few moments he would forget his anger. For a few moments he would respond to her as he used to.

"Very well," she said softly.

— 24 —

He went still. I am a civilized man, he thought, not some miserable savage. *But she wants you!*

He shook his head. He didn't know what she wanted. Slowly he eased his hand from under her and rose to his feet. He saw that her shoulders were shaking, and she'd buried her face in her crossed arms.

"You do smell like a horse," he said, turning away from her to stand by the small fire. "Dress yourself. A lady shouldn't lie about bare-assed."

She wasn't crying, she was too angry to shed more tears. His crude words hit her, and her fury grew. Slowly she turned onto her back and raised herself on her elbows. She was naked from the waist down and made no move to pull her shirt over her body.

"You don't smell too sweet yourself," she said furiously at his back. She willed him to turn around.

He did, and nearly stumbled at the sight of her. "Dress yourself," he repeated.

"Why?" she asked, stretching slightly, arching her back a bit. "You are my husband. As you said, you're thoroughly familiar with all my charms."

She was trying to put the boot on the other foot, and succeeding. He felt a bolt of admiration for her slash through him, and said coldly, "If you don't cover yourself now, madam, I will take you. Very quickly. You won't enjoy it, I promise you that."

She didn't move, only stared at him, her eyes luminous and unreadable in the dim campfire.

He began to unfasten the buttons of his buckskins. "You are willing to risk a babe in your belly when you return to England?"

He was a stranger to her in that moment, and she sought desperately to find the man she loved. "Will you never forgive me? Will you never try to understand?"

His desire was gone, and he wanted to laugh at the irony of it. Even if he wanted to punish her, he doubted he could do it. "I am going to relieve myself," he said, and strode into the darkness.

When he returned, she was covered with a blanket and lying on her side, her eyes closed.

His voice awoke her the next morning. She blinked awake and groaned. The ground, she thought inconsequentially, was not the same as a bed. She gritted her teeth and got to her feet. It was cold, the sun just breaking through the heavy foliage overhead.

"Collect firewood."

She said nothing, and did as he bid. Her muscles eased somewhat with the task. She was beginning to feel human again. How, she wondered, could people live like this day after day?

Delaney watched her moving about, at first stiffly, then more easily. She was as strong-willed and stubborn as a mule. When she returned to the camp, her arms loaded with small branches and twigs, he gave his full attention to making the coffee.

He laughed aloud suddenly, startling Chauncey, the horses, and the birds overhead. He realized he was trying to break her, for whatever reason. He laughed more deeply. If she broke, what would it prove?

"May I share your jest?"

"No," he said. "Build the fire as I showed you. I'm going to pack up the horses."

The coffee was black, bitter, and tasted better than any Chauncey had ever drunk. She gulped it down, burning her tongue. She sighed, shook out her tin cup, and rose.

"I'm ready," she said.

He grunted, not looking up at her.

She studied his averted face a moment, smiling unwillingly at the growth of beard on his cheeks. His hair was tousled, his white shirt no longer clean. She thought he had never looked so handsome.

"I'm going to the creek to wash my face," she said.

He nodded. "We're leaving in five minutes."

"Do you know, Del," she said thoughtfully, her hands on her hips, "if you don't make up your mind what you want, you will surely die of perversity."

"Five minutes," he repeated, for want of anything better to say. Damn her, but she was right, and he knew it.

Five minutes later, Chauncey eyed Dolores with misgiving. "Well, my dear," she said as she stroked her mare's silky nose, "there is no hope for it, is there? If you can keep going, so can I!"

The river wound away from them, snaking its way between narrow bluffs. Delany turned inland. The trees were so thick that the sun slashed through in narrow slivers of light. The silence would have been comforting had there been any conversation between them.

She wanted to ask him about the different kinds of trees she was seeing, but his face was closed. And the birds! So many of them, and she couldn't identify a single one. She saw deer, rabbits, squirrels, even a fox. They seemed to regard her with some disdain. She was, she supposed, a trespasser in their kingdom.

The day dragged on. Chauncey could feel her muscles cramping and wished she could slip her blanket under her bottom. Tomorrow, she thought, no matter Delaney's sarcastic, mocking comments, she would do it.

Delaney stopped in late afternoon, and Chauncey was momentarily surprised to see that there was another small creek near.

"You've come this way before, haven't you?"

The sound of her own voice after so many hours of silence startled her.

"Yes," he said.

He didn't find fault with her fire and she

didn't eye with too much revulsion the plump wild partridge he'd shot. She was careful to turn the partridge continually on the spit, and the result was mouth-watering.

"Either this is the best food in the entire world or I'm starving," she said.

"You're desperate," he said. After a moment he added, "I've always found that food cooked outdoors tastes better. Maybe it's the clean air or the added taste from the open fire."

"Goodness!" she exclaimed, eyeing him in astonishment. "So many words! And all spoken at one time!"

"You know, dear wife," he said, "I find my natural good humor disappearing in your charming company. May I suggest that you try keeping your sharp tongue behind your teeth?"

"Death by perversity," she muttered, and stalked away to lie on her bedroll.

Chauncey had fallen into a light sleep, having made peace with the hard ground, when she felt a hand clamped over her mouth. She jerked upright, struggling.

"Don't make a sound," Delaney whispered, tightening his hold on her. "Don't move. I'll be right back."

She felt a cold lump of fear in her throat. Bears, she thought wildly. Weren't there bears in forests? She pulled the blanket about her and stared toward the dark woods. Snakes? Could Delaney have heard a snake? Stop being a fool, she whispered behind her teeth. Snakes slither, they don't walk and make noise.

She shot up at the sound of three rapid gunshots.

"Delaney!"

There was no answer, nothing! Only the deadening silence. Her derringer! She rushed forward on her hands and knees, grabbing for her valise. She threw her clothes about, and closed her fingers over the small pistol. A foot smashed down on her hand.

She screamed in pain and fright, and the derringer fell from her fingers. An arm closed over her throat and she was dragged back.

It was a man, and he smelled dreadful. She could hear his harsh breathing, hear him grunt in pain when her elbow lashed back into his stomach. He hissed something at her, but she couldn't understand him. She was panting, struggling mindlessly. He jerked at her throat and she couldn't breathe. Her screams became gurgles of sound, but she didn't give up, even as her vision blurred. She kicked back, her boot connecting with the man's shin.

He grunted in fury and jerked her about to face him. She saw him for only a moment before his fist smashed against her jaw. An Indian, she thought vaguely, and fell into darkness.

Her nose twitched. What was that awful smell? She moved restlessly, opened her eyes, and blinked. Her face was pressed against a man's leg, and the filthy odor was from his buckskins. She tried to arch away from him, but a flash of pain went through her jaw, and she moaned softly.

She felt a hand press firmly against the small of her back, and her face fell again to his thigh. I'm going to vomit, she thought. She closed her eyes and swallowed.

The man was saying something to her. It was a string of low guttural sounds that had no meaning to her. She raised her chin, trying desperately to turn a bit so she could see him.

"Delaney," she whispered, the sound of her own voice causing more waves of pain in her head. "My husband! Where is he?"

The man was talking again, turning slightly on his horse's back, to speak to another man behind him.

Her nausea increased. She locked her teeth together. This is all a nightmare, she told herself over and over. This can't be happening. It is a thing woven from rotten cloth. I am going to wake up now. Delaney will be here. He will be all right. Wake up, you fool! She did, with a vengeance. She reared up against the man's hand, yelling a curse at the top of her lungs. For one instant she looked at him straight in the face.

Oh God! Even a nightmare couldn't produce such a terrifying image. Matted black hair hung about his face. His eyes, flat black coals, were close-set, his nose nearly flat against his cheeks, and his lips were parted, showing wide-spaced yellowing teeth.

"No!" she shrieked, and scored her fingernails down his bare chest.

He struck her on the side of the head, and she slumped unconscious against his thigh.

"No, please . . . no! Make it stop. Please!"

Chauncey felt a cool wet cloth on her forehead. I am dead and in hell, she thought vaguely. I won't open my eyes, not yet.

But she did. Kneeling above her was a young

woman. Then her vision cleared and she stared at the woman silently. Her features were flat and heavy, just as the man's had been, but her jet-black eyes held a measure of feeling, compassion perhaps. Her face was perfectly round, her thick black hair braided into two thick plaits that fell over her shoulders. She exuded the same noxious odor, and Chauncey's stomach lurched.

"Where am I?" she whispered, swallowing convulsively.

"You be still, lady," the woman said. "I take care of you."

"My husband," Chauncey said, her voice breaking. "Where is he?"

"Don't know. Chatca no say," the woman said, her voice as flat as her facial features.

"Who are you?"

"Father Nesbitt call me Cricket, after a famous white man. Father Nesbitt let me keep his house and teach me good English."

A priest with a bizarre sense of humor.

"Father Nesbitt dead because Chatca want me to go with him. You drink this, lady, make pain go away."

Chauncey opened her mouth and tasted a thick vile liquid. She gagged and tried to spit it out, but Cricket held her head, forcing her to swallow.

"Chatca say you a demon."

Chauncey fell back, her cheek touching a filthy matted fur. Some demon, she thought, hearing the admiration in the woman's voice. Lying helplessly, unable to fight even another woman. Her mouth began to grow dry, and she stared up at Cricket. "Will I die? Did you poison me?"

"No, you sleep. When you wake up, you feel better. Chatca want you better."

Chauncey slept dreamlessly. When she awoke, she was alone, and to her surprise, she did feel better. Her jaw still ached, but the ripping pain was only a dull throb in her temple. She pulled herself up on her elbows and looked about. She was lying on several filthy furs on a dirt floor. She was in a small lean-to of sorts, and it was dreadfully hot. The door wasn't really a door, she saw, but rather a narrow opening covered with some kind of animal skin. There were several filthy blankets on the floor near her, some ancient tin plates stacked in one corner, and nothing else.

"Delaney," she whispered. The enormity of her situation hit her hard, and she fell back, sobbing softly. He couldn't be dead, he couldn't! She heard again the three sharp gunshots. Had one of them robbed him of his life? She shook her head violently, as if her denial made it true and kept Delaney safe.

Get a hold on yourself!

She drew a deep breath. Indians. She wondered how many of them there were. Why had they taken her? What did this Chatca want with her? She remembered Delaney's words that the Indians were a rather helpless lot. Well, Chatca didn't act at all helpless! She felt a trickle of sweat curl down between her breasts. The cramped lean-to was like an oven. Slowly she pulled herself upright, then onto her knees. There was no surge of pain in her head. Gingerly she rubbed her fingers over her jaw. It was sore, but nothing she couldn't bear.

Get up, Chauncey. You've got to see where you are and how many Indians are outside.

She placed her hands flat in front of her and eased herself upright.

"You better, lady. I tell you so."

"Cricket," Chauncey said, weaving dizzily where she stood.

"You hungry, I bet. I bring you food. You sit down, lady."

"No, wait! I must know where I am! You've got to tell . . ."

But Cricket was gone. Chauncey walked slowly to the entrance and pulled back the animal skin. The sun was high in the sky. Oh God, she thought, how much time had passed since Chatca had taken her?

She forced herself to look about her. There were only three more crudely built lean-tos spaced in a small circle. In the middle of the circle was a good-size fire with a rusted iron pot hung from a hook. The odor of the food, whatever it was, made her stomach lurch. She saw Cricket emerge from the trees surrounding the camp and walk to the pot, slop some of the thick food into a wooden bowl, then straighten.

"Lady! You go inside! Chatca be angry if he find you outside."

"Where is he? Where are the other . . . people?"

"Chatca's brother, Ivan, in tent with his woman. He mean. You not let him see you."

Ivan! Another bit of irony from a priest? Chauncey was on the point of slipping back into the lean-to when she saw another woman, this one older, fatter, and excessively ugly. Her single garment, which hung to her ankles, looked to be made of incredibly filthy leather. It was held together over her massive breasts by a leather thong threaded through holes. The woman saw Chauncey and let loose a high wailing stream of guttural noises interspersed with English curses.

Cricket turned on her and screamed back at the top of her lungs. Chauncey shrank back at the vicious hatred in the other woman's eyes.

"Get inside, lady!" Cricket shouted over her shoulder, her eyes still on the other Indian woman.

Chauncey eased back into the lean-to and eased down on the furs, sitting cross-legged. A moment later, Cricket entered carrying a wooden bowl of food. She handed the bowl to Chauncey, then with all the aplomb in the world drew out a wicked-looking dagger and wiped it off. Chauncey stared at her, her mouth open.

"Tamba crazy jealous," Cricket said matter-of-factly. "I cut her ugly face next time."

"Crazy jealous about what?"

"Chatca take me and make me wife. Old Tamba want him, but he only pull up her skirt when I sick. Eat now, lady."

Chauncey stared down into the bowl. It was a thick brown mixture with chunks of meat floating in it. I have to keep up my strength, she thought, and dipped her fingers into the liquid. To her surprise, the meat was excellent. She couldn't identify the flavor, but it tasted gamy.

She ate in silence. Finally she set the bowl down and said to Cricket, "Why am I here? What is going to happen to me?"

Cricket shrugged. "Chatca make deal and now big fight. Chatca say you demon woman and he want you. He no want to kill you now."

Kill me! No, it was worse than that—he wanted her! "Delaney," she whispered, and dropped her face into her hands. If he was all right, would he even care enough to try to find her? I'm going crazy, she thought, choking down her tears.

"You not blubber," Cricket said in a stern voice. "You no demon woman."

"No, I'm not," Chauncey said, forcing her eyes to the other woman's face. "I'm afraid, Cricket, very afraid. I don't belong here. You must help me. You lived with white people. You know their ways. You know I cannot remain here."

"Father Nesbitt nice man," Cricket said, then added dispassionately, "Even when he beat me with stick, he tell me it is to purify my spirit. Chatca kill him fast. He good man too. I no mind to share him."

"Cricket, listen to me. I am married. I already have a man, a good man. Please, you must . . ."

She broke off suddenly, fear curdling in her stomach at the sight of Chatca standing in the narrow entrance. In the dim light of the previous night, he had looked like a fiend from a medieval book of Satan's followers. In the daylight, he looked worse.

"Demon woman eat," Cricket said, her voice all sweet and submissive deference.

Chatca's black eyes never left Chauncey's face. She stared back at him, willing some feeling, some human reaction in him. He wore only filthy buckskins and leather boots that came to his knees. His chest was bare, devoid of hair, and covered with a greasy substance that gave off a revolting odor. His hair was glistening with the grease and hung in sticky strings to his shoulders. A dirty

band of leather held the hair back from his forehead. His face was hairless. Suddenly he was
grinning widely at her, and she could imagine
the stench from his yellowing teeth. She could
not tell his age.

He turned his eyes to Cricket and said something sharp to her. Chauncey had thought Cricket
had some spirit, particularly after seeing her confront the woman Tamba. But now her shoulders
sagged and she bowed her head.

He is too strong for me, Chauncey thought,
staring again at Chatca. He was not a large man,
but his muscles were tight and sinewy, made
more prominent by the shining grease covering
them. He took a step toward her.

Chauncey jumped back and flung her hands
out in front of her. Chatca growled something at
Cricket.

"Lady," Cricket said, "Chatca want you. He
say he make you wife. He not kill you."

"You're his wife!"

"He take you and have three wives."

Cricket frowned as she spoke. Not waiting for
Chauncey's response, she turned to Chatca and
asked him what seemed to be a question. Chauncey
blinked to see him raise his fist as he growled a
long string of sounds at her.

"What is it, Cricket? What is the matter?"

Cricket turned angry eyes back to Chauncey.
"Chatca want make you first wife. I tell him no."

Chauncey closed her eyes for a brief instant.
This was ridiculous, all of it! This simply couldn't
be happening! Dammit, she was an Englishwoman, a lady! Some lady! She opened her eyes

and looked a moment at her dirty hands. Her skirt was torn and soiled.

"Cricket," she said finally, "please tell Chatca that I am married. Tell him that he must return me to my husband, to civilization. I'm not an Indian. I don't know your ways."

Cricket appeared to ponder her words, then turned to Chatca. What followed was as close to a screaming match as Chauncey had ever witnessed. She cried out, rushing forward when Chatca cuffed Cricket and sent her sprawling to the ground.

"Stop it, you miserable bastard! You damned savage, don't you dare hurt her!"

Chatca grinned. "Demon woman," he said, the words low and pleased and guttural. But she understood, and backed away again. She looked frantically about for a weapon, anything, but there was nothing.

"No," she shouted at him, backing away until she was pressed against the flimsy skin wall.

"Demon woman," Chatca said again, and strode toward her.

— 25 —

Chauncey let out a scream of fear and rage. Chatca's hands gripped her upper arms, pulling her toward him.

"You damned savage!" She brought her arm up and sent her fist as hard as she could into his jaw. "How does that feel, you miserable bastard?"

He was laughing. Laughing! She flung herself at him, raking her dirty fingernails into his neck and shoulders when he threw his head back out of her reach. Suddenly he jerked her tight against him, trapping her arms between them. He bent down and began to nuzzle her neck. The smell of him and his awful breath made her gag. She tried to kick him, jerking and twisting back to give herself leverage.

It was no use.

Her blouse was torn off and her skirt quickly followed. She was sobbing, screaming at him all the curse words she'd ever heard in her life. He took a step back, releasing her for a moment, a wide grin splitting his lips as he studied her.

Chauncey couldn't move. She stood shaking and sobbing, dressed only in her disheveled dirty shift and her boots.

He was looking up and down her body with calm possessiveness. Suddenly he frowned and hurled out a string of the strange guttural sounds. He took another step back, a look of frustration on his face. He was shouting at Cricket now, pointing back at Chauncey.

Cricket answered him, then shrugged. Chacta's voice rose and he gesticulated wildly. He stopped his invective for a moment, his lips curling with both anger and ... disgust. Disgust! Filthy savage—she didn't smell nearly as bad as he did.

Chatca strode from the lean-to without another word.

Chauncey stood still, wondering what the devil was going on. Why had he suddenly left her alone? "Cricket, I—"

"You bleed," Cricket said flatly. "No good for man. Unclean."

Bleed? Chauncey looked down, to see blood staining her shift. She wanted to laugh and cry at the same time. He'd left her alone because of her monthly flow! "Oh God," she whispered, falling to her knees, "I can't bear this."

"No cry. You demon woman. I get cloths to stop blood. Chatca no make you wife until you clean again."

Oddly enough, as she knelt on the ground, she felt a stab of disappointment that she wasn't pregnant with Delaney's child. She quietly, hopelessly, whispered his name.

*   *   *

"Please, Circket, you must let me bathe! Surely no one would mind."

"Water cold and no good. You still bleed."

"I'm filthy!" Chauncey picked up her thick braid and waved it at the impassive Cricket. "Filthy! I can't stand it anymore. As for the . . . other"—she choked a moment in embarrassment—"I don't care. It doesn't matter."

"I ask Chatca tomorrow," Cricket said, and sat down on the dirt floor cross-legged.

Two days. Two nights. It seemed an eternity. Chauncey knew every mound of dirt on the ground of the lean-to, every seam in the animal skins. She was beginning to feel scarcely human. At least Chatca hadn't come near her. Her only companion was Cricket. She'd heard Tamba's loud, angry voice outside the lean-to several times, but she hadn't seen the woman. She was allowed outside for only a few moments to relieve herself, then herded back inside.

"Cricket," Chauncey said after a moment, "please talk to me. I'm going mad."

"Chatca tell me no talk, just watch you."

"Please. I can't bear it. Please. Just tell me how many of you are here in this camp."

"Only eight. No children. Three women."

"Where are your other people? What tribe do you come from?"

Cricket gave her what Chauncey had come to call her what-a-stupid-woman look. "Other Indians dig gold for white man. Many die. Chatca angry and come here to hide and live free." Her chin rose a bit and a gleam of pride lit her black eyes. "We Nisenans, come from tribe of great

Maidu chief, Wema. White man steal lands from us, kill our game, ruin our rivers with . . ." She paused a moment, frowning.

"With their mining equipment," Chauncey said.

"More yellow men now than Indians," Cricket said. "Wema lose to great white father. Chatca save us."

No, Chauncey thought. Chatca didn't have a chance of saving anybody.

"Cricket, how did Chatca find us? Why did he bring me here?"

Cricket shrugged. "No matter. Ivan angry, but Chatca want you. Tamba make more trouble." Cricket calmly began to pluck lice from her hair and crush them between her fingers.

Chauncey wanted to shake her in frustration. She wrapped her arms about her knees and lowered her face. She wondered dully if Delaney had ever killed an Indian. She felt swamped with grief at the thought of him. She felt tears burn her eyes and realized that dirt was making them sting. Some lady, she thought vaguely. An English lady sitting on the rough ground, thoroughly filthy and wearing only a bloodstained ragged shift! She could just imagine Aunt Augusta's face if she could see her.

Delaney. He wasn't dead. She sensed it. But where was he? Was she so desperate that she didn't want to face the truth? What if Chatca had killed him? What if she had to remain here and be raped by the renegade Indian?

"I tell you demon woman no cry. Make Chatca mad."

Chauncey's head shot up. "You can tell Chatca to go to hell!"

"That better," Cricket said complacently, and resumed her task with the lice.

Time passed in a blur. Chauncey ate and slept and dreamed of happier times when she was a child. And when she didn't sleep, she plotted. I must escape, she told herself over and over. But how?

"Cricket," she announced in a very firm voice a day and a half later, "I must bathe. I cannot stand my own stench."

"Bath no good" was Cricket's reply.

"I will grow sick and . . . die."

That got the woman's attention.

"You no die. Chatca not like."

"I will die if I am not allowed to bathe and walk about outside in the sunlight. I will die if you don't give me some freedom."

"You no die," Cricket repeated in her flat voice, but she rose and left the lean-to.

Surely I look like I'm about to die, Chauncey thought. She was thankful that there was no mirror. She would probably die of fright at the sight of herself.

When Cricket returned some minutes later, she was clicking her teeth, a disapproving look on her face. Chatca must have approved.

"You come. I walk with you. Sunlight and freedom."

"What about my bath?"

"Chatca say tomorrow."

Cricket bound her hands in front of her with a thin leather strap. Chauncey didn't care. She followed Cricket docilely from the lean-to. She drew in a deep breath of the clean forest air. The first person she saw was Tamba, standing in front of her, hands on her fat hips, a look of jealousy and scorn on her wide face.

Three Indian men were seated around a small fire handing about a rifle. She smelled rotting flesh and saw a dead deer lying some ten feet away, its belly split open.

She gagged.

"You smell fresh air," Cricket said.

The men eyed her with no more emotion than they afforded the dead deer. Tamba muttered loudly to another Indian woman, but didn't move toward her. The other woman was more a girl, Chauncey thought, but she was so thin, her hair so filthy and matted, that it was difficult to tell.

For God's sake, Chauncey told herself, look around! You must escape! And she knew when she would try—when she bathed the following day. She realized with a calm born of utter despair that she would rather die than remain here a prisoner. She kept her head lowered, but she studied everything. There were three other lean-tos, actually wooden frames covered with animal hides. A couple of horses were tethered to a pine tree at the other end of the camp. They looked as tired and depressed as Chauncey felt. Her eyes widened. She couldn't believe it. Her mare was tethered away from the other horses. Ah, Dolores, you're my hope! She forced her eyes away. There was an assortment of white man's pots and pans lying about, some woven baskets, and little else. Where was Chatca? she wondered.

The clearing was narrow and oddly long, the forest close on all sides. She could see rolling hills in the distance through the tall firs and pine trees that soared upward around the camp. If she were going to be allowed a bath, there must be a creek nearby.

"Cricket," she said, filling her voice with disinterest, "where is the river?"

"Yuba over there," Cricket said, pointing vaguely off to Chauncey's left.

"Then Downieville is there?"

Cricket nodded, then frowned starkly. "You no ask questions."

No, Chauncey thought, no more questions.

She smelled him, and whipped around.

Chatca stared at her with that same complacent look of possessiveness. He grunted some words at Cricket, then tossed Chauncey a bundle of clothes. She clutched the frayed cotton skirt and white blouse. At that moment they were more precious than the finest velvet gowns.

"Chatca exchange your boots for clothes," Cricket said.

There had to be white people near—women! She felt a thrill of hope.

"Tell Chatca that I am grateful," she said.

She watched them converse a moment, then felt the hair rise on her neck at Tamba's furious scream.

The woman was on her before Chauncey could move, tugging at her filthy braid until her eyes watered, clawing at the clothes in her arms.

Chauncey's hands were tied and there was nothing she could do.

Chatca bellowed in fury and cuffed Tamba, sending her reeling into the dirt. The other Indian men laughed.

Chatca kicked her fat bottom, sending her scampering off on her hands and knees.

"She angry because you get clothes," Cricket said.

"Oh God," Chauncey whispered.

"Chatca want you wear new clothes. White woman's clothes."

Chauncey drew a deep breath. "Tell him, Cricket, that I'll wear the new clothes once I've bathed away all the filth. Tell him I must have soap."

For a terrifying moment Chauncey believed she'd gone too far. Chatca's face reddened as Cricket spoke to him, and his black eyes grew even darker. Chauncey forced herself to stand straight, her shoulders back.

Cricket turned back to her. "He get soap. You wear clothes tomorrow. He make you his woman then."

Dear God, she thought, had he been counting the days? Evidently he had.

The next morning, Chauncey, her hands bound again, followed Cricket from the lean-to. The sky was overcast, the air chilly. She didn't care. She looked about the camp. Tamba and another woman were cooking over the open fire. There was no sign of the men. Dolores was still tethered at the edge of the clearing.

"I watch," Cricket said when they reached the narrow creek.

"Fine," Chauncey said, and thrust out her hands.

Cricket looked undecided.

"I can't bathe with my hands bound," Chauncey said.

Cricket untied her hands.

Chauncey looked about, half-expecting to see Chatca lurking in the trees. It didn't really matter, she thought, and stripped off her filthy shift.

She stepped gingerly into the water and gasped at the shock. It was frigid. She clutched the thin sliver of soap and waded in deeper. The creek was only knee-deep at the middle, and Chauncey sat down, gritting her teeth. All I'm washing, she thought, is the gooseflesh!

As she soaped her hair, she kept an eye on Cricket. I am strong enough, she told herself over and over, like a litany. I'll cosh her on the head and get to Dolores.

When she came out of the water, Cricket handed her a thin piece of cloth to dry herself with.

At least it smelled clean. Chauncey dried herself thoroughly and donned the skirt and blouse. They felt heavenly. She sat down on a rock and began to comb out her wet hair with her fingers.

"You come now," Cricket said after watching her for a moment.

"No, not yet," Chauncey said, and continued calmly with her task. She plaited her hair into a thick braid.

"Now," Cricket said, holding out the piece of leather.

Like hell I'm going to let you tie me up again!

She smiled at Cricket and slowly rose to her feet. "Thank you, Cricket," she said, and held out her hands.

Cricket grunted and bent over to tie the leather about Chauncey's wrists. Chauncey brought her fists down on Cricket's temple. The woman gave a small surprised cry and slumped forward to her hands and knees.

"I'm sorry," Chauncey whispered, picked up a small rock, and hit her on the back of her head. Cricket fell in a heap, unconscious.

Chauncey heard a shout of laughter and whirled about to see Tamba standing quite near, a rifle in her hands.

"You kill," she said. "Good. Now you leave."

Chauncey stood frozen to the spot. "I didn't kill her!"

"No matter. You leave. I no get blame."

"Yes, yes, I'll leave." Chauncey darted back to the camp, skirted the perimeter, and eased up to Dolores. At least her mare still wore her bridle. Saddle be damned! She swung up onto the mare's back, clutching at her thick mane. She realized suddenly that the only means of escape was through the center of the small camp.

She drew a deep breath and dug her bare heels into Dolores' side. The mare snorted and dashed forward. Chauncey kept her eyes forward, toward the narrow trail through the trees on the other side. She heard a woman shout. Suddenly she heard Cricket yelling at the top of her lungs. She whipped around and saw Tamba aiming a rifle at her. She threw herself forward on Dolores' neck, but she was too late. She felt a searing pain in her shoulder and it slammed her into her mare's neck. My God, she thought vaguely, that damned bitch shot me!

She heard a scream, and twisted her head back toward the camp. Cricket threw herself at Tamba as the rifle discharged again. The shot went wide, over Chauncey's head.

She fell forward on Dolores' neck, hanging on. Oddly enough, she felt no pain now, only a numbing coldness.

What now, Miss Brilliance? she asked herself.

Back toward Marysville, back toward the river.

Chauncey clung frantically to Dolores' mane, letting her mare pick her own trail. The forest was thinning out, and she realized that Chatca would follow her.

She straightened and looked over her shoulder. Nothing. No one. She blinked. Her blouse was soaked with blood. She could feel it snaking down over her left breast. She pulled Dolores to a halt and ripped off a strip from her skirt. She made it into a pad and pressed it against the wound. Why doesn't it hurt more? she wondered vaguely.

She click-clicked Dolores forward. She had to keep going. She knew she couldn't hide her trail from Chatca. She didn't know how to, and she was afraid that if she dismounted from her mare's back, she wouldn't have the strength to climb back on.

The river! Chatca couldn't follow her if she kept in the water, could he? She guided Dolores into the shallows.

The sky darkened, and the air grew colder.

The hours passed and she forced herself to think about the mining camp she would ride into at any minute.

Suddenly the skies opened and rain poured down, cold rain, so thick she could scarcely see in front of her. No trail for Chatca to follow now, she thought, even if he's a fish!

She was soaked and shivering in a matter of moments. The frigid piercing rain brought out the pain in her shoulder, and she gritted her teeth. Dolores whinnied and shook her head.

Chauncey guided her out of the water to the riverbank. The overhanging tree branches afforded little protection from the lashing rain. Just a little farther, Chauncey said over and over.

Miners worked on the river. Where the devil were they?

Where was the woman who had exchanged the clothing for Chauncey's boots?

She felt light-headed and closed her eyes. Raindrops splashed against her eyelids. She pressed her cheek against her mare's neck. She thought of a warm fire, a thick blanket. She saw Delaney's beloved face, filled with tenderness. Then she saw nothing.

— 26 —

It was the oddest feeling, and she didn't understand it. Surely she couldn't be moving! Chauncey forced herself to open her eyes. She was still astride Dolores' broad back, her arms wrapped around the mare's neck. She tried to pull herself upright, and gasped at the burning shaft of pain that tore through her shoulder. Dolores stopped suddenly in the midst of the tangled undergrowth, and Chauncey gritted her teeth against the jolting movement. "Please, Dolores, we must keep going. We must!" Her voice sounded rusty and hoarse with disuse. She realized that she could scarcely see. No, she wasn't fainting again. It was growing dark. It was no longer raining, but the air felt heavy, pregnant with more moisture. She moaned softly. She knew with certainty that she would never survive if she had to spend the night alone in the forest. She drew on her remaining strength and forced herself upright. She threw back her head and yelled, "Delaney!"

She heard birds chirping and some wings flapping. No human sounds.

"Delaney, where are you!"

She lurched forward at the sound of a rifle shot. Chatca!

"No," she moaned softly. She tried to dig her heels into Dolores' sides, but didn't have the strength. Any moment, Chatca would burst through the trees. He would take her back. She would die.

She sobbed softly against her mare's thick mane. Slowly she slid from her mare's back onto the mossy earth. She lay on her back, staring up at the tall trees. Her mare whinnied. Chauncey heard boots crashing through the forest. She tried to rise. She wouldn't let Chatca take her, she wouldn't! But she couldn't move. The pain in her shoulder was growing stronger, the fangs of some wild beast digging into her flesh.

She moaned softly.

"Chauncey! Oh my God!"

She imagined his voice. She began to tremble. I'm dying, she thought.

"I don't want to die," she whispered. She saw the shadow of a man bending over her, heard his agonized voice.

"Oh God, love."

She blinked, trying desperately to focus on his face. "Del?"

"Yes, Chauncey. You're safe now, love. I'm here."

"How can you be here?" she asked, puzzled

that the apparition was answering her. "I'm dying. I want you to be here, but you can't be."

"I am, sweetheart. Hang on."

Delaney felt as though his guts had been ripped out. He swallowed convulsively as he stared down at her blood-soaked shirt. Carefully he pulled the string loose and eased the material from her shoulder. She'd been shot. He lifted her slightly and breathed a sigh of relief. The bullet had torn its way through her shoulder and out her back. High on her shoulder, through the fleshy part.

"Sweetheart," he said firmly, drawing her dazed eyes to his face, "there's an abandoned miner's shack just a few minutes away. I'm going to lift you now."

"What happened to your head?" she asked, seeing a white bandage wrapped around his forehead.

"Nothing important, love. Can you put your arms around my neck?"

She tried but didn't have the strength.

'Shush, it's all right." He lifted her into his arms and rose. She had to live, she had to! He'd searched and searched. And he'd found her, just when he'd almost accepted the fact that she was dead.

As he shifted her weight, a searing pain tore through her and she cried out. He felt her go limp and froze in fear. No, she was still alive. He held her close against him and grabbed her mare's reins. He began the trek to the river. He could feel the clammy dampness of her clothes. She must have ridden throughout the rainstorm. He bent his head down, listening. Was there congestion in her lungs? Was her breathing labored?

There was no doctor in Grass Valley, the last one having died from pneumonia while panning for gold in the Yuba. There was no one to help her but him.

His own breathing was labored by the time he reached the shack. He kicked the door open and carried her inside the one-room structure. It had one table, one rickety chair, and a fireplace. Nothing else. He laid her on the floor, then brought in the bedrolls.

As carefully as he could, he stripped off her damp clothes and wrapped her in a wool blanket on a bedroll. He spread the skirt and blouse on the floor to dry, wondering as he did so where she'd gotten them. And she'd worn nothing else. He wouldn't allow himself to think about that.

"Please stay unconscious just a bit longer," he whispered to her. Quickly he filled a pan of water from the river and returned to the shack. He built a fire and heated the water. He thought frantically about what to do about the wound. Whiskey. He had just a bit left.

He gently bathed the blood from her shoulder and breast. The bullet wound was clean and, as he'd thought, through the fleshy part of her shoulder. He poured whiskey on the wound and bandaged her tightly with strips torn from his only clean shirt.

He sat back on his haunches and stared down at her pale face. She was alive; she was his; and he would never let her go. He thought of the long days and nights alone. He shook the thoughts from his mind. There was much to do if they were to survive.

He gently eased her next to the fire, covered

her with the rest of the blankets, and rose. He drew a deep breath. One thing at a time, he told himself. He had to find food. He didn't want to leave her alone, but he had no choice. He picked up his rifle and left the shack.

Chauncey awoke to the smell of roasting meat. She felt her mouth water. Her thoughts were vague, disoriented, and for several moments she didn't know where she was. She bolted up, crying out, "Del!"

"I'm here, Chauncey," he said, kneeling beside her. "Lie down, sweetheart. You must rest."

"You're really here with me. I thought I'd dreamed it." Tears formed in her eyes. "I didn't think I would ever see you again."

"I'm like a bad penny," he said. "I'll always keep turning up."

She gasped at the pain in her shoulder and turned her head slightly away from him.

"I know you hurt, love. There's nothing I can do about it. I'm sorry."

"If I hurt, I know I'm alive," she whispered. "How did you find me?"

"That, love, is a very long story. The rabbit is nearly cooked. Let's eat first. All right?"

She nodded weakly. "There's so much to tell you."

"I know. First things first."

He cut the meat in small pieces and fed her slowly. She ate everything. He realized that she was thinner. Her high cheekbones were shadowed, and for a moment he pictured her naked body in his mind. Much thinner, and so pale.

"I'm not pregnant," she said.

He stared at her, not knowing what to say. Suddenly she gasped, her face contorting in pain.

"Del," she cried softly. He grasped her hand and felt her fingernails dig into his flesh.

"Take shallow breaths and breathe slowly," he said. "I'm going to tell you about the last five days. Listen to me talk. Concentrate on what I say, not the pain. Do you understand me?"

She swallowed, and kept her eyes on his face. He was bearded, and there were lines of fatigue around his eyes. The bandage around his head made him look like a bandit.

"It was near dawn, remember?" she heard him say, his voice pitched low and soothing. "I heard movement in the woods and went to see what it was. There were several Indians. One of them shot me in the head. Luckily the bullet just grazed me, but I was unconscious for a time. When I came to, you were gone."

His hand tightened around hers. "I've never been so scared in my life. Unfortunately, the wound in my head kept me lying about for nearly that entire day. When I got my wits back, I knew the odds were that I couldn't track you. I went to Grass Valley and organized search parties. At least ten men have been searching for you the past four days. I came back to where we had camped and searched from there.

"I've been scouring the country for two days now, in first one direction from our camp, and then another. I thought I'd dreamed the sound of your voice when I heard you scream my name."

Her grip on his hand tightened.

"Chauncey, try to listen to me. Can you understand me?"

"Yes," she whispered. "I'm sorry to be such a coward."

"You're anything but a coward, sweetheart. No, don't try to speak again. Breathe slowly. That's right.

"Now, let me tell you something. I've been a thick-headed ass. You were right when you told me I would die of perversity if I didn't make up my mind what I wanted. What I want, Chauncey, is you. I want us to begin again. No more secrets, no shadows between us. I've had nothing but time to think during the past days, to think and worry and hate myself for all the vile things I said to you in my anger."

He grew silent for a moment, gazing into the crackling fire.

"I love you, you know."

His eyes fell to her face. She was asleep. Gently he traced a fingertip over her pale lips, her smooth jaw, her delicate ear. He picked up the thick braid of hair and realized it was still damp. He unbraided it and spread her hair about her head. He cursed softly when he laid his palm on her forehead. The fever was beginning.

He held her tightly against the length of his body, stroking his hands up and down her back, and still she shivered convulsively. The small cabin was terribly hot, and he felt beads of sweat on his forehead and chest. She was burrowing against him, trying to get inside of him, he thought. God, if only he could give her his strength! But he couldn't. There was nothing he could do save try to keep her warm. He felt her lips move against his throat and heard her speaking, slurred sounds that he couldn't understand.

"Chatca," she whispered suddenly, quite clearly. "I won't let him touch me! I'll die before I let him touch me. I'm bleeding!"

She began to laugh, a raspy, pitiful sound that made gooseflesh rise on his body.

"I'm bleeding and he won't touch me! God, please help me!"

"It's all right, Chauncey. He won't touch you, I promise."

Had the Indian raped her? What did she mean by bleeding? He suddenly remembered her whispering to him that she wasn't pregnant. Had she begun her monthly flow? Had that saved her?

She was sobbing softly, and he felt her salty tears against his shoulder. He began to talk, softly and slowly, of anything to keep her mind from her ordeal.

"Did I ever tell you about Mr. Olney of Coyoteville? The miners elected him justice of the peace under the rules of our new constitution. Do you know, he died just last year and left all his money, some six thousand dollars, to the boys, to have a jolly good time. They did, you know. And there was Danny Slengh, who sold his claim for ten thousand dollars. It was over in the Gold Run and Deer Creek area. Then he came back furious because another miner sold a claim that was about an eighth the size of Danny's for four thousand dollars. The other miners laughed at him, and he finally left, ten thousand dollars richer, but still feeling like he'd been robbed."

Was she breathing more easily? He couldn't be certain. He continued stroking her shivering body. "When you're well again, I'll take you to Red

Dog, Rough and Ready, and Humbug. Yes, I swear they're really names of towns near here.

"Did I tell you about Sam Brannan? Not for old Sam to stand thigh-deep in freezing water panning for gold! No, he was far too smart to ruin his health doing that. He bought gold pans for around twenty cents and sold them for sixteen dollars apiece to the miners!"

She grew quiet in his arms and he stopped talking and pressed his cheek against her forehead. She was cooler, he was certain of it. She began to mumble words again, and the name Cricket came out. Cricket, he thought. He must not be hearing her aright. She was growing more agitated, and he began speaking again, calmly and slowly.

"When I first arrived in San Francisco, it was the most ramshackle, flimsy, higgledy-piggledy, haphazard collections of shacks you've ever seen. Big ones, little ones, ugly—and all inflammable. We had six fires in eighteen months. I, personally, lost my first home and a warehouse. But it really didn't matter. We all rebuilt. So many changes I've witnessed in only four years, love. There was litterally nothing in forty-nine, and now we have banks, waterworks, the beginnings of a lighting system, hotels, theaters, churches, schools . . ." He stopped, his mind a blank for a moment. Good God, what else did San Francisco have? He really didn't give a good goddamn. Was she quieter than before? Was his voice, pitched soothing and low, calming her?

"Did you know that men could simply pick gold nuggets up from the ground? I remember the story of old Simon Luther. He was just walking along one day, not too far from here, and chanced to kick a stone out of his path. The kick had a surprising recoil. He picked it up and found that it was pure gold. The record for one nugget is nearly one hundred and forty-one pounds. Then there was John McGlynn. He was a teamster from New York and had brought his wagon with him. He came to search for gold like the rest of us, but he promptly decided that wasn't for him. Things had to be hauled, and there was no one to haul them. His was the only wagon in town. Do you know, love, that very soon he had an entire fleet of wagons? He even had an out-of-work lawyer driving one of his wagons. The story goes that a judge and friend of McGlynn's approved of this, saying that 'the whole business of a lawyer is to know how to manage mules and asses so as to make them pay.' "

Delaney had always laughed at that story before. Now he might as well be reciting a prayer book.

"Do you know the phrase 'a gold spoon or a wooden leg'?"

She didn't answer, of course.

"I remember back in the early spring of fifty-one that flour cost four dollars; by late summer it cost forty dollars. You see, what the merchants did was take risks continually. Would their shipments arrive first? If they did, the profit was enormous, and thus the merchant gained a 'gold spoon.' If he lost, a 'wooden leg.'

"So many absurd things came over on the clipper ships. Can you believe that once we got a whole shipload of omnibuses? Just last year, the sagebrush on the hills was littered with junk that simply didn't sell. The Stevensons' house has a foundation of cases of tobacco. Just eight months ago we used hundred-pound sacks of coffee from Brazil and flour from Chile to fill holes in Kearny Street. Montgomery Street was passable during the rains of fifty because of a double row of cooking stoves sunk in the mud. Of course, several months later, everyone needed cooking stoves. Too late. You can't dig a thing up and use it, once you've sunk it in a mud hole."

That had always seemed amusing to him. Now the stories were just strings of nonsense words. "Chauncey," he whispered softly against her hair, "I'll tell you these stories again when you're well. I want to hear you laugh, watch your eyes sparkle."

What if she dies? It will be your fault, all your fault.

Suddenly Chauncey said very clearly, "I've always disliked you, Guy. Your mother is a witch!"

He smiled against her temple. "I agree with you. Likely a dried old prune."

"Cricket, I must have a bath!"

Who the devil was Cricket? Think! Tell her more stories. She's got to remain calm. His mind was a blank. He shook away his fear for her and said, "It was so difficult and primitive in the beginning. There was so much gold to be found in the rivers and creek beds. You know that gold is seven times as heavy as rock and gravel, thus our use of gold pans. Hell, we even used wooden bowls, Indian baskets, and sluice boxes to free the rock and gravel from the gold. I was very lucky, Chauncey, very lucky indeed. I didn't have to spend the winter freezing in the mountains. I gambled like all the other miners. God, it was so lonely and miserable in the camps. I wrote so many letters back home. My brother told me that only a few arrived eventually. Then, in only two months, I found my fortune. Several huge nuggets, Chauncey, and that day I yelled at the top of my lungs in triumph. But I knew that my real fortune was in commerce. I met up with Dan Brewer in the fall of fifty in San Francisco. He was also one of the fortunate ones. Then—"

"I must have a bath!"

"Yes, love, I know. When you're well, I'll bathe you myself."

"Don't let him touch me!"

"No, he won't touch you. I swear you'll be all right."

He spoke on and on, telling her of the construction of his new house, of how he had found Lin and gotten together with Lucas. His voice became hoarse, his words making less and less sense as fatigue washed over him.

His last thought before he fell into a light sleep was that her forehead felt cool against his cheek.

— 27 —

"You are the most beguiling little ragamuffin I've ever seen."

"And you, sir, look like the most ardent of villains!"

"Hold still, love, there's still that spot of smut on your cheek."

Very gently he wiped her face with the wet cloth, then patted her dry. "Better?"

"Yes, a bit." She turned her head slightly away from him, not wanting him to see her face contorted with pain.

She felt his hand lightly stroke against her cheek and throat. "I know, Chauncey. It hurts like hell itself. Just a few more days and you'll be up and about again. You're young and strong, and there's no more fever now."

She clenched her hands into fists at her sides. Her shoulder felt as if someone had pressed a red-hot poker into her flesh.

"Here, drink this."

He eased his arm behind her head. "It's the last of my whiskey."

The liquid burned a fiery path to her stomach. "Oh my!"

"That will help, you'll see."

He laid her back and pulled the blanket to her shoulders. He rose and looked down at her. "I must find us some food, Chauncey. Will you be able to sleep while I'm gone?"

She didn't want to sleep; she wanted to howl at the damnable pain. "Yes," she said, "I'll sleep."

Still, he didn't leave the cabin until she had closed her eyes. When she heard the door close, she opened them again and cursed. To her surprise, the pain eased somewhat. "I'll have to learn some more colorful language," she muttered toward the fireplace. Why, she wondered, frowning, hadn't Delaney asked her yet what had happened to her? Was he afraid to? Did he believe that the Indians had raped her? Her mind flinched at the thought. No, it couldn't matter to him. He had treated her as if she were the most precious, fragile of women. He was as gentle and caring as he had been when she'd schemed to get into his house and ended up hurt.

She heard two swift rifle shots.

Ten minutes later, Delaney strode into the shack, his eyes drawn immediately to her face. "Did the shots awaken you?"

"No, I was thinking. Del, did Sam Brannan really sell gold pans for sixteen dollars apiece?"

He grinned at her, his white teeth flashing against his bushy caramel-colored beard. "So you did hear me going on and on."

"Just bits and pieces." She watched him place his rifle carefully on the rough-hewn table. He had shucked off his vest and was clothed in a full-sleeved white shirt and dark brown buckskins. Black boots hugged his legs. His face was tanned from the hours he'd spent in the sun, and there were lighter streaks of blond in his hair.

"You are beautiful," she said.

His grin widened. "In my dirty buckskins? And my bushy face? I begin to believe you delirious again."

"I don't think so," she said in a serious voice. "But I can't believe that any number of women wouldn't have tried to abduct you and use you for their pleasure."

"Ah, what makes you think that they didn't? Why, I remember a lush brunette named Brenda. Lord, to remember what she did to my poor helpless body—"

"A brunette named Brenda? And I suppose there was a redhead named Rosalie and a blond named—"

He laughed deeply and she glowed at the wonderful sound. "Del, listen to me, please. Chatca, the Indian who took me—he didn't rape me."

He became very still. "No, I know he didn't," he said at last. "You started your monthly flow and he didn't touch you." He spoke very matter-of-factly, as if they were speaking of the weather.

"How," she demanded, "did you know that?"

He knew her small show of bluster was a result of embarrassment. "You told me you weren't pregnant," he said calmly. His eyes lit with some amusement. "I do know something about how a woman's body functions, you know."

"Oh. Then why haven't you asked me what happened to me?"

"I didn't want to rush you. You're still not up to snuff yet, love. You will tell me when you're well enough and ready to."

She fiddled with the rough edge of the blanket for a moment. "You have forgiven me for all I did to you? For all the awful things I thought about you?"

"Yes."

"You feel sorry for me, don't you? You feel responsible."

"Yes."

"You're being utterly perverse again, Del!"

"And you won't put up with it anymore, right? You're going to jump up and pummel my chest and kick my shins."

"Are you going to send me back to England?"

"No. I'm going to take you to bed once you are well again, and make certain that you become pregnant. Pregnant ladies shouldn't travel, you know."

He paused a moment, aware that his body was quickly responding to his words and thoughts. He was picturing her flat belly rounding with his child. He turned away and began to make coffee.

"When are you going to bathe the rest of me?"

His hand trembled on the coffeepot. "Chauncey," he said over his shoulder, refusing to look at her, "you are flirting with danger."

She sighed. "I look awful."

"Yes, but adorably awful. You're also too thin, and you smell like a wet horse."

The whiskey she had drunk had spread a warm

glow through her mind. The throbbing in her shoulder had lessened considerably. "How long will I take to heal?"

"A couple more days. Then we'll go to Grass Valley."

"Why did the Indians attack us? Why did they take me?"

He handed her a steaming cup of coffee, then pulled it back. "No," he said more to himself than to her, "the coffee will sober you up." He cradled the tin cup between his hands and sat on the floor beside her, crossing his long legs. Then, in answer to her question: "I don't know. Did they tell you who they were?"

"Yes, the woman who guarded me was named Cricket. She said that Chatca, their leader, had broken away from Chief Wema's tribe."

"Ah."

"What do you mean, 'ah'?"

"Nothing in particular, I guess. It's just that the small bands of renegades have nearly all been wiped out. God, what we've done to the poor bastards!" He sipped at his hot coffee, his expression thoughtful. "If you are ready to tell me about it, I would like to know what happened, Chauncey."

"Well," she said tartly, "I can't think of those Indians as poor bastards! They were filthy, smelled far worse than you can imagine, and lived like animals." She sighed. "Perhaps they had no choice. But they didn't have to shoot you and abduct me!"

"I would have abducted you had I seen you."

"No, you wouldn't. You would have waited for me to abduct you." He's made me laugh a bit, she thought. Is he afraid I'll become hysterical? "I fought Chatca and he struck me. I don't know how long I was unconscious, but when I came to and began to fight him again, he hit me again. When I woke up, I was in some kind of odd-looking lean-to—"

"A wigwam, it's called."

"—and this young woman was there. She said a priest had named her Cricket. She was one of Chatca's wives. She told me Chatca wanted me." She paused a moment, getting a grip on herself. The memory was humiliating and terrifying.

"Then he saw that you were bleeding and left you alone."

"Yes. He was very angry. There was this other Indian woman, named Tamba. She wanted to slit my throat, but Chatca protected me. I stayed in that . . . wigwam for several days, until I thought I'd go out of my mind. Finally Chatca agreed that I could have a bath in the stream. Cricket took me there, and I coshed her on the head. The other woman saw me and pretended that she would help me escape. When I was riding Dolores through the camp, Tamba shot me. I prayed I was riding in the right direction."

Delaney said nothing.

"It sounds like such a pitiful tale."

"You were very brave," he said finally, smiling at her. "I am proud of you."

"Why are you looking so morose, if I'm so brave?"

He drank the rest of his coffee and merely shrugged at her question.

"Delaney, what are you thinking?"

"The truth, the tree without the bark on it, so to speak?"

"Yes, the truth, if you please."

"I don't know why the Indians attacked us. They shouldn't have. It is not in their nature to do things like that. I cannot believe it was simply because this Chatca saw your lovely eyes and couldn't live without you."

Chauncey closed her eyes a moment, memory of her conversations with Cricket playing through her mind. "I remember Cricket telling me that there would be trouble."

"With you in the vicinity, I can well understand her concern!"

"Will you always mock me and make me laugh?"

"I will certainly try." He stretched out on his back beside her, pillowing his head on his arms. "Do you know what it was like? I was as helpless as a baby for that entire day, my mind bleary, my body shaking like a leaf in the wind. And then I couldn't find you. I remembered every mean word I'd tossed out at you."

"At least you didn't have a terrifying Indian wanting to make you his wife!"

"All you had to do was tell him that you were already married to the most perverse man in the state."

She giggled and immediately regretted it.

He turned onto his side, facing her. "Easy, love," he said, lightly stroking his fingers over her jaw. He saw her lashes flutter downward as she closed her eyes, not wanting him, he knew, to see her pain. "Please," she whispered between gritted teeth. "Talk to me."

"When I was in England in fifty-one, the Duke and Duchess of Graffton were dead set on marrying me off. I swear to you that I must have attended every soiree, ball, masquerade, and formal dinner in London. There were so many debutantes, all dressed in virginal white, all of them anxious to meet the rich American and simper at him. Lord, what time we would have saved had you only been in London then. You would have abducted me, ravished my poor body, and made an honest man of me."

"Yes, I would have."

"I was even presented to the queen, a plump little lady who had the nauseating habit of continually saying 'we' this and 'we' that. As for her Albert, I found him so stiff and formal that I was certain he'd break if he tried to stand against a strong wind. I suppose I was something of a two-month wonder, this barbarian from the wilds of California who'd struck gold and made his fortune. Do you know that one old fellow—Lord Fanshaw, I believe his name was—practically offered to sell his daughter to me, provided I was willing to change my name. Her name was Bernice, as I recall, a pretty little blond—"

"A blond named Bernice!"

"Well, perhaps it was Alice," he said, smiling down at her.

"Alice the awful?"

"No, Alice with the very pretty, very white breasts." He lightly laid his hand over her breast, kneading gently. "I suppose I have always been perverse," he continued after a moment, resolutely removing his hand. "The prettier the young lady, the more aloof I became. I must have known even then that you were there waiting for me."

"More a nemesis than a sweet young lady."

"A reformed nemesis, I trust?"

"When I am well again, you will see how reformed I am!"

He saw her lips tense, and quickly said, "I figure that you and your fire cost me about four thousand dollars. I trust you will recompense me for damages?"

"Yes, I shall do everything in my power to recompense you completely."

"Will you tear up that agreement and turn all your money over to me?"

She saw the teasing gleam in his beautiful eyes. "So you were after my money all along?"

"Your body first, then your money."

"I . . . I wasn't a terribly good wife to you," she said.

"On the other hand, you never bored me. Such a challenge you were to my masculine ego! Then, with that attempt to remove you from my sphere of influence aboard the *Scarlet Queen*, I realized what passion you had kept from me."

She swallowed, remembering in painful detail her wildness, her utter abandon. "I liked it," she said.

"But for all the wrong reasons," he said quietly. "So you want to know something, love? I avoided you at first because you scared the hell out of me. A man doesn't like to feel that he's lost control, you know."

"So you mean, you miserable wretch, that I didn't have to get knocked off my mare by that damned tree branch?"

"No, that was very well done of you, and probably sealed my fate. Once I saw you in my bed, I was ready to surrender unconditionally."

"You didn't show it."

"I had to win Mary over first."

"You did. I spent a great deal of time angry at her for her defection to the enemy. Del, do you think it possible that Chatca could have tracked me?"

He stiffened, his jaw tightening. "No," he said after a brief pause, "I don't believe so."

He saw that she would keep probing, and quickly got to his feet. "Now, little one, I'm going to change that bandage. Then we'll have another grand feast of roast rabbit."

Chauncey left off her questions, for her shoulder was throbbing again. It took all her resolution not to cry out when he bathed the wound. "Much better," she heard him say. "No sign of infection. Another day, love, and I'll let you do the hunting."

It rained throughout the night, a hard, pounding rain that, strangely enough, soothed Chauncey. She slept deeply, unaware that Delaney held her close against his body.

The next day he allowed her to sit up, braced by a rolled-up blanket against the wall. She watched him clean his rifle and his handgun. She found her eyes drawn again and again to his hands. Strong hands, tanned and callused, his fingers long and blunt. He spoke of his brother and sister-in-law in New York.

"Giana is a woman after your own heart, Chauncey. She hasn't a dependent bone in her body and gives my proud and dominating brother quite a time. I do believe though that she turns into a proper submissive woman in my brother's bed."

"How did they meet?"

"I know the story they gave out, but I don't believe a word of it. Alex hinted to me once that Giana had enjoyed quite an unusual experience in Italy and that was where he had first met her. If they visit us, I hope to get Alex drunk and pry out the whole story. You will like both of them, I think. Alex is a charming dog and Giana is a little whirlwind."

"When you visited them, did they introduce you to all the young ladies in New York?"

"A goodly number. There was one woman whose company I truly enjoyed. She was a friend of Giana's, and married. Her name was Derry Lattimer. Alex wrote me last year that she'd finally given birth to a son, after some five years of marriage."

"I trust your heart wasn't broken," she said somewhat sharply.

"No. Well, perhaps for just a while." He raised his head and grinned wickedly at her. "Then there was her stepdaughter, Jennifer." Before Chauncey could take him to task, he said, "What a shrew! I couldn't believe it, but some six months after I left New York, they'd even managed to marry her off. To a tobacco planter in Kentucky. The poor fellow's probably become a drunkard by now."

Chauncey laughed. "I don't deserve you," she said suddenly, tears springing to her eyes.

"True, but you will have years and years to

come about. I plan to give you every opportunity to become worthy of me."

"Less than an ounce!" she exclaimed, sniffing.

"Less than an ounce of what?"

"Of wit!"

"Such a mouthy little wench," he remarked to his rifle. "I think, madam, that soon you will need another kind of attention. If you are truly winsome this evening, I shall consider shifting all your feelings and sensations a bit lower."

"Is that a promise?" she asked softly, aware that her heart had begun to thump erratically.

"Only if I can convince you to bathe first."

"Del, you just wait until I am well again! And what about you? You aren't exactly like the sweetest rose of summer!"

"You are the rose, love. Think of me as the stem."

— 28 —

Chauncey awoke early the following morning feeling more human than she had since before Chatca abducted her. She lay still for a while, not wanting to awaken Delaney. She was pressed against the length of him, her cheek on his shoulder. She wriggled her nose against a tuft of soft light brown hair. Her shoulder was only a dull ache, and she set her mind to ignoring it. She slipped her hand down his chest to his belly. She loved the feel of him, the texture of his flesh, the ridges of muscle over his stomach. He'd become thinner too, she realized as she lightly stroked her fingers over him. Her hand moved lower, and she entwined her fingers in the bush of thick hair at his groin.

She touched him tentatively, then closed her fingers around him. To her surprise and delight, she felt him harden.

"Chauncey, you'd better consider well what you're doing."

She grinned against his shoulder. "It's most exciting that I can make your body . . . different with but a touch."

"I have told you that men are simple creatures. Their control ceases at the groin. If you keep caressing me, I'll . . ."

"You'll what?" she asked softly, nipping at his shoulder blade.

"Sweetheart," he drawled, his voice cracking a bit, "stop it. I refuse to take the chance of hurting you."

"But you promised last night that you'd shift all my feelings lower."

"I changed my mind after I changed your bandage." Resolutely he removed her hand and brought it to his chest and held it there, palm down.

"Your heartbeat is fast."

"I imagine so. Now, listen to me, you seductive little wench. Depending on how you feel today, I'll bathe you and let you move about for a while. No, love. Keep your hands still or I'll have to get up."

"I love how you smell."

He could feel her warm breath against his shoulder, and his body quickened. He closed his eyes a moment, willing his enthusiastic member to calm. It was like swilling a powerful aphrodisiac, having his wife bent upon seduction. "Thank you," he said. He refused to think about her lovely body pressed against his side. When he felt her thigh moving over his, he gently eased away from her.

"No, Del," she said, clutching at him. "I promise I'll not move again. Don't leave me just yet."

"Lie on your back, Chauncey."

"Why?"

"Just do as I tell you. You are my wife, and it is your duty to obey me."

She pulled at the hair on his chest, then quickly kissed him. Slowly, careful of her shoulder, she turned onto her back and gazed up at him. "Why do you want me on my back?"

He smiled at her, studying her face as he eased his hand under the blanket to her belly. She sucked in her breath. His fingers splayed downward, probing gently until he found her.

"Ah, it is a grave situation, just as I thought."

"What is?" she managed, her eyes on his beautiful mouth.

Her delicate woman's flesh was moist and swelled against his caressing fingers. He felt his own need growing by leaps and bounds, but kept a firm grip on himself.

"Your body, love."

Her hips lifted without her even being aware of it. "You will make love to me, Del?"

"In a manner of speaking. As a responsible husband, it is one of my duties. Lie still, love. God, Chauncey, you feel so warm."

She moaned softly, turning her face away from him. His fingers left her and she shifted back to look at him, her eyes huge with silent question and disappointment.

"I want you to look at me while I give you pleasure." She shuddered at his words, embarrassment at her body's response dissolving when he found her again. "That's right. Believe me, I will let you return the favor once you are well again. No, don't close your eyes. Give me the pleasure of seeing you respond."

She gasped when his fingers took on a purposeful rhythm. Her tongue moistened her dry lips and he saw her eyes begin to take on a glazed sheen. Within moments she felt every ounce of her being concentrated beneath his fingers. "Del," she whimpered softly, biting her lower lip, "it is more than I can bear ... Oh God! Help me, please!"

He felt her muscles tighten, felt the convulsive movement of her hips against his fingers. He thought he would yell at the pleasure of seeing her respond so completely to him.

"Del!"

"That's it, love. Let go."

Her body exploded as wave after wave of intense sensation washed through her. She was crying out softly, panting, unable to control herself, her back arching wildly.

He eased the pressure of his fingers, bringing her back to him very slowly, very gently. Her face was flushed, her lips parted as she sucked in breath.

"So beautiful," he said softly, leaning down to kiss her. "So responsive."

She felt his manhood hard and throbbing against her thigh, and tried to turn toward him. He stilled her. "No, not now. I swear I'll survive. Remember, a gentleman always sees to his lady's pleasure first." He paused a moment, slowly easing his hand back to her belly. "There has been much between us, Chauncey."

"The wrong kind of 'much.' "

"Perhaps. But do you want to know something?

When you were ill in my bed from your elaborate and aborted charade, that was the first time I envisioned truly having children of my own. It was all I could do to keep my hands off you."

"You must have been upset with me when I asked you to prevent my becoming pregnant."

"I didn't wish to be unfair," he said steadily.

"Shall we have an army of children?"

"And all our girl children will be the generals?"

She giggled. "Whatever they are," she said, her eyes twinkling, "they will have the best father in the whole . . . city of San Francisco."

"Mouthy baggage."

"All right, the state of California."

"Most generous, ma'am. Now, my love, I am in desperate need of sustenance and coffee. Tell me honestly how your shoulder feels."

"It doesn't hurt at all."

"Honestly, Chauncey."

"It does throb, but just a bit, I promise."

"Good. I'll bathe you this morning, then set you out in the sun this afternoon."

"You're hoping that like a flower, I'll bloom?"

He grinned at her wickedly. "You already have. The perfect rose."

It sorely tried Delaney's control when he bathed her. He concentrated ferociously, but when she trembled as the cloth stroked between her thighs, he sucked in his breath.

"I can't help it," she gasped. "You're the one touching me!"

He finished as quickly as he could. "Let's leave your hair for tomorrow," he said, rising. "I don't want to take any chances with your coming down with a cold, not now."

"May I dress?"

"Yes, I'll help you."

"Then outside in the sun?"

"Yes, but only to sleep." He paused, then added, "And warm your petals."

She blinked at him, then understood and flushed scarlet. "I thought you said you would help me dress," she said tartly.

"The sun is very warm and bright."

He didn't give her a chance to retort. Once she was wearing the skirt and blouse Chatca had bartered for her, he took her outside onto the planked and sagging porch.

He spread out the bedroll and helped her sit down, her back propped against the shack wall. "You will not move from this spot, all right?"

"I promise, master."

"If you need to relieve yourself, I will be back soon to help you."

"Must you mention things like that?"

He straightened, standing tall and large over her, his rifle snug under his right arm. "Since I know your body as well as I know my own, I can't understand your missish quibbling."

"Well, then, it must work both ways!"

"Does it now?" he drawled. "Next time I'm too ill to see to myself, I'll consider asking your aid."

"One of these fine days, Del, I'm going to have the last word on you!"

He merely laughed, waved his hand at her, and strode away from the shack into the forest.

Chauncey leaned her head back against the

rough wooden wall and closed her eyes. The sun felt wonderful. Petals, she thought, and smiled reluctantly. He was everything she could imagine wanting in a man. And she had almost lost him.

Paul Montgomery. Where was he? Had Delaney's men found him yet? She fought down the spurt of fear. Think about what has happened between the two of you, she thought, and a contented smile came to her lips. It seemed quite natural to be in the middle of nowhere, garbed in tattered and worn clothes, waiting to hear the retort of Delaney's rifle, signaling he'd shot their dinner. Like Adam and Eve, she thought fancifully, and closed her eyes. Yet, she thought as she drifted into sleep, there had been a serpent in the Garden of Eden.

Her dreams were harsh and frightening. She was standing in the middle of Delaney's warehouse, surrounded by crackling loud fireworks, and as they exploded around her, she saw Paul Montgomery emerge through a thick veil of smoke. He was smiling at her. Behind him stood Chatca, his face covered with blood.

She screamed, jerking upright.

"Hush, love."

"Del!" She turned wild eyes to her husband, who was hunkered down beside her. "It was awful!"

"Just a nightmare." He was lightly stroking her face. "Here I give you a bath and make you presentable again, and it brings you a bad dream."

"I saw Chatca," she said, drawing a deep breath. "His face was covered with blood. And Paul Montgomery was there, looking kind and gentle." She shuddered. "Why was Chatca with Paul Montgomery?"

His expression never altered. "They both threaten you, each in a different way. Your weak woman's mind simply put them together for simplicity's sake."

"I should have known you'd mock me!"

"That's better," he said, and kissed the tip of her nose. "Now, I'm going to bring the horses around and give them a good rubdown. Consider it the high point of your exciting day."

"No," she said impishly, "the high point happened earlier, much earlier."

He gave her a slow, intimate smile. "You mean your bath?"

"Yes, of course," she agreed readily, her eyes as guileless as a child's. "There is nothing else I can think of."

"At the time, I don't believe you were thinking at all." He lightly kissed her pursed lips. "No, love, don't say it. It is obviously your fate to have the second-to-last word."

The afternoon passed much too quickly for Chauncey's liking. She knew that their days and nights together were out of time, that despite her wounded shoulder, for the first time in their married life they were enjoying a honeymoon of sorts. She didn't want it to end, though she did swallow a bit convulsively when she saw Delaney plucking the pheasant he'd shot for their dinner.

"You are so bloody likeable," she said suddenly as he rose, his task finished, and brushed stray feathers off his buckskins.

"You would prefer that I beat you?"

"No," she said seriously, squinting up at him.

"I mean that I was so caught up in my vengeance, I was blind to what you were really like. At least," she added, "for a while."

His brows arched upward.

"I mean that I began to feel niggling doubts. Even my ever-faithful Mary was singing your praises, and I wanted to smack her! When I realized that I loved you, I thought I'd die. You see, I felt I was betraying my father, succumbing to his enemy."

Delaney eased down beside her, stretching out his long legs. "I liked your father," he said, brushing a lock of hair back from his forehead. "Damnable greed. You do know, Chauncey, that if it hadn't been for my business proposition to your father, he would likely still be alive."

"No! You won't talk like that!" He was gazing at her quizzingly, and she added, "If it were true, then imagine me as Sir Guy's wife, for it probably would have come to pass."

He didn't like that notion at all. Chauncey saw his lips tighten and his eyes darken. "There, you see what happens when you try to change the past? Actually, when you think about it, if it hadn't been for my godfather, Sir Jasper, I'd probably now be a shop girl in London, barely eking out a living."

"All right, you logical wench, I'll cease and desist."

"Do you still want to be in California's politics?" Chauncey asked abruptly.

"Yes, I do." His left brow shot upward as he remembered their prior discussions about it. "You agreed then," he said slowly, "because you hoped there'd be a way to ruin me."

"Yes, but I simply couldn't think of anything. I fear I'm not a very good plotter."

"But you're excellent in bed."

She smiled at him even as she said in a tart voice, "Is that all you men think about? Bedding women?"

"Alas, there's a great deal of truth to what you say."

"Del, you . . . well, you won't really mind giving up your mistress, will you?"

He gave her an appalled look. "Give up Marie? My dear girl, you expect me to forgo all my sport?"

Her eyes became large and distressed.

"Such a fool you are, Chauncey," he said softly, tweaking her nose. "You know very well that I gave up Marie before we were married."

"Yes, I suppose so, but you were so furious with me and you left that night, remember?"

"Yes, but I didn't go to Marie. Don't ever forget, Chauncey, ever: I love you to distraction. All right?"

"I don't deserve you," she said, and poked him in the ribs when he heartily agreed with her.

The night was cool and clear. Sated, Chauncey leaned back against Delaney's knees, staring into the glowing embers in the fireplace. The pheasant had been delicious. Her shoulder scarcely bothered her.

"I don't ever want to leave here," she said, leaning her head back so that she could see his face upside down.

"That's because I'm doing all the work, madam.

I would expect you to enjoy being waited on hand and foot. Well, hand and something."

She flushed just a bit.

He shifted her around and kissed her lightly on the lips. "I want you to get into your comfortable bed. I, dear one, am going down to the river to bathe."

"All right," she said, her pulse quickening. He helped her ease down into the bedroll and rose.

"I shan't be long. Can I expect you to be waiting for me when I return?"

She yawned dramatically. "I'm awfully tired, sir."

When Delaney returned to the shack some thirty minutes later, he was amused to see that she was indeed sleeping, her face glowing in the soft firelight, her breath even. He stripped off his clothes and started to slide under the blankets with her, but realized he was too wide-awake. He had kept all his doubts and concerns from her, and in the stillness of the dilapidated shack, they flooded into his mind.

Chauncey awoke slowly, not moving. She blinked several times, furious with herself that she'd fallen asleep. She turned her head on the valise—the makeshift pillow—and sucked in her breath. Delaney stood by the fireplace staring as if mesmerized by the jumping flames. He was naked.

— 29 —

Delaney's body glowed golden in the soft fire-light. He was leaning slightly forward, his arm braced against the rough-hewn stone ledge that served as a mantel. His head was bent and she could see the damp tendrils of hair at his neck curling slightly as his hair dried from his bath. He looked so locked into his thoughts that she kept herself silent, content for the moment to drink in the beauty of him.

Her eyes followed the profile of his body, the smooth slope of his back, the taut buttocks, the long, powerful legs. He turned slightly, and she stared at the muscled chest, the firm, flat belly, and the nest of hair at his groin. She wanted more than anything to touch him, to feel the crisp hair of his thighs, to rub her cheek against his belly.

"You are so damned beautiful," she said, scarcely aware that she'd spoken aloud.

He turned abruptly, saw that she was staring at him fully, and grinned. "I am pleased that you like the view."

He made no move to cover himself.

"It is not just your body that is beautiful," she continued after a moment, her eyes drawn downward as his manhood began to respond to her gaze. "You are such a complex man."

He arched a brow at her. "I assure you, my dear, that there isn't a complex thought in my head at the moment."

"I wish that you had some flaws!" she blurted out.

He laughed at that, and she watched the play of muscles in his chest.

"Well, it's true," she said, indignant. "I am nothing but one big flaw, and you ... well, you are so bloody perfect!"

"Oh, Chauncey, I am anything but a paragon. I have been known to sin, you know, and most royally."

"I feel that I've done nothing but sin, and make a mess of everything."

"You're through making messes, love, I promise you."

"Now you make me sound like a puppy!"

"Ah, I knew I could get you out of that serious vein and make you smile. Life is bloody strange." He looked bemused for a moment, then shook off his abstraction. He straightened, a look in his eyes that made her pulse begin to race. His eyes looked as golden as his body. She could feel their intensity, see the shades of feeling.

"I don't want to go back!" she said, running her tongue over her suddenly dry lips. "Ever."

He strode over to her and eased down to his knees. "When we return home, I promise you that what we have learned about each other these past days we won't forget." He held out his hands to her.

She came up to her knees before him. "I love you, Del."

"I know," he said, his voice lightly teasing, "and my body believes you as well."

He drew her gently against him and she felt his swollen manhood against her belly. His hands were lightly stroking down her back, curving around her hips, and raising her slightly.

She clasped her arms around his back and raised her head. He kissed her gently on her lips, his tongue probing until with a contented sigh she allowed him entrance.

He felt her soft breasts crushed against his chest, her nipples taut. His kiss deepened and he brought his hands up to clasp her face between his hands. When he finally released her mouth, she was gasping for breath, her breasts heaving. She nipped at his shoulder, easing down to kiss his nipples, her hand roving through the hair on his chest. She wanted him, all of him. She pictured him loving her body intimately, his mouth covering her until she wanted to scream with pleasure. Could he be so different from her? She eased down lower, giving him light, nipping kisses on his belly. She felt his muscles tighten, felt his entire body stiffen, and she smiled in anticipation. When her lips lightly touched his manhood, he jerked wildly, sucking in his breath.

"Chauncey . . ." he began, his voice raspy.

He slid his fingers into her hair, drawing her

head forward. The soft moistness of her mouth closed so gently around him. She could have no notion of what she was doing to him, he thought, utterly dazed by her marvelous initiative. He closed his eyes, flinging back his head, and let her swamp his body with incredible sensations. But it had been too long, and he could feel himself trembling toward release.

Slowly he pushed her away.

She raised her face and smiled at him. "I love the way you taste," she said, her voice awed and strangely excited. "And the way you feel and . . ." She lowered her head again, but he grasped her shoulders, bringing her upright.

"No! No more, love. I can't hold back."

"Oh," she said, considering his words. "But you never make me hold back."

"That," he said, a wry smile on his lips, "is not quite the same thing. Not the same thing at all."

She snuggled up against him, wrapping her arms about his shoulders. "Please," she said softly.

But he wouldn't be rushed, as much as he wanted to bury himself deep within her. He splayed his fingers over her buttocks, curving until he was probing at her softness. She was ready for him, wanting him as much as he wanted her.

"Oh God," he whispered hoarsely. "Wrap your arms around my neck," he said, easing down on his haunches. He lifted her hips and gently eased himself into her.

She cried out in surprise and pleasure.

"Am I hurting you?"

"Oh no," she cried, kissing him wildly.

He came deeper inside her, his eyes closed with the intense pleasure of her. This closeness, he thought passionately, was what he had always envisioned with a woman, the one special woman he'd almost despaired of ever finding. Her warmth and giving were filling him as he was filling her with himself.

"Lean back against my hands," he told her softly. She obeyed him instantly. "That's right, love. Relax and drop your arms. I don't want to hurt your shoulder."

She flung her head back, arching her back against the support of his hands, her breasts thrust forward. Slowly he eased her onto her back, never leaving her, and supported himself above her on his elbows. Her hips rose to meet his gentle thrusts, and he moaned softly deep in his throat at her response to him. He slipped his hand between them and began to caress her warm swollen flesh. Her eyes flew open, and he saw her desire for him. He began to tremble, thrusting more urgently, more deeply, his breath raspy in the still room. He felt her legs close about his flanks, drawing him deeper, and he tried to slow himself. But she wouldn't allow it.

She gasped his name, feeling his fingers burn white hot into the depths of her, felt him so deep inside her that he was one with her.

She screamed his name, her body tensing, her eyes closing as the convulsing, nearly painful sensations ripped through her body.

He thrust deep, making himself a part of her, spewing his seed into her, thinking at that moment that he had come home.

Chauncey quivered slightly as the gentle spasms

continued to fill her. The feel of him, oh God, she thought, utterly dazed, the feel of him surrounding her, filling her, knowing her . . .

"What's this? Why are you crying? Did I hurt you?"

His soft voice rumbled close by her ear, and she clutched her arms around his back, burying her face in his shoulder. She breathed in the scent of him, pressing her lips against him, and tasted the sheen of perspiration that covered his flesh.

"Chauncey . . ."

"I'm fine, truly fine. I just can't seem to get enough of you."

He arched back and looked down into her face. "You look quite proud of yourself," he observed.

She wriggled her hips upward, drawing him inward. "I shan't let you leave me."

"You know, I begin to believe that having a wife is not a bad thing at all. Particularly a wife who makes me wild every night."

"The wife feels the same away," she said. "Del, no!"

"Sorry, sweetheart." He eased off her onto his side. "Just give me some time to regroup my troops."

"Yes, general, sir." She raised her hand and lightly stroked her fingertips over his bearded jaw. "Del, if Chatca had"—she paused a moment, the word hovering in her mind—"if he had raped me, what would you have done? Would you have hated me?"

It was on the tip of his tongue to tease her and tell her that she was young and silly, but he didn't. She was perfectly serious, and he responded in kind. "I don't understand why a woman could possibly feel guilty if she is the victim."

He felt a slight shudder go through her. "I think I would feel so . . . dirty, so unworthy."

"Do you know, I have heard some men blame women for another man's violence. I have even heard them joke about how they won't enter a field where other men have plowed. In fact, Sam Brannan wondered in all upright honesty how I could have Lin in my house when she'd been a common whore to more men than he could count. As if it had been her decision, her choice! It took months for the haunted look to leave Lin's eyes, to see her stand firm, not flinch when I came close to her. Men are sometimes bastards."

"You wouldn't have minded, then?"

"Of course. I would feel guilty myself that I allowed you so little protection that you could be violated. I would have killed the man who'd harmed you."

She sighed deeply, nestling her face against his chest. "But there's something not right here," she said suddenly, pulling back to look at him. "You're right, I can see that now. Had he raped me, it wouldn't have been my fault. What I don't understand is why men can think that way. After all, if it were not for them, there would be no women who were whores in the first place. Or mistresses," she added, her eyes darkening.

He grinned down at her, lightly flicking the tip of her nose with his finger. "Your logic is terrifying," he said.

"And what's more," she continued, frowning at him, "what is all this about men not wanting to . . . *plow* a field where other men have been. What about women? I don't want a man who's been plowing in other fields."

"Destroyed by my own metaphor."

"Isn't it the same thing?"

"No, it isn't, and it's tough to explain why. Had you not come to me a virgin, I would have been driven wild to know what other man had known you. I would have thought less of you, as unfair as that may sound."

"But I didn't think less of you, and I know you weren't a virgin! You knew too much about things."

"I doubt we would have accomplished much on our wedding night had I been as ignorant as you. It all has to do with you as a lady, Chauncey, that paragon of womanhood whose thoughts and actions must be inviolate. Such a seamy thing as her actually wanting sex is unthinkable. Once she is married, then magically she should be willing to give herself to her husband. She must be pure and utterly innocent, else she's not truly a lady. Does that make sense?"

"I suppose men have ensured that it makes sense. Yet I consider you a gentleman."

"Not the same thing, love. There is a point to it all, you know. You, sweetheart, will carry my children. And as a man whose property and money will go to his children, I want to be certain that they are mine, and not another's."

"Then if I had been raped and become pregnant, you would have hated me because you couldn't be certain it was your child I was carrying."

He stared at her a moment, examining himself,

for he'd never considered such a thing. "I would be a true bastard if that were true," he said finally, "and I don't believe I am. No, I wouldn't hate you, nor would I hate the child, for, you see, the child would be half you. Now, have I given a good enough account of myself?"

"It is all rather difficult, isn't it?" She raised her hand and lightly touched her fingertips to his lips. "I suppose I do understand, yet it seems that women can do naught but slip off the path of righteousness." She smiled crookedly.

"Just so long as when you slip, it is into my arms."

"Ah, and there's another thing, Del."

He groaned. "I make love to you, and in the aftermath I must indulge in philosophical discussions."

She slightly tugged at a tuft of hair on his chest. "No, I am just a simple woman who needs a man to explain things to her. For instance, do you know that at twenty-one I was considered practically a spinster in England? Twenty-one years old! And here you are, a man and twenty-eight. You were a bachelor and that was marvelous! Goodness, even if you were in your thirties, you still could have wed me and no one would have thought it inappropriate that so many years separated us."

"I know what's coming next," he said on a deep, long-suffering sigh. "Chauncey, at twenty you were so much more intelligent, mature, winsome, and marvelous than I was at your age. It takes a man time and years to gain enough experience to make him acceptable. And you know something? I was disturbed that you were so old.

All of twenty-one. A man wants an obedient, malleable wife. I should have found you when you were eighteen."

"You sound like you're jesting, but I know you're serious."

"You're wrong," he said, leaning down to kiss her pursed lips. "I am rarely serious. It's bad for the digestion. Now, watching your eyes glow with pleasure is quite good for the digestion. Hush now, I want to quiet down the rustic dinner in my belly."

His hand slid down to cup her breast, kneading it gently.

"What about my digestion?" she whispered into his mouth.

"It's up to me, my love, to ensure that in a very, very short time, all you'll be thinking about is me in your belly."

Why, Chauncey wondered drowsily sometime later, did he persist in being right?

She slept deeply, her body satiated, the pain in her shoulder so negligible that it didn't pierce the warmth of her rest. It grew chilly during the night, and she went naturally to him, curving herself against his back, her arm around his waist. Her dreams were soft and rambling, filled with light and laughter. The past and the present interwove easily, and she smiled gently, even deep in sleep.

When the door to the shack burst open just after dawn, the shock of it brought her upright, a scream on her lips.

For an instant she was too disoriented to react. There were two men, both holding guns, standing in the doorway.

The taller man she recognized as Baron Jones, the man who had been on the wharf that day in San Francisco, the man Del had fought a duel with. A slender man, black-haired, his features somehow too well-defined for handsomeness, his complexion ruddy. His eyes were cold as the North Sea, a fathomless gray. The other man was mean-looking, almost skinny, and bandy-legged. He was staring at her, his mouth agape, revealing darkly stained teeth.

"Lordy, Baron," the man gasped, "would you look at those tits."

Chauncey's examination of them had taken only a brief moment. She grasped the blanket and pulled it to her neck.

"Del always provides himself with the most prime piece of ass available. Even hitched himself to this one. Isn't that right, Saxton?"

Chauncey felt Delaney's arm go around her back. She turned to look at him and felt her blood run cold.

Never had she seen him so quietly and utterly enraged.

"'What do you want, you filthy son of a bitch?" Delaney asked, his voice so calm that he might have been discussing the weather.

"Why, we've come for the lady, of course," Baron Jones said, his mouth splitting wide to show even white teeth.

"I see," Delaney said, his voice still coldly controlled. "The Indian let you down."

"Stupid fool bastard," Baron spat. "Can't trust those renegades to do anything right. Of course now I can begin to understand his problem. Old Jasper here is right. The bitch has got lovely tits.

I thought she had promise, lots of it, when I first saw her."

Chauncey was stunned. They'd hired Chatca to kill her! But he'd wanted her. And Delaney had guessed the truth. She felt him pull away from her and lurch to his feet, and heard the man Jasper bark out a low laugh.

"No doubt what they were doin' all night, huh, Baron?"

Delaney stood naked, his hands fisted at his sides. "I really should have killed you two years ago, Baron. Ah, indeed, I really should have," he said, his eyes as hard as stone.

"You lost your chance, Saxton. In fact, you're fixin' to lose everything. I wonder if your shoulder still pains you when the weather changes." As he spoke, he rubbed his leg. "The bullet's still there, you know. Every time it pains me, I think of you, Saxton. I didn't hesitate to accept this offer. To even up the score, as it were."

"And just where is Paul Montgomery?" Delaney asked, not moving a muscle.

Baron laughed. "The greenhorn Englishman is safe and snug in Nevada City. Poor proper little gentleman. He can't abide our abominable lack of civilization. I'm wondering what proof we can bring him that we've finally removed his problem once and for all?"

Chauncey found her voice. "Please," she said, coming up to her knees, "let Del go. He has nothing to do with Paul Montgomery. Nothing."

"Well, little honey," Baron said, "maybe we can work out a deal."

Delaney's hand clutched Chauncey's shoulder, hard. "Shut up," he said very precisely and slowly.

She looked up at her husband, her eyes pleading, feeling more helpless than she had in her entire life.

"Lookie, Baron, the little filly has a bandage on her shoulder. Maybe the Indian did try to do away with her."

Baron gave that wide, dazzling smile of his again, and shrugged eloquently. "Well, Jasper, we'll never know, will we?"

"What do you mean?" Chauncey whispered.

"Shot the bastard's brains out, along with those other ragtag savages."

Oh God, they'd killed all of them! Cricket too. Poor Cricket, who'd saved her life.

It all came back to Paul Montgomery. She felt a fury so profound that her body began to tremble. She clutched the blanket around her and rose shakily to her feet.

— 30 —

"Ah, Baron, just a mangy blanket!" Jasper took an excited step forward.

Delaney moved swiftly, planting himself firmly in front of Chauncey. "You won't touch her, you vermin! I'll tear out your throat if you even make the attempt."

Jasper stopped cold in his tracks, but after a short moment his courage returned. "I've got the gun, Saxton, not you! What do you say to me shootin' your balls off?"

"Now, now, Jasper, don't get your dander up. Old Del here, well, he's just tryin' to protect his woman."

Very slowly Chauncey stepped back until she was pressed against the back wall of the shed.

Delaney said, "Do you gentlemen mind if I put my breeches on?"

Baron Jones waved the deadly gun. "Not at all. We wouldn't want your little lady over there gettin' lascivious thoughts."

Delaney was thinking as calmly as he could. They had taken him utterly off guard; he was a complete fool not to have realized the possibility that Montgomery had hired a villain like Baron to ensure that the Indian, Chatca, had done his dirty work. He fastened his breeches and pulled his shirt over his head and tucked it into his pants. He picked up Chauncey's skirt and blouse and very slowly walked over to her.

"Eh now!" Jasper screeched. "Nothin' said about covering up the little honey!"

Delaney paid him no attention. He heard the click of the hammer, then Baron's voice. "Naw, Jasper. It's just a skirt and shirt. Nothin', really."

"Chauncey, listen to me," Del said very quietly as he handed her the clothes. "I want you to stay silent. If you talk, you draw their attention."

She raised wide, frightened eyes to his face. "What are we going to do?"

"I don't know yet. Baron, well, he's the type to gloat. The longer I can make him gloat over me, the better our chance."

Delaney turned and said, "I suggest, gentlemen, that we leave my wife in peace so she can dress herself."

"I wanna watch her!" Jasper said. "I wanna see those tits again."

"There'll be all the time you want for that, Jasper," Baron said, his eyes narrowing with intense satisfaction on Delaney's face. "Now, Del here knows all there is to know about being a gentleman. There's a bucket of water outside. I'm thirsty. Come along, Jasper." Baron waved the barrel of his gun toward Delaney, and he walked swiftly out of the shack. Baron paused a moment, saw Delaney's rifle, and tucked it under his arm. He slung Delaney's pistol and gunbelt over his shoulder. "You probably don't know one end from the other, little honey, but why tempt fate?" He gave her a smile that made her grow utterly cold, and strode from the shack.

She was left alone. It seemed an eternity before Chauncey could make herself move. Her knuckles showed white from strain. *Dress yourself, dammit!* Within moments she was tucking in the blouse and straightening the skirt over her legs. Thoughts of her discussion with Delaney the previous evening about rape tumbled through her mind. Rape was nothing compared to what these men intended. And all because of Paul Montgomery. Delaney would die too, because of her.

Stop it! You're acting like a dithering female!

Chauncey drew in a deep steadying breath and began to search the cabin. No weapon. She quickly bent over Delaney's valise and tossed aside his clothes. She had no hope of finding a weapon, not really, and when she saw her pearl-handled derringer, she blinked, thinking it was an apparition. "Oh God," she whispered to herself, "please let it be loaded." It was. It was just where she'd left it the night Chatca had taken her. She slipped it quickly into one of the large tattered pockets of the skirt. Her heart was pounding. They'll know. They'll know!

She was standing still as a statue when the men returned to the cabin.

"You sit over there on the floor, Del, and keep yourself quiet," Baron said. "You, little honey,

Jasper and me are hungry. Whip us up some grub and coffee."

"She doesn't know how," Delaney said. "As you can see, she was wounded in the Indian camp. I've taken care of her."

Baron looked undecided for a moment, then shrugged. "Very well. Come here, girl. Your husband makes one wrong move, and you'll have a bullet through your pretty head. You hear, Saxton?"

"I hear," Delaney said. He saw Jasper move toward Chauncey from the corner of his eye, and said to Baron, "You seem to have pulled this off pretty well. Tell me, how did you get in contact with Montgomery?"

Chauncey watched Baron Jones straighten, pull back his shoulders, and preen. Jasper stopped in his tracks and watched his partner.

"Well, you see, Del, I know Hoolihan. Ah, surprised you, didn't I? I watched Monk haul him around, Monk and those other scum you hired. But you see, Montgomery was in San Jose and I went to see him, told him you'd captured his man. He's paying me a lot of money, Del, enough to set up my own gambling saloon. Right here close by in Nevada City, I think. Jasper here, well, he'll make sure none of the miners leave the area with too much gold in their pockets."

"You've really thought this all out, haven't you, Baron?"

"Yes, indeed, Del. As for Montgomery, as soon as Jasper and I meet him in Nevada City, he'll pay us and take himself back to England. You know something, though, I would like to know why he wants your wife dead and buried. He wouldn't tell me nothin'."

Delaney carefully set several mugs on the rough table and poured the steaming coffee. He'd thought to fling the hot liquid in their faces, but Jasper was hunkered down near Chauncey. He'd kill her before Delaney could get to him. Or put a bullet through him. Bide your time, he told himself over and over. Keep Baron talking.

"Actually," Delaney said, arching a brow toward Baron, "it's a tale that doesn't make Montgomery look like much of a saint. He murdered my wife's father and stole from him. After dangling my wife on his knee when she was little, he decided she'd learn the truth about him. He should probably remain here in the West. He's a lawyer, you know, and he'd fit right in with the rest of the jackals."

"That ain't a pretty story at all," Jasper observed.

"He tried to kill her before she left England, but she escaped injury. I suppose he was on one of the next ships over. He really doesn't deserve to live."

"Nope, ain't pretty at all," Jasper said again, shaking his head. "Why don't you and I wipe him out, Baron?"

"Honor, my dear Jasper, honor among thieves, I believe the saying goes. Breaking a deal isn't good for a man's reputation, an' things like that get around."

Chauncey spoke up, her voice soft and shaking. "Did you know that he pretended to be my friend after my father's supposed suicide? He even managed tears at my father's funeral."

"Well, ain't that a kicker!" Jasper said in disgust.

"Now, now, Jasper," Baron said, amused contempt in his voice, "the man's smart. Even you should be able to appreciate that. Now, Del, you got anything to eat? I don't like to work on an empty stomach."

"Moldy bread, that's all, Baron. If you want something more substantial, you'll have to go out and shoot it."

Baron sipped at his coffee for a moment. "Well, you know, we don't have to be in Nevada City until tomorrow. I don't suppose it'd hurt to let the two of you have a final meal. Kind of like getting ready for an execution." He rubbed his thigh. "Yeah, an execution."

Delaney felt a spurt of hope, but nothing showed on his face. His expression remained impassive, and he shrugged his shoulders. "Up to you" was all he said.

As for Chauncey, she had to lower her head. She was afraid that they'd see the glitter in her eyes.

"Jasper," Baron said, "let's see if you can hit anything. We'll feed up the little honey here real good. Think of all the fight she'll have if she's got more strength."

Jasper muttered under his breath, but rose.

"First, let's make sure Del here won't try anything stupid." Baron tore strips off the blanket and bound Delaney's hands behind his back, then his ankles. He sent an interested look in Chauncey's direction.

"You leave her tits alone, Baron! I want her first."

"I'll do nothing more than warm her up a bit," Baron said.

I should have thrown the coffee at them and taken my chances. Delaney closed his eyes a moment. Now he was helpless, and he knew Baron would delight more in watching his fury than in actually touching Chauncey. He began jerking and pulling on the bonds.

Jasper stalked out of the shack. "I'll be back in a flash," he called over his shoulder.

"Take your time, Jasper. Take your time." Baron spoke very softly, only for Delaney and Chauncey's hearing. "You know something, Del? With you out of the way, I think I'll teach that little whore Marie a real lesson. The bitch had the gall to tell me that I didn't have anything a real man had. Yes," he added, his voice sounding a bit dreamy, "I'll show her what I can do." He straightened suddenly, and looked purposefully at Chauncey. "In fact, Del, I think I'll practice on your wife. After all, both she and Marie have shared your bed. We'll let her tell us about how a real man acts."

"Don't you touch her, Baron!"

"Now, Del, be reasonable. There's nothing you can do about anything. Grind your teeth all you want. Me, I lied to Jasper. I do want to see those pretty tits again, and without him salivatin' all over me and her."

Delaney yanked with all his strength at the bonds about his wrists, but they didn't give. He gritted his teeth against the pain and continued working them. He watched in horror as Baron moved lithe as a stalking tiger toward his wife. He met Chauncey's gaze, and froze. There was no fear in her eyes. Indeed, if it were possible, he read anticipation there. Fierce urgency.

"Stand up, little honey," Baron said. "I wanna peel off those clothes."

Chauncey rose to her feet. She even smiled a little at Baron. She said in a taunting soft voice, "You need a gun? My husband has never had to use force with me." She shrugged. "But then again, you aren't really ..." She let her voice trail off.

Baron's eyes narrowed. "What are you about? You think to overpower me? Honey, I could break your neck with one hand."

"Is that what you want to do?" she said, her voice still mocking.

He rushed her, flinging down his gun. He clasped her against him, pressing her arms to her sides.

Chauncey heard Del yelling at him, cursing him in language she'd never before even imagined. But she didn't move. She felt his mouth on her cheek, moving toward her lips. His grip on her arms was still too strong. She couldn't get to the derringer. She went limp against him.

"See this, Saxton? Your wife is nothing more than a whore. They're all alike!"

He hooked his leg behind hers and shoved her onto her back. She felt the hard wooden planks biting into her, felt his weight crushing her down. A flash of pain went through her shoulder, but she ignored it. His mouth was all over her, his hands ripping at her blouse. "You love it, don't you?" he said, laughing. He bit her neck and she moaned with pain. He laughed louder.

He tore her blouse free, and leaned up on his

elbow. "Poor Jasper," he said, panting slightly. "I get to touch you first."

Chauncey didn't move. She felt his tongue thrust into her mouth, and forced herself not to bite down on it. Just a moment longer, she told herself. He reared up suddenly and flung her skirt to her waist. He sucked in his breath and stared down at her. "Jesus," he said, licking his lips.

Chauncey raised one arm and laid her palm against his shoulder. "Yes," she whispered, smiling at him. "Oh yes."

Baron began pulling open his breeches. Then he fell forward on her, his heavy manhood pressing against her closed thighs.

Chauncey shut out Delaney's furious voice. She shut out everything. Oh yes, she said to herself. Oh yes.

The muffled sound of the derringer caught Delaney in mid-curse.

He stared at Baron, who had hauled himself up on his elbows. There was a hole in his chest, and blood was spilling out onto Chauncey's bare breasts.

"You scum!" Chauncey cried, and fired the other bullet in the derringer into his stomach.

"*No!*"

Baron fell forward, but Chauncey jerked sideways, drew herself into a ball, and rolled. Baron fell, his face smashing against the rough planking.

She dashed to Delaney and pulled frantically at his bonds. "Quickly," she gasped. "I was a fool. I used both bullets. Jasper will have heard the shots! Quickly, Del! Oh my God, your wrists— they're raw!"

"No matter," Delaney said, his numb fingers ripping off the bonds around his ankles. He heard her draw in her breath and stared at her suddenly colorless face. "Not yet," he said sharply. "Not yet! We've still got Jasper to handle."

Delaney hurled himself across the floor toward the rifle and his gun, but he wasn't in time.

There was an unearthly shriek from the doorway. "You killed him, gutted him! You murderin' little bitch!"

Chauncey froze, every sense suspended as she stared toward Jasper, whose face was contorted with fury. Even as he raised his gun, she didn't move.

"Jasper!" Delaney yelled, and as the man slewed his head toward him, Delaney jumped. He landed a foot from him and grabbed his arms, jerking him against him.

Chauncey watched Jasper struggle. Delaney was the larger and the stronger, but Jasper wouldn't release the gun.

"Please, God," she whispered, watching every movement, hearing every strangled breath from the two men.

The table collapsed as Delaney's body smashed against it. He held Jasper's gun arm, feeling the muscles and bones twisting beneath the onslaught. The man was howling, trying desperately to bring the gun upward.

Jasper kicked Delaney in the groin, and for an instant Delaney's grip loosened. But only for an instant. "I'm going to kill you, you filthy bastard," he whispered between gritted teeth.

Jasper had time only to bring the gun up between them.

Suddenly there was a loud retort.

Chauncey weaved where she stood. Neither man moved.

"Del," she whispered in a strangled voice. Slowly Delaney pulled away from Jasper. Blood covered his chest.

Chauncey screamed.

Then she saw Jasper, his chest ripped open, sink to the floor. The gun fell from his lifeless fingers and clattered across the room.

There was utter silence.

"I'm all right, Chauncey," Delaney said, his voice once again calm and controlled. "It's all over, love."

She flung herself at him, clutching him tightly to her, sobbing violently. She felt his hands stroking over her back, heard him whispering soft, meaningless words to her.

She eased, her breath evening out, her sobs becoming hiccups. She opened her eyes and the first sight she saw was Baron's sprawled body.

"I killed him," she said, disbelief and shock thick in her voice. "I actually killed someone. Oh God!"

"Hush and listen to me, Chauncey. You saved yourself and you saved me. You were very brave and courageous. I love you and I thank you." His fingers were stroking her brows, her cheeks, her jaw as he spoke. "Do you understand? You did what you had to do. I am so very proud of you." His hands closed around her face and he looked deep into her eyes. "Do you understand me?"

She drew a deep breath. "The derringer is so small."

"Yes, but deadly."

"I think I'll retch if I ever touch it again."

"You will touch it again and you won't retch. You'll respect that small piece of hardware now, and you won't abuse it. You will carry it until we have Montgomery. All right?"

She whispered his name. "I never believed a man could be so evil."

"Evil and desperate. Now, I want you to take one of my shirts—unfortunately, they're all soiled—and go bathe in the stream. There's a sliver of soap and a towel on the floor in the corner. You will stay there until I come for you."

She realized that he would bury the two men, spare her that awful sight, and she nodded slowly.

"Good girl. Go now."

— 31 —

Only three hours had passed, Chauncey thought, dazed. Three hours since Baron and Jasper had hurled themselves into the shack. Now they were dead and buried, their horses given to the first miners they had seen.

Delaney hadn't tried to make conversation with her. When he'd fetched her from the stream, he'd simply smiled and said, "Now, love, we're leaving. Are you up for a long ride?"

She nodded, grateful that she wouldn't have to return to the shack.

She didn't particularly notice the beautiful countryside they were riding through. The fir trees jutted high on the surrounding hills. The foothills of the Sierra Nevadas, she told herself. They saw men now, miners, who were working in the creek bed, their gold pans swishing in a continuous circular motion. The air was clear and dry, and not too hot. A fine day.

She turned finally and said to Delaney, "We're going to Nevada City?"

He grinned widely at her. "Not yet, love. First, it's Grass Valley, a small mining town only about five miles west of Nevada City. If you haven't noticed, you and I aren't exactly the picture of elegance. We'll spend the night at the Davidson Hotel, buy ourselves some decent clothes, and then I'll go to Nevada City tomorrow." He paused a moment, his brows drawing together as he stared between his horse's ears. "I want to face Montgomery as I am normally," he continued, "not looking like an itinerant miner."

"What do you mean by 'I'?"

"Just what I said," he replied, his voice clipped, brooking no argument. He heard her draw in her breath and tensed, waiting.

"You, Del," she said, delighting in the fact that her voice sounded so reasonable and calm, "have never before seen Paul Montgomery. I can't imagine that he would be such a fool as to use his real name, either."

"I, on the other hand, believe that he will. He has no reason not to. You will stay in Grass Valley, safe. For once."

"No, I won't."

"I believe your marriage vows included one of obedience."

"Bosh! I can't believe you, Del! Not above two hours ago you were telling me how proud you were of me, telling me that I was brave and courageous. Now I'm back to being a helpless female?"

He didn't look at her. "I didn't protect you. I was a fool not to guess that the Indian was not the only one involved. My stupidity nearly cost you your life. I will hear nothing more about it."

"I don't think you can avoid it. After all, if you ride off, I'll just get lost. Now, I don't consider that much protection!"

He swiveled in the saddle and glared at her. He could hold his ill-humored expression for only a moment, however. She looked like an adorable waif, from her tattered and faded skirt to his huge shirt, to her thick single braid of hair. "Lord, I do wonder what Montgomery would say were he to see you now! Some English lady!"

"At least you're laughing," she said, grinning at him. "That's got to be a step in the direction of good sense on your part."

The smile was wiped from his face. "Chauncey, I've thought about it. I know what I said to you this morning, and I mean it. But I can't face that again. I've never been so damned afraid in my life, nor felt so damned helpless."

"Well, I refuse to let you go alone to face Montgomery. It is my fight, after all, Del. Until this morning you were but a bystander."

"I won't argue with you about it anymore, Chauncey."

"Good!"

They rode in silence until they crested the rise of a small hill and saw the town of Grass Valley below them.

"How lovely it is," Chauncey said. "So peaceful."

Delaney hooted with laughter. "Just wait until Saturday night, when the miners come into gamble and raise hell. There are more saloons than stores or houses in this town. There's no law, but there is a post office."

They rode past scores of rough-garbed miners.

"They've been at it since forty-eight," Delaney said, waving at the men. "We're riding along Wolf Creek. The surface gold here gave out early. You just might meet George McKnight, who came here in fifty. That lucky bastard stumbled on a shiny rock outcropping. He discovered that the rock was loaded with gold. To date, this area is the second-richest find in California. Why—"

"You're just trying to distract me, Del, and it won't work! And so much for your quiet little town. Would you just look at that crowd!"

They'd ridden onto Auburn Street, a fairly wide road lined with wooden buildings. Dust kicked up about their horses' legs, for it hadn't rained much here and the sun was brilliantly hot overhead. As they neared Bank Street, the crowds grew thicker. There were shouts and hoorays from scores of men.

Delaney motioned for Chauncey to rein in for a moment. He dismounted and asked a bearded miner, "What the hell is going on?"

"You ain't heard? Why, Lola Montez just arrived! Lordy! She's a looker. Got her husband with her. Hear she's gonna settle here."

Delaney shaded his eyes with his hand. Sure enough, he could make out Pat Hull standing next to the famous dancer. He looked pleased as punch at the reception his wife was getting.

He returned to Chauncey and told her what was happening.

"Goodness," she said, her eyes sparkling. "The

famous Spider Dance in Grass Valley. What a treat!"

"Given what happened after her first couple of performances in San Francisco, I wonder how long it will be a treat."

Poor Lola, Chauncey thought, her tour in San Francisco hadn't been very successful. Her eyes suddenly fastened on a man who looked so much like Paul Montgomery that she gasped aloud.

Delaney gave her a sharp look. "What's the matter? Is your shoulder hurting you?"

"No," she managed. "I'm all right, Del, really." Never would she tell him about the man; it would only give him more of a reason to leave her behind.

They wove their horses through the crowds and turned onto Mill Street. The Davidson Hotel stood on the corner, a two-story wooden structure that had enjoyed a recent painting.

"Let's get settled in first, then do some shopping."

Chauncey felt terribly self-conscious, but the stoop-shouldered, bespectacled clerk behind the counter didn't seem to see anything wrong with her appearance.

"Ah, Mr. Saxton. Welcome back to Grass Valley, sir."

"Thank you, Ben. Is Hock's still the best store for women's clothes?"

"Yep. Men's too. But I'll betcha that old Bernie is out watching that famous dancer woman."

"We'll give him a while to enjoy himself properly," Delaney said. "Could you send up some hot bathwater for my wife and me?"

"Certainly, Mr. Saxton. Welcome to Grass Valley, Mrs. Saxton."

"It's nice that some things don't change. I didn't think Ben would last, but he's still here. I think Davidson gave him part-ownership to keep him from leaving for the mines. Ah, here's our room, love."

At least, Chauncey thought, her gaze roving about the boxlike room, everything looked clean. There was a simple oak armoire that looked as if it had been built two days before. The wood smelled quite fresh. A small basin on a commode, a good-size bed with a quilted cotton counterpane, and a hooked wool rug made up the rest of the furnishings.

"Ah, to be home," she said, grinning at her husband.

"Have I married a snob?" he asked, a brow arched upward.

"Look at me closely and ask that question again!"

There were several women in Hock's General Store and they blinked at Chauncey's clothes, but their look wasn't at all disapproving, only curious. As for the men, they didn't seem to see anything out of the ordinary. One of them even tipped his felt hat at her. If I were seen like this in London, Chauncey thought in some amusement, there would be a riot! As for "old" Bernie, he was all of forty, as round as he was tall, and had a merry smile.

"We'll fix both of you right up, Del!"

And he did. The two gowns Chauncey decided on were made of sturdy cotton, as were all the underthings. No silks or satins, my girl, she said to herself, smiling at a particularly flashy gingham skirt.

Even as she smiled and nodded or shook her head as old Bernie presented her with different garments, she felt raw fear eating away at her. She wouldn't let Del face Paul Montgomery alone. She couldn't.

"Do you have enough money for all this?" she asked her husband as she eyed the pile of men's and women's clothing atop the counter.

"Madam, I'll contrive," he said.

That evening, they ate in a small restaurant called Curlie's just off Main Street. The food was most plentiful and Chauncey felt her mouth water at the sight of bread and butter. "A feast," she said, rubbing her hands together.

"I've always found that a little deprivation makes one appreciate the more basic things in life."

"You're salivating too, Mr. Saxton!"

"True enough," he agreed, and bit into a thick crust of warm bread.

A harassed waiter brought them thick steaks, green beans, fried potatoes, and huge slabs of apple pie.

"Oh goodness. I think I've died and gone to heaven."

She saw Delaney stiffen and knew he was thinking about their close brush with death just that morning.

"Del," she said sharply, "stop it! We're both alive and quite well and we're going to stay that way."

He gazed at her intensely and she saw the

glittering desire in his golden eyes. She sucked in her breath, her body responding to him, and her forkful of potatoes plopped onto her plate.

"You really shouldn't be thinking what you're thinking," she said, her voice somewhat breathless.

"How do you know what my thoughts are?"

She looked him straight in the eye. "Because I'm thinking the same thoughts, that's how."

"Good," he said, and the caressing softness of that one word made gooseflesh rise on her arms.

They enjoyed their dinner in silence. Chauncey dropped her fork and leaned back in her chair. "Not another bite or I'll pop out of my very fancy new gown! That was the most delicious meal I've ever eaten."

Delaney nodded, still seemingly interested in his dinner plate. "Do you know, Chauncey," he began after a moment, "I will never let another day go by in my life without realizing how sweet it is to simply be alive, and how sweet it is to have my wife by my side, laughing with me, even arguing with me. Life can be too bloody fragile."

It still is! "Yes, it can be," she said quietly. "Del, please, we must talk about Paul Montgomery."

"No," he said quite pleasantly, "not tonight."

"What do you intend to do to him?"

"Love, don't you want more of your apple pie? A bit more wine?"

She frowned at him, her hands clenching. "Treating me like some idiot is not what I call protecting me!"

"Very well, we will speak of it in the morning.

Tonight, wife, my body wants to reaffirm that I am alive. I want you, Chauncey, very much."

Chauncey never doubted that she wanted him equally, but later, in their bed, she found that her mind wouldn't cease its mad flights of fear. So much had happened in such a short time. So much was still to happen.

His hand stilled on her breast. "I had thought to act something of an opiate," he said quietly, nuzzling against her temple.

"We have been very lucky. I am so afraid our luck has to run out."

His hand gently glided down over her belly, his fingers lightly probing. She was moist, but she wasn't ready for him, not really, not until he could ease her mind of her fear for him. Better to face it, he thought. "Listen to me, love. I do intend to kill Montgomery. I have to. If I don't, you will always fear him and so will I. But I don't want you to see it. You've already experienced too much violence and death."

To his surprise, her body went rigid, and she hissed, "He killed my father! I want him dead. I want to kill him myself!"

"No! No, I can't allow that." He felt the resistance in her, the terrible blood lust. He kissed her hard, thrusting his tongue into her mouth, and moved to cover her with his body. Swiftly he shoved her legs apart and lifted her hips to receive him. He had to make her accept him, accept his decision to protect her both physically and emotionally, and his body chose domination. She cried out softly as he drove into her. But he couldn't, wouldn't stop. He had to make her understand! He had to . . . His body exploded and he arched back, a ragged cry erupting from his throat.

She didn't move. He shook his head, his body held stiff above her, his organ still deep and quivering within her.

He felt as cold as his voice as he asked, "Did I hurt you?"

"No." Chauncey felt curiously detached. She wasn't angry, for she probably understood his action better than he did himself.

Delaney eased himself off her and lay upon his back staring at the darkened ceiling. "I didn't mean to do that. I didn't mean to abuse you."

"I know. Tomorrow, Del, we will decide together how we will deal with Paul Montgomery."

Suddenly he began to laugh, a deep, rumbling sound that made her smile. "I should have known," he gasped over his laughter. "I should have known that I would never fall in love with a woman who would docilely and submissively do as I told her. Very well. We will decide together what to do. But you will not kill him, Chauncey. All right?"

"All right."

"Swear to me, else I'll string you up by your toes."

He felt her hand stroke over his chest, downward to his belly. When her fingers lightly closed over him, she said very sweetly, "I swear . . . and I'd rather have you do other things to me."

"Jesus," he muttered, somewhat in awe at his body's immediate reaction, "I'd thought I was dead for the night!"

*   *   *

They left Grass Valley at ten o'clock the following morning. The summer day was bright and warm, not a cloud in the clear sky.

"We'll arrive in Nevada City in an hour," he said, turning in his saddle to face her.

"Yes," she said. "You already told me."

"There's something else that occurred to me. Remember the message I got telling me there was trouble at my mine in Downieville? It was obviously another ruse. Doubtless Baron suggested it. Montgomery probably expected that I would leave you in San Francisco. When I brought you along, he had to make other plans, likely again with Baron's aid. The man is intelligent, I don't doubt that. And an intelligent man is a dangerous man."

"But he is also a man who has no experience outside the bounds of civilization. I remember as a child that he never hunted. Nor can I recall ever seeing him with a rifle or a gun."

"He killed your father."

"Yes, an overdose of laudanum."

There was silence between them for several minutes. "I do have a plan, Chauncey," Delaney said. "I don't particularly like your part in it, but there are practical considerations, such as trying to force a man out of town at gunpoint. I doubt I could pull that off. However, you must promise me that you will do exactly as I tell you."

She gave him a long, thoughtful look. "You are also an intelligent man. And I trust you, now that you've admitted to my true worth. I give you my word."

"There is still an element of danger."

"I have lived with the thought of danger for the past six months. At least now I can look forward to eliminating it once and for all."

"Very well," he said. "Listen."

— 32 —

Paul Montgomery jerked his watch from his vest pocket and stared at it again. Where the hell was Baron? He shoved the watch away again and gazed about the small saloon, empty at this hour save for several drinkers and diehard gamblers at the roulette wheel. He felt as if he'd died and gone to hell. Awful place. Sawdust floor, gawdy lewd paintings of sprawled naked women over the long mahogany bar, circular wooden tables that he wouldn't have allowed in his stables.

Where was Baron?

He wanted the wretched business over with. He wanted to go home, where he'd spend the rest of his life in peace and security. He'd traveled all the way to this godforsaken land to ensure it. He cursed softly, remembering his impotent fury when Elizabeth had escaped the carriage wheels in Plymouth. It hadn't taken him long to realize what he must do. If only Saxton didn't have powerful relatives in England! But he knew what would happen if he allowed her to live. He shivered at the thought of the Duke and Duchess of Graffton. He'd thought about leaving England and moving to the Continent to live like a king for the rest of his life. But it wouldn't work, he knew. Once Elizabeth discovered the truth, she wouldn't rest until she'd avenged her father. He had no choice but to remove her permanently.

And of course, there was the money, so much of it, and all his. Too bad Elizabeth had married, for now the Penworthys couldn't inherit even at her death, and he wouldn't be able to collect a healthy percentage. Married to Delaney Saxton! He could only pray that Elizabeth hadn't discovered too soon that her husband wasn't the evil villain she'd believed him to be. He swallowed nervously at the thought of a letter already posted to the duke and duchess informing them of his treachery. No, dammit, he wasn't too late! He couldn't be too late!

He lowered his fisted hand to the rough tabletop. If only Hoolihan hadn't bungled the job! If only Saxton hadn't captured him and forced him to talk! If only . . .

Where was Baron?

He had the final payment in his pocket. His valise was packed.

"Sir? Mr. Montgomery?"

Montgomery turned to face a skinny boy garbed in too short flannel trousers and bright red wool shirt. "Yes? What is it you want?"

"I've got a letter for you, sir."

Paul Montgomery stared at the folded sheet

for several moments. He dug into his vest pocket and withdrew a coin and gave it to the boy.

Slowly he opened it and read: *Montgomery, Saxton is dead. We're holding the girl at the old Hopkins mine just a mile south of Nevada City. You can kill her. It won't take much. Baron.*

Damn!

He reread the short note. Damn Baron! Bloody squeamish coward!

"Boy!" He rose quickly, but the lad was gone. Damn Baron! Why was he playing this wretched game? Why? *You can kill her. It won't take much.* He shuddered, knowing they'd raped her. Why couldn't they simply finish the job? God, he'd wanted it quick and clean. He'd tried; he'd really tried.

"Damned little bitch! She has more lives than a cat!"

Montgomery sat back down and drew off his spectacles. He slowly and thoroughly wiped the glass lenses with his handkerchief. It was a habit that always soothed him.

Saxton is dead.

He felt sorry about that. But, he repeated to himself silently yet again, he had no choice. No choice at all.

I've got to kill her! How? Put a bullet in her heart? Throw her over a cliff? Strangle her?

He felt his gorge rise. He wasn't a bloody savage barbarian like those wretched Sydney Ducks and Hoolihan and Baron. And Baron *was* a savage barbarian. Why hadn't he killed her?

Damn Baron to hell!

He rose somewhat shakily to his feet, his steps

becoming more purposeful and confident as he strode to the swinging doors of the saloon.

The Hopkins mine had been abandoned a year before by its disconsolate owner, Jeb Hopkins, Delaney told Chauncey, to pass the time. What Hopkins had believed to be a vast gold-bearing quartz vein hadn't appeared. Another Ophir Hill he'd thought it would be. But it wasn't. There simply wasn't enough gold to separate from the quartz.

The main tunnel and the huge shaft dug into the bowels of the mountain weren't yet in ruin.

"It's damp in here," Chauncey said, hugging her arms around her. "And cold."

"Yes, I know. Poor old Jeb is working alongside many other miners today, over at the Ophir Hill Ledge. The underground workings will be something to see someday. He'll be here soon, Chauncey. Everything will be all right, I promise you."

"I just want it to be over with," she said, trying to smile.

"Baron!"

Chauncey leapt to her feet, but Delaney laid a restraining hand on her arm. "Easy, love," he said in a low voice.

"Baron! Where are you?"

"It's him," Chauncey whispered, Montgomery's voice filtering through her mind back to long-ago childhood memories. She raised wide, dilated eyes to his face.

"Listen to me. I can't take the chance that he knows Baron's voice. I want you to scream now, as loud as you can."

Chauncey moistened her dry lips. She let out a shrieking yell that reverberated off the walls of the mine tunnel.

Delaney stepped back into the darkened tunnel. He withdrew his gun from its holster and held it easily in his hand, pointed to the mine entrance.

Montgomery's voice came softly now, closer. "Elizabeth?"

Chauncey whimpered, then cried out again.

"Bring her out, Baron. I'm not coming inside that hellhole."

Chauncey sent her husband a look of panic and consternation.

Think, you fool! "Baron's not feelin' good, sir!" Did he sound like Jasper? Please, God, let it sound so to Montgomery. "He's pukin' his guts out. The girl's nearly a goner. Give us our money and she's all yours!"

"Bridges, is that you?"

Bridges. Jasper Bridges! How kind that name sounds.

"Yep. Ye're wastin' time."

Delaney held his breath. He heard footsteps drawing nearer and nearer. Keep coming, you bastard. Keep coming!

He nodded to Chauncey, and she cried out again. Surely, she thought frantically, he can hear my heart pounding.

Montgomery appeared in the tunnel entrance. "Elizabeth," he said, taking a step inside.

"I'm here."

"As am I, you miserable son of a bitch." Delaney stepped forward, his gun firmly trained on Montgomery.

Montgomery had no time to pull the derringer from his vest pocket.

"No, don't try it, Montgomery."

"Where's Baron?" he asked, his mind fastening on one fact he could grasp.

"Neither he nor Jasper concern you further," Delaney said.

Montgomery drew a deep breath, his eyes adjusting to the gloom of the mine entrance. "The short message—'twas from you," he said.

"Yes. I had to get you out of Nevada City."

Chauncey had said nothing; she was staring at the man she'd known all her life, trusted implicitly until just months ago. Oddly, he looked much older than she remembered. And not as heavy as she remembered his being. His eyes shone through the thick lenses, and she could see his fear and . . . resignation. She asked very softly, her voice breaking, "Why did you kill my father?"

Paul Montgomery turned slowly to face her. "I had no choice," he said simply. "It seems that all choice has been wrenched from me since that time."

"No choice," she repeated. "But my father loved you! Trusted you! I called you 'uncle'!"

"Your father was something of a fool," Montgomery said, contempt entering his voice. "All his life he assumed that money was there for the asking. Only the best for Sir Alec! While he was enjoying himself at Oxford, I was slaving as a damned clerk with barely enough food in my belly! Oh yes, he was my friend. He discovered quickly enough that he needed me, needed my ability to handle his money. He even lowered himself enough to call me by my first name after only five years of acquaintance. But never was I invited to dine with his fancy guests! And if it weren't for me, you wouldn't have been raised so very well. All the finest you had! Beautiful home, servants, stables! Damn you, why didn't you marry Sir Guy! Why?"

She gave an odd, strained laugh. "No choice," she said, her voice a thread. "I was also raised to hold honor dear. A penniless young lady doesn't hold a gentleman to his offer, you know."

"I didn't want to kill you too, Elizabeth, but—"

"I know," Delaney interrupted coldly, "you again had no choice. You knew she would discover the truth."

"That's right," Montgomery said in a strangely calm voice.

Delaney could see Chauncey's pale face, see her eyes dilated. He had to spare her this. He said abruptly, "Chauncey, I want you to leave now. Go wait by the horses."

"But—"

"Go now. Obey me."

Paul Montgomery said nothing. He watched her straighten her shoulders and dust off her skirt. She didn't look at him, merely walked from the mine into the sunlight. She never looked back.

Chauncey carefully placed one foot before the other, her eyes seeing the rocky ground, her mind blank. She reached the nickering horses and reached her hand out involuntarily to stroke Dolores' silky nose. The mare butted against her shoulder and Chauncey moved closer, pressing her face against the mare's neck.

There was one gunshot. Only one.

She felt tears sting her eyes. She realized they weren't for Paul Montgomery; she had already cried for him and what he'd done months ago. They were for her husband. What he had been forced to do to protect her.

Suddenly she felt his warm hands clasp her shoulders.

"I'm sorry, love," he said quietly. He turned her against him and held her close.

"No," she said in a fierce whisper. "It is not for you to be sorry."

Delaney cupped her face between his hands and looked deep in her eyes. "It's over."

"Yes. I have taken so much from you, Del, so much! Please forgive me."

His hands tightened about her face. "There is nothing to forgive. You are my wife, the most important person in my life. You will never forget that, never."

She closed her eyes a moment against the intensity of his gaze. She whispered softly, "No, I shan't forget."

He hugged her tightly. "Now, Chauncey, let's go home."

Home to San Francisco, to live in joy and happiness, never again to know fear.

"Yes," she said, smiling now, "let's go home."

About the Author

When best-selling historical romance writer Catherine Coulter is not at work on her latest novel, she spends her time sailing, playing the piano, or enjoying Mill Valley, California with her husband, Anton.

Catherine Coulter is the author of several historical romances—*Devil's Embrace, Chandra, Devil's Daughter, Fire Song, Wild Star,* and *Jade Star,* as well as of a number of Regency romances—*The Autumn Countess, The Rebel Bride, Lord Deverill's Heir, Lord Harry's Folly, The Generous Earl, An Honorable Offer, An Intimate Deception*—all available in Signet editions.